The
Great
Divorce

BY VALERIE MARTIN

LOVE

SET IN MOTION

ALEXANDRA

A RECENT MARTYR

THE CONSOLATION OF NATURE

MARY REILLY

THE GREAT DIVORCE

Valerie Martin

Nan A. Talese
DOUBLEDAY
NEW YORK LONDON TORONTO SYDNEY AUCKLAND

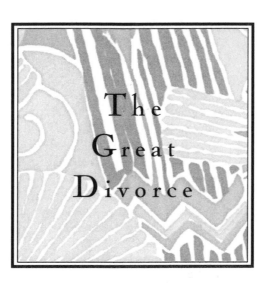

The
Great
Divorce

PUBLISHED BY NAN A. TALESE
an imprint of Doubleday
a division of Bantam Doubleday Dell Publishing Group, Inc.
1540 Broadway, New York, New York 10036

DOUBLEDAY is a trademark of Doubleday, a division of Bantam Doubleday
Dell Publishing Group, Inc.

Library of Congress Cataloging-in-Publication Data

Martin, Valerie.
The great divorce / Valerie Martin. — 1st ed.
p.   cm.
1. Zoos—Louisiana—New Orleans—Employees—Fiction.
2. Women—Louisiana—New Orleans—Fiction.
3. New Orleans (La.)—Fiction.   I. Title.
PS3563.A7295U56   1994
813'.54—dc20   93-5227
CIP

ISBN 0-385-42125-7

Book Design by Gretchen Achilles

*Those who identify with nature
must live with the consequences.*

—WALTER I. ANDERSON

ACKNOWLEDGMENTS

Many books, collections of photographs, old drawings, and maps contributed to my vision of antebellum New Orleans, but none was so useful, so detailed and fascinating as the works of Lyle Saxon, who spent years gathering and documenting old stories of all kinds, about all manner of people, in the city he knew and loved. To two books, *Old Louisiana* and *Fabulous New Orleans,* I am particularly indebted.

The staff and administration of the Audubon Park Zoo in New Orleans were uniformly generous in granting me access to and information about the zoo. In particular I'd like to thank Mark Stetter, Heath Konts, Roger Iles, Eve Watts, Sean MacConnell, and Eddie Green III for taking the time to answer my many questions.

I owe a special debt of gratitude to Sue Mikota, D.V.M., who opened the world behind the exhibits to me, allowing me to follow her on her extraordinary rounds, and who spent hours with me answering questions, reading and correcting the manuscript. Though Dr. Mikota, in her unsentimental and complete devotion to the cause of wild animals, was an inspiration, and though without her generosity and patience my characters would not have had the opportunity to enjoy their brief fictional lives, no character in this novel resembles her.

for John

The contemporary zoo, the "Zoo Eden," is the final irony: a false paradise in which the last representatives of soon to be extinct species are displayed to a public eager to be absolved for their extinction. The expensive exhibits conjure up a world that never did, never will, exist, in which predator and prey gaze stupidly at one another across invisible but effective barriers, while plant life flourishes, water supplies are stable, and all of nature is benign.

Ellen looked up from the magazine. There were more of these essays about zoos lately, and some were in unexpected places. This one was in a magazine Paul had brought her which was usually devoted to articles about the economy or politics. She glanced down to the end of the paragraph to see what the author was getting at. *In nature, as in our own society,* she read, *we will not rest until we have eliminated all possibility of "the wild."*

Was it true? Well, it might be true. Lucius stood up on the

window-sill and arched his back, gazing on his mistress with cold feline eyes, the domesticated cat, bored by surveying, through the screen, his archenemy, Barker, the over-bred, aristocratic collie. No wildness in this scene.

But what exactly did this journalist mean by "the wild?" The sounds of her husband getting out of bed, crossing the landing outside her door on his way to the bathroom, triggered her fingers back through the pages to the beginning of the article, where "The Great Divorce" was printed in large letters and, beneath that, in smaller letters, the author's name. The title intrigued her, for she had used the word *divorce* in her own mind to describe the breakup between the human species and the rest of nature, which like all divorces was causing pain in many quarters, even to the couple's dimwitted friends who refused to take sides, like Lucius, who didn't care, or Barker, who followed his nose in the dull hope that everything would turn out all right.

She slipped the magazine back on the shelf. She could make coffee for Paul, tea for herself; they might have time for a quiet breakfast before the girls got up. But as she rose from her chair the phone rang; of course it was Beth. Gina was on her way from Primates with an infant Diana monkey; the mother had bitten off one of its fingers. "How bad is it?" Ellen asked.

"Gina said it's completely off. I haven't seen it yet. I can have a look and call you back."

Paul was singing now. In a moment he would be in the shower. "No," Ellen said, "I'd better come. I'm on my way."

She would get a cup of coffee and a brioche at Mylie's. In the kitchen she wrote a note on the phone pad: *Hurt monkey, be back soon.* Paul was hitting the high note of Tosca's aria to God: *"Perché, perché, Signor."*

Why do you pay me back like this?

Last night there had been another phone call. Paul answered, gave his diffident hello, his eyes on Ellen because he was mid-sentence with her on the subject of a trip to Saint Francisville he would take next week—he really had found an extraordinary old murder case—then he listened. His expression changed, there was the flicker of a smile, his eyes shifted from her expectant face to some middle ground of air between them, and he said, "No, I'm afraid you have the wrong number." He hung up but he'd lost the thread; Ellen had to bring him back to it. So he had started a new affair and she was bold enough to call him at home. This explained his high spirits of late, his enthusiasm for the old murder case, the necessity for research trips. To his credit he would keep the woman out of town as much as possible and probably get the work done as well, for the combination of guilt and energy an affair inspired was a tonic to him; his confidence soared, he was full of good humor and sympathy for all his fellows.

And she would have some time to herself, a few quiet evenings—if the girls didn't have a crisis to deal with—in which she would drink expensive wine, read and catch up on work, go to bed early, and sleep in the middle of the bed.

In the car she considered a title: "The Rewards of Adultery for the Maligned Spouse," and a list: more time to pursue own interests, ebullient, oversolicitous mate, catch up on children, never have to answer phone, no guilt. It was age and cynicism that turned up such thoughts, no doubt. There was a time when she would have exhausted herself trying to figure out who the woman was and how to put a stop to the affair, how to let Paul know that she knew, that he was hurting her, yet do all this without creating a confrontation. The tightropes of yesterday. Now that seemed so much unnecessary drama. If Paul was going to leave her, he would have done so long ago.

She turned the car into the long, tree-shrouded drive to the hospital, her thoughts converging on the world behind the gate ahead. It wasn't uncommon for a baby primate to suffer aggression from an adult; the attacker was usually an adult male, occasionally another female. Yet Beth had been clear on the phone; this infant had been wounded by his own mother. In a way, Ellen thought, the actual injury was the least of their worries. The mother was doubtless a problem individual, neurotic at best, who would continue to cause trouble. Primates adjusted to captivity more readily than most animals, carrying on, as well as they could, their own peculiar and complicated idea of community. But this community could never be what it was in the wild, because it was closed off, controlled. There was no place for the inevitable outcasts to run. Neither wild nor domestic, they existed in a netherworld of human scrutiny and intervention. Ellen was determined to intervene as little as possible. The baby would be returned to the mother, and with luck, if rejected, he would be adopted by another female.

Ellen parked her car and walked quickly to the hospital door. When she entered the treatment room Gina and Beth were standing before the x-ray screen; the monkey lounged in Gina's arms, a limp mass of fur, his impossibly long arms draped about her shoulders, his bleary eyes fixed on her face as she crooned to him, commiserating, "Your mom isn't very nice to you, is she, poor fellow. You haven't got much of a mom."

2

Paul found the first mention of Elisabeth Boyer Schlaeger, the "catwoman of Saint Francisville," on a microfiche of the New Orleans *Item,* dated April 30, 1846. As was often the case with his best discoveries, he was looking for something else, some record of a property transfer, and here, tucked away on a back page, was a notice of the public execution of a woman, surely a white woman, for the paper listed her full name as well as that of her husband, whom she was said to have murdered. Paul leaned over the strip of film, his mouth frankly agape. To his knowledge—and not many people knew more about such matters than he did—no white woman had ever been executed in the state of Louisiana. And what was to be made of this cryptic allusion to the murderess as the "catwoman," as if every reader was familiar with the case, as if the town had been following a scandalous trial, when, in fact, he had been over the court records of this period more than once and never seen a word about it?

He sat back in his cold library chair and thought hard. This was what he loved about his work, these moments when his brain seemed to blaze with activity and he remembered scenes he had summoned up from old records, letters, diaries, newspapers, a world he wrested back from the dead. Two thoughts came forward, the first a disheartening one, that the records from 1852 to 1860 were woefully inadequate. There were gaps, weeks at a time, lost in fires, to mice, a whole year destroyed in a flood near the river only fifty years ago. The second was that the name Schlaeger was familiar. He had a list of the owners of every plantation from Pointe-à-la-Hache to Natchez for well on a hundred years, and he felt certain that Schlaeger was one of them.

Paul made a note of the date and the two names, Elisabeth Boyer and Hermann Schlaeger, then flicked off the machine and sat rubbing his eyes, smiling to himself. "The catwoman," he said softly. Did she keep a lot of cats? She was French, but her husband, Hermann, was surely not. Not many Germans owned big houses in Saint Francisville. Perhaps he was an American, part of the invasion, and he'd married a Creole to gain access to the salons of his neighbors. But it hadn't worked. Creole society was inbred to the point of genetic exhaustion and determined to remain so. Mlle. Boyer was probably expected to marry one of her cousins. She'd refused, married a German, and found herself excommunicated from her family and from all the lighthearted entertainments, the gay soirées and riding trips along the levees, isolated on her husband's plantation, where the only French she heard was from her own slaves.

Paul gathered up his notebooks and pens, dropped the microfiche at the desk, and made his way out into the humid air that hung like a drapery between the air-conditioned library and his air-conditioned office. He hardly noticed the heat. It seemed to him he could see the list, the very page on which he had read the name Schlaeger. The records in Saint Francisville were in better condition than those in New Orleans; it wouldn't be difficult to find a notice of an arrest. Unless he was wrong and the Schlaegers were not wealthy landowners but poor whites of unknown origins, living on the outskirts of civilized society, not Creole nor free people of color nor slaves nor rich Americans, but something other and excluded by all, left to their own devices on land even a slave would disdain to farm. Then there might be little in the way of records, and the case would not repay his investigations. His readers had no interest in proletarian violence, the banal passions of the disenfranchised or the poor, though if a wealthy man murdered his slave or vice versa, they might be entertained, especially if the details were grisly, as was often the case with such crimes. What they craved were stories of grand passions, of beautiful women and wealthy, cultivated men, of power, greed, treachery, great successes, greater failures. His subject was a doomed world; everyone knew it and read accordingly, with little sense that their daily newspaper offered them a vision into a similar decline. Paul's heart raced on two counts. The first was a premonition that he had stumbled upon something very fine, a bit of history that would serve as a centerpiece for the large important work he knew he must do, the book that was not just a string of connected historical anecdotes, but a serious meditation on the past. The second was the thought of the long drive to Saint Francisville with his attractive young mistress at his side. Donna might have to take a few days from her secretarial duties, but he felt certain it could be arranged to everyone's satisfaction. Her department chair was a personal friend. It could all, he was confident, be easily arranged.

After the last visitor had filed through the entry gates and the zoo was closed for the day, Camille began the ritual of closing out the night house in the Asian exhibit. She did this each day in the same way, though no day was exactly like the others. First she stopped in the yard and stacked the meat sticks from the ice chest into the wheelbarrow. She carried the bucket of fruit for the sun bears over her arm. At the door she put everything down, beat against the metal with her fist, opened the door, and shouted, "Hello, hello," as she had been taught to do, for one could never be too careful around the big cats, particularly Sonya, who longed to tear apart something that would give her resistance. Inside, she flicked on the lights and carried the bucket to the back cages, then pulled the long chains that opened the outer door to the sun bear exhibit. The three bears came in at once: Jojo, the oldest, always first, moved quickly to the far cage and put his front paws up against the feed tray. His mate Jana and their daughter Kim came in behind, doglike and patient; they made concentric circles on the cement while Camille shoved fruit through the tray for Jojo. She watched for a moment as they shoveled in the fruit, licked out their yogurt cups with their strange long tongues. This was the third day in a row Jojo had left his apples. Kim waited until he moved well away, then swept in the two apples with a single stroke of her forepaw, flipped one into her mouth, and stood quietly munching while her mother took the other. Camille wrote the words *no apples* under Jojo's name on the chart attached to the wall. Another day and they would have to tell the vet.

She went back to the wheelbarrow and pulled out a few of the meat sticks, which she dropped before each of the cat night cages. Today there were rabbits as well, which made the cats excited; they knew the feeding schedule as well as their keeper. The night houses had all been cleaned during the day, so Camille went about giving each of the padlocks a perfunctory tug. Keeper-trainees were not always reliable.

There were eight cats to bring in, a total of six steel doors to be opened by means of heavy chains and wheels. As she opened the doors one by one the cats seemed to materialize behind each set of bars. First Paolo and Antonella, the lion and his mate, who came in single file, though never without a quarrel, a growling match; Sonya, the white tiger, the star of every show and the most disagreeable of all the cats; the two Bengal tigers, Clio and her daughter Stella, both geriatric now, hard of hearing and overweight, padding in heavily, lumbering like elephants; the clouded leopard, Maxwell, and his mate Flo, both as tame as housecats, approaching their empty trays amiably, with domestic confidence; and finally Magda, the black leopard, sudden and wild, Magda the powerful. Camille had the rabbit ready for her, as Magda knew she would. When the door creaked open on its heavy chain Magda tore across the concrete like a beam of black light, hit the front bars claws out, mouth open, with enough force to break a man's leg. She snapped up the rabbit from paw to mouth in a motion so rapid that Camille was never able to say she had actually seen it, fell back on her haunches for a split second, then landed high on her stone slab, her imitation of a cliff, where she looked down briefly, her yellow eyes twin stones in the impassive black of her long, serious face, her white teeth sunk deep in her dinner, blood welling up to the gum line and running in a thin stream off her tongue. She took the rabbit between her great paws and began licking it greedily.

Camille stood smiling in the cool aisle between the cages, surrounded by the feeding cats, all so close to her that she could hear their throats contracting over the gobbets of raw meat as they swallowed. Though they never looked one another in the eye, they were all willing to stare coldly at their keeper, so Camille stood in a crossfire of feline eyebeams. Sonya finished her meal quickly and began a low, continuous growl, a wave of sound that set all the others on edge. One after another they lifted their big heads from their dinners and growled back, all but Magda, who was chewing off her rabbit's head, her eyes on Camille, unreadable. It was a scene so unnatural that the oddity of it seemed to speak: a young woman standing quietly among an assortment of the last of the great cats, none of whom had ever been in the wild nor ever would be. Yet the sounds they made seemed to come from a dark continent and their eyes looked out from a world in which there were no bars, no limits of any kind. The young woman had stopped smiling. Her knees were weak, and as there was nothing to hold on to but the bars that kept her from being torn to bits, she had no choice but to sink to the concrete floor. "Oh, Lord," she said, and she brought one hand to her chest, for her heart was racing. She made another sound, not a word but a groan. No one could see her but the great cats who watched her, and they did not care who she was or what she did, as long as the bars stood between. Unlike her charges Camille knew herself to be, for a little while at least, entirely free.

On July 10, 1845, just before dawn on what some accounts were later to call "the hottest night of the year," a Negro boy, still in his white nightshirt, riding bareback and by torchlight on his master's own sorrel mare, arrived at the long oak avenue of the Rosedawn Plantation. He had come twelve miles from his home at Montague at a dead run, his eyes wild and his heart nearly bursting in his chest, to bring the news that his master, Hermann Schlaeger, was dead. He began shouting for help halfway up the alley, and the house servants who were awake heard his cries and the clatter of his horse's hooves as they left the hard ground and came right onto the wooden porch. Roderick Mouton, his master's manservant, who later testified at the trial, threw open the heavy front doors of Rosedawn and shouted to the astounded messenger, "Get that horse off this porch and come to your senses, child!" The boy complied with the request, handing down his torch to Roderick and backing the horse carefully down the steps to the hitching post, where he slid off with the ease of an experienced rider, secured the reins, and, returning gravely up the wide steps to the house, announced, "My master is dead. He been killed in his own house."

The master of Rosedawn was awakened from his slumbers in the dreamy security of his mosquito netting and told of his neighbor's misfortune. He groaned to hear it, dispatched Roderick to wake his sons, but on no account "to disturb the ladies." The three white men made a quick toilette and descended to the dining room, where they took their coffee and French bread while the bewildered boy stood next to the table. They questioned him closely but he knew little more than he had told on his arrival, for he had not been in the house nor seen any signs of the violence that ended in his master's death. His mother, the cook at Montague, had come running back to the cabin and pulled him out of bed, then run with him to the stable, where she and the stable man agreed it would be proper to take the master's own mare, as she was both fast and reliable. The boy was very clear on this point and repeated it, lest he be accused of an impropriety, and indeed, as he had raced through the swamp in the hot, foggy air, it had come to him that if anyone saw him riding so hard on so fine a horse he would be taken for a runaway and shot without question, so he rode low to the horse's neck and prayed God would see him to his destination. His mother had told him only to go to Rosedawn and say our master has been killed. That was all he had to say.

"Did she say he was dead," the master of Rosedawn inquired, "or murdered?"

"She said killed, sir, is all I know."

The boy was dismissed and taken off to the kitchen, where the cook gave him some breakfast and asked after his mother, to whom she was kin. As no one seemed in a hurry to send him home, he stayed the day at Rosedawn, visiting in the cabins, and he slept there that night, for by evening a full story of the strange happenings at Montague had made its way back to Rosedawn. The next morning the same boy carried a written message to the judge at Saint Francisville, and it was only then that two officers were dispatched to arrest Hermann Schlaeger's beautiful young wife, Elisabeth, for the murder of her husband.

"It starts in my mouth," Camille said.

"Can you describe it?"

She shifted in her chair. She had not spoken of it before. "The roof of my mouth. It gets thick and hard. It hurts. My gums ache. My teeth hurt."

"Anything else?"

"Then my hands. My fingers cramp up and they swell. I have to take off my ring. My nails hurt."

"Yes."

She looked at her hands clutching the arms of her chair. Ordinary hands. One of the nails was torn; another had a line of dirt underneath it. "My eyes," she said.

He regarded her steadily. His expression did not betray his feelings, a result of his training—not to show feelings, not to have them if possible.

"Just a headache at first," she said. "Here," her forehead, "and here," she pressed her fingertips against the nape of her neck. "I see patches of light, spots of light."

"Do you feel dizzy?"

"No. There's a blur, but I don't feel dizzy. It's as if another dimension was being laid on."

"Another dimension?" His question was punctuation.

"Heat," she said. "A dimension of heat."

He took in a long breath, let it out slowly. Strictly speaking he did not believe her. They had come too far, too quickly. He had not pushed her, had tried to let her find her own way. This was what she wanted him to believe; therefore, he was not responsible for believing it. They were not lovers, but it was as it is when one lover says, unsolicited, for the first time, "I love you," and the other draws away, satisfied, free of responsibility, a smug little moment.

"You don't believe me."

"What makes you think that?" he said.

"Well. How could you?"

"Let's not worry about what I think. It's not important. Concentrate on what you remember, on what happens."

"My hearing," she said. "Odd sounds. Scratching. Vibrations. A sound like a whisper, but I can't make it out. Magda's breathing. Or it may be her heart."

"You hear her heart?"

"I think that's it. I hadn't realized that before now. I hear her heart beating; then everything gets red. I see everything in shades of red." She pulled her fingers through her hair, a nervous habit she had.

"Are you afraid?"

"Now?" she said.

"No. Then. When it happens."

She closed her eyes. Who wouldn't be afraid to hear the heartbeat of an animal twenty feet away, to have ordinary vision turn to blood and heat? "I'm not so crazy I'm not afraid," she said.

He raised his eyebrows. He didn't want her to use that word, not in his office and not when she was describing an experience they both knew was impossible, her literal transformation from the plain, intense, self-absorbed young woman she was into a wild animal. "Don't say that word," he cautioned her.

"What?" she said. "What word?"

"Crazy."

Camille laughed. A genuine laugh, he thought. It embraced them both with unexpected good humor; it cleared the air. In that moment they could not dislike each other, no matter what came next. Their eyes met, he lowered his, but he was smiling.

"Right," she said.

The juvenile howler monkey was found lying on his back in a corner of his night house, gasping for air, his eyes glazed. By the time the keeper got him confined to a kennel and transported to the hospital, he had begun to seizure. He beat his head against the plastic floor and sides of the kennel, saliva pouring over his lips, which were drawn back over clenched teeth, as if he were smiling. There was no getting him out of the kennel; he thrashed his arms and legs wildly whenever Ellen and Beth drew near.

Beth prepared a syringe of Valium while Ellen pulled on heavy welder's gloves, for the monkey would surely bite if he got the chance. He was making a high-pitched sound, a scream of terror, though his face betrayed no sign of anything, frozen in its deathlike grin. Now his body began a series of spasms, his spine arched high off the floor, then flat, then high again. Ellen hovered over the wire gate, waiting for him to move toward the back of the kennel. His body writhed pitifully, twisting him sideways. He raised his arms toward the metal screen at the top, as if reaching for something to hold on to, and as he did, Ellen popped open the gate, reached in quickly, and caught him just above the biceps. Before he could turn toward her, she had pinioned his arms back in a position that forced him to drop his head forward. She eased his suddenly inert body from the cage, but he kicked at it as he came free, knocking the kennel back on the counter. Beth was ready with the syringe and plunged it into his shoulder. He continued screaming. For a few moments, Ellen held him immobilized while Beth busied herself writing labels for the blood work and x-ray plates. The monkey began to salivate so heavily that water poured down his chest. "Give me two cc's of atropine," Ellen said. "He's drowning us here."

Gradually Ellen felt his taut muscles relaxing, and he hung limp from her gloved hands; his eyelids drooped, though his teeth remained clenched, his lips pulled back in a grimace. Ellen loosened her grip on his arms and carried him gingerly, cradled like a child, to the table. His eyes were fastened to her face, but she didn't think he could see her. The howlers were unused to being touched; she could feel his inward shrinking though he hadn't sufficient control of his muscles to move decisively in any direction. When she laid him on the cold steel of the surgery table, his small perfect hand contracted briefly around her forearm, as if he were asking for help.

For the next hour the two women worked over the dying monkey. Ellen had little hope that he would survive; his vital signs were all unpromising, he was dehydrated, and the rapid onset and intensity of the seizure suggested that a good deal of damage had already been done. She wanted to know what was killing him. She made a mental list: toxoplasmosis, lead toxicity, acute peritonitis, acute encephalitis. Beth packed up her tubes of blood and went down the hall to her microscope. Ellen put the stethoscope over the monkey's flagging heart. He was still now; even his jaw had relaxed. She ran a thumb under his lips to look at the gums, which were pale, edging toward blue. She pulled out the oxygen tubing, clipped on a mask, pressed it over the animal's face, and set the flow. "Breathe," she said. She had rested her hand across his abdomen, so she felt the spasm coming up right under her fingers, into her palm. She put the other hand loosely over his chest so that she could hold him on the table while his body lurched, once, twice, then, after a pause, twice more. There was a gagging sound, an expulsion of breath, his eyes flew open, dropped half closed, and as she lifted the mask and turned his face toward her own, she saw the light leaving his eyes, a dull gray sheen in its place that seemed to flood the eyeball from inside, announcing that life had gone.

"Damn," Ellen said. She was alone in the treatment room, her hands resting lightly on the dead animal, but she could hear the soft tread of Beth's rubber-soled shoes as she came back down the hall. From outside the window the clamor of two jays squalling over their territory tore into the air. Ellen lifted her head to hear it, for it was curiously reassuring, this fury over property so close to the scene of her sudden, unexpected loss. Her hand strayed over the dead monkey's face; she smoothed his fur back over his jaws. Beth appeared in the doorway, speaking before she took in the scene. "Count's normal," she said, then, "Oh. He didn't make it."

"No," Ellen said. She folded the monkey's arms and legs up so that she could carry him back to the kennel like a sleeping child. "He's gone."

In the early hours of that steamy morning in July, when the masters of Rosedawn arrived at the doors of Montague Plantation, they heard to their astonishment the sound of piano music drifting through the French doors and out across the wide veranda. André Davillier recognized the tune as one of Mendelssohn's *Songs Without Words,* a particular favorite of his. It combined classic purity with an unexpected moodiness, a brooding quality he associated with the image of the torches his servants carried up to the house after dark, moving erratically among the great oaks like enormous fireflies. So serious was his mission that he hardly stopped to listen. His sons, Robert and Adrien, hung back on the steps as he crossed the porch and pounded on the heavy cypress door.

There was no answer. The music continued, but no sound of movement came from within. In fact, as the three men stood there an eerie silence settled over the scene, broken only by the strains of languorous music pouring into the heavy, scented air. André looked back at his sons, then up and down the long veranda and out across the yard. Not a slave in sight. He pounded on the door again, more insistent than before; the thudding of his fist against the wood was like a volley of gunshots. After a moment he tried the knob, which, to his surprise, turned so easily that the door seemed to float open before the three visitors, beckoning them inside. André stepped in at once, his sons behind him, and he was on the verge of calling out when his eyes, drawn upward by the graceful curve of the staircase that rose before him, fell on a sight so startling his greeting stuck in his throat and he made only a faint rasping sound.

The staircase was divided by a wide landing, halfway up, a stage designed for a descending lady to pause, arrange her skirts, and look down upon whoever came to her door, admiring suitor or suppliant tenant. It was the master of Montague who used this landing now, and in a macabre way he was looking down upon his guests. He lay on his back, his arms and legs stretched wide, his head dropped over the step, so that, though his face was upside down, he did appear to be staring, for his eyes were wide open. The Davillier clan stood frozen beneath him. Robert made a soft moan, turned it into *"Dieu,"* and fell silent. There was, they explained when they returned to Rosedawn, more blood than anyone could take in without horror. Hermann Schlaeger's long silver hair was black with it. His shirt hung in shreds over his blood-soaked torso, and even from their awkward position at the foot of the stairs, the three men could see that his throat had been entirely torn away.

Yet the delicate piano music still filled the air like an agreeable perfume. It was difficult to know how to react, as if the senses were being purposely disoriented, the eyes riveted by horror, the ears soothed by music. At last André turned from the staircase and strode across the marble hall to the doors that stood open to the drawing room. There he found what he described as "an equally disturbing sight," though it was only a woman playing the piano.

She was dressed in a pale morning gown, tight in the bodice, and her heavy dark hair, which he had always seen wound in a thick coil at the nape, was loose across her shoulders. The unsettling part was her hands, stained with blood to the wrists; they flew across the keys heedless of his entrance, of everything but the rigors of the music. He took a step forward and said her name, "Elisabeth." Then, he said later at her trial, she stopped playing and turned toward him, not with an expression of surprise or of interest; rather, she appeared to be annoyed at the interruption. Added to the inappropriateness of her expression was an additional shock, for poor André saw that she had dried blood on her mouth and neck, that there was a deep stain across her bodice, and that she did not seem to be aware of the spectacle she presented. "What is it?" she said, folding her bloodstained hands in her lap as she had been taught to do at the convent in New Orleans. "Why are you here?"

In the dream Camille was screaming. Her arms and legs were twisted, stunted, and her face was horrible, a monster's face. Yet she was in her own bed. The pain was unendurable; she knew she would not survive it, so she screamed for help and for relief. Soon she understood that she was asleep and that she was screaming to wake up. Louder and louder she screamed, stretching her ugly little arms out before her until, at last, with a thump, she fell back into consciousness and her eyes flew open like windows. She threw off the sheet at once and stood up shakily, holding on to the arm of her sofa bed, breathing hard.

Then she heard a sound that filled her with terror of a more familiar variety, more visceral than the nightmare, a reality, after all, from which she could be awakened. This was the sound of her mother's footsteps moving quickly toward her bedroom. In the next moment the door flew open and the quiet darkness was shattered by brutal light. Camille felt her stomach turn; her knees, already weak from the nightmare, sagged against the cold metal of the bedframe. She averted her eyes, but not quickly enough. As she sank back onto the mattress, she saw her mother in her mind's eye, her wild, unkempt hair matted about her face, her glaring eyes so glazed by alcohol that, Camille sometimes thought, if she got too close to a match they might go up in flames, and her mouth, the mouth of a dragon, issuing smoke. She stood poised in the doorway, one hand on the light switch, the other clutched at her side, dressed only in her loose nylon underpants, her sagging breasts and belly, white and unappealing, her pale, sturdy legs planted well apart, a fury straight up from hell where her slumbers had been disturbed. "What's wrong with you?" she said.

"Sorry," Camille replied, pulling the sheet back, arranging her nightgown to cover her legs, keeping her eyes down. "I had a bad dream."

"You woke me up. It's three o'clock. I'd just gotten to sleep."

"I'm sorry," Camille said again.

"You know how hard it is for me to get to sleep."

"I know," Camille said. "I'm sorry I woke you."

Her mother stood glaring at her for a few moments while Camille studied her own hands, the long crack in the blue Naugahyde arm of her sofa bed, her hands again.

"Well. Do you want the light on?" her mother said at last.

"No. Please."

The light went out, suddenly, mercifully, and Camille heard the door close, then the retreating steps. She'd gotten off easy. She stretched out under the thin sheet, folded her hands over her chest, and indulged in her favorite fantasy, that she was dead. She made her breathing more and more shallow, tried to extend the time between breaths. How shocked her mother would be when she got up sometime in the afternoon, imagining Camille had gone off to her job, and, passing down the hall, would notice the door ajar, would look in and find her daughter dead, completely out of her reach, out of her control. How she would reproach the disobedient corpse.

Camille smiled at the thought and turned on her side, pulling her pillow between her legs. Then, as mysteriously as it had appeared, the smile disappeared and she succumbed to wave after wave of anger. She surveyed the darkness of her ugly room. The windows were too high to see out of and were shrouded in the heavy draperies her mother put over every piece of glass in the small apartment. The room was so small that the opened bed took up most of it, leaving just space enough for her to pass in front of the shabby pine dresser that constituted the other furnishings. My night house, she thought. It was not as large as the concrete cages the cats slept in, but certainly as black. What did they do all night? Did they have roaring matches, filling up the closed compound with a magnificent sound no one ever heard? Did they pace all night? Certainly they didn't sleep much, because they slept all day. Magda was a night hunter; did she spend the long hours gazing into the darkness, listening for anything that moved? There were rats in the night house. They went after the bears' feed, which was stored in an empty cage, and then, apparently, went along the passageway between the other cages. Three had turned up in traps this week. It was ironic, setting rat traps in a building full of giant cats, but presumably the rats were too smart to get close to the big paws. Perhaps the cats didn't bother, or they might actually catch a few and eat them entirely.

Camille rolled over onto her back, the thin mattress sagging beneath her weight, and worked on another fantasy—or was it a plan—that she would spend an entire night in the night house. It would not be as difficult to elude the zoo authorities as it would be to escape her mother's vigilance. A great yawn overtook her. She tried to make it look like Magda's yawning, lips back, canines exposed; she stretched her jaws open until they hurt. Her mother's night house closed over her. She stretched her arms and legs into the darkness and pushed against the imaginary restraints, pushed and clawed, lifting her head from the pillow to assist in the struggle of white limbs against darkness. She was careful to make no sound. I must get out, she thought, I must get out, and she imagined Magda, in her dark cell on the other side of town, lying on her shelf and tearing at the low ceiling, as she had seen her do once, every muscle taut and straining with the same urgency: I must get out.

9

Ellen stood over the opened body of the monkey, snipping out bits of tissue—heart, liver, kidney, a thin slice of lung—dropping each one into the specimen jar. She raised her eyes to watch the piece of lung, which sank like the others, then, halfway down, floated to the top of the clear liquid. Nothing wrong there. The liver was slightly enlarged with some fatty infiltration, nothing serious. The heart and pancreas were normal. She put down her scalpel and surveyed the mess of organs, the spleen, the flat pale lungs, the open stomach, in which she had found two small stones and, curiously, a small plastic button. Then she took up the saw and, holding the monkey's head in place by pressing her palm across his face, cut her way into the skull, where she had suspected all along the problem was.

And she was right. As soon as the bone gave way and she had pried her way into the brain, she knew it. The color was wrong, a sickening yellow brown, and the meninges were thick, hard. She took up her scalpel and cut out a slice of the cerebellum. Probing at the hole she had made, she discovered a small lesion, then another.

The air conditioner cut on, startling her, for there was no sound in the cold bright room but her own breathing and the occasional clink of her instruments. She would tell Gina to put the howler keepers on alert, but for what? Viral infections were tricky. There could be nothing for weeks, and suddenly animals would start dropping like flies. She closed up the monkey's head and folded him back together to fit into the disposal bag, examining her own cliché: dropping like flies. As if flies weren't animals. She screwed the lid down carefully on the specimen jar. Perhaps the lab would have a surprise for her. She looked at her watch.

It was late, nearly seven. Celia and Lillian would be home, lounging about the kitchen, looking for something to eat. Paul was on his trip; he wouldn't call, nor would she call him, though she knew which motel he was in. They were in.

She had watched him packing his slim case with the fastidious care that was so much a part of his character. Everything must be just so. He would unpack it on his return immediately, entirely, putting everything away, never, as she did, leaving the open case on the floor for a day or two, fishing it clean a bit at a time.

But what if he didn't come back?

As he snapped the suitcase closed, the thought struck her like a slap and she'd flinched before it.

"What's wrong?" Paul had asked.

"I just had a feeling something might happen to you."

"What do you mean?"

"An accident," she said.

He set the case on the floor and put his arms around her, pushing her backward over the bed until she lost her balance and collapsed beneath him while he covered her laughing mouth with his own. She held him close, wrapping her arms and legs around his back, feeling the exciting hardness of his body against hers, and so touching was her sense of him, of his dearness, that her eyes filled with tears.

Now she took the saw and scalpel to the sink, turned on the faucet, and watched the bowl turn red as she rubbed the instruments in the running water. She remembered the little monkey's terrified expression when he approached the kennel. He had lost control of everything—even his agile, responsive musculature had deserted him—and all he could do was scream. There was no telling how long he'd been host to the virus that destroyed him, how rapidly his elegant mechanism was undone. Opening a dead animal was often like arriving at the scene of an automobile accident: all she could do was try to extrapolate from the wreckage the trajectory and speed of the vehicles before their collision.

She had lied to Paul, she admitted. It wasn't an automobile accident she feared. It was something else, some change in the delicate balance of their marriage, small now, difficult to detect, but ultimately fatal. Though she was not superstitious, she succumbed to a premonition: the accident that would destroy their happiness had already occurred.

10

Hermann Schlaeger appeared in New Orleans in January of 1842, having come downriver from Cincinnati on the steamboat *Hecla*. He brought with him his wife, Hilda, four slaves, and a small load of furniture. The furniture belonged to his wife: she had brought it with her from Germany some twenty years earlier, and their first order of business on arrival was to find safe storage for it, not an easy matter in the damp, dangerous, bug-infested swamp they hoped to call home.

Hermann was a resourceful man, equal to the challenge of this new environment. He had ambition, energy, and money. The only thing he didn't have was French, and it was this, in an odd way, which finally brought about his ruin. He was a stubborn, proud man, and he found the new society around him contemptible in manners, language, but particularly in efficiency. He had made a fortune through clever, often shady, land speculation, and he wanted now to be what his father had dreamed of being, a gentleman farmer. He left his wife, her furniture, and his four slaves on the boat landing at four in the afternoon. By eight he was back with an ox cart and two sets of keys.

For the next two months the Schlaeger entourage resided at the Saint Louis Hotel. Hermann spent his time and a good deal of his money looking for the house and land that would substantiate his vision of himself. At first he proposed to build the house but soon abandoned this plan. It would take too long, nor was there much uncultivated land for sale, especially along the river. There were grand houses being built on Saint Charles Avenue, the town residences of the invaders, the Americans, who competed with one another for opulence. Creole society was closed to them; all their money could not open the doors of the old homes in the French Quarter or the big houses along the river. They couldn't even buy their way into the Saint Louis cemetery but were forced to establish a new one of their own.

Hermann found himself straddling two worlds: the landed, declining aristocracy of the Creole planters, and the vital, acquisitive, flourishing arena of the American businessmen. His American acquaintances advised him to give up the idea of a plantation and settle in the city, where there was money to be made. But Hermann was not dissuaded. He made frequent trips upriver, inquiring at towns along the way for news of planters in financial straits, or those, like himself, who were childless and without relations. At length he was directed to Montague, the home of François deClerc, who, after an illness that had left him blind and mad, convinced at the end that a fly had entered his nose and laid eggs on his brain, had providentially fired a bullet into his ear on the very day of Hermann's arrival in New Orleans. His only daughter had married a Virginian, a man of business, who knew nothing about cotton and needed the proceeds of his wife's inheritance to secure certain investments of his own. Hermann toured the plantation, which, thanks to a competent foreman, was running smoothly with no master at all, and made an offer at once. Everything about Montague pleased him—the oak-lined drive, the layout of the slave cabins, the access to the river—but especially the house itself, which differed from the others he had seen in an excess of millwork, giving it, in Hermann's mind, an alpine air.

Hermann stayed in Saint Francisville until the sale was concluded; then, one clear, hot morning, he left his horse at the stable that was now his own, walked down to the boat landing that was his as well, and got on the steamer *Doswell,* which carried him back to New Orleans, where his wife lay dying of malarial fever. She lasted long enough to tell him that she hated New Orleans, hated the whole territory of Louisiana, and wanted to go home. A priest appeared at the door—he had been summoned by the hotel management—and while Hermann was shouting that his wife was no papist, that she would have nothing to confess to a French bastard even if she were a Catholic, Hilda closed her weary eyes and died.

So Hermann Schlaeger became a widower, the owner of two thousand acres of prime cotton land, half as many slaves and animals, and a house that was designed to hold a large family and up to thirty guests overnight. If he had any feelings about the passing of his wife, he did not show them. He had her body shipped up to Montague and buried in the cemetery on the property there, and he rode to Saint Francisville to secure the services of a Lutheran minister, who officiated at a brief ceremony attended only by Hermann. When it was over, he walked away without a word of thanks, nor did he make the expected gift of money to the young minister, who returned to Saint Francisville with the news that the new owner of Montague was a coldhearted skinflint who had buried his wife of twenty-five years without shedding a tear.

But etiquette on the river had little to do with personal likes or dislikes. The plantations were held together by rounds of dinners and parties from which no landowner was excluded, and any master traveling to New Orleans or Saint Francisville counted upon the hospitality of his neighbors along the way. Hermann had not been settled in his big house a week when André Davillier rode up the long drive of Montague to welcome his new neighbor. Hermann's manservant, Kirwin Charles, who had come with the property, explained in his halting English that Mr. Davillier would require coffee and spirits, that Hermann must invite him into the drawing room, and that if the master of Rosedawn was traveling, he must be offered a room for the night. Then, with his big, brooding new master following grimly behind him, Charles opened the door and, smiling broadly for the first time since Hermann had arrived, exchanged a few words in French with M. Davillier. Hermann straightened his back at the sight of his elegant neighbor and the sound of the language he found so unnerving; its very softness and fluidity suggested weakness to him, a language for women and slaves. But André addressed himself to Hermann in surprisingly flat English, his accent confined to the occasional misplaced stress, congratulating him at once for having acquired so fine a plantation and expressing sympathy for the unfortunate loss of his wife. The two men sat down to coffee and bourbon in the drawing room, and, an hour later, when André rose and extended his small, fine hand which disappeared in the stronger, coarser paw of his new neighbor, Hermann had accepted an invitation to a dinner dance at Rosedawn the following week. He followed André and Charles out onto the veranda and watched solemnly as André's horse was brought up. Again the Frenchman and the slave exchanged a few impenetrable words, and Hermann, who did not make it a habit to notice his slaves' faces, saw a look exchanged between the two that further unsettled him, for he felt himself to be the subject of it. He was being invited in, he thought, only to be informed that he would always be left out.

He turned back into his mansion filled with a petty, useless, simmering anger. He would have to consult his servant about what to wear to this party, and that galled him, but ask he must, for he did not intend to be left out for long.

1 1

Camille lifted the coffee cup to her lips and peered over the rim at the man leaning against the counter. He was talking softly, almost without animation, to a black man who stood behind it inclined a little away from him, his eyes on the griddle where Camille's grilled-cheese sandwich simmered in a thin layer of grease. The white man was dressed shabbily—an old plaid shirt, pants that fitted him oddly, too loose at the hips, too short at the cuffs, where a few inches of white socks clung to his thin ankles and disappeared into worn sneakers, gray from wear and torn at the toes. Camille passed her eyes up and down the back of the man. Like her sandwich, he was coming to her. She smoothed her fine hair back behind her ears and pulled another hair out of her sweater, short, black, not her own, not human, she thought with a smile. Probably her mother's cat had left it there, but as she rubbed it between her fingers she told herself it must be Magda's. The man had concluded his conversation; he approached her now, carrying the sandwich, which he held out before him disdainfully.

"Thanks," she said when he sat down.

"That looks awful," he said.

Camille bit into the limp sandwich. It was tasteless, an amalgamation of blandness and grease. "No," she said, "it's good."

The man looked about the room nervously. There was no one else in it, only the black man, who was adjusting the heat on his griddle. "I've only got an hour," he said. "The room's a few blocks from here."

"Where?" she said.

"Dauphine, near Governor Nicholls."

"Is it your room?" she asked.

"No. A friend's. He won't be back until tonight."

Camille nodded and finished her sandwich in silence. She licked the grease off her fingers, one by one, her eyes lowered, until the man said, "Why don't you use a napkin?" Then she looked up. He met her eyes, a mixture of contempt and reproach in his own. He was impatient; he wanted to go to the room. She pulled a napkin from the container and wiped her fingers carefully, crumpled it, and dropped it into the plate. "I'm ready," she said.

On the street the man did not touch her. He walked rapidly, and she had to take running steps to keep up. She had been with this man once before. He had not hurt her, and yesterday, when he saw her on the street, he had come up to her at once and asked her if she could come to this room, he thought he could get it, today. He didn't smile nor did he seem pleased to see her; rather, he looked up and down the street nervously as he spoke, softly—she liked his soft voice—urgently. Perhaps he was married or lived with a jealous woman and feared detection. He had the look of a man in trouble.

The room, behind a peeling door at the end of a dim, carpeted hallway, was appallingly ugly, but the man did not seem to notice. There was a mattress on the floor with a thin blanket thrown across it, a single straight-backed chair, and a pile of clothes that had started on the chair but overflowed onto the floor. The one window looked out onto the brick wall of the opposite building. A light bulb hung from a cord that came through a hole in the high ceiling. Mercifully it was not lit, and the unpleasant room was suffused with the gloomy afternoon light from the window.

The man went directly to the mattress, sat upon it, and began unlacing his sneakers. Camille stood just inside the door, watching him. When the sneakers were off she saw that there were holes in his socks. "Come on," he said, patting the mattress beside him.

She sat down next to him and slipped off her own flat shoes. Then she unbuttoned her blouse slowly, not looking at anything, especially not at the man, who turned to watch her.

"How old are you?" he asked.

"Nineteen," she said.

"I only see you on weekends. Are you still in school?"

She looked up at him as she pulled her blouse away. His eyes were instantly fastened to her breasts, the sight of which seemed to please him as nothing in her face ever would. The hard lines around his mouth softened; there was a hint of a smile on his thin lips.

"No, I have a job," she replied. He had taken his own shirt off, revealing his thin, hairless chest, his long smooth torso. He began unfastening his pants. Camille turned her attention to her skirt.

"Yeah?" he said. "What do you do?"

"I work at the zoo," she said. "I'm a keeper."

The man seemed actually to take an interest in this information. "That must be nice," he said. "You're outdoors all the time."

"Yes," she said.

"I never been there," he concluded.

Camille did not tell the man he should go to the zoo. She didn't think he could afford the admission price, four dollars and fifty cents, nor could she imagine him strolling about among the great oaks, over the wooden walkways, having an ice cream while looking at the gorilla; in fact, the idea struck her as disagreeable.

She sat quietly, stripped to her underpants, and waited for the man to get his pants off. When he stood halfway up to pull them over his ankles, she found herself looking at his thin, pale buttocks. When he sat down again, she saw that he had an erection, a shocking sight; she thought she never would get used to it, nor did it seem polite to stare. She looked away. The man touched her shoulder, then her breasts. "You have such a pretty body," he said.

Camille smiled briefly. God knew what this poor fellow had seen. His hands moved to her shoulders again, pushing her back. She didn't resist. She lay half on the ugly stained mattress, her legs and feet stretched across the floor. She looked quickly at his face; he was staring at her crotch fixedly, a bit of saliva had collected at the corner of his mouth. She looked away, at the light bulb dangling over them on its dirty gray cord. Her throat ached. The man licked his fingers, put his hand between her legs, and pressed hard until his fingers slipped inside. Once a man had spit on her there, and she was always cringing at the start lest it happen again. Relax, she told herself. He pushed her legs apart and she did not resist, though a wave of revulsion ran from his fingers to her throat as he slipped to his knees on the floor, brought his face down between her legs, and began licking her, slowly, with a kind of studied insistence that was the opposite of passion; more, she thought, like work.

They all did this and Camille understood it was supposed to be pleasant for her, but she could only think of dogs, always sniffing at one another under the tail or licking their own genitals. She could not overcome her sense that it was degrading and disgusting to be treated in this way, yet she said nothing and stayed very still. After a few minutes the man looked up, moved over her, and fitted his penis between her legs. She closed her eyes, turned her face away, bracing for the sharp pain that she could not deny was strangely pleasurable, especially as it was over so quickly; and then the sensation of his pushing inside her, pulling, back and forth, began. She kept her eyes closed. The man made a low sound; he was moving more rapidly now, and he brought his hands under her hips, pulling her up to him. She arched her back so that her upper body was as far from his as possible, for she disliked having anyone too close to her face. Her throat was tightening, throbbing in time with his sharp thrusts, and she felt a strange swelling in her mouth. Her upper lip drew back involuntarily from her teeth, an amazing sensation, coupled with another, equally disturbing and involuntary, a sure sense of her canine teeth, of their being exposed to the dim figure of the man lurching over her. She could hear the big cats, Sonya and Clio, Stella and Antonella and Magda, especially Magda, who never gave any warning, who would not join the snarling matches that seemed so important to her cellmates, who was, as Camille felt herself to be now, only occasionally possessed of a sudden, inexplicable rage. Thinking of Magda, her long, serious face transformed in sudden fury, Camille opened her eyes and looked up at the man. His face was red, his eyes bulging a little, and his mouth had dropped dully open. He met her eyes and attempted a weak smile, almost apologetic; he was nearly done. Her heart swelled with hatred. She could feel the blood coursing through her limbs, out to her fingertips. All around her the miserable room came into focus, a place where anything could happen and no one would care. The man driving himself into her was faceless, the sort of man no one would ever look for, no one would miss. She fastened her eyes on his throat, exposed to her as, in his final moment, he lifted his head and, with his eyes finally closed, emitted a series of grunts, like a pig, Camille thought, his whole body momentarily rigid. She searched through her memory for his name. She imagined that if she could come up with it, somehow his life, which was worth nothing, would be saved. And as he collapsed over her she found it, gratefully, in some corner of her consciousness where she did not hate him; it was Eddie.

"Eddie," she said tentatively, trying it out.

Eddie pulled himself out of her and rolled over on his back. "Jesus," he said.

1 2

Natural. Another meaningless word, or a word that could mean anything, like love. At dinner last night Celia had said, "I love pasta. I love, love, love pasta," and then, to her father, who had cooked the pasta for her, "And you, Dad. I love, love, love you." Ellen watched the change in Paul's expression, how he basked in the light of his daughter's affection for him, in her "natural" affection for him.

Ellen made a list: natural food, natural childbirth, natural selection. How could one word mean so much or so little? How, given the canine teeth and close-set eyes that declare the human animal to be a predator, had we come up with the notion that oat bran is more natural to eat than chicken? Even our closest relations, the baboon and the ape, would not, in ordinary circumstances, eat oat bran. Yet advertisers suggested that buying oat products, in boxes covered by pictures of fields, sky, rural felicity, would somehow bring us closer to nature, to what is natural for us. And who had come up with the idea that what was called natural childbirth had anything to do with what really happens in nature, where birth mortality is the natural way to control the population of a species? Didn't natural selection mean dead babies, lots of them, dead at birth or deserted by mothers who didn't like the look of them and knew instinctively that they wouldn't repay the investment of mothering? And finally, what perverse twisting of what happens in nature had visited upon women the notion that mothering is a natural instinct, that a woman who does not love her child is unnatural, when the most casual investigation of mothers in the wild reveals that only those with leisure and a plentiful food supply indulge themselves in the luxury of caring for their offspring?

Ellen returned her attention to the book she was reading. It contained a description of lion behavior in one of the great African reserves, written by a naturalist who had witnessed a lioness fighting her starving cubs for a piece of meat. Later that day the writer had seen the father of the cubs kill a small animal, drag it to a hiding place, and bring the cubs with him, carefully avoiding the mother, to have a meal. Meat was scarce. That year, the naturalist concluded, twenty percent of cubs were abandoned at birth, another twenty died of starvation. Ellen read the pages again slowly. Lions were intensely social animals. The females formed friendships that lasted all their lives and, when food was plentiful, were the most indulgent and protective of mothers.

She heard the front door open, close; Paul was home. There was a momentary silence, then his footsteps moving toward the kitchen, where he expected to find his family. Ellen stretched her arms up, yawning, glancing at the clock, which gave her the happy news that it was early, only five-thirty. The girls had gone out to a party. She and Paul would have five and a half hours alone together. Now his footsteps came back to the staircase. He knew she was home; her car was in the driveway. "Ellen," he called out into the shadows, "are you up there?"

"Yes," she said, "I'm here." She heard the slow plodding of his feet up the stairs; he appeared in the doorway. She took him in, smiling, allowing her real desire, which was to cross the room and throw her arms around him, to subside, for his expression was weary, he was a little pale, he might not respond favorably. "Where are the girls?" he asked.

"At a party. I have to pick them up at eleven."

The news softened the lines around his mouth and his eyes met hers at last. "That's good," he said. "We can have a quiet evening."

Ellen got up, crossed to her husband, kissed his cheek.

"You're home early," he said.

"It was slow today," she replied. "All we did all day was weigh the sea turtles." She slipped her arm under his and nuzzled her face against his neck.

"And are the sea turtles heavy?" Paul asked, amused.

"Very," she said. "And they don't want to be weighed."

Paul smiled. "What an unusual job," he said.

She leaned back, looking into his eyes. To her delight he brought his hand to her cheek and drew her forward for a kiss, nor was it a brief, perfunctory kiss, but a slow exploration of lips and tongue. She kept her eyes open, looking into his, while his arms folded around her back, pulling her into him. Then she closed her eyes and gave herself over to the pleasure of his embrace. It was just as she had hoped; he desired her. She ran her hands down over his shoulders, around his back, wondering at how solid yet mysterious he remained to her, after so many years. She was still astounded by his presence in her life. When he released her, she rested her cheek against his chest, toying idly with the loop of his belt, while he stroked her hair back casually. She felt too shy to speak, too diffident to move. He might take her by the wrists and lead her to the bedroom—sometimes he did that—or he might prefer to wait. She felt his lips at her ear and then on her neck, light kisses; nothing could have been more welcome. She wanted to speak, to say, "I love you," but of course he knew it; he must be able to feel it in the tension of her flesh beneath his mouth, in the curve of her body into his. Her heart ached with desire. She imagined that his hand would move up along her waist and close over her breast; she anticipated this with a still, breathless intensity, as if she could will him to think of it, but he did not. Instead, he released her and said, "I'm beat. I think I'll take a shower."

Ellen fell down from her imagining with a solid thud. "Did you have a bad day?" she asked.

Now he stepped away from her into the bedroom, where he began taking off his shoes. "Not bad," he said. "I found out who this Schlaeger fellow was. He bought Montague Plantation, downriver from Saint Francisville. But he only had it for two years before his wife killed him."

Ellen went to the doorway and looked in. *"Did* she kill him?"

"I guess so," Paul said, peeling off his socks. "They hanged her for it anyway. But the question is, *how* did she kill him?"

"And why," Ellen suggested.

Paul shrugged and said, in his best German accent, "Hermann Schlaeger? Hermann Schlaeger, *mein Liebling?"* He was smiling now. "I'll bet she had a reason."

As she had done for nearly a year now, Camille went to Dr. Veider on Wednesday after work. She did not want to go, did not trust this bland, balding professional who looked at her for long moments without speaking, as if he were trying to see through her skull. She went under duress, her mother's, who resented the expense but had been convinced of the necessity, and Dr. Byer's, the family physician, whom Camille feared and hated. Her time with Dr. Veider was a sentence; she had been convicted by an event she could never recall without a flood of shame. Indeed, she tried never to think of it, but every Wednesday evening as she pushed open the glass door to the dreary clinic downtown, the whole miserable business leaped up before her like a sudden shadow cast by a passing cloud.

It had happened over a year ago. She was seventeen, just out of the Catholic girls' school where she had spent four guilt-ridden years. She hadn't yet found her job, her salvation. Because she was plain, she was not a threat to other girls, and so she had a few friends who occasionally asked her to be a blind date for an unsuspecting young man. The encounters rarely went well, yet she never turned them down. This one was a Tulane boy, a chum of her friend's boyfriend, who didn't have a date for a big party uptown, near the university. Camille's mother, who occasionally had a wild vision of her daughter marrying into what she thought of as "society," was excited by the prospect. She stretched their meager budget for a new dress, which she chose herself, surprising Camille, because, though it was not in any way frivolous, it showed to some advantage her small neat figure, her best feature.

The boy was a plain fellow himself, with spotty skin and a bulbous nose. Camille thought he looked raw. She knew by the time they reached the car that he had got in her what he expected, which wasn't much. On the ride over he asked her a few questions —why wasn't she in college, what music did she like—but he accepted her brief answers without comment. Silence fell heavily, thoroughly, between them, and Camille sat looking at the leaf-shaped pattern in her knit skirt. When the boy reached out to flick on the radio she smiled with relief, but he did not smile back. They drove through the dark streets, up Saint Charles Avenue, where Camille diverted herself by looking at the people in the brightly lit streetcars, then along a maze of streets she did not know to a long driveway that ended at a house bigger than any house Camille had ever been in. It was a warm, clear night, and the lawn was dotted with young people who stood in groups talking and drinking from plastic cups. "You do drink?" Camille's date asked coldly as he parked the car near a large oak overhanging the driveway like a canopy.

"Yes," Camille said.

He shoved his car door open and leaped out onto the curb, throwing back to her, as if it were an admonition, "Let's go."

Camille opened her door and followed him up the drive. The big house stood on piers, but these had been closed in on one side to create a large low-ceilinged room, which was filled with people. Camille's date dived into the crowd and she followed, keeping track of him by the color of his shirt, an odd shade of green. He stopped before a long bar and, inclining his head to her as she came up, though not looking at her, asked, "What do you want?"

"Rum and Coke," she said.

After a moment he handed her a glass. She sipped from it obediently; the Coke was flat. He had two beers, one in each hand, which he used as levers to work his way back from the bar to a small space near a staircase. Camille followed, though he made no indication that he wanted her to, and found a space beside him. They stood side by side, looking out into the crowd. "Nice party," he said, and she agreed. Then she saw her friend across the room, standing inside the protective arm of a handsome boy, whispering something to him, her mouth nearly touching his ear. Whatever she said made him laugh. His arm tightened around her shoulder, he kissed her cheek, then her neck. Camille felt a knot of anxiety in her throat. "There's Kathy," she said to her date, who, following her eyes, spotted his friend and began waving one of his beer bottles over his head, calling, "Frank, over here." In a moment the happy couple joined them. Kathy smiled at Camille, admired her dress. Frank and her date fell into easy banter. Camille caught a quick glance from Frank, an appraisal that required barely a moment to be complete and dismissive. She decided to concentrate on her drink. Both young men seemed committed to the matter of replenishing the young women's drinks. Camille soon found that one or the other went to the bar twice as often for her as they did for her friend, and that she derived a certain prestige by virtue of this frequency. They stayed in the narrow space near the staircase for a long time. Camille relaxed and even essayed a small joke, which was greeted with unexpected enthusiasm by the two young men. Kathy had moved back inside the arm of her boyfriend; Camille's date positioned himself against the wall, and as she flushed with triumph over her witty remark, she felt his hand move around her waist, drawing her to him. When she leaned against him, she stumbled and realized that she could not walk without weaving. He pulled her in close to him and kissed her, pushing her lips apart and shoving his tongue, which seemed to her large, thick, unpleasant, as deep into her mouth as he could get it. She clung to him, fighting down a wave of nausea. His hands ran over her entirely; one explored her breasts while the other moved over her buttocks, and he pushed his tongue around, trying to press it between her teeth and lips, then, when she thought she would have to struggle to get free, he released her and stood smiling down into her face. "All right," he said. Camille understood that he was pleased. Music had started up from somewhere, the volume rising steadily, and the crowd jammed between the two bars began to move about to it obediently. Camille thought dancing might help her, though she dreaded falling down. She recognized the music, a local group who laced their songs with the patois slaves had invented to protect their privacy. This was a song about voodoo.

Camille's date turned her toward the bar and, resting his arm across her shoulder, guided her out into the room. She liked the sensation of his arm against her neck, though it was heavy and forced her to lower her head in such a way that she could not see him. At the bar he secured two drinks, handed her one, and moved out into the vibrating crowd, heading for the door. An elbow collided with Camille's wrist, spilling her drink across her skirt. She brushed the sticky liquid away, but it left a dark stain on the light fabric. She felt she was a boat of some kind, being navigated through the crowd and out onto the driveway, where the warm, damp air slapped into her like a wave, then carefully down the drive and into the back seat of the car. This last was accomplished by a combination of an embrace and a shove. She was magically divested of her drink and laid down across the seat, her date falling in over her, another wave. Camille did what she could to go under peacefully. She opened her mouth to his and put her arms around his back. She had the amusing thought *He certainly is fast* as his hands invaded her clothes, one under her blouse, the other, with surprising speed and indelicacy, up her skirt and beneath her underpants. "Fast" was a word her mother used. Women were "fast." Men were just men.

Another wave hit her, but this one made her fight back. She tore her mouth from his insistent mouth and said, "Wait." He ignored her, dropping his face to the seat beside her and gripping her more tightly, but she struggled, bracing her hands against his chest, pushing hard, until he gave in and said, "What's wrong?" Still pushing, she struggled upward. "I can't," she said.

"It's all right," he said, giving another inch. His hip slid over her leg and she felt the lump of his penis pressing against the seam of his jeans. Now she had her shoulders free, but she couldn't get him off her lower body. "Please," she said, "I've got to sit up."

"What?" he said impatiently as she pulled up, half sitting, the best she could do, and, leaning over the floor succumbed to two powerful waves of nausea, vomiting once, then again, while the world came swiftly into focus, drops of sweat poured out across her forehead, and the young man, lifting himself at last entirely free of her, cried out, "Oh, Christ! Jesus fucking Christ. This is my mother's car."

Camille lifted her head, touching the corners of her mouth with her fingertips, aghast at the acrid taste, the foul smell that surged up to her nostrils, and in that moment it seemed to her she might be able to die of shame. However, in the next moment she continued to live, while the young man beside her, muttering his disgust with her, his outrage at his own fate, threw open the car door and bounded out onto the driveway. Her head cleared for a second time. She pushed the front seat forward, opened the door on her side, and, carefully stepping over the shocking mess on the floor, appalled anew at the sheer physical reproach of it, got onto the driveway and sagged against the door of the car. Her date had come to her but did not touch her or seek to comfort her; in fact, he seemed to be stunned into deeper speechlessness than was his habit. "I'm so sorry," she said. "I guess I had too much to drink."

He found his tongue. "I guess so," he said.

Camille raised her eyes to the bright light pouring from the house. "I'd better go find a bathroom," she said.

"Right," he replied.

"I'll get some paper towels," she added. "I'll clean up your car."

"No," he replied, looking gloomily past her at the interior of the car. "I'll take care of it."

She staggered away from him. If she had been able to walk steadily, to walk away from the house instead of toward it, away from the dull young man and his mother's car, never to see or think of him again, she would have been better off. That thought came to her much later. She made her way instead back into the crowd. At the bar she inquired for a bathroom. There were two, one at the far side of the room, the other up the narrow flight of stairs. Carefully she made her way up into the house, along a carpeted hall past two darkened rooms to a third one, lit, with a door that stood open. She veered into it gratefully, wondering that there was no line, as there was downstairs. Perhaps she had been told about this one only because she looked so desperate. It was brutally white inside; even the towels were all white and larger than the ones in her mother's house. Everything gleamed: the big white pedestal sink, the oversized tub, the toilet, which stood facing her at the end of the room with a frank appeal that struck her, even in her misery, as highly comic. She closed the door behind her and turned the bolt in the lock. She realized that her bladder had been full for some time, so much so that when she took her seat on the toilet and attempted to release it, for a few moments nothing happened. Her thoughts moved to the scene that must, at this moment, be taking place in the driveway. Would he tell anyone, ask for help, complain to anyone who would listen? Was she not the butt of some cruel joke already? Her bladder relaxed and she waited for it to be empty, concentrating on the simple task of finding the toilet paper and unrolling a bit. She was sobering quickly. When she was done, she went to the sink, turned on the faucet, and, leaning over it, began laving cool water into her mouth with her hand. She took in a big mouthful, swished it around, spit it out, swallowed some more, aware that it felt pleasant to be doing this, to be alone where no one could speak to her, quietly washing out her mouth. She even slapped a little water onto her cheeks and forehead. Then, drying her face on a hand towel, she found her reflection in the mirror. She could not bear what she saw. She had put on eye makeup for the occasion, not skillfully, and somehow it had smeared in wide black circles under her eyes. It made her look ridiculous, like a raccoon, nor had she any idea how long she had been like this. Had Kathy seen her this way? Her hair was limp and flat, turning up in some places, down in others, and her skin was greenish. She never enjoyed looking in the mirror, but she could not remember ever having found her reflection so discouraging. When she looked down at herself, she saw the new dress was badly wrinkled, and she noticed the dark, ugly stain left by the spilled drink. Her cheap shoes were scuffed from the dust of the driveway; there was a smudge of dirt on her shin. If only there really were some way to disappear. It was a wish that came to her often enough, almost always during these absurd dates, usually when the boy was pulling off her clothes; then she wished he would get the clothes off and find nothing there. No matter what she did or said, the boys did not call again, and her mother, who seemed never to forget their names, would ask, on returning from her job each day, did Jim or Peter or Arnie call, her eyebrows raised hopefully. Camille herself seldom wanted to hear from the boys again, but her mother's tactless inquiries, her expressions of mild disappointment, made it clear that it did not surprise her that her daughter was undesirable. Camille turned over the events of each failed evening, minute by minute, word by word, though there were seldom many words to turn over, in a desperate search for the key to her failure.

As she stood in the cool, bright bathroom gazing at her unhappy young face in the mirror, she concluded that the key was not anything she did but what she was. The boys always seemed to know it on sight. She knew a few girls who were no more attractive than she was, whose manners were, in her estimation, abrasive and loud, but who retained perfectly ordinary boyfriends, week after week, as dull as the ones who pawed over Camille in the back seats of cars, took her home in silence, and never called again. This one, what was his name, even had good cause. Her own body had betrayed her, revealed her for all to see as disgusting. She put her palms on either side of the sink, leaned against it, and groaned. She could not face the ride home in his soiled car; his gloomy accusing silence would fill the air with poison. Perhaps she could just stay in this quiet bathroom. Surely no one would be looking for her. She closed her eyes, breathing slowly, for the despair was giving way to something else; she recognized it dimly, though she had no name for it. It felt like heat. She rolled her head back, then slowly around, trying to loosen the tightness at the top of her spine. Her eyes were open and she took in the details of the scene, the flowered box of talcum on the back of the toilet, the white wicker rack crammed with shampoos, bath oils, the porcelain toothpaste rack, two white toothbrushes stuck into it—how did they tell which was which—the concave soap receptacle on the sink with its fresh cake of white soap, and behind it the old-fashioned double-edged razor propped against a can of shaving cream, next to a thin package of replacement blades. Her eyes came firmly to rest on the package of razor blades. It was as if she had found something she recognized at last, something simple, comforting, a reliable friend.

She released her hold on the sink and reached out for the package, almost shy of it, picked it up, put it down, turned it over, picked it up again.

Dr. Veider was interested in what happened, what she thought about in the next few moments. She went over it for him time and time again. She could get to this point: she was standing before the sink holding the pack of razors in her palm. He suggested that she was angry. Did she want to get even with the boy for something, for being indifferent to her? She admitted such feelings must have been lurking about, but her principal memory was only that she had come upon a good solution to her problems, to all her problems. She opened the package, extracted one of the blades, dragged it quickly across her right wrist, wincing at the pain; then, awkwardly, for she was left-handed, made a quick slash across the left. The blood welled up at once and ran down her hands, which she held over the sink. It was marvelous then, for a few minutes; her sense of release, of relaxation was complete. It even seemed possible that she might never have to leave this quiet, agreeable place. She turned on the faucets, adjusting them until the water was warm, and lowered her wrists beneath them, watching the water wash the blood down the sink. It was a relief not to be drunk any longer. Her head ached from the speed with which she had hurtled herself from confusion to lucidity. She gave herself a shy smile in the mirror. "You look awful," she said, but though she believed this to be an accurate statement, she didn't much care. As she considered the possibility that the cuts really were bleeding profusely, there was a sudden, heart-stopping, insistent knocking on the door. Whoever it was rattled the knob, then resumed knocking, calling, "Come on. Open the door. What's going on in there?"

She turned off the water and stood staring at the vibrating wood. "Open the door," he said again. She didn't recognize the voice. "I'm not going away until you do," he said, and resumed his furious knocking. He was making such a racket, Camille thought, soon the whole party would be upstairs gathered around the door. "I'm coming," she said softly. What to do with her bleeding wrists? She held them up, thinking the blood might just run into her sleeves, but at her first step she saw a red drop appear on the white tile at her feet, so bright and sudden it seemed to have welled up through the floor. "Damn," she said, making her way to the door, where she turned the bolt and stepped back, for it flew open at once and two young men stood gaping at her. She recognized one as the host; her date had pointed him out earlier, when she could still make out people's faces. "Oh, Christ!" he cried out now, and his friend joined him with the exclamation "Shit, man! Look at this." Camille stepped back. "I'm sorry," she said.

Then followed a miserable scene that lasted a long time. Camille remembered some moments of it with brutal clarity: the look on her date's face when he was summoned upstairs to take responsibility for the calamity, his complaining, as they hustled her down a different flight of stairs, that he didn't even know her, for God's sake, he didn't even like her and she was ruining his evening, his car, his life. Another boy was summoned from the crowd, a medical student who had keys to the university infirmary. Camille was told to undo the towel they had wrapped around her wrists and let him have a look. She saw at once that the cuts were not serious, though they were still bleeding, but the young men, who were all drunk, agreed that she should be taken to the infirmary, so they all piled into a car and careened off into the night. She remembered the medical student's question, as he applied butterfly bandages so roughly that the next day she had to pull them out of the cuts, opening them up again, "Have you ever done anything like this before?"

"No," she said. "It's not like me at all."

Eventually she was taken home by her date, who drove through the lovely warm night with the windows of his car open and the radio off, nor did he say one word to her. She huddled against the door as far from him as she could get, the white gauze around her crossed wrists like a bright badge of shame, and she gave herself over to the more horrible scene to come. When they arrived at her house he said only, "Here you are." She got out of the car, which was pulling away even as her feet hit the pavement, and walked alone up the narrow broken sidewalk to the door behind which her mother sat, pouring out another glass of gin, waiting, impatiently waiting, to tell her what she was worth.

14

Paul looked down at the sleeping woman. She lay on her stomach, her face turned toward him, her long blond hair spread over her shoulders, a few strands straying across her cheek. She had one arm curled under her, the other stretched out, her hand open as if reaching for something, for him. The sheet was twisted about her at the waist, but her long legs were clear of it. He allowed his eyes the pleasure of moving from the rise of her buttocks, barely concealed by the sheet, all the way down to her feet. Her skin was tan, smooth; it seemed golden in the seedy light of the motel lamp. He lingered over her strong thighs, recollecting the thrill that went through him when he felt them tightening about his waist. She was big, taller than he was, but lean, graceful; she moved with unexpected ease. He looked at her face; her mouth was slightly open and she breathed softly. Her face was beautiful, especially in repose, the cheekbones high, her forehead wide and smooth; her full mouth open so slightly suggested both innocence and eroticism. He remembered her soft voice in his ear. "Paul," she said as they were falling asleep, their arms and legs entwined so comfortably, so naturally, "I love you."

His heart contracted; tears sprang unbidden to his eyes; he turned away. He looked instead at the ashtray next to the bed, containing the stubs of her inevitable cigarettes. She really should stop smoking. But even the cigarettes seemed dear to him now; there was the open pack she had torn into greedily after their lovemaking, her face flushed with blood, her eyes misty from pleasure. Paul put his hand over his eyes. It was dangerous to look at anything. He had a sense of drowning, of going under with love for this young woman, this Donna, with whom he had started a casual affair to amuse himself, to make him feel alive and strong; and now he thought he was in serious, terrible trouble because he was in love with her and it did seem possible that she was in love with him.

He was forty-seven; she was twenty-five. People would doubtless make fun of the difference in years and he knew as well as anyone that the future of such a union couldn't be bright. He did tiresome calculations: when he was sixty, she would be thirty-eight; when he was seventy, giving in, his body a recalcitrant, unresponsive collection of exhausted muscle and tissue, she would be forty-eight. The thought of what she would be at forty-eight dismayed him. Ellen was only forty, but she seemed already to be entering a resigned usefulness, ambitious still and certainly strong, competent, but not, as this young woman was, excitable, capable of fire. Ellen had the patient look of one who has survived a great passion. She seemed now, he thought, as she had not for the twenty years of their marriage, to be content, to breathe easily. She was preoccupied with her work much of the time; her unconscious was full of sick animals, and often, when she looked pensive and he inquired into her thoughts, she responded with a description of some clinical problem. "The trouble with a viral infection," she had said, only last night, "is that the virus moves on, it's gone, and when you get in there all you can find is the damage. You're left with all this damage."

Perhaps she no longer loved him and that was why he had been able to fall in love. He stood on the ugly carpet in the dinginess of one of the many motel rooms he had passed through, year after year, but everything was different, entirely new; he might as well have arrived on another planet, and in order to keep his terror at bay he stayed very still, gazing into space, and told himself one helpless, desperate lie after another.

15

The Peaceable Kingdom. Importantly the lion stands next to the lamb. Animals who do not exist in the same hemisphere with one another look out at the viewer, serene and imperturbable. In there somewhere, in the crowd, are two children, a boy and a girl. It's not a serious proposition, clearly, but more on the order of a vision. The trees are dark green and gold, flowers bloom underfoot, under hoof and paw; the sky is dark but it looks warm. No hint of death touches the scene; the carnivores all have their mouths closed in dreamy smiles, no teeth in evidence. It's a painting that has enormous appeal to children; they confront it with smiles that match those on the otherworldly faces of the impossible animals who look back at them; they exchange innocent glances. Of course it is inevitable that this picture be reprinted in zoo advertisements all over the world. It's the lie the public requires these days; everything must be seen mysteriously to thrive. In other centuries, when the wild held its own against the forces of civilization, it was enough to look at a miserable, flea-bitten, half-starved lion stalking a cage barely large enough to turn around in, to point at him and taunt him for having been so unfortunate as to be captured; this was a satisfactory attitude toward the wild: bring it down. Now that we have been successful in that quest we want to be told it isn't so, to see wild animals at a safe distance, healthy and strong, as if their existence is not threatened at all.

Ellen pushed the brochure to the back of her desk. That morning she had gone out to the African Plains exhibit to examine a blesbok with an ugly hard cyst on the side of his face. Though she concluded he was not in any danger, the keepers wanted him off exhibit at once; he looked bad. On her way back she had passed through the Asian exhibit, through the inevitable crowd around Sonya, then behind two boys who stood before the two young snow leopards on loan from a zoo in Ohio. One boy read the educational sign on the rail—"Only five hundred left"—to the other, who replied, "Well, that's a lot."

Once when she was complaining to Lillian and Celia about the public's indifference to the extinction of species, of the impossibility of reversing the brutal statistics, a species a day at a recent count, gone, out of existence, never to reappear, Celia replied, "Mom, people just don't care about lions and tigers. They never see them, except in a zoo, and if they never saw them at all it just isn't going to change anybody's life. It's not going to change my life."

Ellen said, "So you two think I'm just some mad romantic on a fool's errand. That's what my work is to you."

Both girls glanced down; they could not look at her. Then Lillian said, "No, I don't think that," and Celia added, "I'm just agreeing with you."

Ellen relaxed. Everything was not lost.

"And what if humans became extinct?" Celia asked.

"That would be a loss too," Ellen said.

Lillian sniffed. "I find that harder to agree to," but Celia said, "I don't," impatient, cold.

This was an essential difference between them. Lillian could imagine a world without herself in it; Celia could not. When Ellen thought about how different her daughters were from each other she couldn't resist the genetic explanation. Lillian was like her; Celia was like Paul. It was Paul's complete self-centeredness that attracted Ellen, for he seemed to be more in himself, less likely to drift away or disappear, than Ellen felt herself to be. He wasn't self-conscious—indeed, he had contempt for those who occupied their thoughts with introspection—but, rather, turned inward. It was more difficult to be Paul or Celia than Ellen or Lillian, because the latter pair never felt themselves to have much at stake. We could live without ourselves, Ellen thought; an impossible locution, yet there was a certain truth to it.

But there was another explanation for Celia's passionate desire to be at the center of everything, and this one was more disturbing, that Celia, as a baby, had not been wanted. Lillian was all Ellen had wanted, one daughter, an ally, and in some ways a guarantor of her father's affection. Of course Paul had not, as anticipated, "settled down" with the advent of a daughter; in fact, fatherhood had had precisely the opposite effect. He had become incautious, almost flamboyant, in his infidelities, yet strident in his insistence that the marriage not be dissolved. So Ellen, beleaguered by the pressures of vet school, anxiety for her marriage, and caring for Lillian, had carried the unexpected, unwanted second daughter through months of sleeplessness and misery, expecting the future to be worse than the present. Miraculously, Celia's birth had changed everything, not at once, but slowly. Perhaps Paul only took pity on his exhausted wife. Unlike Lillian, Celia was a difficult, sickly baby, a condition that strained Ellen's patience to the breaking point but seemed to endear the child to her father. Something in Celia called out to him as Lillian, who was placid and cheerful, did not. Perhaps Ellen's preoccupation with Lillian, the great satisfaction she had found in holding her, nursing her, closing herself off with her, had pushed her husband away, and now Celia, who needed him, who, when she could not be quieted by her mother, was consoled by him, made it possible for him to re-enter his family. Ellen came to admire Celia for the unexpected stores of patience and tenderness she was able to draw from her father; she relied on him and he could not let her down. So, Ellen thought, they knew each other, and at length she stopped resenting Celia, came to love her as she loved her husband, for her very inwardness, her demanding life force, her need for attention, her passionate love of pleasure.

Her resemblance to him caused the pitched battles that erupted now, with disturbing frequency, between Paul and his younger daughter. He battled with Lillian as well, but not with the same ferocity that characterized his arguments with Celia, who, he maintained, was the more unreasonable of the two. He had wanted the Brontë sisters, studious, wildly imaginative, yet docile, and could not understand how his paternal efforts had resulted in these two young women who were so determined to leave behind the world of music and literature, passion and beauty. He loved the past; he had, through his work, found a way to live in it.

And I, Ellen thought, live in dread of the future, of what it will look like, of how ugly and cold it will be, while our daughters sit solidly down in the present, that no man's land where we never go.

She put her head down in her hands. The silence of the house was palpable around her; through it she could make out the smallest sounds, the cat changing position on the couch downstairs, a tree limb touching the window in the next room. She was alone; the girls were staying overnight with friends; Paul was on his trip, not alone. For the second time that day she succumbed to a premonition: she was losing him. It was to be expected, given his age, his dissatisfaction with his work, his inability to let his daughters be other than what he wanted, to let them go, his need for romance, for the unexpected, and her own preoccupation with her work, her dread of the confrontation to come, which made her draw away from him, daily, in self-defense.

She lifted her face from her hands and her eyes fell upon the zoo brochure, the dreamy faces of the animals and people in the fantasy kingdom. In the next moment, she thought, all hell breaks loose. Why do we long for nature to be safe and peaceful when it never has been? How have we come to imagine it? Was it just so harsh, so terrifying, were the nights so black and full of noise, the days so hot, food so scarce, water so hard to come by that after hours of staring into the darkness near the opening of some comfortless cave, falling asleep from exhaustion on the arm of a nervous relative, we entered, unbeknownst to one another, into a sweet communal dream of being safe, warm, well fed, comfortable, at peace?

Many of the guests at André Davillier's dinner dance came up from New Orleans on the steamboat *Doswell,* which rolled ponderously into the Rosedawn landing in the afternoon. A second contingent, largely male, came by horseback after dark. The servants carried torches back and forth to the house, through the maze of trees and greenery, guiding the visitors up from the landing on one side of the house and on the other carrying up great platters of cold meats, heavy iron pots of rice and gumbo, pheasant and quail stuffed and reconstructed in their plumage, and blocks of ice to chill the champagne and to keep the sherbet from melting, for it was a warm night, though clear and unusually dry.

To spare hands, torches had been attached to stakes at intervals along the wide oak alley leading into the plantation from the river road, and it was by the light of these ghostly, sputtering flames that the steady flow of carriages and men on horseback made their clattering way to the front porch. Once their equipages were dispatched to the capable hands of Rosedawn's grooms and stable men, the ladies and gentlemen were greeted by their generous host.

Hermann Schlaeger had started out from Montague in broad daylight and ridden alone on the levee most of the trip, for the guests came principally from downriver. But in the last hour of his journey the sun had set, and he found himself riding through the darkness in a thickening stream of cheerful traffic. The men shouted greetings to one another, and from the open carriages the soft voices of the ladies floated toward him like a vapor, sensuous and maddening, for he could not understand a word of it. As the guests turned into the drive, the agreed-upon pace was the trot. The horses, sensing their destination and their dinners at hand, held their heads high, their ears up and eyes flashing at one another. The high spirited essayed an occasional nip or kick at a passing stranger. Hermann's horse had a miserable trot but a remarkable slow canter, which he set into with ease, so Hermann passed among the bobbing crowd, a big man carried smoothly forward, neither speaking nor smiling to his neighbors, so that the ladies murmured to one another, *"Qui est-il?"* and the gentlemen exchanged looks charged with inexplicable hostility.

André Davillier, who watched this progress from the porch, called one of his sons to take his place, for he saw that M. Schlaeger would require assistance, would have to be taken about and introduced in English, plied a little with champagne to loosen his reserve, treated, though he was hardly more than an acquaintance, as a valued friend. He was an impressive figure as he swirled up the drive on his fine black horse, dressed to perfection, no doubt at the advice of his manservant, and having about his heavy jaw and ruddy cheeks that freshly scrubbed look which struck André as peculiarly German, as if he'd gone after his face with a hairbrush. The two men greeted each other, Hermann gruff, André easy and disarming. He was a man who enjoyed charming barbarians; he took it as a challenge. "Now, my friend," he said, leading Hermann into the blaze of light in the hall, "I will introduce you to some beautiful ladies."

Hermann was taller than most of the men in the room, and his bulk made him seem even larger, for the Creoles were not a muscular lot. Unused to work, fond of eating and drinking, at their best they were compact and sinewy, at their worst red-faced and corpulent. The women, Hermann noticed, were smaller still. Dressed in white or black, though here and there he saw a splash of pale blue or pink, they stood about in small groups, rattling their fans, laughing at the jokes of the men, wide-eyed and excitable, like flocks of birds liable to fly away at a moment's notice. From a passing tray André secured two glasses of champagne, handed one to Hermann, and steered him into a small group, three men and two women, who at the approach of their host looked up expectantly from their conversation. Hermann swallowed his champagne at a gulp as he was introduced, in English, as "our new neighbor at Montague, Monsieur Hermann Schlaeger." One of the men, a bandy-legged, beady-eyed fellow who made Hermann think of a rooster, remarked that Montague was a fine house, that it had been empty too long, and another, M. Pierrot, announced that he planned to call on Hermann soon; in the past he had sent his New Orleans mail to the Montague landing and hoped he might have leave to continue this practice. The women said nothing, but gazed up at Hermann with vague smiles as they were introduced, Mme. Delphine Pierrot and Mlle. Clothier. A tray of champagne floated by and the group helped themselves. The ladies, Hermann determined, had little English and regarded him as a curiosity, though they were too polite to chatter about him before his face. After a few more idle exchanges—the overseer at Montague was a treasure, one of the best on the river; the cotton crop was fine this year, sugar cane had not done so well—André eased his guest out of this group and headed for another. The musicians had set up in the ballroom and the first strains of a waltz drifted out across the hall, an invitation to gaiety that affected the guests like the caress of a warm breeze; they lifted their elegant heads and breathed in the sound. Hermann, who did not dance, was not touched by the music. It was another language that eluded him.

The next group he met was much the same. Everyone, he concluded, had been in his house and knew the exact acreage of his property. It was not as if he owned Montague but as if he represented Montague, which owned its particular place. It was now his obligation to take that place without disturbing the surface of this gay, indolent, artificial society. He had a sense of these people, these Creoles, with their dark Spanish eyes and French manners, as ultimately fragile, liable to crack, like thin veneer.

The evening wore on, filled with music, conversation, the smell of wild roses, which had been placed in heavy vases in every available space. When the party moved into the dining room, the steam from the food rose over the laden table and, mingling with the perfume of the roses, the various scents rising from the bare shoulders of the ladies, turned the tide from gaiety to giddiness. The heavy chandeliers poured a golden, creamy light over everything, and the guests seemed to bask in it, smiling and nodding to one another as if they had just come into the sun. Even Hermann, unaccustomed to good champagne, which he had been drinking like water, felt his senses overloaded with new and delicious pleasure, and as he looked at the burdened table, the glittering crystal, the gold-edged china, pale and thin as the rose petals drooping nearby, the silver dishes and platters heaped with steaming meats, thick brown gumbos in which red crab claws and green okra floated brightly, the carefully arranged feathers of the duck, quail, pheasant surrounded by apples, grapes, and rich, dark plums, his expression softened, the hard lines of his mouth relaxed, and he said to the stranger next to him, "What a fine dinner we are having."

"Yes," the man replied. "But you must come to my house at Christmas. Our table is twice as long."

The master of Rosedawn and his wife stood near the doorway, passing the diners along to their excellent children, who seemed to have the seating arrangements memorized and ready to implement, like a battle plan. Hermann was directed to the top of the table, close to his host. He moved through a thin stream of English that seemed always available to him though rarely more than two people in width. His seat was next to his neighbor, Hector Chauvin of Chester Plantation, who introduced himself "with much pleasure," and turned Hermann's attention to the young woman on his other side, a companion they were fortunate to have, Hector maintained, as she was usually taken up by the delights of the city but had come up just a week ago to visit her aunt and to have a bit of country air, Mlle. Elisabeth Chauvin Boyer. As Hermann made his stiff bow, leaning over the delicate, cool hand this lady extended to him, he heard Hector's continued introduction: the name Chauvin was her mother's, of course, who had been Aimée Chauvin, Hector's father's first cousin, and so he had the pleasure of calling Elisabeth his cousin as well. Hermann made little sense of this genealogy, for as he raised his lips from Elisabeth's hand his eyes found hers at last. She did not smile, blush, or look away, as ladies had done all evening; rather, she met his gaze, coolly, he thought, and steadily, held it as she spoke, her voice soft, her English almost without accent. "Mr. Schlaeger," she said. "Of course we are all so curious to meet you. It must be trying to come into this gawking crowd as a novelty. Unfortunately for you, you are the mystery of the season."

Hermann drew her chair out carefully, bending over her as she arranged her heavy skirts so that she could sit down. "I'm afraid there is nothing very mysterious about me," he said. There was a great bustle about them, the many chairs all being pulled back across the carpet, the guests arranging themselves while the servants, who had been standing silently, invisibly against the wall, were suddenly in evidence, filling glasses and lifting heavy dishes to carry about the table. Hermann used the opportunity to take a gulp of water and another of champagne. Elisabeth, her elbow propped against the table, her small chin resting on her hand, watched him coyly. It was her turn to speak, but she did not. When he turned to her she only smiled, appraising him, he thought, observing that he was nervous, out of place, uncertain how to proceed. "There is no mystery about me," he repeated dully.

It was nearly dawn when Hermann set out from Rosedawn, but he was not the last to leave. Some of the party had planned to stay overnight; those who hadn't but were judged too drunk to walk fell asleep where they sat. Elisabeth, who had come in a carriage, left near three, just as the servants, having cleared the dining table, began to serve coffee and French bread. Hermann walked with her to the porch; he had not left her side since dinner except when he was forced to, when she was asked to dance and he'd stood against the wall watching her whirl about the room, nor had she seemed to want to be away from him, for whenever the music stopped, she returned to him, her cheeks flushed, her dark eyes shining with pleasure. She introduced him to her partners gaily, as if she were showing him off, and he had come to feel, through her influence, handsome rather than hulking, interesting rather than awkward. As he handed her into the carriage he had his wits sufficiently about him to say, "May I call on you?" to which she responded, "At my aunt's? Of course. We'll go riding."

He returned to the dining room feeling as lighthearted as he could, being, as he was, of a somber, dark disposition, and he took his cup of strong coffee absentmindedly, scanning the room for his host, whom he found, to his surprise, leaning in the doorway, cup in hand, gazing back at him with an expression of mild amusement. As Hermann approached, André ushered him into the drawing room, pulled one chair close to another, and indicated his willingness to talk. "You want to know about Mademoiselle Boyer," he began, to which Hermann responded, "You have read my thoughts."

"Not a difficult task, my friend, I'm sorry to tell you."

Hermann looked down into his cup. "I don't think I behaved indiscreetly," he said.

"Oh, no." André laughed. "I'm not criticizing *you.*"

"Elisabeth," Hermann said.

"Elisabeth is a willful young woman," André interrupted. "She is engaged to her cousin René Martin and has been since she was a child. She has taken it into her head not to marry him and she has been sent up here to reconsider her decision. Her father has told her she won't have a cent if she refuses, and he is a man of his word."

"I see," Hermann said. A shout of laughter went up from the dining room and the two men turned to listen. There was a stream of voluble French, followed by a clatter, a chair falling over. André smiled. "They are wrecking my house," he said affably.

"Would it be improper for me to call on her?" Hermann asked.

André shrugged his shoulders. "You are a widower; she is engaged. And then the difference in your ages. *Mon Dieu*. What could be improper in that?"

There was another shout, which brought André to his feet. "You must excuse me," he said, and he left Hermann pondering his answer; was it ironic or serious? He swallowed the last of his coffee. What did he care if Elisabeth had no money; what better way might there be into this closed, myopic society than to oppose it utterly? Her father must relent in time, especially if he were presented with a grandchild. Hermann strode out onto the porch and ordered the servant to bring up his horse. Then he went quickly into the dining room, where, amid the laughter and chatter of the drunken guests, Hermann found the master of Rosedawn perched precariously on a straight-backed chair, beating time with a loaf of French bread for three or four fellows who stood with their arms about one another, loudly singing what even Hermann was able to recognize as a bawdy song.

17

The nobility of the sentiments there expressed. Paul turned the volume up a notch and stood gazing vacantly at the row of dials. Once when Ellen found him standing in this way, moved to tears by a piece of music, she had asked impatiently what it was that so affected him and he had answered with this line about nobility. It struck him as the right answer, then and now, and indeed she had accepted it. She was on the lookout for false sentiment because she was often offended by the sentimentality the public exhibited toward the animals she was trying to keep alive for them to gawk at. She was suspicious of culture, of its ability to disguise or even to glorify destruction and tyranny. Once when he expressed dismay over a newspaper article about a deerhunter's struggle to haul the heavy carcass of his prey out of the woods, she had snapped at him. "Those hunters can take one deer a season and they put the meat in the only appliance they have, which is a freezer. The actual damage they do to the planet is nothing compared to what we do, with our two cars and our wall of books and your record collection."

"Do you mean the only way to save the planet is to give up all that makes life worth living? Art and music? Books?" he protested. "Do we have to live in tents in the woods and hunt wild animals with bows and arrows?"

"That would be a start," she said, but she was smiling at him, at his incredulity. She knew he was serious; such a choice was not to be considered. He would not see his pleasure in this Brahms piano quartet, a new acquisition—he had come to Brahms chamber music only recently—he refused to see his pleasure in it as a threat to the planet. The music swelled and thickened. It was so unexpectedly dense, so rich, finally so interesting, he couldn't think of anything but following it as best he could, for he was not a musician, couldn't read a score, and apprehended music through his mathematical sense and his highly developed sense of drama, of pathos, and nobility.

Now he called upon it to release him from unbearable thoughts, but his effort was in vain; the music seemed to amplify his suffering. Nothing could divert him; even his research had failed him today. Last night, while making love to his wife, he had nearly spoken his mistress's name. He heard it, knew it, altered it at once to *darling,* and he was certain Ellen hadn't noticed, but there it was, a piece of evidence so damning he winced to recall it. Here, before Brahms, he took out the painful fragment of memory and palmed it over once again, as he had done a hundred times already. Surely it was a small matter, nothing serious, a slip of the tongue. But his head ached and his mouth was dry. Suppose he had failed to correct it? Suppose he had spoken her name into Ellen's ear, so near his lips? She had been on top of him, straddling him, moaning loudly, for the girls were out, they didn't have to keep their voices down for a change, and as she came to the end of a long, stunning orgasm, her lips swollen, her eyes rolled up, she had lowered her face close to his, kissing his neck, his cheek; then he had closed his eyes, put his mouth to her ear, and in the next moment heard the D already formed and in the air. Panic seized him, his eyes flew open, he said, "Darling," and Ellen continued her murmuring while the blood drained from his face like a tide. Suppose he had said *Donna* clearly?

Paul didn't allow himself the convenience of believing that this slip must indicate his unconscious wish to tell his wife of his affair. He had never been particularly interested in what his unconscious might or might not want, and even if such a theory was true, what difference did it make, since consciously, with his whole heart and mind, he did not want her to know? His present terror was caused by his certainty that, no matter how he tried or what he might want, eventually she would know. Everything was happening quickly. It would not be long before Donna would require a choice, your family or me, and she had a perfect right to do so. She was young, beautiful; she could have a happy, full life without him, with someone who wasn't always checking the dining room nervously lest they be seen together or leaving her in dreary motel rooms to drive back home in time for dinner. And the thought of that someone, of her long smooth limbs wrapped around his back, of her laughter muffled against his shoulder, her eyes looking into his as she brought his face close to her own to be kissed, this thought turned his knees to water, he sagged against the stereo cabinet, and Brahms only made things worse by pouring him into an andante of unendurable longing.

The volume was turned so high he didn't hear the door from the garage open. Ellen stood in the doorway watching him for many moments while the music filled the room between them, a solid wall of music. She did not really listen to it, beyond noting the appalling volume, which made it impossible to speak. In her opinion Paul was going a little deaf. She wondered how long he would stand so, his face in his hand, strangely bent at the shoulders and knees, absorbed in his listening. His hair, which had once been thick and black, was thinning a little at the crown, was gray at the temples, but otherwise he might pass for a younger man. She took a step into the room, then another, until he detected her movement in his peripheral vision and turned toward her suddenly, his eyes filled with something strangely like terror.

"You startled me," he said as she reached out to him, kissed his cheek. He drew away, almost imperceptibly; it was hardly a motion, but she felt it and dropped back on her heels. It wasn't a rebuff. He might in the next moment be cajoled into a kiss, a long embrace, but Ellen knew herself, for no particular reason, unequal to the challenge. She was tired. She had spent the morning inoculating camels, a dangerous, hateful job. It took four people to hold each one while it balked, spit, screamed, shit, tried to bite or kick her. The dust had swirled up so thickly she couldn't see the syringe, and twice she had dropped to her knees to avoid a well-placed hoof. Doubtless she still smelled of camel and this had caused Paul's reaction. "I'm going to clean up," she said.

Paul looked at her retreating back. Her shoulders were bowed and her hair needed combing. "Bad day?" he said cheerfully, loud enough to be heard over the music.

She turned to him in the doorway. "Awful," she said. "Let's feed the girls and go out to dinner."

He nodded. A quiet dinner, then early to bed. She would be too tired to make love. He would not say Donna's name in his sleep. For one more night they were safe.

18

This man was a painter. Camille had met him through another man, who had an art gallery where she sometimes spent her week-end afternoons, waiting for a man to come and get her. He wasn't a very good painter—even Camille, who knew very little about art, knew this—but the man did not seem to know it himself. As they walked along the street to his apartment, he upbraided Camille for her ignorance; she had never heard of him or his work. He opened the gates to a shady patio and led her back to the slave gallery, up the narrow staircase to the glass doors, where he stopped to use another key. Shelbourne, the gallery owner, had told Camille this man lived comfortably on family money, though the family was displeased with him. They wanted him to become a lawyer.

He wasn't much taller than Camille, but she guessed he was fifteen or twenty years older. His wiry hair was shot with gray and beneath his strong chin the skin on his neck was beginning to sag.

His eyes were dark, hectic, and he looked out of them impatiently. The door came open, Camille stepped inside, and he followed, closing and locking it behind them.

It was a nice place. The walls had been knocked down on one end; this was his studio, scattered with newspapers, tables on which lay tubes of paint, plates covered with blobs of dried paint, jar after jar of brushes. Arranged around the room and on the easel were examples of his paintings. The paint was applied thickly and without much skill so that the colors were muddy. Faces looked out from the smudgy backgrounds, all of them twisted and ugly, some grimacing from what must have been pain. The man gestured toward this part of the apartment. "That's where I work," he said. "That's where I really live."

There was a gallery catalogue on the table next to Camille with his name in bold letters across the top. Apparently the man was actually able to sell his ugly paintings. He didn't notice Camille looking at the catalogue, for he had gone ahead into the little kitchen, which also had no door, just an archway. He was standing at the counter putting ice into two glasses. Through the other archway Camille saw the bedroom. This was in great disorder and crowded with furniture, but there was so much that was beautiful in it she felt she was looking into a picture. The bed, in an alcove all its own, was a big sleigh bed of dark mahogany, unmade, its pillows on either end half hidden by the heavy purple quilted satin coverlet, which looked as if it had been thrown back impatiently. A matching wardrobe stood open, spilling its contents nearby, the drawers down one half pulled open like steps. Next to the bed was a big round mahogany table scattered with books, half-empty coffee cups, ashtrays and plates heaped with cigarette butts, magazines. The floor was covered by an oriental carpet, all dark, winy colors; Camille knew at a glance it was the most valuable thing in the room. In one corner a big brocade and mahogany chair stood invitingly, though the arms were draped with clothes. The two windows were shuttered and the light filtered through the wooden slats, making a cool pattern of shade and light. The man came to her and handed her a glass of bourbon and ice. "What a lovely room," she said.

He gave her a narrow look, then reached out to touch her hair, pushing a loose strand back from her face. "How old are you?" he asked.

"Nineteen."

He smiled. "You don't know anything. At your age you do all your thinking with your cunt."

Camille raised her drink to her lips. She felt she had been slapped. The cold bourbon slipped down her throat; she took it as comfort. When she had swallowed, she put her tongue into the glass and licked the ice. The man rested his hand on the small of her back, propelling her into the room. "Take your clothes off," he said.

He went to the bed and began unbuttoning his shirt, looking back at her coldly. Camille put her drink on the table and pulled off her sandals. She had on only a dress and underpants, so, in a moment, she was naked. The man was still struggling with his socks. She stood watching him, drinking her drink, summoning up her courage. She wished he had not spoken to her crudely. He motioned her to him and she went. He put one hand on her hip as she stood before him, while with his other hand he opened the drawer in the bedside table and took out a fresh pack of cigarettes and a box of matches. Camille looked down into the drawer and saw a small revolver. He noticed her expression of surprise. "I was robbed," he said, slamming the drawer shut and unwrapping the foil top of the cigarette pack. "It's not going to happen again." He fumbled out a cigarette without taking his eyes from her body, which he seemed to be raking over, her breasts, her waist, her crotch, her thighs. She felt his eyes pause over each piece of her like hot probes. "Turn around," he said and she obeyed. Then he let her go, for he needed both hands to light his cigarette. She could hear him, the scratch of the match against the box, the quick sucking sound of his breath. "Do you want a cigarette?" he asked.

"No," she said, "I don't smoke."

"Sit down," he said. Camille turned to him, then sat down beside him on the bed. His penis had become erect and stood up between his legs aggressively. She tried not to look at it, but he caught her shy glance. He took her hand in his and wrapped it around himself, then began working it up and down, puffing at his cigarette all the while, his eyes fixed on her hand. She had a sinking sensation in her stomach and in her chest, a dull revulsion spreading in concentric circles from some central point. When it got to her throat, she coughed. This drew his attention to her face. He released her hand and, holding her by the back of the neck, pushed her head down over his lap. Camille had a moment of real panic. She knew what was expected of her, but she had never done it before. She closed her eyes and, as a preparation, kissed his thighs and abdomen, which seemed to please him. He thought she was teasing, not stalling. Then she put her hand around the penis, stroking it a few times, her eyes opened now. The smell of his genitals offended her; she tried not to breathe it in. He grew impatient. His cigarette-stained fingers sought her mouth, pried it open, and shoved the penis inside. Her throat closed and she gagged, so he released her a little, but then the hand on her neck tightened again and she was shoved back down. What was she to do with her tongue, her lips, her teeth? She moved her head up and down now on her own and the hand released her. She covered her teeth with her lips, directed the throbbing, strangely living thing to the roof of her mouth, and breathed through her nose. The man groaned with pleasure. "Baby," he said.

Baby, she thought. Baby indeed.

As she continued the monotonous operation, he let his hand wander freely over her, stroking and squeezing her breasts, pressing between her legs. She could hear him still smoking the cigarette. At length he put it down in the ashtray, pulled her up with both hands, and pushed her onto her back across the sheets. Then, without speaking, he buried his face between her legs. Camille lay looking about the room, giving herself over to horror. She rubbed her lips with her fingers, as she might have rubbed away an unpleasant kiss. The man had his tongue and the fingers of one hand involved now; he seemed frantic, and Camille, looking down at him, experienced a rare moment of pity, followed by a wave of hate. She closed her eyes, clenching her teeth against it, but a low groan escaped. The man, hearing this, suddenly sat up. His cigarette had gone out in the ashtray so he busied himself lighting a new one. "Turn over," he said.

Camille lay still. "Why?" she said.

He laughed, puffed his cigarette, giving her his cold look. "Just do it," he said, "and I'll show you why."

Camille complied. She lay on her stomach while he ran his hand over her buttocks, then again began pressing between her legs where she was wet from his tongue. He put down his cigarette, positioned himself behind her, and pulled her hips upward. "Come on," he said. "Get up on your hands and knees."

She'd seen something like this in a movie, though it had shown only the couple's faces and shoulders, leaving the rest to the viewer's imagination. Reluctantly Camille yielded her hips to the man's hands, rising up on her knees.

"Bend your back," he said, pushing down at the center of her back, but it seemed to her that doing as he asked would leave her cruelly exposed, so she kept her back arched upward. She felt his penis against her, first touching her legs, being positioned by his hand just inside her. Then, with a thrust so sudden it knocked her off her hands and she fell face down onto the sheets, he was deep inside, so deep it hurt her and she cried out. But he paid no attention to her cry, only pulled back a little and thrust again, this time deeper still. She shouted, trying to pull away from him, but he brought his arm down around her hips and held her fast. He did it again and again, picking up speed. For a few moments she gave in, closed her eyes, gulping in air through her mouth, collecting strength. She felt a thickness in her palate, her gums ached, she was salivating so heavily a stream of water poured out of her mouth onto the sheet. The man was over her, oblivious of her, pounding at her relentlessly, making sounds now that were almost words.

She pushed up onto her hands, feeling stronger now, as if she were waking up. Strength poured into her legs. Her back arched as he had requested, allowing him to drive deeper. He called out his pleasure to her. "That's good," he said, then, "Baby, baby." She made a sound too, a low groan. Now she opened her eyes and looked out into a sea of red. She gasped, closed her eyes, tried again, but to no avail. Everything was red, a wall of blood. She tried to speak but could not frame a word. Her tongue was like a wad of damp leather; she thrust it out of her mouth. Still the man did not sense that anything was wrong. She pushed her buttocks up against him, rising on her knees, and for a moment he was forced to give in to her pressure. "Wait, baby," he said, for he had missed a stroke. She began to turn beneath him, her upper body dropping down low. With one hand she reached across her shoulder and caught him by his hair. Then he saw her face, and his offensive fell apart. "What the fuck," he said, pulling back from her. She released his hair, though reluctantly, so that some of it came away in her hand. She felt the lather at her mouth; some of it flew out and hit his shoulder as she came up under him, twisting away from him. His penis popped out of her with a wet, slapping sound. "What are you doing?" he said, pushing her away with both hands, but he wasn't fast enough; she was inside his arms. She dug her nails into his shoulders, tried to sink her teeth into his neck, but he turned his head to protect himself, and she caught him on the side of the face. She held on while a sensation of such overwhelming pleasure flooded through her, she was weakened by it, and he tore her loose from his flesh, slapping her across the face so hard she bit her tongue. He used his feet too, kicking her away. She lost her balance, fell out of the bed, and landed on her back on the floor. Her head came down last and hit the table leg, making such a crack even the man looked alarmed, but she felt it only as a moment of blackness. Then she lay still, perfectly conscious, looking up at him, tasting the blood from her own tongue as it welled up in her mouth.

He was sitting on the edge of the bed. One hand clutched his cheek so that she couldn't see whether he was bleeding or not, but there were a few specks of blood on his shoulders from her nails. He had an expression of such outrage on his features, it struck her as comic. Even though she knew it would only increase his anger, she could not resist the impulse to smile. She felt oddly peaceful, happy, perfectly serene, but only for a moment while the man found his tongue. "What are you?" he cried. "Some kind of nut?"

She said nothing, so he went on. "Jesus, get the hell out of here." He got up and went to the chair, pulled her dress roughly off the back of it, and threw it at her. "Get your clothes on and get the hell out of here."

Camille sat up and began pulling the dress over her head. The man strolled around in the narrow spaces of his room, muttering obscenities. She came out of the neck of her dress in time to see him uncover his cheek to the mirror. She hadn't drawn blood but there were deep marks in the thin flesh, clearly teeth marks. In a day they would turn to ugly bruises. "Fucking maniac," he said. "Jesus Christ." Without looking at her he strode out of the room to the kitchen, where she heard him running water. She got to her feet slowly. There were several areas of pain: the back of her head, her side where he had kicked her, her tongue, which had stopped bleeding but throbbed, and her eyes, which burned. She found her underpants and sandals, put them on, and stood smoothing her hair. The man came back into the room. He had put on a white robe and combed his hair. "What are you doing?" he said. "Would you get the hell out of here?"

"I'm going," she said.

He went to the French doors and pulled them open, standing inside. "Go right now," he said. "I don't want to talk about it."

Camille did as he asked, wondering if she would say anything to him as she went out. Words came to mind—sorry, I was thinking with my cunt—but she knew she would not say that. Your paintings are ugly—but he would attribute her opinion to her undeveloped artistic sense. I am vengeance. This last thought surprised her. She left without speaking and he followed her, standing on the balcony as she made her way down the steps to the quiet, dreamy patio. There was a fountain in the center of it and she wanted to stop, to put her hand in the water and drink from it to cool her poor tongue, but the man sensed her intention and called, "Don't stop! Keep going." She went to the gate, which suddenly emitted a blaring electric sound, a kind of scream. He had his hand on the button inside the door. She pulled the iron bars open, then turned back to look at him. "And stay away from here," he called out. The street was hot, glaring; she had a sense of being expelled from paradise. As she stepped out onto the pavement and let the gate click closed behind her, she put her hand in the pocket of her dress and pulled out the five-dollar bill she knew was there. She could get a cold drink at the café she frequented on Saint Louis Street. It would be cool there, under the awning. If she sucked on an ice cube, maybe she could get her mouth back to normal.

19

It had been a mistake to paint her nails. As she placed the napkin back on the table, Ellen looked at her fingers and saw that the creamy pale polish only served to throw the gnarled look of her hands into relief. She had thought to remind herself, to remind Paul as well, that she cared for her appearance, took time over it. This was what beautiful women did, and she had been such a woman, or nearly been one, not so long ago. But she'd borrowed the polish from Celia—she no longer had any of her own—and the color was wrong for her, too orange. She slipped her hand back into her lap, looked around the table. No one returned her look.

It was one of Paul's dinners. He did one every month. Ellen knew none of the guests well, though most of them had come before once or twice. The DeMotts, seated across from each other near the end of the table, were regulars, neighbors as well, and their two boys were schoolmates of Celia and Lillian. Joe DeMott was a colleague of Paul's; they'd been friends for years. As she looked at Joe, who was listening to an animated stream of language pouring toward him from a young man whose name, Ellen reminded herself, was Tom, Joe's face crumpled up abruptly, his lips pulled back from his teeth, and two short bursts of air, accompanied by a barking sound, issued from his mouth. He was laughing. Then Paul cut in, an aside. It was a complicated story about a colleague they all despised who had hired his wife as a research assistant. Joe's wife, Peggy, looked from one man to the other, her mouth stretched in a tremulous smile. She was an attractive woman, but she wore too much makeup, and she had a habit of craning her neck when she spoke that made her look like an ostrich. Her chin line was going. She had confided to Ellen her desire to have it tucked up by a plastic surgeon.

The woman next to her, Tom's friend—they did not seem to be married—turned to Ellen and began to speak. She thought it was fascinating that Ellen was the veterinarian at the zoo. As a child she had wanted to be a veterinarian, she loved animals, and she went to the zoo often.

Ellen experienced a familiar feeling of dread. She was about to enter a boring conversation from which there was no escape. She cast a hopeful look at Paul, who was laughing at Tom's wonderful story, his eyes nearly closed in merriment.

"Yes, I'm fortunate," Ellen said. "I love my work."

When she was a girl, the woman said, the zoo had been a very different place. It was all grim cages then and sick, underfed animals baking in the heat, wolves with mange, and eagles in cages too small to let them open their wings, she remembered; they could open only one wing at a time. But now it was transformed; it was a pleasant place to be, even on the hottest days, and the animals all looked so healthy, the displays were so attractive and roomy. It was really a miracle in her estimation, because so few things got better as one got older.

Ellen said that the zoo enjoyed great support in the community.

It certainly did, the woman agreed, and that was what was so wonderful about it, as the rest of the city did seem to be in a decline and there was so much violence now; people were armed all over town. She had been escorted to her car just the other evening after visiting a friend uptown by another guest, a man who carried a pistol, and she knew that this was not uncommon. People uptown lived in fortresses these days; they were so accustomed to having their cars vandalized they weren't even surprised anymore.

Ellen gave the woman a long look as she went on in this vein. It was hardly necessary to say anything. Barker, who was stretched out behind Ellen's chair, changed his position and groaned. The woman smiled down at him and went on. She had a neighbor who put a pistol on the car seat next to her when she drove to work at night. She worked at a hospital, the neighborhood was marginal, a young man had been shot there only last week; perhaps Ellen had read about it, a college student from another state. How his parents must regret having sent him to this city.

Then, to Ellen's relief, the amusing story having subsided at the end of the table, Peggy DeMott caught the part about the college student and rescued Ellen with the news that she knew something about the boy's family. The woman's attention was engaged; she turned away entirely. Later, Ellen thought, this woman will think she and I had a conversation. She looked across the table at her husband, who was listening to Peggy DeMott, a serious, impatient expression on his face. He hated this kind of talk and would change the subject at the first opportunity.

All over the city, all over the world, these wretched dinner parties were going on, this grinning and joking, these exchanges of information and gossip, the gratified host, the gregarious, frankly hungry guests, the conspicuously absent children. Over every table the conversations rose, banal, repetitive, meaningless, a thick layer of fog that prevented anyone from seeing anyone else and protected them all from unpleasantness.

Society—that fortress against chaos—must at all costs be preserved. Ellen took a bite of her chicken, chewed it, gazing hopefully at her husband's face. Suddenly his eyes shifted from the irritating conversation and collided with hers. His eyebrows lifted slightly, an inquiry, a promise. He knew she was watching him, had known it for some time. She swallowed her chicken and sent him a thin smile. Had he read her thoughts? Sometimes he detected her weariness at these affairs and it never failed to irritate him. He looked away—someone had spoken to him—his features abruptly animated by humor. Ellen put her fork on her plate and pushed her chair back carefully, excusing herself to her neighbor. In a moment she was safely out of the room. She walked softly through the empty house, moving in the direction of the bathroom, though she had no intention of stopping there. Instead, she passed through the living room and, careful to make no sound, as the dining room was on the other side of the wall, went up the staircase to her study. Now she was directly above the dinner party. A burst of laughter washed up to her through the floorboards. These houses afforded very little in the way of privacy, the walls were all so thin, yet they were peculiarly airless. She stretched over the desk and struggled to raise the window. As the sash gave and a gust of warm air poured into the room, a movement from behind startled her. She stepped back, her hands raised involuntarily to protect herself, but even as she experienced the rush of panic, her knees giving out, a giddy lurch in her heart, she saw it was only Lucius, who had leaped onto the desk and was already settling in the open window, his back against the screen.

"You scared me," Ellen said, smiling at him, but he only gave her his blank stare, his eyes glittering in the darkened room. He was a singularly unfriendly cat, a loner who would endure affection now and then, even seek out a little head-scratching, but he never sat in anyone's lap and would not tolerate being carried about. Paul had never liked him.

She stretched her arms over her head; her back ached. Then she looked at the phone. She was on call; why didn't it ring? Now was the time for a medical emergency. How pleasant it would be to drive out into the night, away from the laughter and noise downstairs—why were they so excited in one another's company?—to arrive at the hospital, confer with Beth, who would be there waiting, over some small problem, nothing big; she wasn't wishing for anything serious. A cut to clean, a little suturing, a simple fracture to set. She allowed her mind to wander over the current problems, the persistent mouth infection of one of the sun bears, the otter who had somehow damaged his hind leg and was in the hospital overnight, the young orangutan Didi, who was off her feed. This last was the most worrisome.

There was another burst of laughter, almost a shout from downstairs, and at the peak of it the phone rang. Ellen grabbed the receiver to stop the noise—such an unpleasant urgent sound; why have we been so willing to let this into our lives?—held it to her ear, and said, "Hello." Whoever was on the other end did not speak but listened. She said hello again, then set the receiver back in its cradle.

This one was certainly determined.

As she passed through the hall she looked into her daughters' bedrooms; Lillian's all confusion, clothes everywhere, books and records scattered on the floor, and Celia's, rather orderly in spite of the pictures of dangerous, hostile-looking young men whose raison d'être was surely to strike terror into the hearts of the mothers of teenage girls. The rooms were the opposite of what one might have expected, given Celia's exuberance and Lillian's steadiness. Ellen had a sense that Celia's room, like so many things about her, was a lie, a cover for a profound disorder within. Paul was like this too; everything in its place.

When Ellen returned to the table there was a pause in the conversation. They were recovering from a bout of laughter. Paul, his eyes damp, shot Ellen a questioning look. "Did the phone ring?" he asked.

"Yes," Ellen replied. "It was just a listener."

Peggy averred that she had such a caller, most annoying.

Ellen kept her eyes on Paul. "We've only had this one a few weeks," she said. Paul shifted his gaze, first to the tablecloth, then to Joe DeMott's face. There was a clear though momentary exchange of looks between the two men. So Joe knew about the affair. Had he told his wife? Ellen examined Peggy's bland, anxious features as she recalled a story of a graduate student who had suffered a nervous breakdown the year before and in the decline preceding his incarceration had gotten it into his increasingly irrational head that Joe was trying to block his career. "He was failing my course," Joe put in. "All his papers were these insane racist tirades. All this genetic-purity stuff. In his view Hitler was a visionary. It made me sick to read it."

After plaguing the DeMotts with phone calls, sometimes waiting silently on his end for ten minutes at a stretch, the young man was dismissed from the university on a plagiarism charge. This sent him over the edge. He wrote mad and threatening letters to the English professor who had discredited him, as well as to the dean, the chancellor, even the board of supervisors. He drove to the English professor's house late at night, parked in front of it for hours, sat watching night after night, until the police were called in and he was arrested for loitering as well as, of course, resisting arrest. "The police who came to get him were both black," Joe said. "You can imagine how he responded to that." The young man spent a little time in a mental hospital, then was released. Mysteriously, he fell silent and no one had heard from or seen him in some months.

"He's probably at Harvard," Joe concluded, "perfecting his theories."

It was a sad case, everyone agreed, though not that unusual. Racism was certainly on the rise.

Ellen listened to this conversation moodily. It struck her as ironic that the same people who allowed themselves to be escorted to their cars by men with pistols should express this knee-jerk concern about the rise of racism. But she said nothing and the conversation turned to an amusing academic squabble taking place at some Northern university, where a white professor had published a study "proving" that blacks are genetically inferior, especially as regards their ability to perform on any kind of standardized test, even those modified to accommodate a cultural bias. At the same time, at the same university, a black professor had published a paper contending that whites exhibited consistent personality traits that were clearly genetic in origin, to wit: anxiety, an obsession with goals and personal achievement at the expense of the community, and the verifiable absence of a sense of humor.

Everyone laughed at this last assertion. Paul stretched his arms above his head and leaned back in his chair, smiling upon his clever guests. The forks and knives lay across the empty plates at each place; they were nearing dessert.

Paul's expansive good humor swept down the table and settled on his wife. "Shall we clear up?" he said.

The guests remained seated while Paul and Ellen moved among them, taking plates they passed along. Barker had posted himself in the kitchen door, his long, sad face lowered; he knew better than to beg, but this was the moment he had been waiting for all evening. As Ellen passed he turned and followed her, casting furtive glances at his dinner bowl. "Yes," Ellen said to him, "this is for you." She busied herself scraping the bits of food on the plates into one plate, separating out the salad, which he wouldn't eat, and the chicken bones, which he wasn't allowed to eat. Paul filled the kettle and measured out the coffee into the pot. The voices of the guests drifted in; Ellen could hear them clearly. They were talking about dogs, having been amused by Barker's manner at the door. The DeMotts had a spaniel who was capable of stealing food right from the table. Then, as she worked, Ellen felt her husband's hands on her hips, his mouth against her neck. She smiled, leaning into him, though her hands continued the business of pulling chicken from bones. "Is everything okay?" he said, his mouth close to her ear.

"Yes," she said. "Of course." His hands moved up along her sides, closed over her breasts. "This is a lovely dress," he said. "You look great tonight."

Against her will a bubble of sadness rose up from her chest, then burst behind her eyes, which filled with tears. She blinked them away; Paul did not see them. A wave of resentment followed hard on, and a volley of angry words swelled up in her throat: No, everything is not okay; how could it possibly be when you force me to live in this lie, to answer the phone so that your mistress can hear my voice, to sit at the dinner table with your hypocritical friends who know all about it, and then you put your hands on my breasts and tell me I look good. Well, I guess I just don't look good enough, do I? She made an effort not to listen to these words, though they were coming in loud and clear, as if someone were standing next to her ear, yelling. Paul released her and returned to his coffee pot. Her mouth was dry, her head, quiet now, throbbed. She put the dish down on the floor and patted Barker on the back as he set to it, her vision so clouded she could hardly see what she was doing. Paul was humming over his work, a snatch from a duet she recognized, in which one man describes to another his vision of a goddess. Ellen went to the sink next to him and stood washing the chicken grease from her hands.

2 0

Paul turned the tape player up a notch and rested his hand on Donna's knee. He slipped his fingers under her skirt and squeezed the firm flesh there, just below her thigh. The car was flooded with Mahler. Donna, who had not heard this piece before, sat listening intently. They were heading out across the causeway, passing over the dark choppy water of the lake on a long river of white. Ahead, the clouds were building, thickening. It was raining on the north shore and they were driving right into it. The music was building as ominously as the clouds, with an edge of such sadness, such longing, it was difficult to bear. Paul glanced at Donna's face, then back at the road, noting with a pang of satisfaction that made his chest ache the glistening of unbidden tears in her eyes.

At times like this he thought it might be possible literally to die of beauty. He wanted his life, what was left of it, to be spent in the pursuit and the presence of such moments. Everything else seemed a waste of time—his writing, his family obligations, his students. He could not think how it had happened, how he had allowed himself to be shackled to so much that was tedious and unrewarding, when always, in his heart, he had wanted to be free, to be in pursuit of beauty.

And here was this miracle, this Donna, whom he had found by accident, or by some fatal stroke, who not only possessed beauty but shared his love of it. She had not known a great deal about music; now she seemed to be taking it in like a starved child. What a pleasure it was to open to her this world, in which he had wandered happily, though solitary, for so long. It was cruel to have found so complementary a match so late. She didn't want children; he never really had. She wanted to travel, to see all the beautiful places they could find, to make love in hotel rooms in foggy exotic cities, Venice, Istanbul, Luxor, to stand in the Colosseum at Rome or before the Pyramids at Giza, her strong hand clasped resolutely in his.

It all seemed absurdly possible. What was less possible every day was giving her up. He would have to find a way to explain this to Ellen. He'd given his life to his family, his youth, his energy; he must make her see that he had a right to this happiness.

For some weeks now he had revolved variations of these arguments through his consciousness. He went home in the evenings buttressed with resolutions, armed for the horrible combat, but something always silenced him. He stepped into the kitchen and found his daughters at the table, eating one of the chocolate cakes they often made together, and Celia, smiling, jumped up to get him a plate. "Come sit with us, Dad," she said. "Don't you want some cake? There's some coffee left," and her face was so alive with affection for him his heart contracted. How was he to do it? Or in the evening, as he sat at his desk going over his confession, Ellen wandered into his study, a book in hand, to read him a paragraph, her hand resting on his shoulder for a moment—here, this fellow thought the whole *idea* of nature faced extinction, that an idea could go out of existence just like a species—and then, before she wandered away, she leaned over to kiss his forehead, his cheek, her eyes unfocused and her expression softened by a kind of sleepy preoccupation that had always attracted him, and as she turned away he had to catch his breath, for he could not bear the thought that he must lose her, that to do what he wanted to do meant she would no longer love him. How could she? This silenced him and he sat late into the night over his books, the music turned up, trying so hard not to listen to his own thoughts that his head pounded from the effort.

Mahler, weeping for the earth, faded away, forever, forever. Donna stirred, reached forward, and clicked off the tape deck. "That was beautiful," she said. Paul could not speak. "I'd love to hear that in a concert," she said. "Have you ever heard it?"

"Yes," he said, "I have. Only once. A long time ago."

2 1

In his brief but intense courtship of Elisabeth Boyer, Hermann Schlaeger never once asked himself whether there was enough sympathy between him and his proposed bride to make a successful marriage. Like everything else in the new, strange world he had come to conquer, Elisabeth was so mysterious, so exotic, so given over to self-indulgence, to what seemed to him whims and fancies, that he spent most of his energy trying to keep her attention. When she exhibited behavior he knew would be intolerable to him, he told himself, as many a foolish man had done before him, that he would bring her into line after he married her.

Her passion for music was a peculiar trial to him. When she was visiting her aunt it was not so difficult; he had only to sit and watch her play the piano, which she did for hours on end, or he drove her to the houses of her friends and her endless relations where they made up small groups and played together. Music meant little to Hermann. These afternoons bored him, but often enough he was given some good coffee or a glass of wine, and once Elisabeth had finished playing it was pleasant enough to exchange gossip and news with whoever was present.

But when she moved back to New Orleans and Hermann was forced to keep a hotel room to continue his courtship, the music became a serious impediment to his suit. Elisabeth required him to sit every night at some entertainment. Often enough it was the opera, which confused him utterly and left his back stiff and his temper ragged with boredom. If he was not sitting next to her while she listened to music, he was standing against a wall watching her while she danced to music. She never inquired whether he might be tired or in need of refreshment, and if he complained, she admonished him gaily: he was uncouth, a barbarian. Hermann endured it, as he endured the impenetrable streams of French to which he was occasionally subjected, in obdurate silence. Once he had her at Montague, he would put an end to all this frivolity, but for now he tried to fall in with her ways. He promised her a piano when they married, a promise he intended to keep, for even a barbarian could see the social advantages of having and displaying a beautiful and accomplished wife.

Another weakness in Elisabeth's character which Hermann had every intention of eliminating as soon as the opportunity appeared was her attachment to her *griffe* hairdresser, Lucinde. Hermann had seen the woman only once when she passed through the big double parlor of M. Boyer's house on Royal Street, where he sat waiting to drive Elisabeth to yet another ball. He heard a rustle near the doorway and turned to see her moving across the room, but in a most curious fashion, for instead of walking across the carpet, as the heavy furniture had been arranged to allow, she hovered close to the wall. She was a small, quick, foxlike woman; her dark eyes were never still, and she lifted her chin when she spoke to Hermann, peering down her straight sharp nose at him, her nostrils flaring, as if, he thought, she were sniffing him. "You are Monsieur Schlaeger," she said. Hermann nodded. He did not get to his feet, as she was clearly a servant of some kind, though what kind he could not imagine. She was dressed in green silk, a respectable dress but for the color, and her reddish hair was drawn back under an orange *tignon,* all at odds with the dress. The wonder of being addressed by such a person left Hermann speechless; he sat dumbly while she scrutinized him. At length she said something in French; it seemed to be a prediction or a summation, for she pointed her finger at him as she spoke and kept the finger out before her, as if she could hold him in place with it, though this was certainly ridiculous, since Hermann was twice her size. She continued her wall-hovering, moving out into the room only when forced to by an intervening piece of furniture, keeping her front toward Hermann at all times, until she arrived at the opposite doors and backed out of the room.

Hermann sat glumly after she was gone, going over the encounter. She was one of the free people of color who were everywhere in the city, and every time he saw one he was uncomfortable. He did not see why they were tolerated. Worse than that, they were recommended. When Hermann told André Davillier of his plan to stay at the Saint Louis, André had encouraged him to stay instead at the house of one of these women, a Mme. Haydel, on Chartres Street. "A fine establishment," André assured him. "Her rooms are the most comfortable in town. She was the mistress of a very wealthy man who gave her the house when he married. No expense has been spared." Then, as Hermann did not reply, he added, "Really, only Americans stay at the Saint Louis. Mademoiselle Boyer will think better of you if you stay at Madame Haydel's."

These people were creatures of the city; they seldom left it. Few had any English. The young men were sent by their white fathers to Paris, where they attended art schools or learned to make fine furniture. They came back, arrogant and difficult, to set up their little businesses. They rarely married their own kind. The quadroon women would not have them; in fact, they rarely married at all. Perhaps they would die out eventually, which in Hermann's opinion would be an improvement. He never knew how to address them, and it was possible to be introduced to one of them in a perfectly respectable parlor.

When Elisabeth came in Hermann said, "I have seen your hairdresser."

"Ah, Madame L'Abbé. I'm not surprised. She wanted to have a look at you. She has been advising me about you."

"I think she put a curse on me."

Elisabeth smiled. "I don't think so. She is too fond of me. But if she did, you may as well give up; you won't survive it."

And this was the third passion of his future bride that Hermann had every intention of subduing: her infernal superstition. If anyone in the house was ill, M. Boyer sent for a doctor and Elisabeth sent for her hairdresser. Once when they observed a young couple dancing dreamily at a masked ball, Elisabeth told Hermann, "Look, there is Aimée Tranchepain with her Philippe. He was in love with his cousin, but Aimée went to Lucinde and now they are back together."

Hermann, not taking her meaning, blurted, "What? Because of her hair?"

"No." Elisabeth laughed, patting him on the arm. "You really are a child. She went to Lucinde for a charm."

Hermann believed that this superstitious streak was partly the result of Elisabeth's Roman Catholic upbringing, which he abhorred. Accustomed to worshipping statues as she was, it was not surprising that she also believed in evil spirits and the magical powers of powders made from roots. To have his suit accepted Hermann had been forced to hide his distaste for many things, but this, his hatred of her religion, was the most difficult. The Boyer parlor was frequented by a priest, Père Pierre, who held out his small girlish hand to Hermann as if he expected him to kiss it and engaged in high-pitched banter with M. Boyer on the possibilities of converting this "poor heathen" to the wisdom of the one true church. This church had also thwarted his original intention, which was to marry Elisabeth without her family's consent, for she had told him she could defy her father but not God. M. Boyer had received information about Elisabeth's cousin, René Martin, whom she had been intended to marry, that allowed him to look more favorably on his daughter's disinclination to the match. René was a violent, reckless young man who had formed such an attachment to a quadroon woman he kept on the ramparts that he was bankrupting his family. His father was set on the marriage, maintaining that Elisabeth would bring the young man to his senses, but M. Boyer, whose fortune was secure though not inexhaustible, had already succumbed to certain suspicions when Elisabeth returned from her exile in the country with her big, awkward, wealthy German in tow. He made further inquiries. Then, as a test, he lowered his daughter's dowry, saying that recent business reverses made it impossible to do otherwise. The Martin suit cooled instantly, but Hermann responded that he would have Elisabeth with no dowry; it was a matter of no importance to him. Would he become a Catholic? That he could not do. Would he agree to have his children raised in the church?

This was the sticking point. It was a horrible idea to Hermann, like sending his children out to a witch doctor. They would be made strange to him, as strange and dark as the swamp that hemmed in this sinister, fabulous city. At length he decided that to marry Elisabeth he could make this promise, then break it when the children were born. He knew enough about the Catholic church to be sure that once a child was conceived, the marriage could not be annulled. It wouldn't matter what he did—Elisabeth could have married Satan himself—the church would be forced to stand by the union.

So one hot afternoon in June, Hermann called upon M. Boyer and agreed to all his terms. Elisabeth waited in the parlor, imagining herself the mistress of a truly grand house. What parties she would give. They would take a town house as well so that she would be able to come in for the opera, the Mardi Gras, and any important weddings, and, of course, to consult with Lucinde about her destiny. When Hermann and her father came out they stood for a moment in the doorway, looking at her. She sat quietly, her hands occupied in some needlework, but her face was flushed with expectancy; this was an exciting, an unusual match, and everyone knew it. "Well, Elisabeth," Hermann said. "We can be married."

Elisabeth looked him up and down, her eyes full of merriment. Her husband. He was a big bull, but she would make a lamb of him. He had already proved so easy to manage.

And Hermann frowned at his future wife, as he might have frowned at a fine young filly he intended to own. He believed she was exactly what he wanted. Once her high spirits were broken, she would suit him down to his shoes.

2 2

Shelbourne, the art dealer in Pirate's Alley, had heard all about Camille's encounter with his friend the painter. She knew it as soon as she stepped into his shop, for he looked up from the rack of pictures he was rearranging and gave a low, catlike moan. "Here comes that little hellcat," he said.

She threw herself down in the wicker chair near the door. "What did he tell you?" she asked.

"Not much. But his face is black and blue and you left a few holes in his shoulder."

Camille could feel herself blushing. She pushed her skirt down over her knees. "I didn't like him," she said.

"Evidently." Shelbourne grinned at her, as if, she thought, he was pleased with her. "You don't have to cover your legs. I know you're dangerous, but I still like to look."

Camille pulled the skirt back up. Shelbourne positioned himself so that he had a clear view, though he did not come closer to her. "Open your legs a little," he said. She did as he asked. "That's better. Now we can talk."

Camille gazed at him gloomily. He was a big man, with a big belly, a pink babylike complexion, and short gray hair, which he kept in a crew cut, and which gave him a crisp, military air. Camille did not like him to touch her, but sometimes she let him paw over her in the back room of his shop. It seemed to make him absurdly happy to put his fingers inside her or fondle her breasts. He never tried to do more, perhaps because he could see how his touch nauseated her. The painter was not the first of his many friends he had introduced her to. On weekends, when she came to see him, he would sometimes let her sit for hours, plying her with glasses of lemonade that he brought from home in a jar and kept in a cooler. Sometimes she tried to imagine his other life; he had a wife and children, a house in the suburbs. She was certain he never tried to imagine hers. He talked about sex all the time, acquainting her with gossip about anyone who might wander in. Once he had introduced her to two women who were lovers and he went into a kind of ecstasy after they left, describing what he thought they did when they were alone together. Another time he'd told her some of the young women he knew in the Quarter liked to masturbate with electric toothbrushes. He seemed to think this was ingenious, another instance of the endless charm of the female. He had, he said, a great love of anything that had to do with women.

The pictures he sold were the worst sort of trash, paintings of flowers and patios. He had a steady supply of them from local artists, many of whom had attended the same art school a few blocks away. Camille wondered how he made a living doing this. She rarely saw a picture actually leave the shop, though he was constantly rearranging them, as if he might find the exact method of display that would draw in the hot, foot-weary tourists and make them empty their pockets of traveler's checks. Now, from the long shutter facing the alley, he took down an ugly picture of a patio and replaced it with an ugly picture of Jackson Square. "Jack thinks you're crazy," he said amiably. "He thinks I ought to throw you out."

"I am crazy," Camille replied.

Shelbourne turned to face her. "He said you foamed at the mouth."

Camille laughed.

"I like the idea myself. I'd like you to do that for me."

She looked past him across the alley, through the iron fence, at the statue of Jesus, his hands raised before him, as if he were waving to someone in the street. It was a cool day—the weather had changed in the night—and the azaleas against the fence, which had only yesterday been faded and limp, looked fresh, invigorated. She noticed this rather than notice Shelbourne. His remark had turned up the memory of her struggle with the painter. It made her stomach ache and her throat feel tight and dry. It was true. She had felt the saliva thickening in her mouth but had told herself he hadn't noticed it. She framed the wish that she would never have to see the painter again, addressing it to Jesus—make him die, give him a stroke or something—then she looked back at Shelbourne, who was smiling at someone walking up to him.

It was the painter. He didn't see Camille, but in the next moment he did, and his expression changed from his habitual frown to a scowl. "Here's someone I know you'll be pleased to see," Shelbourne said, but Camille couldn't tell which one of them he was addressing because she couldn't raise her eyes. She was covered with confusion, as if a heavy woolen blanket had been dropped over her. The impulse to bolt was strong, but to do this she would have to get past the two men, who stood blocking the door. "She's afraid to look at me," the painter said. "She's ashamed to see what she did." Camille kept her eyes down, taking in the bare skin of her own knees. She did not look up, nor did she move, though it was not shame that fastened her to her chair. The two men standing before her loomed over her, casting a shadow over everything. Their expectations were impossible. They wanted her to yield up her body, all of it, whenever they required her; now she was supposed to give them her eyes as well, and she was not allowed to struggle. She felt as she often did in her room at night when she heard her mother's footsteps in the hall, smothered in a suffocating darkness from which there was no escape. "What's wrong with you?" the painter said, adding to Shelbourne, "Why do you let her hang around here? You should get her out of here."

"Are you afraid of her?" Shelbourne asked.

The painter ignored the question, intent on berating Camille. "You can't even look at me," he said. "Will you look at me."

Camille thought about the big cats. Though they were often willing to stare into human faces, they almost never looked one another in the eyes. If they did, it meant a fight must ensue. She had seen this happen once at feeding time when Magda's meat stick had fallen close to the adjoining cage and Flo, the clouded leopard, came over to the bars to see if she could get any of it. Magda dropped her forebody down low, and Flo, her attention on the meat stick, suddenly found herself looking directly into the eyes of her neighbor. Then, as if on cue, both cats charged the bars that stood between them. Magda got one paw through, catching Flo on the side of the head, a blow hard enough to send her screaming back to her dinner. Camille, standing before the cages, saw the moment when the eyebeams of the two cats crossed, like twin rays of fire, and the state of relations between them was declared.

If only things could be that simple. She would not mind looking at the painter if there was any chance that he could read the import of her look. But what was agony to her was a joke to him; if she tried to fill her eyes with the hatred she felt, he would only find her laughable, another object worthy of his persistent world-weary derision. Despair settled over her. There was no way to express what she felt. It wasn't acceptable, therefore she did not feel it. She raised her eyes to his shirt, then to his face, which was full of impatience and fatigue. His cheek was badly bruised, turning yellow now. It gave her a twinge of pleasure to see it; it was something anyway, though not much. "What do you want from me?" she said.

"I want an apology," he replied.

"For what?"

"For attacking me," he said. "What do you think?"

She returned her attention to her knees, carefully pulling her skirt over them. "I don't know what you're talking about," she said.

The two men stood before her at a loss for words. She imagined their thoughts—well, this proves it; she's out of her mind; she's a little idiot. She felt she could hear the slow-grinding cogs of their thoughts, always eager to label and dismiss. Taking a stand on an obvious lie confounded them, but they were mistaken if they thought their astonishment the result of the intrinsic honesty of their sex. She had no doubt these two could lie quickly enough when the occasion warranted it.

She looked up, making her face an expressionless mask, her smile implying a perfect vacancy: no one home. "I've got to leave now," she said, getting up. They allowed her to pass, not speaking. Perhaps they would exchange a few sentences about her; the painter might advance his theory that she was thinking with her genitalia; and then they would forget her. They thought she was crazy, but she thought she was not as crazy as they wanted her to be, for she'd gotten away without apologizing. Yet strangely, the certainty that she had not, could not, please them worried her, made her feel unworthy. She could not see what they were, though she hated them, only what she was or was not. She was not able to say, *Who cares what they think?*—as she had noticed some women were perfectly capable of saying. She went over the humiliating scenes as she walked along the alley, out past the cathedral and into the square, first the humiliating struggle in the painter's apartment, then this new one, in Shelbourne's shop. When she came to a bench she sat down and gazed out at the tourists and the pigeons milling about, marking only that they seemed alike, aimless and needlessly agitated. Then someone separated from the crowd and stood before her, his back to the sun so that she couldn't make out his face at once. "Camille," he said. "How are you doing?"

It was Eddie. He appeared pleased, even eager to see her. She thought he must have a room. He took a seat beside her at once, inclining his long body toward her. He stretched his arm out along the back of the bench. He looked different, better. His clothes were neat, a white T-shirt and black pants, and he was shaven, his hair trimmed close to his neck. Even his fingernails were clean. "You haven't been around in a long time," he said. "I look out for you, but I haven't seen you."

"No," she said. "I guess we didn't cross paths."

He took this in. He had, she thought, a slow reaction time, which she liked. Perhaps it was only that he listened to what she said. "I guess not," he replied. "Probably because I've been working a lot."

"You have a job?"

"I do," he said. He seemed pleased with this news, with the opportunity to give it. "I'm cooking at this new place on Dumaine."

"I didn't know you could cook."

"It's just short-order stuff. I can do that. It's just a counter place. But it's pretty busy so I've been working a lot. I got a room with it. It's okay. I even have my own bathroom and I can eat at the place, so that takes care of everything."

Camille smiled at him. He had a job, a bed, a bathroom, food, everything he could want. He seemed stunned by his good fortune. She had thought him furtive and assumed he was hiding something, but it appeared he had only been frightened. Now his manner was changed entirely. When she did not speak, he looked out across the square, his eyes moving over the people, the statue, the pleasant arrangement of benches and plantings, as if he could not get enough of it. "It's a great day," he said. "This cool air is great."

"Yes," she said, "it is."

"You want to take a walk to the river?"

Now she was slow to respond. She had the sad realization that no one had ever asked her to go for a walk before. And his proposition did seem innocent, for surely if he had something else in mind he would have suggested going to his new room. "Sure," she said. "That's a good idea."

They got up and walked across the square side by side. At the street he surprised her by taking her hand, which he retained after they reached the sidewalk on the other side. This was another new experience for Camille. She wasn't sure how to do it. Should she relax her hand in his or hold it tightly? They made their way through the promenading tourists, up the wide staircase. At the top a pleasant breeze greeted them, carrying the light scent of the crape myrtle trees, which were flowering all around them. They could see the wide, brown, churning expanse of the river and on it the ferry from Algiers, making steady progress against the powerful current, though it looked small and flimsy, as if it might be swept away at any moment.

"Are you still working at the zoo?" Eddie asked as they stood leaning on the railing overlooking the river.

"Yes," Camille said.

"What do you do there?"

"I'm a keeper," she replied. "In the Asian section. I take care of the big cats."

"You do?" Eddie said. He sounded impressed, interested. "Lions and tigers?"

"Yes, and leopards. And three bears. We have three sun bears."

They passed down the steps to the lower level, where there were a few benches. Eddie steered Camille toward an empty one, his hand touching her shoulder, then her waist. They sat down, gazing across the water.

"So, have you ever touched a tiger?" Eddie asked.

Camille laughed. "Only when he was unconscious."

Eddie nodded. "So they're not tame."

"No. Well, one of the clouded leopards is tame. She likes to have her head scratched. And the lions are old, so they're not real excitable, but they're not tame. They don't want anybody to touch them."

Eddie considered this in silence. "I never been there," he concluded. "Are they in big cages?"

"Only at night," Camille said. Then, because he appeared interested, she began to talk about her work. She described the exhibits, how they looked to the visitors and how they looked from the inside, and the routine of the cats. He wanted to know just how big they were, how much they weighed, and how much they ate. She told him about Sonya's bad temper and Magda's ability to get up on a ledge at the top of her exhibit by executing a series of leaps that required her to do a complete turn in midair. It was a relief to talk about this world of strict routine and responsibility, the world in which, though she was surrounded by large, dangerous, and temperamental animals, she felt safe. It seemed odd to her that Eddie did not grow bored. She waited for him to change the subject, pausing at the end of each anecdote, but he responded by asking more questions. He really did seem to want to picture not only the zoo but Camille in the zoo, and she felt drawn to him, to assisting his eager imagination. She realized that she was describing it well.

The Cathedral clock struck behind them, and Eddie, looking back over his shoulder as if he could see the face of it, told Camille he had to go to work. "But maybe you could come by sometime and I'll cook you something." He told her exactly where the new café was and how long he would be working. He said he was glad he had run into her, that now she knew where he was, she could come and find him. Camille agreed, this was true, she would come to him. As he got up he passed his hand around her shoulder to her cheek; then he brushed her lips with his own, catching her unawares, so that she took in a quick breath of air, closed her eyes, and opened them to find him already turning away. "See you later," he said, ambling out into the flow of pedestrian traffic.

" 'Bye," Camille replied, but she did not think he heard her.

She sat for many minutes without moving. This was something entirely new, something to be considered. She was especially pleased by the manner of his parting kiss, which because of its brevity had seemed more familiar, more personal than a long embrace. This was the way married couples parted, knowing they would meet again soon, that there was time and that the opportunity for private embracing would not be denied them. The very brevity of the kiss said, We will meet again. She examined the possibility that Eddie, whom she had not previously distinguished from the dark knot of men who made claims on her body, actually liked her, liked her particularly. What would the future be if this was truly the case? Might she not someday soon find herself in light conversation referring to him as "Eddie, my boyfriend," as she had heard other young women do? The thought made her shiver. She imagined going to the movies with this new Eddie, or meeting for coffee. After a while he might complain that they were not together enough, that they should combine their resources and find a small apartment where they could live together. Camille calculated the amount of her savings; it wasn't much, though she'd been putting away what she could for over a year in the hope of saving enough to move out of her mother's house. She knew that when the time came to tell her mother, she would be in for a scene so hysterical and of such duration that she wondered whether she would ever find the courage to begin it. If her mother knew she was moving in with Eddie, she would be even more enraged; there was no telling what she might do. The only way to get out would be to marry Eddie; then and only then would she be allowed to leave and to live in peace. At some point she would have to explain this to Eddie. It seemed possible that he might understand. If he cared for her, as he must, he would want to save her from her mother's rage.

Camille sat manufacturing from a few scraps and threads an enormous tapestry, a tableau in which she stood at the center, arrayed in white with flowers in her hair and in her hands, green grass underfoot, blue sky overhead, the cooing of doves in the distance, happily mated, approved by all, desired, loved. The unpleasant business with Shelbourne and his friend the painter disappeared, and it seemed to her that this was a wonderful day, a day in which a new world of felicity and peace, previously hidden from her though she had always suspected its existence, was suddenly opening before her. At last she got up and wandered back across the square. She would not, she decided, show up at Eddie's job today as he had suggested she might. It would be better to wait. Though she had no experience in such delicate matters, she knew instinctively that it was important never to appear to push for her own happiness.

23

Paul and Ellen had gone to a restaurant recommended by a friend, but they were suspicious, expecting the worst. Then the salad was particularly good, a delicate balance of simple ingredients, and the soup had an unidentifiable spice in it. What is it, they asked themselves; when Paul said, "Cumin," they gazed at each other in cheerful agreement. The meal was good. Everything was perfect. They walked out into the street with an air of triumph. A passerby might have thought they'd brought off a marvelous feat, a trick of some kind, instead of what they had actually accomplished, another in an endless series of good meals. Ellen leaned on Paul's arm; he forged ahead, guiding them to the car. They stopped for another drink on the cool porch of an old hotel on Saint Charles. Their conversation was largely alternating streams of free association. Occasionally they strayed into areas of contention, but never for long; they knew when to change the subject. Eventually they wound up at home. Ellen checked on the girls, found them both peacefully asleep; then she went into the bathroom, brushed her hair, washed her face, brushed her teeth, casting a look now and then at Paul, who sat on the end of the bed flipping through the TV channels. After such a pleasant evening she felt lethargic and affectionate, but Paul seemed agitated, distracted. She took off her blouse in the bathroom and came out to join him wearing only her skirt. As she stepped through the doorway she pulled her shoulders back—he might be looking, might be pleased—but he hardly noticed her. His eyes flickered over her, then returned to the television. She lay down on her stomach across the bed and watched with him the tyranny of images that paraded across the screen. If there was something mildly erotic, he paused over it, then, impatiently, moved on. Ellen had the dull recognition that romance between them was dead. She knew because she shared his desire to find the erotic image. She hoped together they would find what excited him. She did not contain, in herself, that image, though once she had embodied it to perfection and they both knew it. It was in the shadow of what she had been to him, this aimless searching. Good-naturedly she lifted her head to comment on the strange scenes that went by. There were the remains of a good actor. This was a young woman who could not sing but could dance and preferred perversely to think of herself as a singer. The commercial with the cat walking through history had a certain lighthearted charm. Eventually Paul grew bored and clicked off the set. Ellen thought he might turn to her. She kissed his fingers, his wrist; he was leaning on his hand and he smiled down on her, accepting this childish affection as if it was his due, to be expected, but unreturned because he was clearly so restless. "Don't you think it's hot in here?" he said, getting up, walking around the room.

"Do what I've done," she suggested. "Take off your shirt."

There was a noise in the hall. One of the girls had gotten up to go to the bathroom. The sound of water running in the pipes filled the air. Ellen pictured Lillian, then Celia, standing at the sink, gazing at her sleep-weary reflection. Which one was it? Lis-

tening closely, she followed the footsteps to the clicking doorknob.
Lillian.

She looked up at Paul, who was listening as well. His expression was alert but annoyed. He had taken her advice; he was pulling at his shirt, unfastening the cuffs, pulling it away from his chest. Ellen gazed at his shoulder, his back, as he turned away. Her amorous feelings disappeared entirely, as if someone had squeezed the tip of a burning match, suddenly, thoroughly. If he came to her now she would turn away. Her stomach ached; she'd eaten too much. The banality of the dinner, their conversation, her desires, which he did not share, the cool, inconsiderate way he chose to let her know he did not share them, the needless hostility he poured into the room; did he tell himself he was trying to hide his feelings? All of this left her enervated. She wondered whether she had the energy to get up and take off her skirt. He was going now, into the shower to cool himself down. Perhaps he would come out in a better humor. She considered the possibility of asking him, when he came out, why he was so unhappy, so hard to please. He would complain about his work. The research wasn't going well, he couldn't find a record of some property settlement, or perhaps his students were lazy and demanding. There were always a dozen superficial reasons for not being cheerful.

The phone hadn't rung lately; perhaps his affair was coming to a close.

Then Ellen thought it really was unfair to assume that because the phone rang or did not ring, Paul was necessarily responsible. It was possible that he wasn't having an affair at all; she had no proof. His coldness could be attributable to his being depressed because he was *not* involved with another woman and because the tedium of his work, the tiresome obligations of family life, were wearing him down. Ellen felt this as well, that her life was so irrevocably settled and full it would be pleasant to leave it behind, to become, even for a few hours, someone who was never on call.

She got up from the bed, went to the closet, and hung up her skirt. For a moment she looked down on her body, clad only in black underpants. Everything was holding up well, though she looked thinner every year, as if her skin were tightening down over the skeleton. She could never look at any human skin, even her own, without feeling a certain sadness about the absence of fur or anything resembling a hide. She put on her robe, a puffy terry-cloth affair, and her ugly furry slippers, much too warm for this climate but her feet were always cold, and wandered out of the room, across the landing to her study. There, she sat at the desk, gazing at the poster of *The Peaceable Kingdom.* Of course the children who sat among the animals were clothed, though the clothes were odd, diaphanous, Grecian-looking gowns, and the little girl in the left-hand corner was carrying a red cloak across her shoulder. They would look too ridiculous without their clothes, too pathetically naked and defenseless, next to the wolf, the leopard, the lion, even the big, thoughtful-looking steer. Her mind wandered from these imaginary animals to the real ones, the thousand or so for whose health and safety she was largely responsible, and to the ideal of beauty, which they might be said to embody in various degrees. The public agreed that lions and tigers were beautiful. They stood before their exhibits with admiring faces and even greeted the occasional jaw-cracking yawn with gasps of astonishment. But the more an animal resembled a human, the more they seemed to view it as ludicrous. Even the gorillas, which Ellen thought astonishingly beautiful, elicited guffaws and shouts of derision.

If she took a vote among the public, Ellen thought, they would all agree that Sonya, the white tiger, was the most beautiful animal of all. She embodied even a schoolchild's ideal of beauty, strangeness, wildness, power. Her coat was thick and gleamed with health; her eyes were blue ice; her paws were enormous, for she was young; and her teeth, when she showed them, were ivory white. If all cats were beautiful, she was the most beautiful of all cats. Her admirers came to see her again and again, passing the lions, the clouded leopards, the yellow-eyed recondite Magda, and stopped dead in their tracks before Sonya, the magical white tiger. They took in gulps of air, repeated her name to one another. The director had a telescope installed. They plied it with quarters and stood in line to have a closer look at her.

To Ellen she was cross-eyed, knock-kneed, a great disaster of inbreeding, impossible in the wild and pointless in the gene pool, a freak who drew in the crowds and pleased the investors. She had a miserable, truly vicious disposition, possibly the result of the strictness of her diet, for she had a big appetite and a slow metabolism, which resulted in a tendency to put on fat. Her keepers were elaborately cautious of her; even the other cats steered clear of her. Presumably they did not find her more beautiful or exotic or in any way more wonderful than they were. Nor when she stretched out on her fake rock platform and gazed coldly at her appreciative audience was it likely that she was aware of herself as inspiring. Presumably animals have no aesthetic sense. They do not appreciate the beauty of a natural scene. Horses may look out upon a field, but even a cursory knowledge of equine psychology precludes the possibility that they are admiring the sunset. How ironic that the only animal capable of appreciating natural beauty is the one bent on destroying it, the only one capable of actually creating ugliness. Ellen reflected on the concentrated ugliness of contemporary life, a subject that was often on her mind, the tawdriness of fast-food franchises, the obscenity of the supermarket, with its wretched imitation of music piped in to keep the shoppers from being able to think about the nightmare of the scene before them: whole aisles of poisonous cleaning products, the repulsive creatures grinning luridly on cereal boxes, the solid wall of meat.

Ellen gazed past the poster through the window, where the darkness lay like a sheet of black paper against the glass. There was no seeing into it. It must be true, she thought, that in spite of our protests, we don't really like nature at all. Why do we imagine we can care for the planet when we measure the progress of our peculiar civilizations by how much they allow us to be free of it? Aren't we the animal who fears nature? Our notion of caring for it is to stand on the seashore or before a bubbling brook or on some hill overlooking a green pasture and think, "I'll build my house here."

She heard the bathroom door open and gave up her reverie. Paul had finished his shower and gone back into the bedroom, presumably undisturbed by her absence, possibly pleased. He would be propped up on the pillows reading; she didn't hear the television. She sorted through the papers on her desk, rearranged the stack of mail she was so far behind in answering. She heard a soft step on the landing, looked up, and found Paul standing in the doorway, wrapped in his robe, barefoot, his damp hair flat against his scalp, wide-eyed, frowning. "What are you doing?" he said.

"Nothing," she said. "Just thinking."

"What are you thinking about?"

Ellen smiled; it was hard to explain. "The ideal of natural beauty," she said, "and the ugliness of contemporary life."

She thought he would give her the pleased, indulgent look that meant he thought it was a fine thing to have a wife who sat up late thinking about the ideal of natural beauty, but he didn't. He continued his frowning and staring; he looked miserable. She turned in her chair to face him. "What is it?" she said. "What's wrong?"

"What makes you think something is wrong?"

"You seem so unhappy lately. So agitated."

This annoyed him. "This is agitated? I'm standing in a doorway looking at you."

"You don't have to be defensive. I just wondered if I could help."

"I'm fine," he said, turning away.

She followed him, switching off the study light and the hall light as she went. He climbed into the bed, took up his book, and lay looking at the cover. Standing inside the door, aware of herself as an unexciting vision in her bulky robe and absurd slippers, gazing at the gloomy face of her husband, who would not raise his eyes to her, Ellen had a sure sense of her options—she could push it, he was ready to unburden himself; or she could ignore his mood, climb into bed beside him, turn her back to him, and go to sleep. He might even pat her on the shoulder, kiss her hair or cheek, determined to bear his burden in silence. She was overcome with an enormous weariness from which she thought there was only one exit: oblivion. How long was he going to sit like that, gazing blankly at his book, every line of his body a cold address: if you push me, I will meet you.

"I really can't stand going on like this," she said. She stepped out of her slippers and crossed the room to the bed, clutching her robe about her as if she were cold. "I know something is bothering you. You're so irritable, and so cold. Are you in love with someone else?"

He lifted his eyes at last, looked at her, then past her, at the window. She knew what he was about to say. He would say no, he wasn't. What made her so suspicious? What was it that she wanted from him?

His eyes came away from the window, settled on her anxious face as she climbed in beside him for what they both knew was to be a long and miserable night.

"Yes," he said, "I am."

Ellen stood at the counter, her shoulders bowed, her head inclined over the steam rising from the electric teapot, in full battle with her feelings. She had gotten, tight-lipped and dry-eyed, through a hurried breakfast with her daughters, who were so intent on the reassuring dullness of their morning, their choice of cereal, the banana they divided, Lillian's tea and Celia's coffee, the last-minute examination of books and book bags, that it did not occur to them that their mother, who leaned against the counter mechanically chewing a piece of dry toast, had anything more serious than a morning of inoculations on her mind. They were off, leaving her two quick kisses and an empty, silent kitchen. Paul mercifully was upstairs, still asleep. The kettle began its high-pitched scream, and for a moment she only looked at it, unable to remember what to do. Barker, who lay under the kitchen table, raised his head—the whistle hurt his ears—and this reminded her: the thing had to be unplugged. She poured the boiling water over the tea bag in her cup and watched the dark color bleeding like a wound. That's my heart, she thought, managing a wan smile. Then the tears she had been fighting overflowed. The smallest attention paid to them would result in wretched sobbing, so she did nothing, did not even bother to brush them away. They rushed down her face, pooled at her neck, but she concentrated on getting the milk and sugar into the teacup.

The warring factions behind her eyes carried on at full pitch. In a way it was like some terrible music, small themes repeated and tossed about, now high, now low, some only a whisper, others full in the brass. One was plaintive, rich with self-pity: How would she live? How could she bear it? She could not imagine a life without Paul in it, not one at any rate she would care to live. Another line was outrage: Why was he doing this? Was he mad? What did he expect her to do? It was intolerable. Behind this were a dozen little operatic swells suggesting violence, murder, suicide, revenge. A thin note of resignation, hard-earned and steady, sounded as well; there was nothing to be done about it but accept it. Let him go quietly, salvage what she could of her self-respect. No scenes, be-yond the one she had endured all night, were required. Whether she was loved or not was a matter of indifference to the universe. The proper way to suffer was to treat her broken heart as an animal would a broken limb: use it if possible, stay off it if neces-sary. She sat down at the table with her cup of tea, took a sip, then another. The tears had stopped. She wiped her face and neck with a napkin.

Ordinarily this was her favorite time of day. She made a reso-lution: it would be again. She was weak from emotion, so much so that she knew she could not face her cheerful colleagues at the zoo hospital. She would have to phone, say she would not be in until afternoon. By then she might have reduced this cacophony to a thin whine of pain.

Paul had said repeatedly that he did not want to hurt her. This was a joke, of course, and she had responded, "Then don't."

But he said there was no way of avoiding it: he was determined to leave; things had not been good between them for some time; surely she knew that; he had not been happy.

No, she said, she had not noticed. She'd thought things were as they had always been. She knew he was having an affair—how could she not know when the woman called the house and hung up if he did not answer?—but it wasn't the first time that had happened, was it, and they'd always gotten through such things before.

She knew? He was genuinely surprised.

"Oh, for God's sake," she'd said.

Now she heard him moving around upstairs. The bedroom door opened, the bathroom door closed. Why couldn't he just stay in bed? She had nothing to say to him. The trouble with his going was that it could not just happen, just be over. A year from now she might be able to sit at this same table, her nerves collected, contemplating the day ahead with equanimity, but that would not be possible any time soon. Now they all had to live in hell. It would be horrible for the girls and for Paul too, even though he was going to get what he wanted. But there was a special hell reserved for her, the abandoned wife. Their friends would draw close, everyone would have an opinion, she would be encouraged to do all sorts of hateful things, to meet marriageable men, to talk with a therapist. Paul, without a doubt, would be dismissed as a man having a crisis. Nothing better was to be expected; his decision was banal, even predictable, yet each time a husband behaved as he had, the flimsy fabric of society stretched and vibrated through every thread, as if the whole thing were suddenly in danger of unraveling because Paul Clayton had left his wife and family for a younger woman.

Was he really to be dismissed in this way? He clearly did not feel himself to be in the grip of anything ordinary. He wept at the thought of giving up what he had as well as at the thought of what he wanted. He could not tell Ellen he did not love her. She had asked him to; it would help, she said, but he refused. His vision of himself was of a heart, even a will, divided. She heard his footsteps on the stairs; then he stood in the kitchen door, his body sagging against the frame in an attitude of misery, as if he wished to be invisible or simply very small.

"Hello," Ellen said.

"Morning," he replied.

Not *good* morning. They both knew that would be pushing it. Ellen kept her eyes on her teacup. She did not want to look at him. There was an abyss between them. It seemed to Ellen the kitchen floor had cracked open and a wall of cold air had issued out of the widening fissure. It was marvelous, really; she had never felt like this about him before. "Celia left some coffee for you," she said.

This allowed him to move into the room. "Good," he said. It was as if she could control his movements. She looked at his back as he stood over the stove, but when he turned to get the milk from the refrigerator, she looked away.

"Are you going to work?" he said.

This meant, please go to work, she thought. "No, I'll go in later. I don't really feel up to it," she said, then, ironically, "for some reason."

He stood gazing into the refrigerator. "Do you want an egg?"

"Sure," she said.

Barker got up from his station beneath the table and lumbered into the middle of the room, where he stood looking from Paul to Ellen mournfully. He feels the draft, Ellen thought. She patted her knee, which brought him to her side. It was an ordinary morning in every way, but a dog could tell everything was different. Why was it necessary to carry on this charade? Paul filled the little pot with water and set it on the burner; he turned his back to the stove and stood facing his wife and dog. Ellen was amazed at the complexity of feelings, some of them entirely new, crowding her view of him. She imagined him as she would soon find him: absent. Then she allowed herself to see him.

He looked exhausted. He had not slept and his expression was grim. He must have been screwing up his courage to face this scene for weeks. He was waiting for her to speak, prepared to be calm, to accept the blame for acting badly, yet determined to stay firmly on his course. He wanted a new mate, and he was going to have her.

Now was the time to say anything she felt like saying, yet no words came to mind. Over the years she had often thought that marriage was largely a matter of holding one's tongue, of sparing Paul the capsule summaries of his character that rose to her lips when she was angry or hurt. She had never been able to stay angry long because he fascinated her and because she found him so attractive. Even now, she thought, when it could not be denied that he looked awful—his eyes were puffy, his hair needed washing, he was hanging his head from shame or weariness or both—she admitted that she found him curiously attractive. She knew so much about him: his little obsessions, his habits, what he liked to eat, how he felt about his job, his ambitions, his taste in clothes, in pictures, his passion for music and for history. She would have to unlearn him. But how was that possible?

The first thing to do was to stop looking at him. She looked instead at Barker's head. His eyes flickered; he'd taken in the subtle movement of her eyes, knew she was now paying attention to him. He leaned into her leg, transferring his weight, in the hope that the hand resting on his shoulder would begin to scratch him. Paul's pot of water had begun to boil, and he turned away to put the eggs in. He set the timer. "Do you want toast?" he asked.

No, she couldn't answer. She scratched Barker's shoulder, stroked his ears. Paul was pulling the bread from the wrapper, waiting for an answer. How absurd that he had spent the night telling her of his intention to leave, because he had to, he simply could not stay, he wasn't happy and he had a right to be happy; and now he was asking her, as he had done a thousand times before, asking her if she wanted toast. She met his eyes, which registered his impatience at her reluctance to answer his simple question: Did she or didn't she? It occurred to her that in the thousand or so times he had asked this question, she had never said no. She never ate a soft-boiled egg without toast, never. So obviously he knew the answer, yet he stood there holding a slice of bread anxiously, as if its fate, to toast or not to toast, were really in question. Ellen felt hysterical laughter rising through all the other emotions, even above the anger, which, in the face of so much absurdity, was as useless as trying to soak up the ocean with a sponge.

She smiled at him. His anxious expression changed to deep puzzlement.

"What I want," she said amiably, "is for you to go out of existence."

This surprised him, but only momentarily. He put both slices of bread into the toaster—she was having toast now whether she wanted it or not—then turned back to her. "Do you want me to leave at once? I thought you wanted to wait until I found a place."

"That was what you wanted, I think."

"I'm just trying to make it easier on you. And the girls."

Ellen groaned. He seemed to think his daughters would accept the news that he was leaving with the same indifference they showed toward his being there, but she knew it would be, for both of them, probably for the rest of their lives, the worst thing that ever happened. Being abandoned by a father was the same as being abandoned by God; nothing ever filled the gap.

"Don't you think it's pretty ridiculous to think anything *you* could do could make the truly miscrable thing you're *doing* any easier?"

"No, I don't think it's ridiculous."

"Tell them tonight," she said. "And leave tomorrow."

The toast popped up; the timer went off. Paul busied himself with the eggs. Ellen watched him sullenly. He was trying to uncreate what he had created. He imagined that he could take it apart one bit at a time, and that would somehow be better than just putting a stick of dynamite at the base and blowing the whole thing sky high. Perhaps he was right, but either way, the thing was gone. She thought of divorce, a word she usually associated with another couple, the divorce that had so preoccupied her she didn't see this more conventional one in the works, the divorce between humanity and the rest of nature, which was proceeding as Paul wanted his own to go, one bit at a time. Toward the end, in spite of all efforts, the pace accelerated, and this would happen to Paul too. For a while he would concern himself with his family, try to keep some ties to them, no matter how pathetic. He wouldn't forget his daughters' birthdays; he would come round at Christmas; but eventually these attentions would become so perfunctory, so meaningless, they would be no more than gestures. The analogy made her smile. Then we'll visit our marriage the way we would visit a zoo, she thought. It will become a living tribute to what's gone, a memento mori.

Paul brought the food to the table. They ate in dismal silence. "Don't you want to be with me when I tell the girls?" he said.

She chewed her toast, examining the broken shell of her egg. "No."

"It might be easier on them if you were there."

"I don't think so," she said. "I'm going to work late and I want you to tell them before I get home. They should be here by five."

"I'm just going to tell them you and I have agreed to separate," he said. "I don't want to tell them about Donna yet."

Ellen let her spoon clang against the egg cup. "Coward," she said.

"No," he responded at once. "I'll tell them in time; it's not that. I just think it's better to go slowly."

Ellen felt her temper, like a taut band of steel, snap in two. She pushed her chair back and staggered to her feet, certain that if she did not get away from Paul at once she would try to hurt him. He looked up at her in blank amazement, as if he honestly did not understand what all the excitement was about. She got to the kitchen doorway and held on to the frame. "You're disqualified from knowing what's better for us, Paul," she said. The struggle to keep her voice from rising to a scream was exhausting. Though she was looking at him, she could hardly make him out. She turned away, gazing out into the dining room, astounded by the power of her anger, which seemed to sweep everything away before it, as if she were standing in the path of a hurricane. Barker, who had followed her, lay down at her feet. Outside the open window she could hear mourning doves cooing to one another in the cool morning air. Her head throbbed. This is how people get murdered, she thought. On quiet mornings, on pleasant, peaceful streets, suddenly shots ring out. She imagined shooting her husband. But then there would be prison; the girls would have no parents; terrible things would happen to her. She might even have to pay for his life with her own. She could hear the gates of the prison cell clanging shut. So punishment really was a deterrent to crime. Her hand, which was gripping the door frame, had begun to hurt, and she saw that she was holding it so tightly the edge of the wood was cutting into her thumb. Her blood pressure had soared, she knew it, and the adrenaline pumping through her system burned like circulating ground glass. She concentrated on releasing her fingers from the door frame; then she let her hand drop to her side. Gradually the world came back into focus and she regained a wavering sense of proportion.

Through all of this Paul sat chewing his breakfast, mulling over her remark. He looked at her back but made no reply, nor did he sense the mental turbulence going on there, right before his eyes. He saw only that she stood very stiffly in the doorway; then she walked away, up the stairs to the bathroom, where he heard her running the tap.

Later Ellen sat down at her desk and examined the conversation that led to the few miserable moments she had spent clinging to the door frame. She did not want to be reduced to such a condition again. She concluded that it was the name of her rival, coupled with the reference to her children, that had triggered her fury. Doubtless at some point this woman would actually meet her daughters. Ellen too would be forced to say her name, possibly, eventually, to shake her hand; and then, like a tired old lioness, she would turn her back on the new, the reigning couple, summon whatever dignity she could muster, and quietly walk away.

2 5

Ellen left the zoo with her head full of death. In the last two weeks she had lost two more monkeys, and though the necropsy results were conflicting, it was possible that the deaths were connected. Then, this afternoon, two of the three red wolf pups had started to seizure in their exhibit, and by the time she got them in, one of them was dead. Ellen treated the other with Valium and moved him to the isolation area, where he stabilized quickly. The three pups had been apneic at birth, so the seizures could have been related to that anoxia, but she didn't think so. When she opened up the dead cub she found the same lesions on the brain, the same yellow-brown color and thickened meninges she had seen in the first howler weeks before. Again she prepared samples for virus isolation, though the results from the howler's test had been negative. It could be toxoplasmosis, but she would have expected to find some infiltration in the liver or lungs. She didn't think the cub's death was connected to the monkey's death, though it was possible.

She drove across the city lost in conjecture. She'd heard a report once of a similar outbreak in a Florida zoo. They'd lost twelve animals, three of them big primates, before it was over, and they had never figured out what caused it. One of the apes had lasted six months, subject to regular seizures and white blood counts that soared up and down. He'd been kept alive on a drip and before it was over lost both his eyesight and his hearing. It was a pitiful story.

She turned into her street and her thoughts drifted to the other, more metaphysical death, the death of her marriage. Her foot was light on the gas pedal; she did not want to arrive at home. Everything was quiet. This was a safe neighborhood, just on the edge of the city, and an older one. The big oak trees closed in places over the pavement so that even on the hottest days the light was soft, cool. There was the constant, ubiquitous hum of air compressors; people rarely opened their windows. The houses were set back on the lawns, pleasant, bland fronts built in the early fifties, mostly by contractors, but here and there evidence of an architect's hand cropped up in an archway, a dormer, or an added wing. The yards contained cats and dogs, but few children. Most of the couples, like Paul and Ellen, had been here over ten years, and their children were all teenagers.

Ellen pulled the car up slowly in front of her house. Paul's car was in the driveway, poised, she thought, for flight. She turned off the engine and sat there, unable to move. Out here she was safe, but once she went inside she was trapped in a drama, and she felt she hadn't the energy to play her part. Did actresses feel this way, going through the same empty speeches night after night, taking a stand or giving in, all passions required to be grand, all conversation charged with wit or pathos? She sat in the wings, the outraged wife, the protective mother; it was all laid out for her, and all she had to do was put a foot in her own front door and the hateful scene would begin. The audience came only to see how well she would perform. Everyone already knew the plot.

The garage door creaked suddenly and began to rise, as if by magic. For a moment she saw no one; then from the rear of the garage Celia appeared, pulling her bicycle along beside her. Ellen waved, opened the car door, but as she did she noticed that Celia's eyes were red, her face was crumpled with anger, and though she saw her mother, she did not speak to her. As Ellen got out and stood on the curb, her daughter straddled her bicycle and took off in the opposite direction, her dark hair flying out behind her, her long, thin legs pumping the pedals furiously.

So he told them, Ellen thought. Now to see what's left. She went through the garage and into the kitchen. There she found Lillian sitting at the table stirring sugar into a cup of tea, ponderously calm. She looked up and smiled weakly at her mother. "Hello," she said. "Want some tea?"

Ellen nodded. "I'll get it." She put her case on the chair and busied herself at the counter, her back to Lillian. "Where was Celia going?" she asked. "I saw her riding off on her bike."

"Just for a ride," Lillian said. "She's pretty upset."

"Your father talked to you?"

"Right," Lillian said. "Great news."

"Where is he?"

"He went upstairs," Lillian said. "He and Celia started screaming at each other, then she ran out, and he started crying. I told him it was no wonder he felt like crying, but I didn't want to see it, so he went up there and I decided to have a cup of tea."

"Good decision," Ellen said.

"Really."

Ellen fished the tea bag out and brought her cup to the table, where she took a seat across from her daughter.

"It's a lie, isn't it?" Lillian said.

"What?"

"That he's leaving because you don't get along anymore."

"Is that what he said?"

"He said you needed to be apart." She opened her hands on the table. "Space. You know."

"Right," Ellen said.

"But it's really that he's got a girlfriend, isn't it?"

Ellen nodded.

" 'Cause I said, 'Dad, you and Mom get along just fine,' and he couldn't look at me."

"He wants to break it to you gently," Ellen said.

"How old is she? Twenty?"

"No. Twenty-five. A grownup."

"A student."

"No. A secretary."

Lillian made a choking sound with her tea. "A secretary!" she said. "Jesus, Mom."

"That's what I said."

"What are you going to do? Are you going to divorce him?"

"I don't know. I think I'm in shock."

They sat quietly, sipping their tea. Ellen felt absurdly grateful to her daughter for her practicality, her open disgust with the world of adults she was about to enter, although she knew the level-headedness with which Lillian greeted all things was partly a sham. Later she would cry alone in her room or take a long walk. She'd nurse her wounds in solitude, and when she was better, she'd put the past behind her. Celia would be another matter.

They heard the bedroom door open, then the sound of Paul's footsteps on the stairs.

"Here he comes," Lillian said, and they exchanged rueful looks.

He stood in the doorway. This quest for happiness was certainly wearing him down, Ellen thought. He looked worse every time she saw him. "Oh," he said, "you're here."

"Yes."

He glanced anxiously at Lillian, who kept her eyes on her

teacup, then at Ellen. "Could I talk to you for a few minutes?" he said, lifting his chin toward the bedroom, where he proposed the conversation take place.

Ellen got up without speaking and followed him up the stairs, but at the top she turned into her study. Paul followed, closing the door behind him. There was one chair in the room, Ellen's desk chair, and she took it. She had a sensation of unreality as she swiveled to face her husband, who stood with his back to the door. Who was this anxious, miserable man? He seemed unable to speak.

"What do you want?" Ellen said.

"I told them," he announced.

"Yes, I know," Ellen replied. "Lillian and I were just talking about it."

"What did she say?"

"She said she didn't believe you were leaving because you . . . need space. She thinks you have a girlfriend."

Paul's expression changed from misery to vexation. "And what did you say?"

"I said she was right."

Now he was angry. "Why did you tell her that?"

"Well, I guess because it's true. She's going to find out sooner or later, and if I lie about it now just to please you, she'll have two parents who can't be trusted instead of one."

"I haven't told them anything that isn't true," he protested. His face was contorted, a mask of pain.

Ellen put her hand over her eyes. He was ashamed of himself; that was what all the equivocation was intended to conceal. He knew there was an angle from which his actions could be seen as the worst possible cliché, the stuff of women's magazines and group analysis. She could go out tomorrow and find a few articles on getting her husband through midlife crisis, or others explaining how to forget entirely a man who has revealed himself to be such a cad. There were names for what he was, for this part of what he was anyway, a Peter Pan, an adult-child of something or other, the victim of a "syndrome" or a "dependency." But Ellen had lived with him for twenty years, and although, like everyone else, there were moments when it seemed he could be reduced to a cartoon, he was more than the sum of these, his most recent actions. All day long she had thought of him, when she allowed herself to think of him, as a fool. Now, faced with his inappropriate anger, which scarcely concealed his appropriate shame, she did not want to dismiss him. She refused all the feelings she was supposed to have, those sanctioned self-serving feelings recommended by a hypocritical society obsessed with the idea of the individual, though it required that each individual resemble, in thought as well as in deed, every other. She brushed away the tears that had risen beneath her hand and said in an unsteady voice, "I will never stop loving you."

The sentence hung in the air a moment while they both examined it. Was it true? It certainly did seem an inadequate, even an odd response to Paul's lie about telling the truth. It had brought tears to Ellen's eyes and at the back of her neck she could feel the first dull throbbing of what would doubtless be a spectacular headache. She went on. "I'll just say that now and ask you to remember it. It may not seem like it in the next few weeks or months or however long it takes." She looked away from him, out the window, where she could see Barker chewing a stick in the yard. "I'm so angry with you." She caught her breath; it was difficult to speak. She concluded weakly, "I have to tell myself I don't care what happens to you."

Paul had not moved throughout this speech. His impulse was to put his arms around his unhappy wife, but the impossibility of being both her comforter and the destroyer of her happiness kept him where he was, pressed against the door. He thought about the weeks to come, the dreariness of apartment hunting, the wretched packing, how they must stand in the kitchen dividing up pots and dishes, the grim, disapproving looks his daughters would give him as he struggled down the stairs under the weight of his clothes; it was too horrible to contemplate. He tried conjuring up a vision of Donna, but her face stubbornly refused to come into focus, and he had the slight though persistent misgiving that he hardly knew her, that he was taking a foolish, unnecessary risk. But the thought of risk, any risk, reassured him as vows of everlasting love could not. It was risk he wanted, and the tedium of a safe, quiet, ordinary life he wanted to leave behind. He thought of timid Joe DeMott, whose doglike features knitted with worry at the very idea of what Paul was about to do, who was anxious, clearly threatened, and told Paul he should see a psychiatrist or do some joint counseling with his wife, as he and Peggy had done some years ago when they found themselves in troubled waters. No, his situation was clear. He could be a coward and continue, as Joe did, a kind of death in life, or he could give it all up, take a chance, leap as far and as fast as possible from the sinking ship of the present, and come up wherever he came up, ready to swim for his life.

Ellen woke at dawn and looked out drowsily into the soft gray light of her bedroom, her thoughts unsorted and strangely resistant, so that she knew she had been dreaming. Ordinarily she greeted the daily recovery of consciousness and wasted as little time as possible in the process, but now she experienced an appalling dread of what she must hear when she gave ear to her thoughts. She closed her eyes and instructed herself to return to sleep, but in the effort she turned onto her side and found the source of her discomfort, the vast, deserted landscape of sheets, the untouched pillow on what had been for so many years Paul's half of the bed.

She sat up, shifting her legs over the side, not yet ready to stand but willing. Her daughters were sleeping and would be for hours to come. On the carpet near her feet Lucius was crouched, gazing up at her reproachfully. His favorite sleeping place, the chair in Paul's study, was gone. "I'll get you a new one," she said.

Pulling her robe up from the end of the bed, dragging her fingers through her hair, fumbling on her slippers, she got up to face a new world, one, she told herself, not entirely without possibilities, only empty of one.

Yesterday Paul had come while they were all away—the girls at school, Ellen at work—and moved out those possessions they had agreed were his to take. Most of the rooms were intact, with small things missing, but his study yawned as empty as a tomb, a kind of eerie hollowness to it, and Ellen realized when she stood in the doorway that he had filled it over the years as no other room in the house was filled with the force of his personality, his love of books, of music, and of the past. He must have stood, as she did, looking into it, perhaps forlornly, for he had closed the door on leaving, as he never had in his tenancy. When Ellen stepped into her own study, the only room from which he had taken nothing, she occupied her thoughts with a plan for the empty space, a room for the girls where they could invite their friends, a few old couches and chairs, a stereo, perhaps a small refrigerator. She sat down at her desk before the stacks of papers and books, the things that interested her, letters that needed to be answered or articles she intended to read. There were photographs of Lillian and Celia smiling at her from wooden frames, and another of both of them, their arms around each other, looking worriedly into the camera. Ellen remembered it was a cold day and they had left their coats in the car. She looked from these pictures out into the yard, where she caught the movement of an animal in the split base of the plantain trees, probably a rat. As she gazed sleepily at the tall, luxuriant trees, which were not trees at all but giant leaves, she felt eyes looking down at her from the corner of the room. She looked up. It was a photograph of Paul that she had hung there years before in just such a position that he would seem to be smiling upon her when she sat at this desk. Or gazing upon her, for it would not be accurate to describe the slightly open mouth, the poorly focused eyes, as a smile. He disliked having his picture taken.

Ellen stood up and took the picture down from the wall,

laying it on the desk before her. He was very young, hardly recognizable as the same person. It was taken when he was in graduate school; Ellen didn't know by whom, but it had a professional look about it. She had found it among his few photographs shortly after their marriage. It had drifted around the various houses they shared for years. One day Ellen decided to frame it and put it up here. She could not recall when or even why. He had on a white shirt with a wide collar and a vest of some kind; it was hard to tell because the picture was black and white. His hair was longer than she had ever seen it. In many ways he was better-looking now. In the picture he looked poor and shabby, improperly nourished, uncertain. Over the years he had arrived at his present sophisticated, only slightly professorial style.

Unbidden, the memory of their last night together rose before her and cast a mist over the photograph. The young man in the picture seemed to be staring into his future, but Ellen was certain, no matter how he might squint and peer, that he could not imagine he would spend the next twenty years of his life moving relentlessly toward that night.

They had reached a truce, or so they thought, that allowed him to stay home until he found an apartment, which task he accomplished in under a week. When Ellen asked why he did not move in with his girlfriend, he gave her a sour look and said it was too soon for that. He wanted a place where his daughters could visit him. "You're right," Ellen said. "God forbid you do anything impulsive." He had given her his patient, suffering look. He had difficulty adjusting to the scorn in which she now held him; he hoped it would pass.

They spent a few hours going through the house, coming to an agreement on what he could take. Ellen felt little interest in the project. "Take whatever you want," she said, but he insisted that she would resent it later if she did not oversee his selection. When this was done and the girls had come home, they sat down to a last dinner. The words *our last dinner* seemed to hang over the table, as if they were written on a banner, and the conversation was strained. Celia alone did not accede to the unspoken code of civility, but sat sullenly, slumped over her plate, pushing her fork around in her food dispiritedly, excusing herself at the first opportunity, and rushing up to her room, where she closed the door with more than the strictly required force. Lillian went off to do her homework while Ellen and Paul did the dishes together. Then, as often happened, he went to his study and she went to hers. The difference was that he was putting the last of his books into boxes, and she was sitting at her desk with her head in her hands, unable to read or even to think. Everything hurt, her eyes, her head, her stomach. She wished she had not eaten. The hours went by slowly. Celia, her eyes red and full of resentment, came in to ask about an overnight party across the lake the following weekend. Could she go? She had a ride both ways. Lillian came in later to say good night.

At last it was midnight. Ellen thought she had never been so exhausted. She brushed her teeth, washed her face without looking at herself, stripped off her clothes, and climbed into the bed. It was a hot night. The air conditioning didn't seem to do much against the heat, and Ellen had the dull thought that the compressor was going and would probably have to be replaced, at absurd expense. At some point they would have to divide the money, decide who owned the house, a thought she pushed away with such force it brought tears to her eyes. One streamed down her cheek, then another. She looked out into the darkness, through the haze of tears, her heart and head for once in unison, filled with emotions— anger, pain, fear, but most persistently a sense of intolerable sadness, so deep and so strong it seemed to press her down into the mattress. She could not move. Sleep didn't interest her; her eyes remained steadfastly open. After a long time she heard the sound of Paul moving through the house, switching out lights as he went, letting the dog in, the cat out, climbing the stairs. The bedroom door opened, and in the shaft of light from the hall he saw that she was awake and she saw that he saw it. The light went out, he entered the room, took off his clothes in the dark, and got into the bed beside her.

For a few minutes they lay still, both on their backs looking out into the room, not touching. Paul turned on his side, facing her. "You can't sleep," he said.

"No," she answered. The effort at speech produced a rush of new tears, so unnecessary as to be amusing, and she added, laughing through them, "I don't much feel like it."

He touched her shoulder tentatively, then her cheek. His fingers strayed near her lips. She had only to keep still or turn away and they would pass the few remaining hours of this night as they would pass the rest of their lives: apart. But she hadn't the strength or will to do anything but seek comfort. She caught his hand in her own, brought it to her lips, and kissed it. "Ellen," he said softly. He stroked her hair back from her face as she turned to him. His arms came around her waist, hers around his neck. She hid her face in his shoulder, which was immediately wet with tears. "I can't stand this," she said, then gave herself over to sobbing. His hands stroked her back and arms; he kissed her hair. She thought of Celia, who as a child had often come running into the house in tears, angry, outraged, and of Paul holding her stiff, unyielding little body, stroking her back and her hair, just like this, until she relaxed and the tears subsided. Ellen drew up the edge of the sheet and wiped her eyes with it. She raised her face to Paul's and found his lips with her own. His mouth opened over hers as she uncurled her legs and pressed her body against the length of his. She let one hand stray down over his shoulders, his torso, and as she did he brought his leg over hers and tightened his hands across her back. She felt an odd convulsion in his chest, a gasp in his throat. She drew her mouth away from his. She touched his cheek and found it damp with tears. "Don't cry," she said, and he laughed, for it was useless now. He held her close, her face again hidden in his chest while a racking wave of sobs washed over him. She could feel his tears in her hair. Their bodies, from long familiar habit, fit and refit against each other. Ellen kissed his shoulder, his neck, his chest, and she passed one hand down across his back, pressing him to her. When she got to his buttocks she gave a light slap, then another, and said softly, "Stop that crying." He lifted her chin to kiss her, but before he did he looked long into her face—he seemed to be memorizing it—and wiped away the last of her tears. "I will if you will," he said. Gradually they began to make love. Everything was familiar —they did not consciously move from one stage to the next—yet it was entirely new because each touch, each motion had stamped upon it the brand of the last time. Ellen felt her skin burning from his mouth and she allowed herself to be entirely open to him, in some deep unexplored core of her imagination where he was both her husband and a stranger, the beloved and the unknown. She felt greedy for his body, which he was taking from her, and he, sensing her desire, turned her this way and that, going through the long repertoire of their marriage. She wept, but asked him to go on, and she felt his tears on her breasts and back, but she said nothing, only encouraged him with her kisses and the involuntary motion of her hips.

They went on in this way for hours, falling still, silent, even asleep now and then, only to wake, one or the other, their arms and legs entwined, and begin again. The sky outside the window began to lighten, and Ellen, catching sight of it across Paul's shoulder, closed her eyes against it. A whole new surge of endless, pointless weeping overtook her. This was the morning she had never wanted to come. Minute by minute the room grew light, cool, for during the night there had been a complete change of the temperature outside; a wave of dry, cold air had rolled down over the lake and driven out the stale, hot malaise that had been hanging over the city for weeks. Though they could not feel the freshness of it in their closed room, the quality of the light was different, soft and diffuse. The objects on the dresser and the night table seemed to sparkle, mocking the agony of the couple who lay knitted together, exhausted in the tear-soaked pillows of their marriage bed. They separated their bodies a little at a time until they lay side by side, speechless, filled with dread. At last Ellen sat up and reached for the clock, turning off the unnecessary alarm. Her eyes were swollen and sore, but it did seem that they were finally dry. She turned to

Paul as she got up and pulled her robe from the bedpost. "I think I understand the expression 'vale of tears' now," she said. Paul smiled weakly. His eyes were red and puffy, and his skin was pale. "Do I look as bad as you do?" she said.

"I doubt it," he replied.

Now, as she studied the photograph of her husband, his slightly parted lips seemed ready to speak to her, and she felt she had no idea what he was about to say. Lately he was called upon to speak only in his own defense, which he did poorly. He never apologized; he thought it was contemptible to do so, and perhaps he was right, as he did not regret what he was doing nor had he any intention of changing his mind. He knew he would pay a price for his actions, but this did not daunt him, as he believed it was liberty he wanted, and liberty, as we all agree, comes at a premium but is always worth the expense. Yet there was something lifeless in Paul's determination, something already dead in his eyes. Ellen thought of the zoo, where there was so much that was wild but none of it at liberty. Of course many of the animals were as habituated as Barker and would not leave if the gates were opened. Others were in between, unable to live in the wild but not reconciled to captivity. But Ellen was thinking of those few, the leopard Magda, for example, whose nature could not be compromised. When the big gates rolled shut in the night houses each evening and the animals settled down to their nightly routines, these were the ones who did not look, as Paul looked, crazed and desperate, longing to be free. Their eyes were as they always were, wild. Liberty could be neither taken from them nor given to them; it was their essence, and when the public came to gawk at them, that was what they saw, that was what made them step back in awe and look nervously at the informational signs; that was liberty. Magda would lose her liberty only at the moment of her death, which she would never see coming. Even death would be forced to take her, and others like her, by surprise.

2.7

"You'd better lock me up," Camille said.

"What purpose would that serve?"

"I'm going to hurt somebody."

He said nothing.

"You don't believe me?" she said.

"I believe you want to hurt somebody."

"You don't think I could. You think I'm not strong enough."

He was silent.

"Magda only weighs sixty-five pounds but she could easily kill someone. She could kill a man."

"Oh," he said, "as for that . . ."

Camille looked at her hand. "You have to bite hard to break the skin."

"Why are you talking like this?" he said. "Are you trying to make me think you're dangerous?"

"I am dangerous!" she exclaimed.

"It sounds to me like you were the one who got hurt. You got hit on the head and kicked in the stomach. It sounds like you wanted to hurt yourself but you know you're not supposed to want that, so you got this man to do it for you."

Camille frowned.

"Am I wrong?" he asked.

"Why would I do that?"

"Maybe you don't like being a woman," he said speculatively.

It was unusual for him to talk this much. Camille distrusted him, but his reply provoked her. "A woman," she said. "I don't like being a human."

"And why is that? What is it you don't like?"

"You name it. I don't like it."

"No. You name it."

"The way we look," she replied at once. "The way we smell. What we're up to, which is nothing most of the time, or just destruction and greed. The way we look down on each other, the way we look down on animals. The way we're always talking, always so agitated and talking about it. For what?"

"You mean talking to me?"

"For example," she said.

He was quiet a moment. Then he said, "You're awfully hard on us."

"Is that what's wrong with me?"

He looked away, at his box of tissues.

"Is there something wrong with me?" she asked seriously.

"Yes," he said at once.

Camille bit her lower lip, fighting tears. Of course, she thought, she knew it was true, so why did it sting so much to hear him say it?

"It's getting worse," she said. "I don't think you believe me. My mouth feels completely different and it must look different. This man saw it. He was afraid of me."

"I don't doubt that," he said.

"But you don't believe me."

He sat up straight in his chair and leaned a little toward her. He began in the usual way. "It doesn't matter what I believe," he said, but then, to her surprise, he went on. "But if you want to know, no, I don't believe you. At least I don't believe you are turning into a leopard or any other animal, for that matter. I don't believe it because it's just impossible. You might wish it were possible and there was a time when people thought it was possible. You could probably find some people today who think it's possible, but I'm not one of them. People can't turn into animals and animals can't turn into people. Scientifically, biologically, it can't happen and we know that. We even know why it can't happen. So that's that."

Camille listened with her head bowed, as if she were taking a beating. It seemed easy enough to admit that he was right, here, in the ordinary daylight of his impersonal office, but she knew that, when the time came, no such confession would help her. She raised her hand to her eyes, rubbing against the remarkable hardness of her eyeballs while tears welled up beneath her fingers. "What am I going to do?" she moaned. "It's not getting better. It's getting worse and worse."

He opened his hand before him, a gesture of acquiescence. This much he believed.

She reached for a Kleenex, dabbed at the tears, then gave up, for they were flowing with a pent-up force that would not be stanched. "I'm afraid," she said. "I'm afraid of what's going to happen."

He said nothing. She sat weeping quietly, sunk in a pit of such black misery she had no wish to describe it. After a few minutes he turned his little clock toward her. "We've run out of time," he said.

Outside the clinic the sun was blazing. Camille put on her sunglasses to hide her red, swollen eyes and shield them from the glare. She felt weak, wounded, and she walked along the busy street with her shoulders hunched forward, as if to protect her heart. It was time to go home; her mother would be waiting, having prepared a heavy, tasteless meal for them to share while perched high on uncomfortable stools at the Formica counter in the kitchen. She would be on her second martini, a little expansive, but the sight of her daughter would drive her on to another drink and another frame of mind, contemptuous and censorious. Camille did not feel up to the nightly lecture on her many failures, the chief of which was her attitude. It was her mother's conviction that Camille's attitude was responsible for everything that was wrong with her and that a change in this abstract condition could be easily made. An attitude, it seemed, was something like a force. If Camille tried to defend herself, the charges only escalated. Proof of her bad attitude was any suggestion that she believed herself to have a good attitude. If she said nothing in her own defense, the diatribe took on color and texture. Details of her past were rehashed and vilified until finally the accusation billowed like a sail in the wind and covered not only Camille, who sat pushing a fork disconsolately through the mush on her plate, but her whole generation. Wednesdays were particularly bad because she had to listen to a description of just how embarrassing it was, how humiliating, to have a daughter who was so self-centered and gloomy she had to talk to a psychiatrist. No one in her mother's family had ever been reduced to such a pass. The expense was outrageous, and she could not see that it was worth it, as Camille was, if anything, more intractable, more self-indulgent and willful than ever. Everyone knew that these so-called doctors encouraged you to blame your parents for everything that didn't go just right. Freud, she concluded, should have been strangled in his crib.

Camille walked along the sidewalk to the bus stop while her mother's voice raged on inside her head. Dr. Veider had told her, when she expressed her fear that her mother couldn't afford these visits, that the bills were paid for by the insurance her mother carried at her job. Camille wanted to tell her mother she knew this; every week she vowed to use this information as a countercharge, but she could never summon the courage to contradict the enraged dynamo who sat across from her each night at dinner. It would only make her worse, Camille thought. She had arrived at the bus stop. Even as she stood there, the big bus came in to the curb and the doors snapped open before her. She looked up at the driver, a black man, older, a long, serious, inquisitive face: Was she getting on or not? If his eyes were yellow, Camille thought, he would look a little like Magda. The idea made her smile, and to her surprise the man smiled back at her, as if he had read her mind. "No," she said softly, shaking her head. The doors closed, the bus gave an exhausted cough, the engine groaned as it pulled slowly away from the curb. Camille stood for a few moments, lost in thought. Then she crossed the street and set out resolutely away from her original destination. She was headed downtown, toward the Quarter, shyly framing the hope that when she arrived at the café on Dumaine, Eddie would be there and he would be glad to see her.

28

The café was in a pleasant old building with French doors opening onto the street and a battered tile floor. There were only a few
people inside, huddled in conversation over the dark wood of the
tables. The steam from their cups of coffee rose up before them like
whispers, Camille thought. She spotted Eddie behind the long
counter at the back of the room, but her enthusiasm sparked and
checked in the same glance, for he was leaning over the counter, his
head dropped down between his shoulders, speaking earnestly to a
young woman whose face Camille could not see. She stopped, then
took one cautious step forward.

Eddie looked over the woman's head, reluctantly at first, but
when he recognized Camille he came completely up from the
counter and his earnest expression changed into a look of pleased
surprise. "Camille," he said, "so you found me." He raised his
hands, indicating the room. "What do you think?"

Camille moved easily toward him on a little wave of relief. "It's very nice," she said. "It's great." Eddie seemed to dismiss the woman. He moved away from her, and Camille took his cue, so that they met across the other end of the counter. Her hands were shaking, her heart raced; she didn't know why. Eddie reached out to her, touching her cheek briefly with his fingertips, a gesture that so pleased her she had to keep her eyes down lest he see the inordinate pleasure he had given her. "This is a good time," he said. "I get off in an hour. Let me fix you something."

"That would be good," she said. "Anything. A grilled cheese."

He frowned. "Do you live on grilled cheese? I've never seen you eat anything else."

"I just like it," she said. She tried to remember when he had seen her eat anything. It could not have been more than once.

"I'll dress it up for you," Eddie said. "I'll put a slice of tomato on it. Do you want coffee?"

"Yes." Camille glanced around the room. The woman at the counter had left a few dollars and some change, and Camille looked back in time to see her going out the door to the street. "Is there a phone?" she asked.

Eddie was tending to the coffeepot. "Over there," he said, lifting his chin to direct her. She found the phone in the paneled alcove that led to the bathrooms, dug a quarter from her pocket, and tried to brace herself for what she was about to do: call her mother. She would say she had run into Kathy, a high school friend, and they'd decided to have dinner together. It didn't really matter what she said, because she knew her mother would not give her permission but would tell her to come directly home. Either way she was in for it. She reasoned that calling might temper the force, as her mother would not sit wondering where she was, perhaps trying to hold the dinner and passing the evening drinking on an empty stomach. Camille would give her a reasonable hour, say nine, nine-thirty; it was already six-thirty. She dropped the quarter in carefully and slowly dialed the number.

Everything was as she expected. Her mother's response to the sound of her voice was an accusatory "Where are you?" Her excuse was rejected out of hand as a lie, or if not a lie, an affront. Camille kept her voice low, her back to the room, where Eddie was preparing her sandwich. When she named the time of her expected arrival, she received a gale of dire predictions: rape; death by gun, knife, or drunken driver; at the very least, mugging. She listened quietly, holding the phone a little away from her ear. When the fury seemed to abate, she said she would be careful, that she would be home by nine-thirty. Then, quickly, saying goodbye, she hung up.

She leaned against the wall and looked out into the pale light of the small café, which seemed to her a place of limitless possibility, freedom, and hope. She made her way back to the counter, where Eddie waited for her, holding the coffeepot until she was sitting in front of him so that her coffee would be as hot as possible. "Is everything all right?" he asked.

"Fine," Camille said. "I just had to call my mother to tell her I'll be late." She stirred milk from the creamer into the cup and dreamily brought it to her lips. Eddie smiled down upon her; then he went back to the grill to turn her sandwich over.

This was how she wanted to spend the rest of her life. She would stop seeing Dr. Veider. Instead, she would come here after work, spend the hours until Eddie got off reading the paper and drinking coffee. They would have dinner together, here or somewhere else, then a movie perhaps, or they might have friends to meet. The peacefulness of these imaginings filled her with a sense of well-being. When Eddie brought her sandwich, she allowed her eyes the pleasure of running over him, his face, his long torso, his arms, his hands. She let her hand touch his as he set the plate before her, and he returned her gesture by touching her cheek, brushing back her hair, before he moved away to serve another customer. She was charmed by his soft, deep voice as he said, "Can I help you?" Yes, you can, she thought and for the first time she experienced the delicate catch at the throat, the drawing in of breath, a kind of sigh in reverse, that announces the condition of desire.

The hour passed swiftly. Eddie's replacement, a black man named Sammy, arrived, and the two of them were busy chopping vegetables and reorganizing the narrow galley. Camille drank more coffee and ate a piece of pecan pie, which Sammy, who was high-spirited and affable, insisted she try. The other customers who came in noticed that hers was a privileged position, for the two men directed their amusing remarks to her, and whenever there was an opportunity Eddie took his place before her, attentive, she thought, even concerned. "Go ahead," Sammy said during a lull. "Go off with your girl." Eddie, smiling, came out from behind the counter and ushered Camille into the street, which was dark now, coming into its nightlife, its real life. "I need a drink," Eddie said, steering her along by her elbow. They walked a block, toward Bourbon Street, where the stream of pedestrian traffic had already begun, and turned into a dark, cavernous bar. "This is a good place," Eddie said. He took what was clearly a familiar bar stool, and Camille climbed up on the one beside him. He ordered a beer; she, after a moment's hesitation, asked for a rum and Coke. "How can you drink that?" he said when the drinks arrived. She shrugged. "I like it," she said.

They drank and talked in a desultory fashion. Eddie asked if she had come straight from work, and she lied, saying that she had. She did not want him to know about Dr. Veider nor did she want Dr. Veider to know about him. She would wait until the time was right, when she and Eddie joined forces and she could present an accomplished fact: she was loved. Pleasant fantasies revolved in her imagination as she listened to Eddie, who was talking about his room, which he proposed they go to in short order. She agreed. They finished their drinks and went back out into the street, back the way they had come. Eddie used a key to open the iron gate next to the café, and Camille followed him down the dark, narrow alley that led to the back courtyard, which was hardly a courtyard at all but a strip of concrete between two high walls. Facing this was a dilapidated slave quarter, its peeling shutters opened and sagging away from the inner doors so that the whole structure looked as if it might collapse in the next moment. Eddie had another key for the French doors on the right. He motioned Camille in under his arm as he pushed the door open and switched on the light.

Although her expectations of the room had been neither elaborate nor optimistic, Camille saw at once they had been too high. A bare light bulb, a mattress on the floor, a rickety table and two chairs, damp, cracked plaster on the walls, the odor of mildew; this was the room Eddie had spoken of as "nice." "So this is it," he said, looking about in his pleased way. "I gotta get some stuff for it, some sheets and stuff. You want a beer?" He left her for the bathroom, which had been cobbled in at the back corner, giving the room itself an awkward L shape. Camille could see him, pulling a can loose from a six-pack he had in the sink, apparently to keep it cool. She took the opportunity to look at the room more closely. The floors were good, wide oak boards that only needed a cleaning, and the cross beams exposed in the ceiling were attractive. The room wasn't hopeless, she thought, but Eddie was. He came toward her carrying two beers. "I'm glad you came to see me," he said. "I was hoping you would."

Camille smiled and accepted the beer. In spite of the dreary room she felt comfortable, unafraid. Eddie had left the light on in the bathroom, and after handing Camille the open can of beer he went to the switch and turned off the overhead bulb. "Is that okay?" he asked. The room, relieved of the cruel glare, lost much of its harshness. Camille walked over to the mattress and sat down on the edge gratefully. "That's better," she said. "That's good." She realized she was enormously tired. Eddie sat down beside her and began rubbing her neck and shoulders, casually at first, but when she sighed and relaxed beneath his strong fingers, he got up on his knees behind her and began working the tight muscles with a nearly professional concern. "Gee, that feels good," Camille said weakly.

"You're all tensed up," he said.

It was true, she thought. It was always true. She had never been touched in this way, with so little force and so much interest, and she did not know how to respond. Eddie's hands moved around her back and covered her breasts. She felt his lips at her neck, but she did not detect beneath his hands and his mouth any resistance. His hands moved down to her waist, over her hips, pressing, but not too hard, then back up again. He sat beside her and bent down over his legs, unlacing his shoes. Camille kicked off her own shoes and began unbuttoning her dress, which she pulled over her head. For a moment her face was hidden but for her eyes. Eddie smiled at her. When he lifted his hips from the mattress to pull off his pants, she pulled the dress free and shook it out before her, then folded it carefully and put it next to her on the corner of the mattress. She did not look forward to what would come next; neither did she dread it. Eddie knelt before her, stroking her breasts. As he leaned toward her to cover her mouth with his own, he said, "You sure are pretty." His lips teased hers in a way she did not at first like, but a pleasant languor kept her from pulling away. It pleased her that he seemed so taken by her body. She could feel his gathering excitement through his hands, which were moving over her carefully, as if taking measurements. When he released her mouth and fell to kissing her breasts, her hands came up around his head and she held him there, stroking his hair back from his face while a strange and new sensation invaded her from head to foot, one she struggled to recognize, but could not name. Eddie's arms were around her, pulling her body in closer and closer. She wrapped her legs around his back and held him tightly as he lifted her so that he could get up off the floor and bring them both down across the mattress. She saw his face, alive with concentration and excitement, though he did appear to see her through it, for he gave her the same almost shy smile she had seen before. Then he set about arranging her body beneath his own.

She closed her eyes, expecting a wave of revulsion, for Eddie was kissing her stomach now, moving down, but she found instead a wave of a different kind, not overpowering but insistent, more like urgency. She opened her eyes and stared at the ceiling, then at the table and chairs, which seemed curiously delicate and far away. There was no red anywhere. Eddie came up from between her legs, raised himself over her, and, using one hand, fitted his penis inside her, but only a little way. He looked at her as he did this and she was overcome with shyness. She closed her eyes and turned her face away. A sigh escaped her as he pressed deeper and deeper inside. It did not hurt at all, not even, she thought, slightly; her hips raised up a bit, inclining to meet his, and she drew her arms about his shoulders with a sense of taking him in willingly. She was alert, experiencing with quiet amazement a barrage of sensations in her body and in her thoughts as well. She heard her own voice saying *oh,* softly, and then again, *oh.*

Oh what? she thought, smiling to herself. Oh, let us go on like this forever? Eddie was picking up speed and intensity; she held on to him with all her strength. She opened her eyes, expecting the edge of red to close in, to block out these extraordinary feelings, but all she found was the dim pearly light from the other room, not red but blue. Eddie groaned once, and stiffness seemed to invade him; she could feel it under her hands. Then, with another groan, he collapsed over her, his face turned away. They lay still for a few moments. Camille listened to Eddie's heart, which she could feel against her chest, beating rapidly. She hoped he would not speak. Over his shoulder she saw the long rectangle of light that poured across the floor from the bathroom, missing the mattress but covering the wide oak boards all the way to the French doors, where it seemed curiously to be stopped by the glass panes, so black they no longer looked transparent. Eddie turned his face toward her and kissed her shoulder. "You're very sensuous," he said.

Camille smiled. She did not think this a true assessment of her nature; in fact, it was so far from what she knew to be the truth, it was nearly a joke. But she saw no reason to correct Eddie, or anyone else, for that matter, including Dr. Veider. It seemed to her the world was full of people who were willing, even eager, to tell her what she was like, what was wrong with her.

Eddie was mistaken, but at least his view of her was generous. He had said the word *sensuous* as if he thought it a fine thing. There could be no doubt that he was pleased with her, and for this pleasure she was absurdly grateful. She patted his shoulder, kissed his cheek, wishing she never had to leave, that she could stay in this unexpectedly peaceful territory forever.

Later, she knew, she would get up and later still she would go home. She would not be too late, but it didn't matter; her mother would be angry. She would be in her robe and slippers, enthroned in her chair before the television, her drink at her side, having spent the evening embroidering her own version of Camille's night out. If she believed the story about the dinner with Kathy, she would accuse Camille of being a lesbian. If not, she was a liar and a tramp. Camille would not defend herself, and with any luck she could go off to her room before long and struggle with the sofa bed for a few minutes before she stretched out on the sagging mattress and drifted into the uncharted, sometimes dangerous, territory of sleep.

Tonight, she thought, she did not dread that prospect; there would be no bad dreams. She was tired. Eddie's eyes were closed; he was drifting away. In a little while she would slip out from under him and get dressed. She might even take a shower if the bathroom was not too awful and she could find a towel. On the weekend she would take some money from her savings account, go downtown, and buy him some sheets.

29

The next morning Camille was careful to arrive at the zoo before eight, because the clouded leopard, Flo, was scheduled to be taken to the hospital for a birth control implant. She wanted to have all the cats out in their exhibits by the time the vet arrived. Whenever there was a change in their routine, they seemed to sense it in the works and they put on a grand display of growling and irritability. When Camille stepped into the night house, she was greeted with snarls. Both Magda and Flo began flying around their cages in a fury, and Sonya rushed the bars with a roar as Camille came by. She was amused. "Yes, I am early," she announced over the racket. "Do you have clocks?" Magda threw herself against the steel gate to her exhibit and screamed. "All right," Camille said, stretching up to pull the big wheel that raised the gate like a drawbridge. "You first." As soon as the gate was high enough for her to squeeze under, Magda was gone. The others, still anxious but persuaded by the sound of the gate that routine might prevail, all went to their exhibit gates and waited their turns. One by one the gates opened and the great cats disappeared into the cool early morning light of their exhibits, all but Flo, who waited more patiently than the others because she was always last and because she was the most tame. But when the night house was quiet and her gate still did not open, she understood that she was being held back. Camille went to the front of her cage and spoke to her while Flo clawed the gate, making her high-pitched cry again and again. "You can't go," Camille said. "You have to go to the hospital, poor girl." Then Camille left her, going to the back section of the house, where the sun bears were pacing about in their small maniacal circles, as they always did when they were nervous. Once they were out, Camille took the broom and pan into their cage and began cleaning up the night waste, waiting now herself for the vet and her team to arrive.

News traveled fast in the closed community of the zoo, and although he had been gone only a few weeks, even Camille knew Ellen Clayton's husband had left her for a younger woman. Camille had seen Ellen only a few times, at her initial job interview, which had lasted ten minutes and taken place in a feed barn, and during the occasional visits Ellen made to attend one of the animals in Camille's care. She was always accompanied by a technician and usually a supervisor, and her attention was absorbed by them and the animal in question, but Camille had noticed that she always addressed her by name and asked her opinion of the animal's condition. This time there would be little to say because Flo was not ill. Still, Camille experienced a low churning in her stomach at the thought of the encounter. Ellen seemed to come down to her from another world, the world of science, of the hospital, which Camille had seen only from the outside, and now the world of emotional suffering, for everyone knew about Ellen's family, her pretty daughters, and her handsome, popular husband. Camille had seen newspaper photographs of Ellen and Paul, standing together at the elegant fundraising party given by the zoo each year or at the occasional exclusive functions of the state historical society, their drinks raised in their hands, smiling or laughing, caught off guard by the camera, Dr. and Dr. Clayton, the historian and his attractive wife, the zoo veterinarian. Would she look different? Camille wondered. Everyone agreed it must be awful for her, the faithful, abandoned woman; everyone knew that she loved her husband. Would the sadness show on her face or in her manner?

Camille heard the outer door creak on its metal hinges and the sound of voices. She recognized Ellen's, the only woman's voice, and though she could not make out what was being said, she understood it was an inquiry; then she heard Ellen, on receiving an equally inaudible reply, laugh. She carried her broom and pan into the passageway so that she might see and be seen by the approaching trio. They were all dressed in the dull brown uniform Camille wore herself, but they carried themselves so differently, with such authority, that Camille had a sense of herself as too small and drab to warrant their attention. Ellen did not seem to see her. She stopped just inside the door and set down her black valise, which contained the blow dart for the anesthesia. Camille's supervisor, a tall, cheerful man, one of the few men in the world for whom she did not harbor mixed feelings, called to her, "Camille, good morning. Here we are." She put the broom and pan into the closet and went to join the group, crowded well away from the panicked leopard's cage.

Ellen was kneeling on the concrete, unpacking the dart. The technician, a fair young man Camille had never seen before, had opened his own black bag and was occupied in loading the syringe. They could hear Flo charging wildly around in her cage, emitting a series of high shrieks.

"Flo's not too pleased by our visit this morning," Ellen said.

"She knows something's up," Camille observed. Ellen looked up from the dart and met Camille's eyes. She had a close way of looking that made Camille nervous. It seemed to her Ellen was either completely unaware of her existence or completely focused on it, with little in between. "No problems with her lately?" Ellen asked.

"No. She eats well. She's fine."

"Good," Ellen replied, returning her attention to her dart. "We're using Tiletamine today instead of Zolazepan. We get less body rigidity with it."

"Seizure-free." The technician chuckled.

"So they say," Ellen said. "We'll find out. I used it on one of the wolves last week and it was pretty good."

The dart was loaded. "We're ready." Ellen turned to Camille. "You can come with me to watch if you want," she said. "But stay back a little."

Camille nodded. The invitation flattered her, though she knew it was only because Flo was accustomed to seeing her keeper and was less likely to panic. She followed Ellen down the long hall lined with empty cages to the one in which Flo, who usually pressed herself against the bars in the hope of being petted, paced up and down, her ears flat against her head and her tail wrapped down tightly against her legs.

Camille stepped away from the cage while Ellen, the blowpipe pressed against her lips, alternately crouched and stood up, trying to get a clear shot on the excited leopard. Flo responded by picking up speed. She charged the back gate, throwing herself against it so hard she bounced against the floor, then scrambled to her feet and took off, flying around the cage like a mad creature, her mouth open wide, issuing a strangled, terrified sound, something between a snarl and a scream.

After a few minutes Flo came to a sudden halt, her back to her audience. Ellen stepped back, still holding the tube to her lips, waiting. Camille thought she could feel the tension between the woman and the leopard. A palpable stillness filled the air; no one spoke. The next move would be Flo's, and she seemed to know it. She tilted her head from side to side, her ears cocked toward Ellen. Her hearing was so acute she could detect even the smallest movement, the crooking of a finger or an uneven breath, but Ellen was motionless. How long would they both stand thus, suspended in their concentration on each other? Camille was fascinated. When it seemed one of them must move, but neither did, a stubborn resolve set into the stillness, as if a contest had been declared. Camille took the opportunity to look closely at Ellen. There were dark circles under her eyes, but otherwise she did not look unhappy. She was clearly not thinking of anything but getting the dart into the leopard. Her mouth was set in a thin, determined smile; the lines of her body were all bent toward the animal, poised for the necessary move.

Then, very quickly, it was over. The leopard turned on her haunches and strode purposefully toward the front of her cage. In the same moment Ellen stepped forward, brought the blowpipe up against the bars, and angled it toward Flo, who turned toward it as if on cue. There were two soft sounds, the expulsion of breath followed by the light thud of the dart as it entered the leopard's shoulder. Camille whispered, "Good shot," and the tension was broken. Flo sat down abruptly, the syringe flopping against her flank, looking already a little dazed, stupefied. Ellen checked her watch; then Camille followed her to join the others, who stood waiting in the passageway.

They were relaxed, speaking to one another with friendly expressions. The technician began packing up the bags. Ellen suggested they bring in the gurney on which Flo would be transported over the block or so of sidewalk and narrow back street that separated the Asian domain from the hospital. "Stay here and watch her," Ellen told Camille. The three went off down the concrete hall and their footsteps and voices filled the air, drifting back to Camille, who went to Flo's cage and gazed at the now unfocused, nearly uncomprehending leopard. She had not moved, but she seemed to sag, as if the animated cat inside had withered and the outer cat was now too big. Her lower jaw dropped open and a stream of drool poured out from the side, falling on her forepaw, which she tried but failed to move. Camille felt an unusual sympathy for her; it was not in a leopard's nature to be anything less than alert, and Flo was mystified by her inability to command her own lithe and highly strung musculature. She swayed from side to side; her head fell forward. With a visible effort, she lifted it, for she could hear the sound of the door opening again and the clatter of the metal wheels being rolled into the hall, but the drug was too much for her. Her head dropped forward again. By the time Ellen and her team had the table in place, the leopard had sunk to the concrete floor, her legs stretched out stiffly, though she persisted in trying, with little success, to raise her head.

"How's she doing?" Ellen said as she joined Camille.

"It won't be long."

They stood side by side, watching the leopard give up consciousness. Camille wanted to speak to Ellen but could not think of the right thing to say. She certainly couldn't say, *Sorry to hear about your husband,* which was what came to mind. Ellen seemed calm and purposeful. Nothing in her manner suggested that she was thinking of her personal life, though those around her might be. Camille gave herself over to a sensation of awe. She wished the moment she was standing in would not pass.

"Do you want to come over to the hospital with us?" Ellen asked.

Camille did not immediately understand that the question was directed to her, but she found Ellen's cool eyes resting on her face. "Sure," she said.

Ellen looked past her, at her supervisor. "Can you spare Camille for an hour?" she said. "We're short-handed today." Camille turned to him in time to see his curt nod of assent. So it was decided that simply. Camille tried to keep her amazement from showing. Ellen consulted her watch. Flo lay immobile now, her back legs pressed up against the gate. The technician poked at her side with the catchpole; then, at Ellen's nod, he raised the heavy latch on the door and began sliding it open. He eased himself inside, pushing Flo away from the gate with his foot and lowering the loop on the catchpole over her head. The leopard lay quietly on the concrete, a pool of saliva gathering around her mouth, her closed eyelids showing a little white at the corners. She was aware that the humans were closing in, that she was being lifted by her shoulders and back legs, but she was unable to make even the smallest move to stop them.

30

The zoo hospital was a long, low building, hidden behind a screen of trees and a maze of wooden bird enclosures. On the lawn next to the enclosures various hawks and owls stood fastened by leather jesses to low perches, gazing intently at the passersby. Sometimes they hopped down to drink water from the pottery bowls set in the grass before the perches. Camille had been this far before. Most of these birds had been injured, shot by hunters or run afoul of power lines and brought in by anxious citizens who had found them on the roadside, more dead than alive. Some would recover; others would never leave, never fly again. They watched people and animals come and go all day; it kept them from going mad with boredom, though some of them were so accustomed to the traffic they watched impassively, scarcely ruffling their feathers. As the hospital crew rattled down the sidewalk, three humans pushing a rolling table on which lay a large, unconscious cat, the birds stretched their necks, opened their powerful beaks, and made sounds of distress and interest. At the hospital door, Ellen, who was in the lead, stepped ahead and held it open while Camille and the technician maneuvered the table inside. Flo's head bounced as the wheels bumped over the threshold, and Camille touched her shoulder to steady her. The leopard felt stiff, hard, dead; and she looked dead, for her mouth had sagged open and her drooping eyelids still showed white at the corners, giving her a flat, dull look. They wheeled her into the x-ray area, where they shifted her easily onto the table. Ellen and the technician put on lead aprons while Camille stood near the unconscious cat. She touched the stiff fur on Flo's shoulder again; then she passed her hand over one half-opened eye, thinking that she would close it, but there was no reaction, not the slightest flicker of muscle or nerve. On impulse her hand moved to the animal's chest, where she pressed against the rib cage and found a slow yet steady beat. Ellen had turned back to the table, and Camille met her oddly expressionless gaze. "You'll have to step outside," she said. "Just until we finish the x-rays."

Camille nodded, did as she was told. The door had a small window in it, and once she was outside she stood on her toes looking in. Everything in the scene interested her. She watched the technician making labels for the x-ray while Ellen arranged the leopard on the table. She could see them speaking to each other but couldn't hear them; indeed, the world seemed suddenly very quiet and still. There was a great deal of equipment in the room, shelves littered with boxes and trays, a lot of gleaming metal. Across from the x-ray table was another high metal table and next to it a big contraption with tubes of all sizes coming out of it: the operating table, Camille guessed. The machine must be used for anesthesia. She watched Ellen turning the cat over and the technician lowering the x-ray column. Their expressions were calm, businesslike; this was a familiar routine. Ellen stepped back and took off her apron.

Then she came toward the door, and Camille, feeling shy, dropped back on her heels. The door opened; Ellen looked out and said, "You can come back in now."

While the technician was loading the film into the developing processor, Ellen and Camille moved the cat back onto the gurney and over to the operating table. Ellen hardly spoke. She gave directions with her eyes and hands. Camille felt unusually alert. She was seldom curious about other people, but Ellen excited her interest; she seemed self-possessed, calm, and complete. The technician joined them, placing an IV into the cat's back leg. Camille flinched as the needle slipped in under the skin and the technician taped it in place. "We want to keep a vein open," Ellen said, "in case anything goes wrong." Camille, who watched Ellen holding a clear plastic packet containing the implant, determined that this remark was addressed to her. Ellen held up the implant, a plastic cylinder the size of a piece of chalk. "Look at this thing," Ellen said. "It's huge. Why is it so big?"

"They're new," the technician said, his attention on the bag of clear liquid he was attaching to the drip. "We just got a batch of them."

Ellen concentrated on the unconscious cat. She ran her finger under the dark lips. A gush of water poured out over her hand. She pulled the eyelids open. "Give me two cc's of atropine," she said. The technician turned to the tray of syringes and began unwrapping two of them. Camille stood by, feeling useless yet so curious she was aware of her own heightened pulse. She tried to take everything in: the deathly stillness of the animal, the preoccupied manner of the two humans working over her, the bright, still air flooded with sunshine, the heavy scent of vegetation coming through the open window, the gleaming equipment, all arranged so carefully, everything labeled and in order. She watched the technician draw a tube of startling red blood from the cat's jugular vein as Ellen injected the clear liquid from the second syringe into the animal's hip. Ellen went to the sink, where she washed her hands and arms vigorously, while the technician shaved the thick fur on

Flo's shoulder with an electric razor, exposing a patch of dark, leathery skin. "Now to get the old one out," Ellen said. She pulled on thin rubber gloves and leaned over the cat, palpating the flesh until she found a lump under the skin. Camille drew closer as Ellen took up a small scalpel and brought it down against the lumpy area. Her hand tensed with the pressure it took to press through the flesh; then the scalpel came away, leaving a small slice edged in red. Ellen's face, bent intently over her work, expressed only concentration. Camille wanted to speak but could think of nothing to say. Flo's head, resting solidly against the cold steel of the table, seemed somehow enormously heavy and sad, helpless. What a change has come over this animal, Camille thought. She almost said it but checked herself. Ellen eased the old implant from the cut, which hardly bled at all and opened into a kind of pocket. It was true; this implant was a few inches shorter than the new one. Ellen took up another scalpel, a thinner one mounted on a long stem, and worked it down into the pocket. For several minutes Camille and the technician watched her scraping away at the tissue at the back of the pocket to make room for the new implant. The only sound was the cat's unsteady breathing. The air rasped in her throat. Her mouth twitched, once, again. She lifted her head a few inches from the table, suddenly, but only momentarily, so that even as Camille registered the movement in her peripheral vision she heard the dull thud as the head fell back against the table. All three humans watched the cat's mouth drop open. Her mouth twitched again.

"I thought this Tiletamine was seizure-free," the technician said.

"I guess Flo didn't read the insert," Ellen replied. She gave up her scraping and turned to the machine behind her. As the technician began attaching a flexible rubber tubing and adjusting valves, Ellen fastened the end of the tubing to a rubber cone. "This is where you come in," she said to Camille. She pressed the cone over Flo's face and showed Camille how to hold it there. The twitching stopped at once.

Camille watched the rest of the procedure from this vantage, her attention moving back and forth from the cat's face beneath the black cone to the incision in her shoulder, where Ellen was occupied. After a few tries she squeezed the new implant into the pocket of tissue. She took up a curved needle and suture the technician had prepared for her and, gathering the edges of the cut together carefully, sewed them closed. Camille noticed that the flesh seemed to pull apart and the stitches had to be placed close together, creating a puckered red ridge of flesh. When Ellen reached for another suture, she met Camille's fascinated eyes and gave her a surprising, shy smile, as if she had been caught doing something mildly shameful. "This is the part I like," she said. Camille smiled back. She felt she had been taken into the confidence of this powerful and intense woman who lived on a higher plane, breathed a different, richer air. It was such a simple confession; any woman might have made it: she liked to sew.

In the beehive world of the zoo, Ellen had the reputation of being professional, strict in her observance of regulations, even cold. Whenever she entered the various domains, the keepers were anxious lest she find something amiss in their supervision. Camille had always thought of her only as "the vet," and was often torn between her need and her fear of Ellen. But now, as she watched Ellen's hand pulling the stiff cord back and forth through the leopard's torn flesh, she felt irresistibly drawn to her. The extraordinary vision before her, a woman sewing up a leopard, was made ordinary; the operatic stage of Camille's imaginings, where lives were charged with passion, was revealed to have a homey, kitchen atmosphere.

For a moment the cool, fresh light of reality filtered through the shutters that protected Camille's dark, moody interior world, the world where anything was possible. She flicked the shutters and turned away, nor did she mark the event with anything that might be called recognition. She did not think, *My visions of power and transformation are only the impotent fantasies of a sad, lonely young woman;* what happened was nothing so grand as that. But the lie of the hidden world had been exposed, and for a moment Camille knew she resembled the woman sewing more than the unconscious leopard under her hands. She had no wish to deny it; for the first time in her life she was not ashamed of her own kind.

When Hermann Schlaeger brought his young bride to Montague, the first present he gave her was a piano, which, during the couple's brief honeymoon on the Gulf Coast, he had installed in the drawing room. Elisabeth had wanted to go to Paris and had envisioned herself at the center of admiring circles, dressmakers by day and opera lovers by night, but Hermann had insisted he could not absent himself from Montague for more than a week. Such a trip was a needless extravagance, as there were perfectly good dressmakers and operas to be had in New Orleans. He promised her Paris in a year or so, after Montague was refurnished and redecorated. It was not the first promise he had given her that he had no intention of keeping.

As in the old story of Bluebeard, the symbol of power and death in the marriage of Hermann and Elisabeth was a key. But unlike his predecessor, Hermann had no interest in testing his wife's devotion by offering her a choice. He was the keeper of all the keys at Montague, and he locked and unlocked doors at his pleasure. Elisabeth thought he feared being robbed by his slaves, until the morning when, having finished her solitary breakfast— for she did not get out of bed early enough to join her restless husband—she crossed the wide front hall to the drawing room, where she often spent the morning playing her piano, and found the heavy cypress doors locked against her. She understood that it was not fear that caused her husband's preoccupation with locked doors, but something else, something she had never seen before.

She did not lose her head. She stood before the locked doors, her hands resting lightly on the curved brass handles, and considered her options. She could get on a horse, ride out to the field where Hermann was supervising his farm, and demand the key. That would humiliate him in front of his slaves, which she knew would enrage him. He couldn't afford humiliation. He was uneasy with his slaves; he trusted none of them. Because such large numbers were required to bring in a crop, as compared with the small staff necessary to run a town house, and because the owners were isolated from one another and news traveled more slowly and runaways were more likely to take their chances, plantation life was more precarious than city life. It was a simple fact, and everyone knew it, that field hands, no matter how they were treated, were excitable and easily aroused to insurrection. Most of the owners of Elisabeth's acquaintance solved the problem by creating a network of spies, trusted slaves, often brought in from the city, who had been with the family for more than one generation and might be motivated by promises made, and occasionally kept, of freedom for a particular child or relative, or perhaps the right to live with a chosen spouse, or just uncomplicated access to food and a regular allowance of money, given in the form of gifts. Even with such a system, plantation life was perilous, and if he chanced to be alone, no master slept until his big house was locked from top to bottom.

But Hermann had no such system, and now Elisabeth understood even she was not to be trusted. Her second option, to walk out to the veranda and throw a brick through the glass of the locked French doors, lost its clear, elemental appeal when she turned away from the doors and found Charles, the mulatto butler Hermann had bought with the house, watching her calmly from the hallway. It had been her contention that Charles could be trusted, that he should be provided with a full set of keys, which would give him the necessary power over the rest of the house servants to make thing run smoothly, but Hermann had refused. Charles, who knew everything, knew this. His quiet, interested expression told Elisabeth that she could now, with a word, a French word, at this moment take him into her confidence and create an ally in what she had begun to see as a battle with her husband. But she was reluctant to do this; it was, she thought, a last resort. Too many things could go wrong. Instead, she crossed the hall to the staircase. As she passed Charles, who did not move but stood tensely, as if his nerves were tightly strung, she said only, "Mr. Schlaeger has forgotten to unlock these doors." She went up to her room, where her own girl, Bessie, was busy making up the bed, threw herself down in the pink satin armchair she'd brought from her father's house, and burst into tears. Bessie, who did not like to leave her mistress's room, because Hermann had taken a dislike to her, backed up against the bed and watched Elisabeth anxiously. "Go and get me a cup of coffee," Elisabeth said through her sobs, and when the girl did not move at once she added impatiently, "Oh, go ahead. He's not here. No one is going to hurt you." Bessie slipped out, leaving Elisabeth to drown herself in tears.

She was bored with life in the country, bored with her stern, overbearing, demanding husband, bored by his big, drafty house, his tedious conversation, always in English and largely on one subject, the responsibilities of "the wife." Often at night, when the servants had gone to bed, he came into her room and forced his body into hers, another of her responsibilities, and she lay beneath him stiffly, her eyes closed tight, waiting for him to finish, which he did quickly enough. Then he got up and went back to his own room, leaving her restless and bitter. She got out of bed, lit the lamp, and washed her body with the cool water in the night pitcher, crouching down on the carpet to press the cloth between her legs, trying to rid herself of all traces of her husband. She had, she realized, been a fool. She'd entered her marriage with no idea of what marriage meant. She had always been spoiled, adored, given, as far as a young woman could be, her liberty, and she had grown up among people who only wanted life to be agreeable and easy. Her husband was a dark creature from another world, a world where pleasure was forbidden and appearances were more important than reality. Hermann seemed to his wife driven by malignant, uncontrollable forces. During their courtship Elisabeth had seen his unfathomable gloom as gruff self-confidence, his desire to have power over people he despised as a touching wish to be accepted into the bright, cheerful circle she herself ornamented so casually. Now she knew the truth, and it was gall to her. Last night she had asked him not to come to her room. She was tired, she said, and needed sleep. He had seemed to accept the request as reasonable; he had not awakened her. But today he had locked her piano away, and the message was clear: if she denied him her body, he would deny her her music.

It was a puzzling equation. When her tears subsided, Elisabeth stayed in her chair, considering how best to proceed. Though she had never seen her husband lose his temper, she was afraid to provoke him. The easiest solution she knew was to appear at lunch as if nothing had happened, speak to him pleasantly, inquiring about the state of the crops or the slaves, then, on leaving the table, lean over his chair and whisper, "I hope you will come to me tonight." The doors would be opened immediately, and she could spend the afternoon looking over the new Schubert pieces her cousin had sent from the city.

But she scorned this solution. She wanted to win her point, to have understood between them her right to turn him away. The more she considered it, the more important it seemed. She thought of her own mother and father, and she felt certain her mother had this right, for once or twice in the early morning she had gone to her mother's door and found it locked. How had she managed it, and why hadn't she told her daughter what to do? Lucinde, she remembered, had wanted to tell her, but she was too excited, too sure of herself to listen. Even as she had arranged Elisabeth's hair for the wedding, Lucinde told her, "Once you have married him, your husband will not care for your wishes so much." Elisabeth had laughed at her. "Hermann is easy to manage," she said. "He's madly in love with me."

She stood up and began pacing up and down her bedroom. Lucinde knew everything about men, how to get them, how to keep them; there were rumors that she had even assisted a client or two in getting rid of an unwanted man entirely. Elisabeth would go to the city on some pretext: the wallpaper samples Murray's had sent were too small, and none was really what she wanted; she must visit M. Béjan, who got his paper directly from Paris. While she was there, she would have a consultation with Lucinde.

For now she would ignore the matter of the drawing room doors. When Hermann came in for his dinner, he would find her in the dining room already with her bolts of cloth draped over chairs and her paper samples spilled across the floor. She could make a few of the drawings that so fascinated him of possible arrangements for furniture, or different patterns for upholstery and curtains. She possessed a flair for such things that gratified her rough husband, who could not draw a box. No, she would exclaim, there was nothing for it. She had been at it all morning, and she would have to make a trip to the city; it was so tiresome, but she knew exactly what she wanted, and she didn't see why she should settle for less. Her hair would be loose around her neck, her sleeves rolled up, her hands on her hips. She would turn to him just so, in such an appealing way, and ask whether he might not come with her and they could make a little holiday of it, if his cotton crop could spare him, just for a day or two. But, of course, he wouldn't be able to leave, so she would go alone, and once she got to her father's house she could extend her visit, see an opera, go out, as she longed to do, with old friends to dance the warm, torch-lit nights away.

Her plans filled her with energy and a pleasing sense of resolve. She smoothed her hair back, splashed a little cool water on her eyes, and went out to the landing, where she found Bessie laboring up the stairs beneath the coffee tray. "Turn right around and take it to the dining room," she said. Then she followed down the wide staircase, pausing on the landing to cast one cold look at the drawing room doors. She saw herself sunk on the floor before them, her hair disarranged, her fists raised and pounding against the wood, and she knew her husband stood just behind her, a grim smile on his stubborn face. But she shook off this momentary vision; it was absurd. Surely she would never be reduced to begging for what was rightfully hers.

3 2

Elisabeth passed the morning among her swatches and samples in the dining room. What began as a subterfuge distracted her from her grievance so successfully that when she heard her husband's heavy boot steps in the hall she did not immediately recall her plan and strike her pose. She only noticed something odd; he was coming not as he usually did, from the front veranda, but from the back of the house. In the next moment he stood in the doorway, glaring at her, holding before him, as if he intended in the next moment to dash it in her face, a plate laden with thick slices of ham. "She's a thief," he hissed. "I won't have her in this house."

Elisabeth straightened up from her work, dimly aware that her back ached from bending over so long. "I beg your pardon," she said.

"That girl of yours," Hermann continued. He strode into the room and set the plate down hard on the table. "I found this in her room. I knew someone was stealing from me; Charles knew it too, and now we've caught her."

"That's ridiculous," Elisabeth replied. "Why would Bessie steal food? She eats like a bird."

"Why?" Hermann shouted. "I don't care why. She's done it; here's the proof. I'm going to turn her in to the police and let them deal with her. She can be hanged for stealing food from her own master."

Elisabeth frowned. "I don't believe it," she said. "Let me talk to her."

"Have you lost your mind?" Hermann bellowed. "A slave steals food from your table and you want to talk to her? Nobody's talking to her. She's locked in her room and she can stay there until the police come to take her to jail."

Though Elisabeth had occasionally raised her own voice in anger, no one in her memory had ever yelled at her. She clutched the edge of the table, nearly reeling from a sudden flash-fire of outrage. She could feel the blood rushing to her face. Bessie was locked in her room; her piano was locked in the drawing room. What would he lock away next? She thought she would scream, but then she saw through her anger a thin silver thread of reason. She drew herself up and spoke calmly to her bullying husband. She wanted to be certain he understood her. "You can't lock her up," she said, "and you can't turn her into the police. She isn't yours. She's mine."

But Hermann wasn't listening, or if he was, he wasn't interested. "I can do what I like in my own house," he said. "She's a thief. She stole from me. That's all I need to know." He left the room, dismissing his astounded wife, and went back down the hall, brandishing his plate of evidence before him. Elisabeth followed him to the hall and found herself gazing at the drawing room doors and at Charles, who stood before them looking after his retreating master with an expression of such dismay that Elisabeth snapped at him, "What are you worried about?"

His eyes then settled on her and she thought they turned cold.

His face seemed to harden. "Did you have anything to do with this?" she said. He shook his head slowly, not lowering his eyes from hers. Again, though he said nothing, Elisabeth had the sense that he offered himself to her as an ally.

She considered him. Could she be well served by such an alliance? No. Not yet. She went back into the dining room and began gathering up her materials. As she did, she formulated a plan. Hermann would have to send a rider for the police, but they wouldn't set out from Saint Francisville until the next day. Even her vigilant husband had to go to sleep sometime, and when he did she could sneak out to the barn, take her horse, and ride to her aunt's. It was a long ride, but she would be there in time to take some breakfast and catch the steamer that stopped at her aunt's landing the next morning. Once she was in New Orleans, she could deal with Hermann from a position of strength, surrounded by her family and, most important, her family's lawyers. He would see he'd gone too far.

As for Bessie, she would be arrested, possibly beaten; but Elisabeth felt certain that if she moved quickly, even Hermann Schlaeger was not a clever enough bully to have Bessie hanged.

33

Some things were harder than others. Paul's empty closet was a particular trial. Ellen spread her own crowded wardrobe into the space once filled by his carefully laundered shirts and pants, his neatly arranged shoes. He was fastidious about his clothes, so much so that he did his laundry himself. Would he continue to do so, or would Donna be entrusted with this important labor? Ellen gathered up an armful of shoes and threw them into the closet, then slammed the door. When she was at work these bitter thoughts didn't assail her as they did at home. Nothing had changed there, though everyone seemed to think she had changed, and she felt she was in a glass case, exhibit B, the deserted wife. People who had hardly noticed her before now felt the need to inquire after her health or tell her she was looking well. There was a good deal of enforced jollity among the men, insincere sympathy among the women. What they really felt was curiosity, also a measure of fear.

People who hardly knew her asked personal questions: How had she found out about her husband's infidelity? How were her daughters "handling" the breakup? And, invariably, did she have a good lawyer? These questions, Ellen concluded, revealed a general pessimism about human nature, coupled with a paradoxical conviction that individuals should somehow rise above our expectations of the species. Ellen realized she shared this conviction. Her own rather strict view of the world wasn't the result of moral rectitude, but of an abiding cynicism and of moral despair. Certainly history suggests that the less one expects of humanity, the easier one's life is likely to be. But though it is not difficult to expect the worst from the human mob, the fact that the individual so often runs true to form drives us mad. We expect something better from those we have chosen to love, and finally, fatally, from ourselves.

She heard the door from the garage open, the sound of voices and footsteps, bags being thrown down, the refrigerator door opened—her daughters arriving home from school. She went to the landing and called down, "Hello," received two replies, like echoes, one friendly, the other indifferent, with a hollowness that worried her. Celia wasn't "handling" the breakup well at all, though she denied that her moodiness and plummeting grades were in any way connected to her feelings about her parents. She had told the school counselor she didn't care what her parents did; they were stupid and she was not interested in hearing about their problems. She told Paul she did not want to see his new apartment, and when he suggested that he might like her advice on furnishing it, she had snapped at him, "Why don't you ask your girlfriend?"

Ellen went down the stairs and joined her daughters in the kitchen. Lillian, who stood inside the opened refrigerator door unwrapping a piece of cheese and sniffing it, asked, "What is this, Mom? Cheddar?"

"Monterey Jack," Ellen replied.

"Good," Lillian said. "My favorite."

Celia stood at the counter, her back to the room, fussing over the coffeepot. Ellen watched her, taking in with an ache of recognition and sympathy the slight trembling of her hands, the dejected slope of her shoulders. She wanted to touch her, really to hold her, but she knew better than to try. Celia showed a marked aversion to being touched, especially by her mother. In some way, she blames me, Ellen thought. "Don't eat too much," Ellen said. "I'm going to fix dinner."

"I'm not hungry," Celia muttered. "I just need some coffee."

"We could eat late?" Ellen suggested.

Lillian, stacking cheese onto a cracker, said, "Okay with me."

"What are you cooking?" Celia asked, her voice flat.

"Pasta. Red sauce."

Celia turned to her mother, her expression intent, as if she were considering a complicated proposition. "I could eat some pasta," she said.

Ellen noted the dark circles under her eyes, the rigid set of her mouth. "You look tired, baby," she said. "Try to get to bed early tonight." She expected an impatient reply—*There's nothing wrong with me,* or *I can't, I have too much homework*—and she felt a mild surprise, an increase of anxiety, when Celia drooped against the counter and said, "You're right. I will."

The phone rang. Lillian, who was closest to it, answered, nodded to her sister, who took off up the stairs, saying, "I'll take it in my room." She seemed to pull behind her a thin ribbon of nervous tension so that the kitchen was altered by her absence, as if someone had tuned out the static in the transmission of some otherwise serene music. Ellen sat down at the table with Lillian and helped herself to a cracker. Lillian handed her a slice of cheese.

"How are you doing?" Ellen asked.

"Okay," Lillian replied. "I kind of like my bio teacher. I heard she was tough, but she's really pretty good. She makes it interesting."

"Biology is interesting," Ellen said.

Lillian smiled. "I know you think so."

"I do," Ellen agreed. They were quiet a moment. From upstairs they could hear the hum of Celia's voice. Lillian lifted her chin, indicating the sound. "The kids she's running with at school aren't so great."

At these words, which Ellen noticed did not come as a surprise, she felt an inescapable gloom gathering around her. "Do you know them?" she asked.

"I know who they are."

"Have you talked to her about them?"

Lillian sniffed, finished chewing a cracker. "Nobody can talk to her about anything lately."

"I know," Ellen said. "Do you think I should try?"

"No, I don't think it would do any good. She's mad at you and Dad. You're about the last person she wants to take advice from."

"Well," Ellen said, "I guess I can't blame her for that."

"No," Lillian agreed.

"Are you mad at Dad and me?"

"No," Lillian said, "I'm not mad. It's just kind of pathetic."

Ellen looked away from these words, out the open window; it had begun to rain. It was light, a drizzle; then, as she watched, the drops increased in weight and frequency, and the air cooled. "Is Barker in the yard?" she asked. She got up and went to the back door, where the dog stood waiting impatiently, his manner accusing. He rushed inside to Lillian, as if, Ellen thought, to complain about having been left to get wet.

She stood in the open doorway watching the rain, thinking over her daughter's remarks. Pathetic. She agreed. Instead of tragic. There was nothing grand about it. Was that why it seemed so hard to bear, so humiliating? In a way she and Paul and all her friends, all these people in their forties, were like teenagers, like Lillian and Celia, trying to figure out how to enter the next, unpromising stage. They didn't feel old or even mature; but a deceptive impetuosity, something more intense and perhaps a little desperate, something less attractive than the bloom of youth, was supplying unmanageable energy. It was easy to panic, to snatch at this second half of life and try to make it one's own, to make it different. That's what Paul had done, and in the process he'd changed her life and his daughters' lives, betraying her trust and throwing off responsibilities. She was wounded, outraged, enormously sad, but her anger had subsided; this was to be the way it was. Her thoughts wandered, disconsolate and slow, subdued by the pleasant torpor of the rain. She thought of the zoo, of the animals who stood about in their night houses, listening vacantly to the rain. The rhino, Conrad, had a bad cold that seemed to be moving into his respiratory system. She would have to go out to see him in the morning. And there were the otter physicals to do; they would take most of the afternoon. The hawk someone had brought in from downriver, its wing badly mangled, a spray of rifle shot lodged in the humerus, and a strange crepitation in its legs, would not, she suspected, last the night, so there would be that necropsy to do before she left. Then, she had consented, after begging off four or five times, to have dinner with the DeMotts that evening. It would be unbearable. She had run into Peggy in the grocery store and submitted to a brief, tasteless inquiry: How was she doing? How were the girls? Was there anything Peggy could do. It was as if, Ellen thought, Paul had died. In a lowered voice that suggested she was sharing a dark secret, something that she shouldn't tell, Peggy had confided that Joe was very angry with Paul. Dumbfounded, Ellen had said nothing. Then came the first of the dinner invitations.

Certainly there would be difficulties ahead, but for the moment it was hard to turn away from the comforting lull of the rain. Ellen closed the door reluctantly. The evening stretched out pleasantly before her, simple cooking, a quiet meal; she had a bottle of good Chianti and a new book, a fascinating study of elephants by a woman who had followed one family for thirteen years. An armchair trip to Africa, complete with pictures, while her daughters, safe from harm, busied themselves upstairs. Somewhere out there Paul was looking out at the same rain, a thought that gave her a quick stitch of pain. Perhaps he was in a restaurant with his girlfriend, fitting together puzzling little pieces of the new life he had chosen. After dinner they would rush out into the rain, laughing, high-spirited, back to his new apartment, which was a dreary place; he'd taken it in a rush. Ellen stretched her arms over her head as high as she could while she entertained the unexpected and surprising thought: better him than me.

When she stepped back into the kitchen, Lillian was gone. She'd wrapped the cheese but left it on the table, the kind of thoughtlessness that always irritated Paul. Barker sat next to the table, his eyes riveted on the cheese, his whole posture tense and miserable. While Ellen had watched the rain dreamily, he had been alone here, deep in the throes of a moral dilemma. His eyes flickered over to Ellen, then back to the cheese. "Make the right choice, boy," she said encouragingly, though there was no chance that he would take the cheese in front of her. His agony was over. He let his eyes wander away from the table, to the chair, a spot on the floor, anywhere that was not Ellen or the cheese. She went to the table quickly, broke off a good-sized chunk of the cheese, and handed it to him. For a moment he couldn't believe his luck and stood looking up at her hopefully. Then he took the morsel carefully in his mouth and carried it away to the dining room, his head held high so as not to drop his treasure. Ellen sat down at the table, still adrift in a dreamy complacency, content for the moment, at ease; even, she thought, like Barker, a little hopeful.

34

Camille was shocked by the price of sheets. She thought she had enough money for pillows and pillowcases and she had envisioned buying something masculine and stylish, such as she had seen in magazines. Instead, she found herself condemned to the sale table, where the selection was limited to ugly patterns—little yellow daisies every foot or so, or ugly checks—and a few solid colors. It was just as well, she thought. It might seem too much to arrive at Eddie's café with a cumbersome package of bedding, and certainly designer sheets would look ridiculous in his bare and dreary room. She chose a set of pale blue, with dark blue piping across the top sheet.

When she got back to the street, her package folded neatly beneath her arm, she succumbed to a wave of anxiety. Suppose Eddie was not in the café? Could she go around to the back and knock at his door? What if there was no bell and the gate was locked? She didn't remember seeing a bell. Or suppose she did get in and he wasn't alone? The thought sent a shudder down her spine. Or suppose he just wasn't there at all. Should she leave her present at the door, or in the café, behind the counter? Should she write a note, and if she did, how should she sign it? Could she sign it *Love, Camille?* No. Perhaps *Your friend, Camille.*

She agitated herself over these questions throughout the long walk, oblivious of the scenes around her, the street musicians and milling tourists, the antique shop windows along Royal, crammed with beautiful, expensive objects. She didn't notice that it was a pleasant day for a walk, warm and clear. She wanted Eddie to be pleased—surely he would be—but beneath her optimism there ran a current of doubt that threatened her happiness, so that she walked quickly, eager to get past the presentation of her gift, an event that had now, mysteriously, become another in a long line of ordeals.

Outside the café she stopped to check the gate. It was locked and, as she feared, there was no bell. She pushed open the café door, conscious of a dull pain growing behind her eyes. Of course he wasn't there, nor did she know the unfriendly-looking older man behind the counter. It occurred to her that he might be the owner and that asking for Eddie would get him in trouble. She sat at the counter and ordered a cup of coffee and a piece of pie, which she ate slowly, her package and purse balanced awkwardly in her lap. The café was not crowded, a few people at the counter and two young women at one of the tables. The man busied himself making a sandwich at the grill, his back to the room. When he finished, he brought the sandwich to a very thin man, then, brandishing his pad and pencil, went down the counter writing out checks. Camille smiled at him but failed to catch his eye. She said softly, "Is Eddie here?"

"What?" he said.

"I'm looking for Eddie. Is he coming in today?"

The man spoke without looking at her, but he did not move

away. "He don't work weekends," he said. "He don't come in till Monday night."

Camille was downcast. What was she to do with her present? She couldn't take it home; that much was certain. As the man did not move away, she was emboldened to speak. "Do you think he's in his room?" she asked.

"Jeez, I don't know," the man said. Now he was annoyed. "Why don't you knock on the door?"

"Well, the gate's locked," she said. "And there's no bell."

The man gave her a long, serious look. She felt she was being evaluated against some standard. She opened her purse and dug through it, taking out money for the check. He'd put it all together now, she thought. He knew she had only ordered the coffee and pie to try to get to Eddie. She felt the heat of a blush rising from her neck to her face. She counted out the change onto the counter, leaving a large tip, unable to raise her eyes. The man was fidgeting with a set of keys that hung from his belt. "You can come out this way," he said at last, moving away along the counter. Camille slipped off the stool at once, clutching her package and her still open purse, following him. He took her through a door at the back of the café, through a small, nearly empty storage room, to another door, which he unlocked with a key. "If he ain't there," he said, "you can go out the gate. It locks itself as soon as you close it. But make sure you close it all the way."

"I will," Camille said.

The man pushed the door open, and Camille, stepping through, found herself on the narrow concrete strip that ran between the café and the slave quarter. Without speaking, the man pulled the door closed behind her, and she heard the key turning in the lock. For a moment she stood still, unable to believe her good fortune. She could have a few moments of privacy to brush her hair and remove the price tags from the sheets before she went to Eddie's door. She opened the package carefully—the paper bag was frayed at the end from being bunched up in her hands—and picked off the sticky price tags on the plastic wrapping of the sheets. Then, clutching the package under her arm, for she did not want to put the bag on the dirty pavement at her feet, she took her brush from her purse and carefully brushed her hair. She looked at her face in the small compact mirror, but it was hard to see much except that, as usual, she was pale and tired. Then she closed the purse, straightened her skirt, and walked softly, as if she feared detection, to Eddie's door.

She could see into the room through the glass panes of the door, and what she saw reassured her. Eddie, dressed in a T-shirt and boxer shorts, lay across the mattress, his face turned away from the door. Camille felt her heart race ahead. Now her simple fantasy was about to come true. She rapped her knuckles once against the glass, but stepped back, startled at the sharp, loud sound she had made, like a shot being fired in the quiet morning air. Eddie sprang up from the mattress at once and bolted toward her, but his speed belied his condition, for he had been sound asleep. He stood for a moment looking confusedly through the glass at her. Camille smiled, raised her hand in a helpless, self-conscious greeting. He began dazedly fumbling with the lock, and she heard him say, "For Christ's sake."

So he wasn't pleased to see her.

"I'm sorry," she said, when he had opened the door. "Were you asleep?"

Eddie staggered back to his mattress, where he threw himself face down. "You nearly gave me a heart attack," he said.

Camille closed the door, followed him, and sat down on the edge of the mattress, clutching her package and her purse. "I'm sorry," she said again, this time to the back of his head.

He lifted his head from the mattress, turning his face toward her. "How did you get in here?" he asked. "Is the gate open?"

"No," Camille said. "The guy in the café let me in through the back."

"Al?" he said, opening his eyes wide in surprise. "You got Big Al to let you in here?"

"He didn't seem that big to me," Camille replied. Her shoulders slumped beneath the weight of a sudden dejection. She let the package and purse slide off her lap onto the floor. She wished she had never come up with the ridiculous idea of buying sheets for Eddie.

Eddie frowned. "You must have really wanted to get in here."

"I guess I shouldn't have come," she said.

He raised himself up on one elbow. "No," he said. "It's okay. I'm starting to wake up now."

Camille pushed at the bag with her knee. "I brought you a present," she said.

Eddie gave his attention to the package. An expression of surprise mingled with suspicion animated his sleep-weary face. "You did?" he said, reaching across her leg. "What is it?"

Camille lifted the package, allowing it to come open a little. "It's not much," she said. He turned the bag on its side so that the plastic-wrapped sheets spilled out across the mattress. A smile played around his mouth as he understood what she had brought him, but it was not, Camille observed, a smile of pleasure. "Sheets," he said flatly.

"You said you wanted to get some."

"Did I?" he said. He meant he had said it in passing, for something to say. "Sure. I can use these."

Camille folded the paper bag carefully, put it on the floor, and stacked the sheets on top of it. She had imagined a scene in which Eddie was pleased and touched by her gift and insisted on opening it at once. Then, when they had put the sheets on the mattress, he made love to her slowly, intensely, so that she knew he understood her gift was meant to begin their future together. His response, or lack of response, made it clear to her that he saw her gesture as a trap, that he believed she intended to invade his room and take over his life. Sheets were the beginning, his wry smile said to her. Next, it would be curtains on the door and a picture on the wall. She felt small, miserable. Eddie fumbled with the belt of her dress. "It's funny to see you in the morning," he said, trying to draw her down next to him. He was going to overlook her mistake, this time. She put her hand on his cheek while she swallowed a hard lump of humiliation and anger. She allowed herself only a momentary vision; her hand was a black paw raking sharp claws into the flesh of his face. The image was bloody and quick; she blinked it away. Then she smiled, patting his cheek. Her fantasy had ended with his voice whispering in her ear, *Camille, I love you.* As far as she knew, men did say such things to women, though no one had ever said anything of the kind to her. No, she thought, allowing herself to be pulled down in the circle of his arms, Eddie wasn't going to say anything like that today or any other day. One of his hands slipped under her skirt; the other began unfastening the buttons down the front of her dress. She pulled her hair away from her neck so that she could feel his warm lips there, and she pressed her body against his, resigning herself, as she had done before, to taking what little she could get.

35

When Hermann entered the dining room that evening he was braced for a weepy, hysterical scene. Instead, he found his young wife talking composedly with Charles, both of them bent over a dish of vegetables that apparently was not properly prepared. Though Hermann could not understand what they said, it seemed clear that Charles was in agreement with his mistress, that he was shocked and embarrassed to have such a dish appear at his master's table, for he took it up, holding it out before him as if it were distasteful to have it so close, and went out to the kitchen, muttering beneath his breath. Elisabeth gave her husband a smile accompanied by a sigh of dismay. "I don't know what is wrong with that cook lately," she said. "She has actually burned the okra."

Hermann stood for a moment taking in his beautiful wife. She was dressed in a pale violet dress he particularly liked, and he detected at the edge of her dark hair, pulled back loosely over her ears, the glitter of the diamond studs he had given her at their marriage. She appeared neither angry nor tearful; indeed, her complexion was so smooth and delicate, her eyes so bright and full of playful irony, that he recalled that first evening at André Davillier's dinner party. He was himself tired, uneasy. Plantation life confounded him. He couldn't seem to manage it all, and he was afraid of losing money. The sight of this young woman, who took everything, including the thwarting of her own wishes (for in the matter of Bessie and of the locked door he knew he had tried her sorely), with such gracious, conciliatory good humor, lifted his spirits and softened the habitual hardness of his expression. "I don't care at all about okra," he said. "Not when you look so lovely."

This brought a smile of real pleasure to Elisabeth's lips, a sidelong coquettish flash of her eyes. "Then I shall tell the cook she's been saved by my beauty," she said.

The kitchen door opened, and Charles came in bearing a covered dish, the contents of which evidently pleased him, for he set it on the sideboard with a flourish. Elisabeth watched him as he lifted the lid. A cloud of steam carrying a tantalizing aroma rose from the dozen or so perfectly browned little birds arranged on a bed of wild rice and sliced oranges. Charles busied himself opening the other dishes and serving them onto the plates while Hermann took his seat. "These quail were sent over by my cousin Louis," Elisabeth said. "They came this morning, so I thought we should have them at once."

Hermann poured himself a glass of wine, then filled his wife's glass as Charles set the laden plates before them. "They look delicious," Hermann said. He took up his knife and fork and began sawing at the little birds. Quail was a favorite of his. When he had rendered a forkful, he stuffed it into his mouth and followed it with another draft of wine. Elisabeth sat watching him, an expression of approval in her eyes; her mouth was compressed in a thin smile. Hermann didn't notice her until he had swallowed two more mouthfuls; then he looked up and nodded toward her plate. "You should eat," he said. "They're getting cold."

Elisabeth took up her fork and gave herself a few grains of rice.

"After dinner," Hermann said when he had swallowed another bite, "perhaps you will be willing to play for me a little."

Elisabeth used her fork to brace the quail against the plate and bore down on the breast with her knife. "Nothing would please me more," she said.

So they passed a quiet domestic evening, neither referring to the dramatic events of the afternoon. When they retired to the drawing room, the doors were already unlocked; Hermann must have seen to that on his way in. Elisabeth took her place at the piano while Hermann pulled up a comfortable leather chair so that he might see as well as listen to his wife. She selected a few sheets from the stack she was continually accumulating on the carpet next to her velvet piano stool. She began to play at once, eagerly and with great feeling; even Hermann, who cared little for music, could hardly resist the spell of her serious attention to the score. It unnerved him, for she seemed capable of escaping entirely into the world of music, and he watched her anxiously, jealously. There was nothing in life, save Elisabeth herself, that could ever so captivate him. When Charles offered him a brandy, he took the bottle as well and sat quietly and steadily drinking, for a long time, while the music gushed into the room, out across the hall, where Charles had taken his station against the wall, his favorite post, for he could hear but not be seen. The music swept past him, into the back of the house, past the kitchen, to the narrow bedroom where Bessie lay, weeping on her thin moss palette. She lifted her head to hear it, but it gave her no comfort. Her mistress would not stand up for her, and Mr. Schlaeger, who detested her, though she had never done anything to cross him, would have her hanged. The music only proved they had settled it between them and now gave no more thought to her.

36

A few hours before dawn Elisabeth slipped out of her bed, lit the candle on her nightstand and another on the washstand, and carefully opened the doors of her armoire. She took out her riding skirt and boots and began dressing in the dim, cool room. Hermann had come to her, as she expected, silent, a little drunk, pulling the coverlet away from her and pinning her down rudely, though he muttered endearments into her incredulous ears. She lay still but not stiff; she let her body relax, and in a few moments his breathing became labored, he gasped her name, his body stiffened, and it was over. He went away, and she got up to wash herself. Then for more than an hour she lay awake in her bed, going over her plan—what she would say to her aunt and to her father—until she felt sure Hermann must be asleep.

When she was dressed, she opened the door to the hall and stood listening, perfectly still in the great, dark house. She had one key, which Hermann had given her ceremoniously on their arrival at Montague, as if it were all she would ever need, and it *was* all she needed at the moment, for it opened the front door. She crept down the staircase, pausing at each step, but no sound answered the light creaking of the wood beneath her feet. She had considered whispering through Bessie's locked door, to tell her that she would not allow her to be hanged, but the risk was too great. If Hermann woke up and found his wife in a conspiracy with a slave, there was no telling what he might do. He might lock them all up, forever.

Elisabeth turned the key carefully in the lock and pulled the door open, amazed at the sudden racing of her heart, the pounding in her ears that made it difficult to hear anything else. In the next moment she was outside; the door was closed behind her. She had a sense of space looming wide around her and she plunged into it eagerly, for it seemed to contain numerous and wonderful possibilities such as she had never imagined. She was defying her husband, permanently and irrevocably. When he woke up to find her gone he would understand that she was not, as he had imagined, a pliable, spiritless creature who could be flattered and bullied into submission. She walked quickly along the narrow path that led to the stable. Once out of earshot of the house, she broke into a run. Her eyes grew accustomed to the darkness; the moon was full, the air fragrant and damp. At the barn she threw open the tack room door and burst inside, nearly colliding with the confused and terrified stable boy, who had been asleep on the feedbags he fashioned every night into a bed on the floor. She caught him by the arms and hissed into his wide-eyed face, "Hector, listen to me. Saddle Leon. There's an emergency. I must go at once."

"Yes, ma'am," Hector cried out, rushing into the barn where the horses, startled by the noise, stood straining their long necks over their stalls to see what the fuss was about. While Elisabeth paced up and down the small tack room, the boy lit the two lamps, set them on their stands, got a halter onto the reluctant Leon, and led him out into the aisle to be saddled. This was so unusual, the horse was such a creature of routine, that he resisted, pulling the boy up from the floor by raising his head high and stamping his hooves about dangerously. The boy spoke to him calmly, and when his feet were on the ground again he fastened the rope neatly at the hitching post. Still speaking in a reassuring voice, he patted the horse's flanks, his shoulders, and his neck, until the big head came down and Leon allowed his face to be scratched just below the ear. He was Elisabeth's horse; she had brought him from New Orleans, and he had the best disposition of any horse in the barn. He kept his head down and received the bit between his teeth easily, remaining still while the boy fitted the straps along his face, careful not to rub them against his eyes, easing the loops over his ears. As he was fastening the buckles at the base of Leon's jaw, the boy could hear Elisabeth moving about in the tack room. When he looked back he was startled to see her walking toward him, carrying her own saddle and blanket before her.

"I'm coming, miss," he said, hurrying to relieve her of her burden. She gave it up at once and went ahead to the horse, running her hands over the bridle to make sure that it was fastened properly, that none of the straps chafed the animal's face, that the longer hairs around his ears were not being pulled uncomfortably, speaking to him softly as she did. "Leon," the boy heard her say, "no rest for you tonight, I'm afraid. You have to help me. We have a long way to go."

The boy came up beside her and began arranging the blanket across the animal's high, somewhat narrow back. In general he was more frightened of his mistress, who was high-strung and short-tempered, than of any of his equine charges. Even Hermann's temperamental stallion was no match for Elisabeth when it came to unexpected displays of aggression. But tonight, as they stood together in the wide, dim aisle of the barn, the other horses snorting and stamping in their stalls at the strangeness of it all, the boy sensed that Elisabeth was not dangerous. As he lifted her saddle across Leon's back, she went to his other side and brought down the cinch strap herself, passing it to him beneath the horse's belly, adjusting the flaps against the blanket and snapping out the stirrup so that it lay flat. She came around to his side and watched him fasten the cinch, then ran her hand under the woven strap to check the tightness of it. Wherever she was going, the boy thought, she was in a hurry to get there, but her solicitude about the horse suggested that she intended to arrive without accident. "Open the door," she said. She unfastened the bridle, bringing the reins up over the horse's head, while the boy ran down the aisle and lifted the long bar that lay across the big double doors. He pushed one door open, set the hook in the eye against the outer wall, and went back to open the other. Elisabeth was leading her horse, and in the flickering lamplight it seemed to the boy that she was a pale, commanding spirit coming out of a mysterious world of spirits into the black, cool night, leading her fine, ghost-white horse, whose wide brown eyes shot off thin streams of gold. He stopped to look at her, but he didn't feel afraid of her; she wasn't after him. She motioned him to her to hold the reins while she mounted. He stroked Leon's face and gazed into one of his big, calm eyes. If he could have any horse in the barn for his own, he knew this one would be his choice, this mild-mannered gelding who he now saw was not a spirit at all but a patient, serviceable beast of burden. Elisabeth was in place; the boy led the horse a few steps past the threshold. Then many things happened at once. The reins were jerked suddenly upward, so that he lost his grip. Next, a terrific blow across his back pitched him face down into the dirt. He heard the rushing intake of the animal's breath and Elisabeth's startled cry. As he rolled over, he saw Leon's front hooves come down hard against the earth, then go up again, but not so high. In the same look he understood what had happened, though he could not comprehend how it had happened, for directly in the path of the startled horse and rider another spirit had materialized. But this one was a man, and he was standing his ground.

Elisabeth spoke to the horse; the hooves came down again, and though he danced to one side, then the other, he had come back under his mistress's control. The boy sat up in the dirt and brushed at his shirt. The man, he knew, had come from the house.

He approached the horse and rider. Elisabeth spoke sharply to him. "What are you doing here?" she said.

"I saw the lights," he replied.

"You should have stayed in the house where you belong."

The man said nothing, but he stepped aside, and the boy had the odd sensation that he was giving Elisabeth permission, though he knew this couldn't be true. Elisabeth's pale face seemed very high up now, from his vantage on the ground, and he saw her expression, haughty, impatient, yet troubled, as if she too recognized this man's right to block her path. She squeezed the horse's side, and he stepped forward slowly until she was next to the man. "Tell Bessie he can't hang her," she said. "He can't even sell her. She belongs to me." And with that she gave the horse a firm kick on his right flank, and he leaped forward, carrying her smoothly away, almost as if she were flying. It couldn't be denied; she was a fine rider. The man watched her for a moment as she galloped down the path to the wide road that led to the levee. He waited until he saw her make a turn downriver. The boy's chest ached, and he wasn't sure he could stand. The man came to him, extending a hand. "Are you hurt?" he asked.

"No, sir," the boy said. "He knocked the wind out of me is all." He took the proffered hand and got to his feet.

"My name is Charles," the man said.

"I know," the boy said. "I seen you at the funeral when Monsieur deClerc died. My *maman* told me you and me is kin."

Elisabeth reasoned that even if Hermann got on his horse as soon as he found she was gone, she would still be in New Orleans several hours before he could arrive. The steamer *Doswell,* which she intended to catch at her aunt's plantation, would pass the Montague landing very early, probably before Hermann discovered she was missing, unless Charles told him. If that happened he'd flag down the ship and be there waiting for her when she boarded at her aunt's landing.

But she didn't think Charles would tell Hermann. No slave wanted to give his master bad news or appear in any way responsible for his difficulties; it was borrowing trouble. Elisabeth knew the saying "Servants got to see and don't see, hear and don't hear," and she suspected Charles, with his quiet manner, his way of suddenly appearing in a room, was the embodiment of that homely advice. With luck Hermann might not even look for her until the noon meal, for often enough he did not see her until then, by which time she would be well on her way to the city. So she rode along the levee road at a steady pace, while the moon poured down a milky light over the hard ground beneath her horse's hooves and the same light glittered upon the wide, churning river that ran beside them. Her head was filled with strange fantasies; her spirits were dangerously high.

One of her fantasies was that she would never return to Montague. Another was that her husband would die. Then she would sell Montague and buy a town house, where she would do only as she pleased. She would not make the mistake of marrying again.

The steady pounding of Leon's hooves against the road lulled her, though she was too excited to feel sleepy. Leon knew where they were going; he'd been on this road before. He had settled into his gait like a somnambulist, though the slightest movement of Elisabeth's hands or legs would rouse him instantly to attention. His powerful shoulders had begun to gleam with sweat. When they arrived at her aunt's, he would have to be walked for an hour to cool him down.

Gradually the sky began to lighten, and the dull gray landscape was suffused with a greenish glow that rose up from the soil. They had come to the landing and turned down the narrow lane leading from the river to her aunt's great house. There was another, wider oak-lined alley that would bring her to the front door, but this way was shorter and led directly to the stable. Everything was quiet and still; the plantation had not come to life yet, but Elisabeth knew the stable boy would be up. Horses and their keepers are early risers. In fact, the barn doors were open and the boy stood watching her approach, for he had heard Leon's hooves on the path and come out to see who could be arriving at such an hour. Elisabeth could not repress a smile when she saw his puzzled face; he feared she must be bringing trouble. "James," she called down to him, "take Leon and cool him down. We've come all the way from Montague."

"Yes, ma'am," he said, taking the reins over the horse's ears.

Leon dropped his head, tired, sweating, his mouth dripping a green froth. He stretched his hind legs out from his body, as if he were being looked over by a buyer. Elisabeth alighted from the saddle and strode away, heading for the house and leaving the boy to whatever explanations he could imagine; she didn't care. The less he knew about what she was doing, the better.

Her aunt, who was already up and in conversation with her overseer—for she ran the plantation herself and had done so for the ten years since her husband's untimely, accidental death—greeted Elisabeth with no show of surprise or curiosity. She was a woman of habitual serenity, disinclined to pry into her family's affairs. She invited her niece to sit down to breakfast, listened quietly to Elisabeth's explanation; she said only that she had entered a property dispute with her husband and needed her father's counsel. Her aunt assured her that she had time to catch the steamer and would arrive in New Orleans before nightfall. Elisabeth was calmed by her aunt's influence and began to see her mission in a less romantic light. Such disputes were bound to come up, after all, and once Hermann understood that he had not simply purchased another slave when he acquired a wife, they would resume an amicable coexistence. Her aunt did not even raise an eyebrow when Elisabeth revealed that she had come away without any money for her travel expenses. After they finished their meal, she led her niece into a small office under the wide curving staircase, opened a heavy metal cash box, and counted out several bills, which she folded into an envelope and handed to Elisabeth, saying pleasantly, "You can repay this when your business is settled." Elisabeth sensed that her aunt knew exactly what she was up against, that the proffered envelope represented this strong woman's sanction. She took the money gratefully, her head inclined slightly, as she had stood as a child to receive a blessing from her confessor. Her aunt called a houseboy and bade him run to the landing and get the flag up; then the two women followed him, walking slowly along the path where all manner of azaleas and camellias bloomed gaily, and the air was rich with oxygen, pure and bright, for the sun was well up now. As they rounded the bend they could see the river. The boy was already running back, having raised the flag that would signal the ship to draw in for a passenger. Elisabeth could see the big white steamer, its great paddle wheel rolling and rolling, drawing up the brown water, its deck lined with people, rich and poor, slave and free, and she recalled how often and under what happy circumstances she had arrived at this landing with no more serious question than which dress she would wear or upon which young man she would smile. Now all that was gone, and she was going home to confess a failure of sorts and to find a way out, though not back.

Her father would not be pleased. He would doubtless tell her she had made her bed and must lie in it, and her mother would give her a sympathetic version of the same advice. But they would give her counsel on the matter of her property, that much was sure, and if she could get to Lucinde, she could get the other advice she needed: how to deal with her husband. She contrasted the thought of her former happiness and freedom with her present unhappiness, which she characterized as defeat but not surrender. She had a brief vision of herself as a doomed creature, betrayed by the people she loved. She drew away from her aunt as the boat pulled gracefully into the landing, and she searched the faces of the passengers leaning against the rails, smiling down at her. No. Hermann was not among them; she would get to the city before he did. Her aunt took her hand. She turned to receive a dry, perfunctory kiss on each cheek, the murmured words *"Bonne chance,"* and then she walked out to the ship, for the deckhands had thrown down the plank and were calling to one another, to her, waving her onto the ramp. The steamer rocked perilously, a huge, ungainly elephant who could pause only momentarily, for his master was the river, which ever gave one command, and that was to submit to the strong current and roll on, without protest, to the sea.

38

Ellen had taken an immediate dislike to her lawyer, a thin, well-dressed, mean-looking young woman who advanced upon her as she entered the office, her teeth bared in an artificial smile, her hand extended to take Ellen's in what she knew would be a bone-crushing grip, the overzealous handshake of a politician or a salesman. She was competent and avaricious, eager to inform Ellen of her rights, of the low, self-serving tactics Paul and his lawyer would doubtless use to take advantage of her, of the necessity for just such a hard, cold, single-minded young woman as she was to protect the hopeful, naïve potential divorcée from the snares of her ex-husband. Ellen explained that Paul knew himself to be in the wrong and that she did not expect him to protest any fair settlement of their mutual property. She herself wanted nothing from him, though she hoped to find a way to hold on to her house. He loved his daughters and wanted to provide for them.

"I hope you're right," the lawyer said, but it was clear that she had no such hope; rather, she had expectations, and she expected the worst. She gave Ellen a printed page containing a breakdown of her exorbitant fees.

By the time she left this woman's office, Ellen was filled with resentment toward Paul. He was putting her through new and unpleasant experiences she had never wanted to have, forcing her to put her fate in the hands of such people as this lawyer, whom she neither liked nor trusted, and all because he couldn't bear the tedium of ordinary life, because he needed to live dangerously. If he'd just told me, she thought, I could have locked him up with one of the tigers for a night or two. This idea so delighted her that she laughed and shook off the encroaching shadow of melancholy and self-pity the visit to the lawyer had cast over what she now discovered was a perfect day, clear, warm, unusually dry. Unless an emergency came up, she had nothing but paperwork to do at the hospital, and she had agreed to have lunch with the Primates' supervisor to talk over the expansion of the gorilla exhibit.

As she drove along the tree-shaded avenue, she indulged in the dangerous pastime of turning over the bones of her dead marriage. She was amazed by how completely devoid of life it was. Like those enormous reconstructed skeletons of dinosaurs in museums all over the world, the marriage seemed to her to have been shattered and buried a million years ago. Yet the evidence was undeniable, their daughters, struggling to adjust to the new world, the house they had shared for so many years, filled in haphazardly to disguise Paul's absence, the half-empty bed, the missing toothbrush: this dinosaur had once lived and breathed, had dominated the landscape, oblivious and stupid, meandering aimlessly toward extinction. Could anything have been done to save it? That question, Ellen admitted, was giving way to a more interesting one: Should anything have been done to save it? Increasingly she knew the answer was no; she did not want Paul back. Though he had been gone only two months, the memory of their daily commerce was fading. Her battle with him, which had at times consumed all her energy so that she woke up exhausted from dreams in which he betrayed her, openly, brazenly, as he had actually done, as she thought she had always known he would—this battle was over. And who was the victor? Oddly, Ellen did not believe Paul had won.

And it was stupid, really, to characterize their marriage as a battlefield. There had been long periods of peaceful coexistence and even of passion. It would be cruel to deny this now, cruel to her and to Paul. She had never stopped desiring him, and she knew that if he saw her, even now, he would desire her, more than ever probably, because he had put her out of his reach. This was the part of their marriage that had survived. It was frustrating to admit it. She made a conscious effort not to think about sex, but the thought of Paul, just his name, Paul, was connected to sex, was synonymous with sex, so that sitting in the hateful lawyer's office talking about Paul had the perverse effect of filling her with desire. Yet she no longer desired Paul. He had betrayed her, and she was too stunned and too proud to long for his embrace, so this desire was a nonspecific aching directed at no one in particular. At night, lying in her empty bed, she tried to return to the imaginative world of her childhood, in which she had lived alone, without sex, neither desiring it nor not desiring it, rather innocent of it. She remembered sleeping in her narrow child's bed, in that pleasing solitude children accept so naturally, reluctant to share anything, toys, food, especially one's bed. Considering the universal loneliness of children, she drifted into sleep, but as soon as she was asleep she plunged into dreams of unrelenting and startling eroticism. She often dreamed of having sex with animals, a phenomenon that amused her when she woke, for the dreams were highly satisfying; she had confidence in these dream animals, in their uncompromising devotion to her, a confidence she knew she would never have with a human lover again. Then she thought of Paul bitterly, for she felt he'd reduced her to this, knocked her back to zero, so that even her poor unconscious could not willingly frame a sexual attachment to a man.

Paul, she said softly. Submitting to a reflex, one she was coming to rely upon, even in a detached way to appreciate, with the equivalent of a mental shove she put Paul out of her thoughts and turned to a less aggravating, though equally puzzling problem, the persistent skin infection one of the tamarin monkeys had contracted, which was proving peculiarly unresponsive to antibiotics. It had started in his armpit a few weeks ago and spread slowly but insistently down his side. Yesterday she noticed a new patch starting between his toes—dry, red, flaking skin—some hair loss already. He didn't scratch it, didn't seem to be aware of it, but there was no doubt that it was spreading. She would take him off of the sulfa and try an antifungal, starting today. He was miserable in the isolation area, off his feed; he'd lost weight and his tiny, human-looking face was drawn with worry. His keeper came to see him two or three times a day, bringing him bits of fruit, which he took willingly enough, but he chewed them lackadaisically, as if he ate only to be polite. The other patient she had to look in on was a lizard, who had been in the hospital for two days because his keeper had noticed he'd stopped moving. He was dehydrated, his blood count suggested he was already dead, and Ellen fully expected to find him dead when she went in. Reptiles generally responded slowly to treatment.

So she passed the morning, busy and preoccupied. The lizard was dead and she had him put in the cooler in the necropsy room; the tamarin looked about the same; the stack of correspondence and paperwork on her desk was intimidating. She switched on the phone machine and sat down at her desk with a good will, making steady progress until noon, when she saw Gina, the Primates' supervisor, a pale, delicate woman who, when she moved among her charges, did not appear to be in any way descended from them, smiling at her in the doorway. "Give it up," she said, and Ellen groaned. "Yes. Gladly. Let's get out of here."

The restaurant was crowded; it was a popular spot, a little farther afield than Ellen usually went for lunch, but she and Gina had agreed they both wanted seafood and needed a change from the uptown menus. They had to stand at a long noisy bar for a few minutes, shouting at each other and drinking beer, another indulgence Ellen didn't usually allow herself at lunch. She was in a good humor, and Gina entertained her with stories about the primates and their keepers. It amused her that anyone listening would not guess that half the characters in Gina's stories were monkeys. When the bartender called Ellen's name and they turned to follow the waiter through the room, crowded with diners, tables, other waiters balancing trays laden with delicious-smelling food, Ellen was laughing. Her eye caught that of a man at the end of the bar, a good-looking man, she noted, who responded to the contagion of her laughter with an indulgent smile of his own. This provided a further lift to her spirits, and she felt herself to be attractive, light-hearted, carefree. She followed Gina to the table, sat, and looked around the room happily. This restaurant was a good choice, she told Gina, who agreed. She glanced over at the bar where the attractive man had turned back to his drink, then at the door. The crowd was thinning, more people going out than coming in, though the stream was steady; the door barely closed before it opened again. She watched a couple with two children maneuver their way through the crowd going out. Then the door opened from outside, and Paul and Donna stepped in.

Ellen felt the sudden downturn of every line in her face. Her mouth dropped slightly open. Involuntarily she put her hand up to cover her eyes. Her heart raced; she could hear it inside her head; and her mouth went dry.

"What's wrong?" Gina said.

Under the awning of her hand she smiled weakly. "My husband just walked in with his girlfriend."

"Oh," Gina replied. She strained to see over the crowd, but she was not facing the door and couldn't make out anything without moving her chair.

"My ex-husband, I guess I should say," Ellen added. "It doesn't matter really. It's just that I've never seen her before."

"Do you want to leave?" Gina asked.

"No. I don't think so." Ellen took a swallow of beer, then another. She looked back to where Paul and Donna were standing, directly in her line of vision. Paul was giving his name to the bartender. Donna was watching him.

So this was Donna.

She was so tall! When Paul spoke to her, he looked up to meet her eyes. And of course she was pretty, very young, blond, long-limbed, eager-looking, frisky perhaps, but eager to please. She had a wide, quick smile that showed all her teeth. She had put her purse on the bar and was digging through it, but her attention was entirely on Paul; her head was cocked in his direction, and something he said provoked the big smile once, then again. She pulled out a pack of cigarettes and began tapping one out into her palm. She was dressed in Paul's favorite style, straight, nearly tight skirt, silk blouse, stockings, heels, an outfit that revealed her figure, which was worth revealing. Ellen took all this in quickly; hardly a moment had passed, and in the next one she looked at Paul.

He looked fine, happy, even pleased with himself. His attention was absorbed by the woman at his side. He was not casing the room, as was his habit. He was lighting her cigarette carefully, and as she bent to take the light, her long hair fell over her cheek and he reached out to protect it from the little flame of the match. She pulled back, holding the cigarette to her lips, drawing in the smoke, taking it away, blowing out smoke, smiling her too-big smile.

Ellen tried to read her menu. The words seemed to swim in front of her, and her thoughts, in a temporary riot, cast up odd bits: Paul hated cigarettes. Another had to do with his shirt, a new one; she knew she'd never seen it before. It was a color like rust, an unusual, expensive-looking shirt.

"Ellen," Gina said, "do you want to leave? I really don't mind."

She looked up at her friend. She hadn't expected it to be so painful and so confusing. "No," she said. "With any luck they'll get put in the back dining room."

"No. I don't think so." Ellen took a swallow of beer, then another. She looked back to where Paul and Donna were standing, directly in her line of vision. Paul was giving his name to the bartender. Donna was watching him.

So this was Donna.

She was so tall! When Paul spoke to her, he looked up to meet her eyes. And of course she was pretty, very young, blond, long-limbed, eager-looking, frisky perhaps, but eager to please. She had a wide, quick smile that showed all her teeth. She had put her purse on the bar and was digging through it, but her attention was entirely on Paul; her head was cocked in his direction, and something he said provoked the big smile once, then again. She pulled out a pack of cigarettes and began tapping one out into her palm. She was dressed in Paul's favorite style, straight, nearly tight skirt, silk blouse, stockings, heels, an outfit that revealed her figure, which was worth revealing. Ellen took all this in quickly; hardly a moment had passed, and in the next one she looked at Paul.

He looked fine, happy, even pleased with himself. His attention was absorbed by the woman at his side. He was not casing the room, as was his habit. He was lighting her cigarette carefully, and as she bent to take the light, her long hair fell over her cheek and he reached out to protect it from the little flame of the match. She pulled back, holding the cigarette to her lips, drawing in the smoke, taking it away, blowing out smoke, smiling her too-big smile.

Ellen tried to read her menu. The words seemed to swim in front of her, and her thoughts, in a temporary riot, cast up odd bits: Paul hated cigarettes. Another had to do with his shirt, a new one; she knew she'd never seen it before. It was a color like rust, an unusual, expensive-looking shirt.

"Ellen," Gina said, "do you want to leave? I really don't mind."

She looked up at her friend. She hadn't expected it to be so painful and so confusing. "No," she said. "With any luck they'll get put in the back dining room."

the uptown menus. They had to stand at a long noisy bar for a few minutes, shouting at each other and drinking beer, another indulgence Ellen didn't usually allow herself at lunch. She was in a good humor, and Gina entertained her with stories about the primates and their keepers. It amused her that anyone listening would not guess that half the characters in Gina's stories were monkeys. When the bartender called Ellen's name and they turned to follow the waiter through the room, crowded with diners, tables, other waiters balancing trays laden with delicious-smelling food, Ellen was laughing. Her eye caught that of a man at the end of the bar, a good-looking man, she noted, who responded to the contagion of her laughter with an indulgent smile of his own. This provided a further lift to her spirits, and she felt herself to be attractive, light-hearted, carefree. She followed Gina to the table, sat, and looked around the room happily. This restaurant was a good choice, she told Gina, who agreed. She glanced over at the bar where the attractive man had turned back to his drink, then at the door. The crowd was thinning, more people going out than coming in, though the stream was steady; the door barely closed before it opened again. She watched a couple with two children maneuver their way through the crowd going out. Then the door opened from outside, and Paul and Donna stepped in.

Ellen felt the sudden downturn of every line in her face. Her mouth dropped slightly open. Involuntarily she put her hand up to cover her eyes. Her heart raced; she could hear it inside her head; and her mouth went dry.

"What's wrong?" Gina said.

Under the awning of her hand she smiled weakly. "My husband just walked in with his girlfriend."

"Oh," Gina replied. She strained to see over the crowd, but she was not facing the door and couldn't make out anything without moving her chair.

"My ex-husband, I guess I should say," Ellen added. "It doesn't matter really. It's just that I've never seen her before."

"Do you want to leave?" Gina asked.

Paul, she said softly. Submitting to a reflex, one she was coming to rely upon, even in a detached way to appreciate, with the equivalent of a mental shove she put Paul out of her thoughts and turned to a less aggravating, though equally puzzling problem, the persistent skin infection one of the tamarin monkeys had contracted, which was proving peculiarly unresponsive to antibiotics. It had started in his armpit a few weeks ago and spread slowly but insistently down his side. Yesterday she noticed a new patch starting between his toes—dry, red, flaking skin—some hair loss already. He didn't scratch it, didn't seem to be aware of it, but there was no doubt that it was spreading. She would take him off of the sulfa and try an antifungal, starting today. He was miserable in the isolation area, off his feed; he'd lost weight and his tiny, human-looking face was drawn with worry. His keeper came to see him two or three times a day, bringing him bits of fruit, which he took willingly enough, but he chewed them lackadaisically, as if he ate only to be polite. The other patient she had to look in on was a lizard, who had been in the hospital for two days because his keeper had noticed he'd stopped moving. He was dehydrated, his blood count suggested he was already dead, and Ellen fully expected to find him dead when she went in. Reptiles generally responded slowly to treatment.

So she passed the morning, busy and preoccupied. The lizard was dead and she had him put in the cooler in the necropsy room; the tamarin looked about the same; the stack of correspondence and paperwork on her desk was intimidating. She switched on the phone machine and sat down at her desk with a good will, making steady progress until noon, when she saw Gina, the Primates' supervisor, a pale, delicate woman who, when she moved among her charges, did not appear to be in any way descended from them, smiling at her in the doorway. "Give it up," she said, and Ellen groaned. "Yes. Gladly. Let's get out of here."

The restaurant was crowded; it was a popular spot, a little farther afield than Ellen usually went for lunch, but she and Gina had agreed they both wanted seafood and needed a change from her energy so that she woke up exhausted from dreams in which he betrayed her, openly, brazenly, as he had actually done, as she thought she had always known he would—this battle was over. And who was the victor? Oddly, Ellen did not believe Paul had won.

And it was stupid, really, to characterize their marriage as a battlefield. There had been long periods of peaceful coexistence and even of passion. It would be cruel to deny this now, cruel to her and to Paul. She had never stopped desiring him, and she knew that if he saw her, even now, he would desire her, more than ever probably, because he had put her out of his reach. This was the part of their marriage that had survived. It was frustrating to admit it. She made a conscious effort not to think about sex, but the thought of Paul, just his name, Paul, was connected to sex, was synonymous with sex, so that sitting in the hateful lawyer's office talking about Paul had the perverse effect of filling her with desire. Yet she no longer desired Paul. He had betrayed her, and she was too stunned and too proud to long for his embrace, so this desire was a nonspecific aching directed at no one in particular. At night, lying in her empty bed, she tried to return to the imaginative world of her childhood, in which she had lived alone, without sex, neither desiring it nor not desiring it, rather innocent of it. She remembered sleeping in her narrow child's bed, in that pleasing solitude children accept so naturally, reluctant to share anything, toys, food, especially one's bed. Considering the universal loneliness of children, she drifted into sleep, but as soon as she was asleep she plunged into dreams of unrelenting and startling eroticism. She often dreamed of having sex with animals, a phenomenon that amused her when she woke, for the dreams were highly satisfying; she had confidence in these dream animals, in their uncompromising devotion to her, a confidence she knew she would never have with a human lover again. Then she thought of Paul bitterly, for she felt he'd reduced her to this, knocked her back to zero, so that even her poor unconscious could not willingly frame a sexual attachment to a man.

in which she had told Paul she would never stop loving him. It had seemed true at the time. She could not then have imagined the complexity of emotions that would lead to this moment and the revelation it contained: she was, after all, going to stop loving Paul. He was sitting in the next room, basking in the affectionate attention of his new love, secure, confident, perhaps a little guilty about discarding his wife, a little sad about leaving his daughters; but all in all things were going along very well. He was in love and he was free to be in love. He did not sense Ellen's love flickering and fading, but for her it was as if the lights in the room had been dimmed.

The food arrived. Ellen chewed the shrimp mechanically and tried to concentrate on her conversation with Gina. Finally, when they began to discuss the exhibit expansion, she was able to engage herself completely, and the vision of Paul in his happiness faded. It was nearly pleasurable to give her consciousness over, bit by bit, to a practical matter. They had coffee, Gina ate a custard, then they went out into the street, clambering into Gina's truck, heading back uptown. In the zoo parking lot they parted. Gina had completely forgotten about her friend's discomfiture, or perhaps she made no mention of it out of courtesy. Ellen watched her small, thin figure crossing the bright shell lot, walking quickly along the sidewalk past the administration office, eager to get back to work, to what she called her "monkey business."

Ellen turned toward the hospital. It was a short walk, but she experienced a series of emotions—sadness, frustration, loneliness, anger—so abrupt and confusing that she stopped beneath a bottle brush tree and stood in the shade, unable to move. Was this to be it, then? Would this be the content of her solitude from now on, this sensation of being unable to find her way, this paralysis of intention? It was unbearable. She gave it a name; it was despair. Not the despair that longs for death, which she now understood to be a paltry, self-serving emotion, but that which longs for life. How had she arrived at this barren place, shut off from so much that she loved? She felt she was standing on the bank of a broad, turbulent

Gina nodded, studied her menu, giving Ellen time to recover, for which she was pitifully grateful. Her appetite was gone, but she read the familiar names of the various dishes. They served what they called trout in this restaurant, but it was really an inferior farm-raised fish, tilapia. All the restaurants in town were using it because the once plentiful trout, like so many other animals, were now scarce. Ellen allowed herself to think about this for a moment; it cleared her head. She glanced up again and saw, to her relief, that her wish had come true: Paul and Donna were following the waiter down the bar to the back room. Donna was leading the way; Paul had rested his hand on her hip, a habit he had. Ellen recalled exactly how it felt. Neither Paul nor Donna looked out into the dining room, and in a moment they were gone.

The waiter appeared, a big man with a dour though not un-friendly manner. "What can I get you ladies?" he asked. Ellen listened to Gina's order, then ordered the same thing for herself; shrimp, at least there were still shrimp. When he was gone Gina gave her a sympathetic look. "Are you okay?"

"Yes," Ellen said. "They've gone."

"How long have you been separated?"

Ellen thought Gina knew exactly how long; everybody did. "Two months," she said.

"Were you married a long time?"

"Twenty years."

"Ouch," Gina said. "That is a long time."

"That's true," Ellen said. Mercifully, Gina began to talk about herself. She had been married, but only for two years, when she was very young. Her husband had been in a rock band when they met. He was rebellious and sexy, had long beautiful hair. Gina thought of him as an outlaw. Then the band broke up, he cut off all the hair, and went to law school. It was too much.

Ellen asked a few specific questions, a trick she used to relax herself. People liked to be asked questions; it made them feel inter-esting. She gave to Gina's answers half her attention. The other half was engaged by an unwonted recollection of the conversation river, and that for some reason, it didn't matter what, there was no turning back. She was now required to jump in and swim across. She looked this way and that. Somewhere there must be a boat or someone to help, but there was nothing and no one, just the dark water and over there in the distance the dull gleaming of the opposite shore. She summoned up all her courage, said farewell to the unattending world, took a step into the cold, swirling shallows, then another. This was it, she thought. When this was over she would know herself better than she had ever wanted to. Whatever happened now, she was going in and coming out alone.

39

"I've done a little better this year than last," Paul said. He pulled from his briefcase a thin sheaf of papers covered over with numbers and squared it next to a similar stack, equally scrawled upon, but in a finer hand, on Ellen's kitchen table. Ellen, her back to him, was standing at the counter pouring coffee and hot milk into two cups. Paul glanced at her, noting with pleasure the steam rising from the milk. No one made better coffee than she did. He almost spoke. He wanted to say he had been looking forward to this coffee all day, but as the words reached his lips she turned to bring the cups to the table, and something about her, perhaps the grim set of her mouth, made him call back the remark.

"But my expenses have been higher as well," he continued, feeling suddenly, childishly nervous. "So I think my self-employment will cancel out."

Ellen put one cup in front of him, then took a seat across the table. She occupied herself in opening an envelope containing a number of tax forms, which she flipped through disconsolately. "I hope I got all the right forms."

"It shouldn't be too complicated this year," Paul said. "I picked up an extra Schedule C in case you forgot."

Ellen took a sip of her coffee. She had been dreading this meeting all week, but now that it had come it seemed surprisingly ordinary. Paul was always optimistic at tax time, she was always apprehensive; in this respect nothing had changed. It was interesting to look at him after not seeing him for so long. He seemed both exactly the same and entirely different. There was something fluttery about him, alert and defensive, though she knew he would not remain defensive if he felt himself to be under attack. His strategy was always to shift quickly to the offensive, and it was so instinctive with him that nothing, not even actually being in the wrong, could change it. He took a sip of his coffee, lifting the top sheet of paper and reading the one beneath. Then he put the cup down before him and nodded at it admiringly. "What good coffee," he said.

So Donna didn't make very good coffee.

Ellen gave him a blank look; she wasn't up to compliments. Neither of them had mentioned Donna, yet Ellen felt her presence as clearly as if she were sitting between them. She made Paul cumbersome; he took up too much room and looked out of place in what had been for so long his own kitchen. Ellen handed him the envelope containing her W-2 form. "How's your new book coming along?" she asked.

"Very well," he said at once. "Very well. I think I'll be finished by August."

"It's still about that murder?" she said. "That German?"

"Herr Schlaeger," Paul reminded her. "And Elisabeth the 'catwoman.' Yes."

"So did she really turn into a tiger?"

"A leopard, I think. That's what I'm calling it, anyway. Well, who knows?" he said; then, "I mean of course she didn't, but she thought she did."

"Have you finished the research?"

"Not entirely. The book isn't just about the Schlaegers. There are some stories connected to theirs, but the strangeness of that case, well, it's fascinating. The rest of the book opens out around Elisabeth. She's sitting at the center of it, very mysterious, unknowable, like a big black cat."

Ellen smiled at this idea, a book with a leopard in the middle of it. "It sounds good," she said. "It sounds different."

"Completely different from anything I've tried before," Paul said. "I may try to find a bigger publisher for it, a New York house. Donna thinks it will attract a much wider audience . . ." Paul's voice faded out. For a moment they sat in silence, listening more to a fact than to a sound, the fact that Paul had mentioned his lover's name. He was himself so stunned by what he had said that he sat gazing into the air, his mouth ajar.

Ellen felt she was seeing right through him. So this was what it was all about. It was one thing that Donna was young and beautiful and probably exciting in bed, but this was the kicker, the deciding factor: Donna thought Paul should have a larger audience. It was so obvious and in its way so pitiful, it made her smile. Paul was fingering the W-2 form, studying the figure that represented Ellen's yearly income.

She said, indulgently, as if encouraging a child, "So that's what Donna thinks?"

He looked up, then away. "Yes. Well, she's very interested in my work."

"I've seen her, you know," Ellen said. Why not, she thought.

Paul gave her his full attention. "Where?"

"At Mandina's. A few weeks ago. You were there, but you didn't see me."

"Really?" he said.

Now, she thought, she should make some remark about what she had seen; she should say she's very pretty or isn't she rather tall. What she wanted to say was *How could you be such a fool?* She felt bored, weary. She fished through the forms in her hands, pulled out the thickest one; it was practically a book, bigger every year. "Here's the 1040," she said. Paul opened the form and began filling in the boxes, writing in Ellen's social security number as if it were his own. "I'll be moving again next month," he said.

"Oh? Where?"

"Actually not far from where I am now. Perrier Street. Near the park."

"A better place?" Ellen asked. She understood they were still talking about Donna.

"Yes," he said. "Much more light. My apartment is too dark. This one's bigger."

Ellen said nothing. They both knew the next sentence; she could have said it with him.

"Donna will be moving in with me there."

Ellen laughed weakly. "What a surprise," she said.

"You don't have to be snide."

"Have you told the girls?"

"No," he said, "I will. The next time they visit."

They heard voices in the garage, then the soft tread of leather heels against concrete: the girls, as if on cue, arriving home from school.

Ellen raised her eyebrows at Paul. "I told them you would be here," she said. Barker got up from under the table and made his way, stretching and yawning, to the door. Greeting family members was his most sacred duty. He stood anxiously, his tail moving back and forth slowly, until the door opened and Lillian, then Celia, pushed in past him, saying his name and giving him the requisite pats on the shoulders and back. The sisters were in the midst of conversation. Lillian was making one of her faces, imitating a teacher perhaps, and saying, "Ms. Clayton. What did you expect?" and Celia was laughing. Ellen watched Paul as he turned to speak to them, his face animated with expectancy and pleasure in their good humor, blissfully unaware of how rare it was these days to see Celia laugh.

"Greetings, parents," Lillian said, swinging her heavy book

bag onto the counter. Celia, whose laughter had disappeared completely, leaving not even a trace of a smile, edged past her sister and, giving her father a cursory nod of recognition, disappeared into the living room.

Paul sat up in his chair. "Celia?" he called reprovingly. Ellen looked at Lillian, who was frowning at her books. There was a moment of silence; then Celia appeared in the doorway, her shoulders drooping forward and her head down so that her hair covered her face. She said nothing. "Don't you want to tell me hello at least?" Paul said.

Celia had visited her father only twice since his move, both times at his insistence, and Ellen gathered the visits had not gone well. Paul said only that she was sullen; she would get over it. Celia complained that his apartment was dreary and she didn't want to sleep there. Ellen watched now as she shifted her weight from one foot to the other, deciding whether to answer her father or not. It was a gruesome, horrible decision, one Ellen felt she should not be required to make. Giving in, forgiving, smoothing over, the options Ellen and Lillian embraced, were not available to Celia. She was, after all, like Paul; she bore grudges and contemplated revenge. At last she straightened herself, lifted her eyes, and, as she concentrated her features into an expression of consummate boredom and contempt, hauled up the strap of her book bag and walked silently away.

Paul let out a long sigh of exasperation and turned to Ellen, who sat fumbling with a pen, her eyes wet with tears. Then he looked to Lillian. "What's wrong with your sister?" he demanded.

"I guess she's not too crazy about you right now, Dad," Lillian said.

"Well, maybe I'm not too crazy about her," he replied. "Does that mean it's no longer necessary to be civil to one another?"

Right, Ellen thought. Let's drag out the great code of civility, that old standby in times of difficulty, that bulwark against chaos.

"Don't take it out on me, Dad," Lillian said testily.

"Oh, for God's sake," Paul said.

Lillian took up her bag and shuffled past her father, saying, in a measured voice modulated to a perfect neutral, "Well, I'd better get started on my homework."

Paul returned his attention to the tax form, muttering about the ingratitude of his daughters. Ellen sat watching him, wiping her eyes with her knuckles, for the tears that had been provoked by the sight of Celia's indecision hadn't stopped. She made an effort to control herself—it was ridiculous, she thought—but to no avail. Her nose began to run as well. She got up and pulled a paper towel from the roll, then sat down again, blowing her nose and wiping her eyes carefully.

Paul watched her. He was irritated now; no one was acting as he thought they should. His daughters were hostile, and here was Ellen in tears. "What are you crying about?" he said.

Ellen blew her nose again and folded her towel to dab at her eyes. "I don't know," she said. "I think I must be exhausted."

"Have you been working hard?"

"It's not that. I'm worried about Celia. And it's you. It wears me out to watch you."

"Yes?" Paul said. "Well, fine. Just fine." He began gathering up the papers in front of him. "I think I have everything I need here to do this on my own. Since it's so exhausting and unpleasant for everybody—including me, by the way—to have me here, I think I'll just take it all home and I'll let you know how it turns out."

Ellen stopped crying. It was fine for him, she thought. He could go off in a huff and tell his girlfriend how unreasonable his family was. "I hate living without sex," she said coldly. "I wish I had a lover."

Paul glared at her but continued stacking the papers. The words *well, get one* rose to his lips, but he did not say them, not from any reticence but because he was so shocked by what she had said that he couldn't speak. He had expected Ellen to persuade him to stay, to tell him that he was being silly, that he was not unwelcome. He had been from the start happy to see her, willing to sit for a while and talk about those things which concerned them both; it was unfair to find himself cast in the role of the man responsible for all the misery in a house full of love-starved women. She wouldn't look at him now. She had rested her chin in her hand and was gazing into the empty space at the edge of the table. Most irritating, he thought, was how beautiful she looked. He'd noticed it as soon as she opened the door, and he'd said hello sheepishly, like a boy on a blind date who finds he's had a bit of luck for a change. She was wearing a black T-shirt and jeans, a pair of sandals; her cheeks were flushed from the heat, and her eyes were bright, full of busy intelligence. It lifted his heart to see her looking so well. She was so small; he'd forgotten that. As he followed her into the kitchen he'd suffered an exhausting bout of desire and frustration. How was it that he could no longer catch her up and press her against the wall as he had always done when he felt like this, alone in his own house with his own wife? He couldn't make sense of it. How could the woman he had made love to passionately and often for twenty years now sit across from him and say she wished for a lover? She'd changed her hair, he thought pointlessly. It was drawn back in a braid, but loosely, so that a few strands strayed around her face. He needed to speak because he was sick with desire and he knew if he did not speak he would walk around the table and try to take her in his arms. Then all hell would break loose. "You sound like you're looking for a piece of furniture," he said. "Or a new appliance."

"It is like that," she said. "People put ads in the paper, you know, looking for lovers; really, that's all it is. I find myself reading them." She laughed. "It's absurd."

Paul entertained a momentary vision of Ellen in the arms of one of these advertisement men, someone with a gold chain around his neck, or a thick mustache, or even a tattoo. His stomach was queasy from the range of emotions he'd run through: anger at Celia, then desire and horrible jealousy. There was nothing he could do about any of it, but especially nothing he could do about the jealousy, because his rival was imaginary, and, even if he wasn't, when a man abandons his wife he abandons his rights. When a new man came along—and he understood now that this was a distinct possibility; it was inevitable—he would not be asked for his approval. "Don't do that," he said, but Ellen's mind had wandered away from her own offhand remark, and she replied, "Don't do what?"

"Answer an advertisement."

She gave him a long, cold look, allowing her eyes to rest on his face. It was laughable. He wanted a say in the matter of her loneliness, but she didn't feel amused; rather, she was weary. The room was filled with a familiar agitation, the agitation, she thought, of Paul's restless soul. If she let him know how much she wanted him to take this tortured knot of conflicting needs and desires out of her kitchen, he would be hurt, confused, and angry. In the past this consideration would have tempered her response, would even, in some way, have altered her feelings, have made her care; but now she felt a strange, not unpleasurable desire to cause him pain, which, combined with physical fatigue, caused her to lower her face to her hands, rub her aching and irritated eyes, and say, "I thought you were leaving. I thought you had everything you needed."

The pages were stacked neatly. All Paul had to do was put them in his briefcase. He stood tapping the edges against the table top, recalling an earlier thought, that he might be asked to stay to dinner, and his care to keep the evening free for that eventuality. Donna would be pleased to hear from him. Ellen was looking at him now, her face a study in indifference; he was certain she had never looked at him in quite this way before. He pulled the brief-case up on the table and slid the papers inside carefully; he did not want his impatience to show. "You're absolutely right," he said. "There's nothing I need in this house." He made his way to the kitchen door, feeling awkward and strangely blown out, as if he were walking out of a storm. He paused, holding the door open, looking into the garage, which, he noticed, was in its usual mess. "I'll call you when this is done."

Ellen hadn't moved. "That will be fine," she said. Then he closed the door and went out.

She sat quietly for a few moments, listening to the sound of his car engine starting up, the return of silence as he drove away. She got up and took his empty coffee cup to the sink, put the pot back on the stove for herself. Then she stood at the window. The yard looked hot; the azaleas were limp, bleached out by the sun. It was just like Paul to conclude from her confession of surprise that she should actually find herself reading the grotesque personal ads in the newspaper that she intended to answer one, and, having completely misunderstood what she had said, advise her against a course of action she had never had any intention of taking. She turned on the tap, rinsed out his cup, and set it on the drying rack. "Idiot," she said.

Dr. Veider resisted the idea that Camille discontinue her weekly sessions with him, but her insistence, which took the form of a stubborn refusal to talk about anything else, wore him down. Or so she thought. There was no way to measure the level of his real interest, but she guessed it wasn't high. They scheduled three final meetings and passed these hours more amiably than any they had shared before. Camille found herself in the peculiar position of giving assurances: that she was, as she put it, better; that she had no desire to do anything but live. Dr. Veider was clearly skeptical. At their last interview he extracted promises that she would call him, that she would feel free to return to him should the need arise, and his manner was so earnest that she was both touched and alarmed.

"I haven't had one of those attacks in a long time," Camille reminded him. "I'm doing well at work. I wouldn't say I was a happy person, but really, who is?"

Dr. Veider frowned. "That's all superficial."

"But I want to be on my own, to take care of myself. That's different, isn't it? That's not superficial."

"It's not that easy, Camille," he said.

"Well, if you think I'm not better than I was when I first came here, I might as well quit because it isn't doing me any good, right?"

"You have to be careful," he said. "People like you. You're going to have to take it one day at a time."

"What do you mean, people like me?"

"People with personality disorders . . ."

Camille laughed. "Is that what I've got?" she said. "Well, at long last."

"It's not a joke," he said.

Camille glared at him. She didn't think it was a joke either, and she was angry with him for saying it. She felt he'd classified her, neatly and pointlessly, and now he wanted to pass his dismissal on to her so that she would see herself as one of those people, the ones in the group stamped "personality disorders," whatever that meant, who had to be very careful or—what? What would happen if she wasn't careful?

He sat waiting to hear what she would say next, though his expression was not attentive, rather abstracted, as if he were trying to solve a problem in mathematics. He looked confused, Camille thought, and her anger dissipated. Given their respective jobs, she preferred her own. Day after day he had to sit here and listen to all manner of pain, hysteria, misery. He probably knew the worst about people and didn't want to hear any more, but now he was in it and he couldn't stop listening. "Don't you think people can get better?" she asked seriously. "Don't you think they can change?"

He looked surprised. He knew the answer, she thought, but he wasn't sure whether to give it to her or not. There were so many considerations: who she was, who he was, what he should say to someone in her condition, what he wanted to say, what people had said to him. She had a sense of his going over all the possible answers, though they both knew there were only two, and, as the moments ticked by, a kind of gravity accrued to his choice, so that when he finally spoke, it seemed to both of them imperative that he give her nothing less than the truth. "No," he said, "I don't think they can."

Though Camille said nothing, she registered a conscious reflex of denial. If this was true, he had condemned her to a lifetime of servitude. She looked at the clock; they had only a few minutes left. "I think I'll be all right," she said weakly.

"I hope so," he said.

She cast about for a safe subject, something to get them to the hour, but nothing presented itself. Oddly, he did not seem to mind. He sometimes asked a question or made comments that provoked her, but now he just sat there, leaning a little forward in his chair, his hands folded between his knees. Camille rarely looked at him closely, but she took this last opportunity and saw to her surprise that he was not well. There were dark circles beneath his eyes; his fair skin was greenish. As she watched, he brought his hand to his mouth to stifle a sudden, dry cough. "Are you sick?" she said.

He smiled, waving his hand lightly as if to dismiss the idea. "No," he said. "Just a cold." The clock made the final click into the hour. "I guess that's it," he said. "It's time." She stood up at once, eager to be away from this room, and he followed her to the door, where they shook hands awkwardly. She walked quickly across the lobby and down the long gray hall to the glass doors, which she pushed open hard with both hands, bursting out into the street the way, she thought, Magda burst out into her exhibit each morning; she wasn't going to be free, of course, she knew that, but at least the street provided a change of scenery.

It was a warm afternoon. She shrugged off the sweater she had worn to defend herself against Dr. Veider's air conditioner, and her spirits lifted. She would never have to sit in that frigid room again. She shrugged once more, this time shaking off his parting words. He was like her mother, always expecting the worst of everyone. As she turned toward the French Quarter a celebratory mood animated her step, and she experienced a mental alertness that delighted her. She had a few hours before she had to return to her mother's house, and she hoped to pass them in Eddie's company. She often went to him on Wednesdays, though sometimes he wasn't there. His work schedule was erratic. Lately he spoke of leaving his job. He disliked his boss and wanted to work only at night, an idea that worried Camille. She knew he was perfectly capable of moving without telling her. Vacillating between optimism and anxiety, she made her way through the busy streets. She walked down Bourbon Street where the strip-show barkers were just coming on, pulling open the doors to passersby, all girls, all nude, all the time. She allowed her eyes to wander over the photograph montages displayed under glass outside each door, each with black rectangles taped over the genitals of the couples, men and women, women and women, or women who had been men or were still partly men. In one, a naked woman stood with her legs spread apart. Before her, kneeling on the red, slippery-looking floor, a naked man reached up to her, his hands resting on her hips. The place where his head met her crotch was covered by a black rectangle. The expression on her face was hard to read, somewhere between pleasure and boredom. These pictures made Camille uneasy. They suggested a world she knew nothing about, a kind of tear in the fabric of life through which she could discern unfathomable depths, a strange, lewd, black abyss into which anyone who wasn't careful might fall.

She crossed the street, conscious of the fragility of this unusual mood, this heightened sensibility. If Eddie was at the café, and she thought he would be, then everything would be fine. She would thoroughly and deliberately forget Dr. Veider. She turned the last corner and her heart leaped. There, just ahead, coming out of the café, was Eddie. He was speaking to someone behind him, still inside the half-opened door. Camille shouted his name, and he turned to see her, smiled, waved, stood waiting for her, still holding the door open. As Camille quickened her step—she was nearly running—a young woman came out, frowning at the glare of the pavement. She stood beside Eddie and watched Camille, who slowed down, then came to a stop. She was close enough to touch them both.

"I got off early," Eddie said.

Camille stood breathless. The woman looked her up and down carefully, then looked at Eddie, who seemed to be the only one with the power of speech. "Camille," he said, "this is Cindy."

Camille looked at Cindy. She was pretty in a boyish way. Her face was sharp. She looks like a fox, Camille thought. "Hello," she said.

Cindy only nodded. Eddie said, "I was going to get some dinner."

Camille struggled with the implications of this bold statement. Did he mean, *Cindy and I are going to get some dinner together, without you.* Or did he mean, *I'm going alone.* Or, *I'm going and you can join me.* She couldn't think of anything to say that would clear up her uncertainty without revealing her insecurity. Her head ached. Cindy shifted her weight from one hip to the other. Camille said, "Oh." She looked behind her, back down the street, where a pedestrian was cursing a passing motorist. Cindy said something very softly, a question, to Eddie, but Camille couldn't make it out. When she turned back, Eddie was smiling ruefully. Was he enjoying Camille's suffering? "No," he said.

Then, abruptly, it was all over. A man came out of the café and squeezed past the three of them, displacing Cindy, who said, "Well, I have to go home." Eddie said, "See you later," and Camille, recovering her breath, managed a wan smile and said, "Goodbye." As Cindy walked away Eddie put his arm around Camille, leaning down to kiss her cheek. "Are you hungry?" he asked. She sagged against him. Her knees were weak and her forehead damp and cool. "Yes," she said, "I'm starving."

They went to a crowded restaurant, a few blocks away, where they were the only white people. The waitress seemed to know Eddie; the boy who likes white beans, she called him, and laughed. Camille drank two cold beers and ate a bowl of gumbo, feeling more euphoric with each bite. This was the life she wanted. In saying goodbye to Dr. Veider she was a step closer to an honest life with Eddie.

Eddie complained about his job, his boss. "It's a personality problem," he said, and when Camille replied, "You hate his personality," he laughed and said, "That's it. That's just it." She drank her beer quietly, indulging herself in the pleasure of being his confidante while he went into the details of his grievance. He bragged of the contemptuous responses he made to his boss's oppressive demands. He left early, without properly closing out his shift; that was what he had done today, and he knew the boss would hear about it because Sammy, who followed him, was so annoyed, he said he'd complain.

As she listened—she was not required to say anything—Camille came down to earth with a thud. He was going to be fired, she understood, possibly soon. He would be outraged when it happened, but it was clearly what he wanted. And then what? He didn't have another job lined up, nor did he appear to have any ambitions to have one. He would go back to living off the few friends he had, staying in borrowed rooms. There wasn't any point in trying to dissuade him from the course he was on. She tried a mild, placating remark, and he responded coldly: she didn't know what she was talking about. She had a nice job. She didn't have to work for an idiot.

When they had finished and split the bill, they walked back to Eddie's room. The little bare patio threw off waves of hot air like a radiator; Camille could feel it through the thin soles of her shoes. Eddie left the French doors open and went straight to the bathroom, pulling off his shirt and muttering about the heat. Camille sat on the edge of the mattress and began unbuttoning her blouse. When he came out, carrying two lukewarm beers, he threw himself down beside her. The sheets she had given him lay in a crumpled pile on the floor, where they had been for a few weeks and would remain until, Eddie said, he remembered to take them to the laundromat.

Camille unfastened her skirt. "Aren't you going to close the door?" she asked.

"It's too hot," he said. "Nobody comes back here anyway."

While Camille removed and folded her clothes, Eddie pulled himself up and took off his pants, shorts, and socks. They stretched out together side by side, and Eddie handed Camille one of the beers. She took a swallow and set the can on the floor beside the mattress. The room was grim, though the sun was finally going down and the softened light from the patio relieved her eyes. Eddie ran one hand down her side, then leaned over and fastened his mouth to her breast. She stroked his head absently, neither repelled nor excited, trying to remember whether she'd taken a pill from the plastic dial pack she kept hidden at work. She gazed out the door as Eddie turned her on her side, facing away from him. His fingers were probing between her legs, and she reminded herself to relax, not to pull away from him. He was kissing her shoulder, then pressing his tongue into her ear, a sensation she hated, but she did not resist. She felt absent—from her body, from the room, from her life. Eddie didn't seem to notice. He pushed her this way and that, stuck his tongue in her mouth, then between her legs, did the same thing with his penis, and she accepted everything without protest or enthusiasm. She even felt a distant, dim affection for him, because she was used to him now. He wasn't going to hurt her, and he seemed to enjoy what he was doing. As he became more and more urgent, she responded to him with sighs of encouragement. She reached up to brace her hands against the wall so that her body would not slip away from his and he would have something stable to drive himself into. No images rose to her mind, no visions of red, no strange sensations in her mouth, no fear for his life or her own, just a dull desire for this to be over, as it certainly would be in only a few moments. He groaned once, then again while his arms came down across her shoulders, and he pulled her in to him so tightly she lost her breath. For a moment she feared her head would be slammed against the wall, and he seemed to realize this possibility too, for he pressed one hand over her forehead as if to protect her. In the next moment it was over and he was still, though he moaned once more, softly, and he still held her body tightly against his. They were both sweating and slippery, a sensation Camille liked. Eddie released her, rolled away from her. "It's too hot," he said. "I thought I was going to have a stroke."

Camille lay still, her knees pulled up near her chest, gazing through the open doors at the dim light from the patio. It would be dark soon and she would have to get up and go home. She heard Eddie fumbling on the floor for his beer, then swallowing. "That girl," he said. "That Cindy?"

Camille turned her head toward him to show that she was listening. "Yes," she said.

"She thought you were my wife."

"Why did she think that?" she asked.

She felt her cheeks flush with pleasure. Surely this remark was a promising one.

Eddie sat up and began fishing in his pants pocket for his cigarettes. "I don't know," he said offhandedly. "I guess she thought you could be her. She's never seen my wife."

Camille didn't move. She felt a sticky wetness between her legs, his semen pouring out of her, but she ignored it, concentrating instead on what Eddie had just told her. She listened to him lighting his cigarette, puffing at it. He leaned back to her, kissed her shoulder, and said, "I thought you were going to hit your head there at the end." He laughed, then sat back up again, and she heard him drinking from the beer can.

"You're married?" she asked. Her voice was soft, controlled.

"Yeah," he said. "Two kids, too. Two little boys. Why do you think I never have any money?"

Camille tried to picture Eddie sitting at a kitchen table with two boys running around on the floor, a faceless woman setting a cup of coffee in front of him.

"So, you're separated."

"No," he said, "not really. I don't stay there every night. But most nights I do." He gestured at the ugly room. "I sure couldn't stay here all the time, could I?"

"Why didn't you tell me before?"

"You never asked," he said.

Camille closed her eyes. Of course, she thought. Of course. I should have known. She could hear her heart beating steadily in her ears. If only it would just stop. "Just stop," she said.

"What?" Eddie said. He put down his beer and stretched out beside her. She did not speak again. When she opened her eyes, she saw a lizard poised uncertainly in the doorway.

"Does it make any difference to you?" Eddie said.

Camille rolled onto her back and looked at him. He had one hand behind his head; the other held the cigarette close to his mouth. Smoke was pouring from his nose. He was pleased with himself, she thought, absolutely smug. A glittering dagger of hatred stabbed her behind the eyes; it felt like an electric shock, once, then again. She sat up, pulling her blouse from the end of the mattress. As she shoved her hands into the sleeves, she watched the lizard dart purposefully into the room. What had prompted his decision? Was he looking for something to eat, or was he attracted to the smooth wood of the floor? He was green, but in a few moments he would be brown.

She stood up next to the mattress and walked away from Eddie, toward the bathroom. "A lizard just came in here," she said.

She closed the door and ran warm water in the sink. First she washed her face, then she wiped away the wetness between her legs. She recalled the amused, incredulous smile she had seen on Eddie's face when he responded to Cindy's question: Was Camille by any chance his wife? How could anyone have drawn such an improbable conclusion? his smile said. Couldn't anyone see what Eddie clearly saw, that Camille was nothing like a wife?

She wanted to leave but not to go home. She resolved to say nothing to Eddie; she didn't want to give him the satisfaction of knowing how badly he had hurt her. She buttoned her blouse and went back into the room, where he lay propped on one arm, smoking his cigarette, pleased with himself. She pulled on her underwear without looking at him. "I have to go," she said.

He watched her, saying nothing. She fastened her skirt, pulled on her shoes. He would probably get fired this week, she thought. Then she would only run into him on the streets.

"Everything okay?" he asked. She could hear the amusement in his voice. He'd leveled her; he knew it. Now he was interested to see how much she would squirm, what pathetic resistance she would put up. She willed herself to look at him, but it wasn't easy. She only managed to pass her eyes quickly over his face. "Sure," she said. "But it's getting late. I have to go home." She picked up her purse, went to the open doors, where she paused, looking back quickly.

"I'll see you," Eddie said.

"Sure," she said again. Then she went out, across the ugly patio, down the narrow alleyway to the street. She closed the gate behind her hard, but not as hard as she wanted to. She took a few steps, stopped, and leaned against a wall. Her head contained one long scream, and she searched helplessly for a way to let it out. Tears came to her eyes. She clenched her fists at her sides; pounded one against the wall. A couple, arm in arm, walked past her. She kept her head down; when she felt the woman's eyes rest on her, she pretended to remove a pebble from her shoe. The simple action calmed her, as if there really had been something in her shoe and now it was gone and she could go on. The scream turned into a mocking refrain: *You should have known.* It was dark and the streets were thick with slow traffic, people searching for parking places. Camille walked slowly along a few blocks, across Dauphine and Bourbon to a bar she knew on Chartres, where she found a small empty table beneath a framed painting of two hands, one dropping coins into the other. She had seen the painting a hundred times, but this time, as she sat down, she noticed a hill in the background and on the hill three crosses. Of course, she thought. Judas. That explained the thick drops of what looked like motor oil dripping from the coins. It was blood.

There she sat, drinking quietly and steadily for a long time. She forgot entirely her optimism and high spirits on leaving Dr. Veider. This day would live in her memory only as the one on which she had learned that Eddie was married. This information, though somehow not surprising, seemed to be growing in her brain like a tumor. Everything had to be rearranged to accommodate it. Eddie's question—does it make any difference to you?—repeated itself, a bad joke, so insistent and so devoid of humor that after her third drink she asked it out loud, of her table, of the wall next to her: "Does it make any difference to you?" She gave a dry laugh.

The joke, she thought, is on me.

The room was filling up with people, all talking and laughing, greeting one another. A woman got up from one table of friends and moved to another. Camille's waiter, a thin elderly man whose hands shook pathetically, materialized before her. Did she want another drink? Yes, she told him. She decided to go to the bathroom. She wanted to determine how drunk she was.

The answer was clear as soon as she got to her feet: very drunk indeed. She was conscious of weaving as she passed among the tables, but she made it to the bathroom without upsetting any furniture. She used the toilet, washed her face, drank water from the tap, combed her hair. It wasn't bad at all, she thought. The alcohol made it impossible to remember anything from one minute to the next. She got back to her table to find a drink waiting, and gulped it down quickly, examining her wallet to see how much money she had. There was enough, she felt sure. She always carried a little more than usual on Wednesdays in case Eddie was broke.

This time when her waiter appeared she asked for the check. She didn't want to go home, but she had no other place to go and she had begun to feel weary. Once she got past her mother's tirade she could have a bath and crawl into her sofa bed. She counted out the bills carefully onto the plastic tray the waiter had left; then, concentrating on the floor to find her way among the tables, she went out onto the street.

The bus stop was only two blocks away but it seemed to Camille a long, unmanageable distance. The last drink had released a torrent of bitter thoughts, all on the subject of Eddie and her own foolishness in having imagined that he cared for her. She was an aside in his life, an occasional entertainment, but he had not failed to notice that he was the center of her meager existence and had made up his mind, with how much or little calculation she would never know, to be rid of her, or if not to be rid of her, to apprise her of her true status, for she felt certain that if she showed up next week and he was still working in the café, they would go on as before. He would not say another word on the subject of his other, his real life, unless she insisted, and if she insisted he would close the subject firmly; he would tell her that it was boring or that there was nothing, really, to say about it.

She arrived at the bus stop and stood alone, holding on to a lamppost, counting out the proper change from her pocket. There were few pedestrians about, but the wide street was thick with cars pouring their poisonous exhaust into the damp night air, their occupants occupied with the idea of a destination, as if, Camille thought, there really were someplace to go. A gray sedan pulled up at the stop light in front of her, and she noticed a black dog sitting alertly in the passenger seat, his big mouth open in what looked like laughter but was probably just heat exhaustion. His dark brown eyes engaged Camille's; then the light changed and he was gone. The bus came just behind, lumbering and slow, but bright inside and cold. Camille climbed up the metal stairs and poured her coins into the rattling machine. It wasn't crowded. She found a window seat midway, behind a tired-looking woman with two whining children. She slid gratefully into the inhospitable plastic seat and leaned against the window, breathing in the unnaturally frigid air that poured from the air-conditioning vent beneath her nose.

The bus had gone only two stops when the man got on. He was very big, fat, cruel-looking; his shabby clothes strained to cover his unappetizing bulk. Camille kept her eyes down, hoping he would not choose the empty seat next to her, but of course he did. She wondered if he could tell she had had too much to drink. She made herself as small as possible, for he overflowed his own seat. She closed her eyes and leaned against the window. An acrid smell rising from his clothing combined with the cold air from the air vents to make her head swim. She opened her eyes, and things cleared up a little. He shifted in his seat, taking up more of the narrow space available to her. It felt as if he was leaning against her, an idea that filled her with alarm. She stole a furtive look at his face; his bleary eyes were fastened on the back of the bus driver. She tried again to make herself smaller, but it didn't work. Through the cloth of his pants she could feel the moisture from the heavy flesh of his leg pressed against her own. She looked out the window; perhaps he would get off soon. The bus was close to Canal Street, where it connected with several other lines. Camille tried not to notice the man's heavy, phlegmy breathing, but it was all she could hear. She watched a couple on the sidewalk coming out of a parking lot, hand in hand. They looked rich, elegant, excitable. The woman pointed down the street, and the man, smiling indulgently, changed direction. Tourists, Camille thought. They think it would be exotic to live here.

Canal Street came and went, but the man did not move. The bus filled up with passengers, warming the air with their breath and their cheerful voices. Gradually Camille became aware that the man's big hand, which had been resting on his thigh, had moved. It was now part of the general pressure being exerted against her own thigh. She looked at his face again, but he was still staring intently toward the front of the bus, apparently unaware of or uninterested in the position of his hand.

She leaned her face against the window, stifling a groan. She was still dizzy and disoriented from drinking, but as the man's hand moved again, the fingers now stretching over the thin material of her skirt, she experienced a rush of nausea that she knew had nothing to do with alcohol. For a moment she convinced herself that she was mistaken. She could not bring herself to look down at her lap, which the hand was now invading audaciously. Outside the window she saw nothing but cars. The bus was pulling into the long curve around Lee Circle, causing the passengers to lean first one way and then the other. Tears filled her eyes, but she blinked them away, for she was rigid with horror. The man pressed his hand along the inside of her thigh, beneath her skirt, edging up toward her underpants. She managed a sound, but it was barely audible. "Please," she said. "Please don't." Now the tears flowed down her cheeks. She kept her face averted, pressed against the glass, and she allowed her eyes to take in the dimly lit scene outside, the occasional pedestrians walking on the sidewalk or huddled together in conversation, waiting to cross the street, the quiet fronts of the houses and stores; it seemed innocent and calm and safe. She could feel the man's fingers now, pulling together the cloth of her underwear. She winced as he reached his goal; he was touching the soft flesh of her vagina. She pressed her legs together as tightly as she could; then, much too late to save her from the torrent of shame and humiliation in which she had to struggle for breath, she was able to move. She raised her arm and pulled the cord over her head, signaling the driver of her intention to get off at the next stop. She pulled herself up by holding the edge of the seat in front of her; the man gave way at once. He was so big she could not get past him, so he got to his feet and stood back in the aisle while Camille slipped out quickly and walked to the front of the bus. The driver had already pulled up to the curb; the doors snapped open before her; she rushed out onto the sidewalk. As the bus pulled away, she was left in one final puff of exhaust, like a dismissal, which she gulped down obediently. Then she stood in the dark, drying her eyes on her sleeve. No one was around; the traffic moved slowly in the street before her. She remembered her sweater, which she understood she'd left somewhere, at Eddie's or at the bar. Her mother would remember it too; that much was certain. There was nothing to be done about that now, nothing to do about any of it. She had to wait for the next bus, which would probably be along in half an hour or so. She was tired and nervous; her eyes burned. She wanted to lie down, to pull a blanket over her head, close her eyes, get this day behind her, but she couldn't; it wasn't over yet. She still had a long way to go.

41

When she woke to the sound of the phone ringing and, with a glance at the clock, confirmed her suspicion that it was two on a Saturday morning, Ellen's first thought was to let it ring. There was no one she wanted to talk to, and she wasn't on call. Then she remembered that Celia was spending the night at a friend's; she would have to answer. She switched on the light and staggered across the hall to her study, where the phone was squalling like a baby. She picked it up to shut it up. "Hello," she said weakly.

"Is this Mrs. Clayton?" a gruff male voice inquired.

"Yes," she said.

"This is Sergeant Womack of the New Orleans Police Department."

Ellen glanced up hopelessly at the dark spot on the wallpaper where Paul's picture had once hung. "Yes," she said again.

"Your daughter Celia Clayton has been arrested for illegal possession of narcotics. We have her here in the Juvenile Division. Do you want to come down and get her out?"

"Yes," Ellen said a third time. "I do. But where are you?"

"Broad and Tulane," the man said.

Ellen pictured the corner. It was the prison, a huge frightening place, a square block with horrific rolls of razor-edged wire all around it and a guard tower at the center. They had Celia in there. "In the jail?" Ellen asked.

"We're right next door," the man said. "Juvenile Division."

"I'll be there as soon as I can. I'll be there right away," Ellen assured him. "Is she okay?"

"Sure," he said. "She's all right. She's in a lot of trouble, that's all."

"I'm on my way," Ellen said. She placed the receiver carefully back in the cradle, as if, she thought, it were Celia's hand.

"Oh, Jesus," she said. The room was nearly dark; only the light from her bedroom filtered in dimly. It crossed her mind that she could do this alone, but her fingers were already moving through the card file on her desk, searching for Paul's new phone number. She had a bitter thought: he owes it to me. And another: this is all his fault. She switched on the desk lamp and began punching the number into the phone. There was a pause, then the phone ringing, once, again, three, four times. "Wake up," Ellen said. A woman's voice, husky with sleep, said, "Hello."

Had she dialed the wrong number? No. Of course not. This was Donna. Our first conversation, Ellen thought. She couldn't speak. "Hello," Donna said again.

"Hello," Ellen got out. "This is Ellen Clayton."

The voice struggled to consciousness. "Yes," she said.

"May I speak to Paul? It's an emergency."

"Yes," Donna said, "I'll get him."

There was a pause. Ellen listened closely. Was she simply turning over, or had she actually gone to another room to find him? Ellen clenched her jaw. It was demeaning to have to go through another woman to get to Paul. She could hear a voice but couldn't make out the words. It was Paul. The receiver crackled as he picked it up. "Ellen," he said, "what's wrong?"

"It's Celia. She's been arrested."

Another moment of silence. What was he doing? "But she's not hurt?"

"No," Ellen said, "she's okay."

"Thank God," Paul said. Ellen sighed and covered her eyes with her hand. The hostility and jealousy she was struggling with evaporated instantly in the face of this, the right response.

"I'm sorry to get you up," she said. "They told me to come get her and I didn't want to do it alone."

"No," he said. "Of course. I'll come get you. What did they arrest her for?"

"Drugs."

"Did they say what?"

"No. They said possession of narcotics."

"I guess that means she didn't have enough to sell."

"God," Ellen said, "I hope not."

"Well, just let me change and I'll be there. Maybe twenty minutes?"

"I'll be ready," Ellen said.

"Does Lillian know?"

"No," Ellen said. "I called you as soon as I found out. She's asleep. I'll leave her a note in case she wakes up."

"Just say you went to pick Celia up," Paul said. "Don't tell her why. Celia may want to tell her herself."

"Right," Ellen said.

"Okay." They hung up. Ellen switched off the desk lamp. It never failed, she thought. Celia brought out the best in her father. As she crossed the landing, she looked into Lillian's room; she could see her hair and one hand. The rest was covered by the big quilt she slept under, even on the hottest nights. Ellen closed the door carefully and went to her room to get dressed. As she did, she thought of Celia. Had they searched her? Would she be sullen or frightened? Was she with the friend she'd said she was visiting, or was that a fabrication too, as so much of her life seemed to be of late? There was a sense in which this two A.M. catastrophe was both expected and a relief. Now it was out in the open: Celia needed, possibly even wanted, help. Ellen felt absurdly confident that there was no hole deep or dark enough that she would not find her way in and pull her daughter out. Like the father in the story of the Prodigal Son, she felt a swelling of passionate love for Celia, and she knew it was partly because Celia wanted to reject her, to go out and take a pounding from the world, just to prove she could.

Ellen went down to the kitchen to wait for Paul. She made a pot of coffee and ate two pieces of toast; hungry, she thought, because she was nervous. She went over the brief conversation with Paul, which had seemed to her satisfactory, as their conversations rarely were these days. She wrote the note to Lillian and propped it on the kitchen table. It was unlikely that Lillian would even wake up before they got back. Ellen was wide awake, strangely elated. It would certainly not be pleasant, but in the end Celia would be home, safe, dragging herself up the stairs to her bed, where she would sleep probably well into the afternoon. There was a sound of heavy footsteps on the stairs. Was Lillian up? Ellen turned, but it was only Barker, who came down the stairs drowsily, his head lowered, his eyes barely open. He stumbled into the bright kitchen and collapsed theatrically near her feet.

"Ever on the alert, eh, boy?" Ellen said. He lifted his head and looked toward the garage. It was several moments before Ellen heard what he heard, Paul's car on the street moving toward the house. Barker got to his feet and stood dully at the garage door, too sleepy to show enthusiasm but determined to be at his greeting post. Ellen rinsed her coffee cup at the sink, took up her purse, and eased out the door past the patient dog. "No, boy," she said. "You stay here. Go back to sleep." She pressed the garage door button and watched as the heavy door rolled upward. She saw Paul's car turning into the driveway.

As she got in beside him, Ellen wondered if there would be some evidence of Donna in the car, a scarf perhaps or an umbrella, or cigarette butts in the ashtray, but there was nothing. Paul's car was always spotless, the tapes perfectly organized and stored in their plastic boxes, never spilled across the seat as her own so often were. No soft drink cans, no magazines or empty envelopes. She knew he had a container of change in the glove compartment, a map of the state, the car registration, a flashlight; that was it. She smiled at him and, to her surprise, he leaned over to kiss her cheek. "Parents' night out," he said.

"Right," she said. "Big fun. Let's drop in at the police station and check out the action."

"Sounds great." He backed out of the driveway and turned toward the city. Ellen opened her window, breathing in the warm night air. She was thinking of Celia, of her dark, moody expression, the way she wore her hair now so that she could hide behind a sheet of it.

"So what will we have to do?" Paul said. "Post bail or something?"

"I don't know," Ellen said. "They didn't tell me anything but come get her, which I guess means we *can* get her out of there tonight."

"How could she be so stupid?"

Ellen frowned. "This has been coming," she said. "She hates us because we split up and she hates authority, and, really, why shouldn't she?"

"Oh, for God's sake," Paul replied impatiently. "So it's our fault we have to go get her out of jail in the middle of the night."

Ellen smiled. "Something like that," she said. "You're getting it." Paul's profile was set in a stubborn frown. How had Donna taken the news that her exciting lover had to go out and attend to his teenage daughter's crisis? She had the feeling it hadn't gone well. He looked tired, edgy. It amused her, seeing Paul with someone else to answer to. Ironically, he was now more at liberty with his wife than with his girlfriend, and that was what the kiss, the cheerful greeting had been about. He was sneaking off to be a parent, which was certainly not as much fun as sneaking off to be a lover, but it did give him that self-righteous sense of doing as he pleased, which was so dear to him.

"The place is on Broad, right?" he said.

"Yes. Right next to the 'big house.' "

Paul looked more grim at these words. "I've never been arrested," he said. "How did she manage it."

"I hope they didn't search her," Ellen said. Then, both imagining Celia, stripped, her palms pressed against a wall while cold, unfriendly hands ran over her small, thin body, Paul and Ellen exchanged quick, frightened looks.

"Celia," Paul said, filling his daughter's name with sadness.

They had searched her, but perfunctorily and with her clothes on, and they had questioned her, fingerprinted her, and put her in a cell next to two young men who had tried to hold up a liquor store. These boys frightened her more than the police, for they shouted insults and threats at her, and one of them took his pants down and masturbated, leaning against the bars to her cell, telling her what he would do to her if he could get to her, while Celia huddled as far from him as she could get, her eyes closed, her hands over her ears. When the policewoman brought her out into the noisy bright office where Paul and Ellen stood waiting nervously, she tried for a moment to be sullen, rebellious, but she was scared, her hands were trembling, and when Paul put his arm around her she hid her face in his chest.

She had not been with the friend she was supposedly visiting, but with an older boy—Ellen had seen him once and didn't like him—who had an apartment uptown. Paul turned pale at this revelation, which Celia spilled out in the car, her voice flat, resentful, now that she was safe. There were other friends along as well, a group, she explained, and they had gone to a club in the Quarter to hear a band. At the door Celia had opened her purse to take out the fake identification she carried; this was another blow to her parents, but she glossed over it, determined to tell the whole story as quickly as possible. There was a policeman standing next to the bouncer—this bar was popular and it was a big, dangerous, hostile crowd—and as Celia opened her purse he glanced inside it and saw a plastic bag of marijuana, which Celia said one of the boys had given her to carry. It wasn't even hers, she complained. The policeman arrested her on the spot.

She was angry. It was stupid, she said; she hadn't done anything, and of course her friends abandoned her at once and the police were hateful. They told her she couldn't call anyone because she was a minor, and they said many parents, when informed of a teenager's arrest, left them in the jail overnight to teach them a lesson. Then they put her in the cell next to the two criminals. At this point she began to cry. She told the rest of the story in broken sentences, her voice low and hurt. Ellen leaned over the seat and tried to take her hand, but she withdrew from her touch. Paul was driving slowly, leaning against the seat back to listen, and Ellen noticed that his hands clenched the wheel so tightly the blood drained from his knuckles.

"It was stupid," Celia said. "I knew he couldn't hurt me. I should have just laughed at him." So she reconciled herself. This was how she would tell the story, to Lillian surely, and to her friends. But she hadn't been able to laugh, and she wasn't the tough, hard young woman she wanted to be. Instead, she was a girl of fourteen, one who had spent a sheltered, happy childhood, who had no experience of the world and no resources to call upon when confronted with the pointless, random hatred of a stranger.

As Ellen watched Celia wiping her tears on the sleeve of her blouse, she opened her purse, took out a handkerchief, and passed it over the seat. Celia took it and began blowing her nose at once. "Thanks," she said, folding the cloth over carefully, then patting her eyes with it.

"I would have been terrified," Ellen said. "What a nightmare." Paul shot her a quick, speculative look. He didn't think that was the right thing to say.

"I was pretty scared, Mom," Celia said, addressing herself to the handkerchief, from which, Ellen observed, she was deriving a considerable amount of comfort. "Pretty scared."

Outside the car the city was quiet and dark. It was nearly four o'clock. Paul drove through the streets, putting mile after mile between Celia and the scene of her humiliation; he felt he was laying down the distance in a wide ribbon.

"I guess I'm grounded," Celia said.

"I guess so," Ellen said.

"What about the trial?" Paul said. "What do we do about that?"

"Get a lawyer," Ellen replied.

"Perry Winslow got busted for marijuana," Celia said. "He got off with just a fine. I could find out who his lawyer was."

"This is going to be expensive," Ellen said.

"I'm sorry," Celia said.

Paul braked abruptly at a changing light. "How could you be so stupid?" he said.

Celia whined as if stung. "Dad. Don't you think I feel bad enough?"

"No," Paul said. He turned to glare at her over the back of the seat. "No, I don't."

They drove the rest of the way in silence, each lost in bitter, recriminatory thoughts. Ellen looked out the window as the cemetery went by. The big monuments were especially ghostly in the haze of early dawn and incongruous as well—a giant stag, a fireman holding an axe, a woman in a Grecian robe on her knees before a marble door, an angel raising a sword. When the girls were younger, this cemetery provoked a game: What do you want on your grave? Ellen always said she wanted an angel, but now she thought, I want a woman, blindfolded and holding a scale. *Justice* was another word, like *natural,* that meant everything and nothing.

It always wound up in strange equations, for example, "with liberty and justice for all." Only one thing was certain, lawyers were as confused as everyone else about what justice actually meant. Now Ellen would have two lawyers in her life, negotiating for her so-called rights, the divorce lawyer and Celia's lawyer. It was a thought that made her wince.

When they got home Celia surprised them by a brief but sincere display of gratitude. "I couldn't say anything in that place," she said, "but when they brought me out of the cell and I saw you two standing there, I was so glad to see you . . ." She paused. For Celia, Ellen thought, this was the finest eloquence. "Well," she concluded, "I really want to go to bed."

"We'll talk about it tomorrow," Paul said. "I'll call you in the afternoon." Celia kissed them both and went wearily up the stairs. Paul turned to Ellen. "Coffee?" he said.

Ellen looked at him curiously. He seemed in high spirits and pleased with himself, as if something important had been accomplished. "Isn't it a little late?"

"Too late, I'd say," he replied. "I won't sleep, so I may as well stay up."

Ellen felt wide awake herself. "Well, I've got to sleep. I've got a lot to do tomorrow. So I'll just have hot milk and you can have coffee. There's some left." She led the way to the kitchen.

"Great," Paul said, following her. In the kitchen he sat at the table while Ellen busied herself at the stove.

"You don't mind my asking why you're in such a cheerful humor?" Ellen said.

"Am I?" Paul replied. "I wasn't aware of it."

Ellen turned from the stove and leaned against the counter, crossing her arms before her. "Aren't you afraid you'll get in trouble when you get home?" she said. "Or maybe that's what excites you. Is that it?"

"No," Paul said quickly. "It just cheers me up to be treated with unnecessary hostility."

Ellen laughed. "I'm not hostile. You amuse me."

"That's good," he said. "Now you can be in a good mood, since you've put me in a bad one."

Ellen resisted the urge to say something placating. She paid attention to the coffee again, and, when it was ready, set a cup in front of Paul.

"So how long should she be grounded?" he said as Ellen sat down across from him.

She sipped at her cup of milk. "The rest of the school year," she said.

"That long?"

"Sure," Ellen said. "This is big time. Anyway, I think she wants to be grounded. This group she's running with is tough, Lillian told me that, and they're all older than she is. Tonight she saw they don't give a damn about her, and she was truly frightened by those boys at the jail."

Paul shuddered. "I can't think about that," he said.

"I'm going to have her come in to work with me after school," Ellen said. "There's plenty she could do there to help out and I think it would be good for her."

"That's a good idea." Paul looked dazedly into his coffee cup. He was losing interest fast, Ellen thought. "I want you to take care of the business with the lawyer," she said. "The court stuff, all of that."

"I can't," he said quickly.

"Why?"

"I don't have time. I've got classes and I'm working hard on the book now. I'm making real progress, but I have to keep going up to Saint Francisville."

"Well, make time," Ellen said. "I'm not asking for much."

"Ellen. Be reasonable," he said.

"I am being reasonable," she snapped. "Who's going to spend every evening closed in here with a sullen, miserable teenager? Who's going to make sure she's home every day after school? I'm going to have to talk to counselors over there; she could get kicked out for this, you know. All I'm asking you to do is engage a lawyer and spend a few hours in court."

"I can't do that sort of thing," he said. "I won't do it right, and you'll be angry."

"That's ridiculous," Ellen said. "You don't want to do it because it isn't going to be much fun and you know it."

"Sure," he said. "That's just like me, isn't it? That's why I got over here as fast as I could in the middle of the night; that's why I'm sitting here trying to figure out what we should do."

"What I should do," Ellen said. "Where's the part where you do something?"

"I thought you weren't hostile," he said.

"Is there some reason why I shouldn't be?" she replied.

Paul swallowed the remains of his coffee. "Right," he said. "I'm off."

"Good," Ellen said. "I'm getting so I prefer seeing the back of you."

Paul got up from his chair and stood for a moment staring glumly down at Ellen. This was the pass they had come to; they could hardly bear to speak to each other. She was angry, he thought, because of Donna, because he was happy, because in every way that was important to her, he was gone. All that was left was the occasional show of solidarity for the girls, a sham act at best, and they both knew it. He seldom thought of going back, though he missed her, his life with her. Often and at odd moments, unexpectedly during the day or even at night when he slipped into bed beside Donna, he thought of his wife sleeping alone across town, in the bed he would always think of as theirs. He referred to her now as his ex-wife, though the divorce would not be final for months. The "ex" functioned as an erasure of the word that came behind it. Now he saw that he couldn't go back even if he wanted to, no matter what happened. The erasure was complete; the world of their marriage was gone.

Ellen looked up at him at last. She seemed to hear his

thoughts, for her anger was gone. She gave him a wan smile. "Go ahead," she said. "I'm just tired. Too tired to talk. I shouldn't even try."

"All right," he said. "We'll talk tomorrow. I'll call you from work."

She watched him as he went out the kitchen door, pulling his car keys from his pants pocket, his getaway keys, she thought. Now he would run to Donna, and if she was awake he would make love to her. Her thoughts veered to the two boys who had threatened Celia. She gave herself over to a few moments of castigating men. Their passion for liberty knew no bounds, and it never occurred to them that their freedom always came at someone else's expense. They raped women, countries, the planet, all in the service of their passion to be pulled forward by the force between their legs, like murderous teenage boys on motorbikes. They thought women were sly and calculating, but that was because they never willingly spent a minute contemplating the consequences of their actions. They felt scared, trapped; they ran from pillar to post, woman to woman; they wanted to be in control of something, anything, everything but themselves.

This tirade relaxed and amused Ellen. She put the empty cups in the dishwasher and switched out the lights in the kitchen. Now she would have a few hours of what promised to be deep and dreamless sleep. As she went up the stairs she thought of Celia and of the lawyer she would have to call on Monday. She felt she was picking up an enormous weight, pulling it up on to her shoulders, her head down, knees bent to keep from hurting her back, a good, reliable, willing, mildly stupid but serviceable beast of burden. Barker stood at the top of the stairs, waiting for her, encouraging her. Though there was certainly a way in which he was only another link in the endless chain of responsibilities that sometimes threatened to drag her down entirely, she experienced a warm fellow-feeling for his quiet companionship. "I'm coming, boy," she said. "You can get some sleep now. All I have to do is get to the top of these stairs."

42

Elisabeth woke from the nightmare to find a dear, familiar sight, an old cobalt-blue glass vase that had stood on her bedside table since she was a child. Her mother had filled it with fresh, creamy roses yesterday, because Elisabeth was home. She knew there was a chip in the base of the vase; she'd broken it herself when she knocked it over once, years before. She looked out sleepily through the mosquito netting, which made the whole beloved room seem pale and dreamlike. She had never been so happy to be in it. The nightmare faded; she knew only that she had been afraid and now was safe. Then, as she turned over, she saw a thin red cut on her arm, just inside her elbow. The whole confusing, terrible memory of her escape from Montague, her arrival at home, and the strange journey with Lucinde flashed before her so vividly that she closed her eyes against it, giving out a low moan.

Her parents had not greeted her with enthusiasm, though

they did agree, after hearing her story, that Hermann had no right to discipline Elisabeth's slave. After a somber dinner, during which her father explained to her the many reasons that her flight had put her in a weaker rather than a stronger position, Elisabeth had gone to her mother's sewing room and tried to tell her what she had not told her father, that Hermann would not allow her the privacy of her bedroom. But her mother seemed unwilling or unable to comprehend this outrage. "You must speak to him," she advised, which only proved to Elisabeth that her mother had never had to oppose her will to that of an accomplished tyrant.

In the afternoon her father went off to consult his lawyers while her mother retired to her bedroom to take her usual rest. Elisabeth dispatched a boy with a message to Lucinde: "Come at once. I need you," and went off to the drawing room to practice piano until the hairdresser should arrive. Though she had begged to stay a few days, her parents had insisted she return to Montague the following morning. Her father supervised the composition of a letter to Hermann explaining that Elisabeth had been called to the city abruptly but would return at once. The letter, sealed with her father's stamp, was carried away by a runner, who promised it would be delivered before Hermann had breakfast the next day. If he was still there, Elisabeth thought. He might have followed her; he might appear at any moment. Her fingers flew over the keys of the old piano as if they could carry her away from the image of her husband climbing down from the high back of his bad-tempered stallion and striding across the oak boards of the hall, calling her name in that gruff, hateful accent of his, which she had once, how long ago it seemed, found quaint, even charming.

How had she been so deluded? Was she expected to live the rest of her life the captive of her uncompromising husband? She played faster and louder, trying to put up a solid wall of music between herself and the sound of Hermann's footsteps, which she knew would follow her forever. Didn't she hear him now, opening the front door? She lifted her hands from the keyboard. It was true, the door had opened—she heard the metallic click as it closed

—but the step in the hall was quick and light; she was part Indian, everyone agreed. She moved like the wind itself. Elisabeth rose from the bench and turned to find Lucinde already standing in the doorway, her sharp features alert to every movement around her, posed like a great raptor with the power to tear out hearts if necessary, and no shred of pity or mercy for anything weaker than herself. Elisabeth flew to her, allowed herself to be enfolded by the strong arms and comforted by the reassuring voice, murmuring, in her soft Creole French, "Who has hurt my poor child? How can Lucinde help her now?"

Elisabeth drew her friend to the comfortable loveseat and poured out her story of disillusion and despair. Lucinde listened closely, putting in a question now and then: How far was her bedroom from her husband's? Where was the stolen ham usually kept? Elisabeth concluded with a description of her escape. Surely Lucinde would agree she had had no choice but to run away, to come home, though her father insisted it was the worst thing she could have done.

"I know what your father is thinking," Lucinde said. "You must be very careful. If your husband declares you insane, then no one will be able to help you, not your father, not even me. And everything you own will become his."

"But I'm not insane," Elisabeth protested. "That's ridiculous."

"Not yet," Lucinde said ominously.

"What can I do? I can't bear it. I don't want to go back there. I hate Montague and I hate Hermann."

"He won't let you go," Lucinde said. "He is on his way here now, to take you back."

"How do you know?" Elisabeth begged. "Are you sure?"

"Oh, yes, I'm sure. I see it." Lucinde narrowed her eyes, and Elisabeth thought, *She sees more than she's saying.*

"Lucinde," Elisabeth said, "what must I do?"

Lucinde's black eyes settled on Elisabeth's face. "There is something you can do," she said. "But it is very difficult. You will be frightened. You will have to find it in yourself not to be afraid. How much do you want to get rid of this husband?"

"I'll do anything."

"These things take time," Lucinde concluded. "You must be patient. We will go to see Mambo Pitou this night and she will tell you how it can be accomplished."

Elisabeth had never heard of Mambo Pitou, though she felt certain every slave in the house knew who she was. "How will we get there?"

"In my carriage," Lucinde said. "I will meet you on the Cathedral steps at nine. You will be back in your bed by midnight."

"I knew you would help me." Elisabeth sighed.

"It won't be to your liking, my help," Lucinde said, rising to leave. "But you will be rid of your husband."

So Elisabeth spent the rest of the day in a state of exquisite tension, hoping that the hour of her appointment would arrive before Hermann appeared at the door. She presented a calm, willing, filial courtesy to her parents and sat through a long, tedious supper listening closely to her father's advice on the matter of Bessie. Then she begged him to allow her to visit a cousin who kept an evening every week. Because she was to have only one night in the city, and because this cousin was an older, steadier head who had in the past exerted a reasoning influence over Elisabeth, her father gave his permission.

Elisabeth kept her word, passing an hour with her cousin, who described the latest round of parties and marriages. Just before nine Elisabeth climbed into her carriage and rattled through the narrow streets to the Cathedral, where she had her driver pull up into the shadows so that she could watch the street without being observed. The oil lamps were lit, and there were a few pedestrians, appearing and disappearing briefly from the dark byways, their voices raised against the eerie stillness of the scene. When they had passed, there was only the incessant drone of the mosquitoes, perhaps the sound of a dog barking or a sudden shout of laughter in the distance. The clock chimed, filling the air with its sweet, reassuring announcement, another hour gone in another dangerous night, and as the last stroke faded Elisabeth sat forward in her seat, for she could hear the clatter of hooves and carriage wheels coming toward the church from the back of the Quarter, where Lucinde had her tidy, charming bungalow. In a few moments the carriage turned onto the flagstones before the Cathedral. Elisabeth spoke briefly to her driver; he was to wait for her. She climbed down to the banquette, pulling up the hood of her black evening cape, which billowed around her as she rushed across the flags, so that Lucinde's coachman, who sat watching her approach, saw a ghostly apparition swirling toward him through the fog, casting up a sudden shadow, like an impatient fist against the white façade of the Cathedral. Lucinde held the carriage door open, and Elisabeth disappeared inside. The carriage pulled off at once, turning back the way it had come, down Chartres Street, past the Ursuline Convent, where Elisabeth had spent so many quiet, carefree hours and where even now, she knew, a few of the nuns were in the small chapel ceaselessly telling the beads of their heavy rosaries, to Esplanade Avenue, where a group of men stood arguing in the flickering light of a streetlamp, then away from the river toward Bayou Saint John, where, Elisabeth knew, no one but runaways, criminals, prostitutes, and desperate people, like herself, ever ventured. She did not fear being observed, for if she saw anyone of her own class in such a place it would be understood at once that to speak of a meeting must implicate the speaker as well in some insalubrious adventure. The road had narrowed; it was little more than a path between trees and tall grass, through which Elisabeth could see the black, glittering surface of the lake. They passed an occasional shack, set up on piers at the water's edge. A humid, sultry, unhealthy breeze served to animate the plague of mosquitoes and gnats. The carriage pulled up before one of the shacks, larger than the others, Elisabeth observed, and hung with skeins of brightly printed cloth. Two black men sat on the front steps, swatting themselves aimlessly. Lucinde touched Elisabeth's arm. "We're here," she said. The two women alighted from the carriage, Lucinde leading the way. At the door she spoke to one of the men, who nodded; then, giving Elisabeth a slow inspection, he laughed at her and said something to Lucinde in a patois Elisabeth couldn't penetrate. As they went up the steps—apparently the men had given them permission to enter —Elisabeth whispered to Lucinde, "Why don't they speak properly? They know I can't understand," to which Lucinde replied, as she held aside the curtain for her client to pass through, "No one cares what you understand here." Her voice was low, and it struck Elisabeth's ear as harsh, even hostile. It occurred to her that Lucinde might not be her friend, but whether this was true or not no longer mattered, for she was inside the room, which was intolerably close and hot. The walls were lined with men and women who stood or squatted on the floor, talking volubly and drinking from gourds they passed among themselves. Elisabeth thought she recognized one, a free woman who had worked for her cousin, and another, a slave in a neighbor's establishment, who would be severely beaten if he was caught on the street after the curfew. They were all people of color, though some were so fair they might cross the line. In one corner a man she could barely make out crouched over a drum, filling the air with a pulse like a heartbeat. Elisabeth drew back, but she found Lucinde's hand placed firmly at her waist, and heard her sharp whisper, "You can't go back now."

The room was lit only by candles, which stood in pools of wax on the sills of the windows and on wooden planks along the walls. In another corner, connected to a battered pipe that went out the ceiling, was an iron brazier glowing red from the fire inside it, the flames visible through the grate like a miniature hell. It filled the room with a stifling, nearly unbearable heat, consuming all the available air. It was madness, Elisabeth thought, to be running such a stove on a night that was already uncomfortably warm. Elisabeth felt her stomach tighten with anxiety as she passed her eyes across the indifferent crowd to the strange tableau in the center of the room. There were two wooden crates, also studded with flickering candles, which, Elisabeth noticed, were all black. Between the crates, on a straight-backed chair, sat a large black woman dressed in a red robe that flowed out over her body like a big curtain to the floor. Her hair was tied back in a multicolored *tignon,* which she had begun to unravel methodically, muttering to herself. There was a jug between her bare feet, and a gourd. Before her was a long wooden box with slats across the top like a shutter. The woman kept her eyes fastened on this box as she shook out her hair until it fell wildly around her face. She was speaking to the box, Elisabeth concluded, though not in any language she recognized.

"That is Mambo Pitou," Lucinde said, pushing Elisabeth deeper into the room. "I have told her about you. She knows why you are here."

Then Elisabeth remembered herself and her mission. This was certainly a frightening place—Mambo Pitou looked neither friendly nor rational—but whatever happened here would take only an hour or so, and once it was over she might be free of Hermann forever. How horrified he would be if he could see his wife in this room, if he understood even for a moment what she was willing to go through to be rid of him. He had ridiculed Lucinde and spoken slightingly of her power, but Elisabeth knew he feared her, just as he feared his own slaves, because he understood how much they hated him and because he knew they had another life, a secret life, in which, no matter what he did to stop them, they found a way to get beyond his reach, to be free of him. And here she stood, in the world he feared, a supplicant to any power that might lay her husband low. She straightened her spine and lifted her head, breathing in the smoky, rancid air of the little cabin, and as she did Lucinde drew up beside her, her hand still resting on her waist, but gently now, encouraging her. "What must I do?" Elisabeth asked, her voice calm.

"Go and kneel before Mambo Pitou. Don't say anything. She will tell you what to do."

Elisabeth did as she was told, though the big woman who mumbled and rocked back and forth in her chair frightened her. She fixed her wild eyes on Elisabeth and poured out upon her a look of such hatred, Elisabeth felt she was pushing her way forward against a wall of flames. At last she was before the wooden box, where she dropped to her knees awkwardly, casting her eyes down at the slatted cover. Something was inside, something moving slowly and sinuously; then, as if it did not care to be observed, it was still. Mambo Pitou poured herself a gourd of wine and swallowed it greedily; some of it ran over her lips and down her chin. Elisabeth looked up at her, dizzy with fear. The woman held the gourd out before her, as if offering Elisabeth a drink. But though her throat ached with thirst, she knew she would not be able to drink anything offered her in this room. Mambo Pitou made no such offer. Instead, she drew back from Elisabeth, hissing strangely and rolling her eyes. The gourd clattered to the floor. She was speaking again her unearthly language; darting an icy look at Lucinde, who stood a few steps behind her kneeling client, she said clearly, "There is too many bones here. I can't make it out. Too many bones."

Elisabeth heard Lucinde step forward, then felt her hand on her shoulder. "Get up," Lucinde said softly, "and follow me." She got to her feet, keeping her eyes down, though she could still see Mambo Pitou, who was bent over her long skirt, searching for her gourd. She could see the gourd as well—it was behind Mambo Pitou's left foot, half hidden in the skirt—but she said nothing. She followed Lucinde to the door. She was disappointed, annoyed. Was this all there was to it? Lucinde opened the door and ushered her onto the porch. "I don't understand," Elisabeth whispered, though there was no reason to be quiet; they were alone on the porch but for the two men who had laughed at them and who were absorbed in an argument they carried on by speaking loudly and at the same time. They showed no interest in the women. Lucinde took Elisabeth's elbow and steered her into the shadows behind the door. "You have to take out your stays," she said.

"My stays?"

"Those are the bones. They cover your heart. She can't get through them, so you have to take them out."

"Lucinde," Elisabeth complained, "I can't take my clothes off on the front porch."

But Lucinde was already loosening the hooks on the bodice of Elisabeth's dress. "Don't be stupid," she cautioned. "Mambo Pitou can help you, but not if you don't do what she tells you."

Elisabeth leaned away from her friend's rough fingers but didn't resist. She allowed herself to be pushed against the wall, her dress opened, her shift loosened. She turned away from the two men while Lucinde pulled out the long stays one by one. She was dizzy; without the stays her dress was less confining, yet she felt she couldn't get her breath. Lucinde laced her back up and fastened the bodice. Elisabeth thought she seemed nervous. What was it to her? Was there prestige attached to bringing a white woman out here, a Creole from an old family? Would the entire town know about it tomorrow morning? "Go back in now," Lucinde was saying as she pushed Elisabeth through the door into the heat and noise of the room. "Go back and kneel down. Don't say anything."

Again Elisabeth took her place before Mambo Pitou. Her eyes were accustomed to the darkness now, and as she gazed through the slats of the wooden box she saw that the creature inside was a large snake. Because she did not want to look at it, she raised her eyes to Mambo Pitou, who had found her gourd and was drinking from it. Her eyes slowly focused on Elisabeth. She seemed to remember her from some time long ago and then to remember that she hated that memory. Her hair still stood wildly about her face, and her eyes were edged in red. She was like Medusa, Elisabeth thought; no one could look at her without becoming too horrified to look away again. She began to speak in her own peculiar language, and Elisabeth watched her lips moving for some moments before she realized that she understood what she was saying. She was talking about a man who wanted to take Elisabeth's soul. This man was following her now, would follow her everywhere; she could not escape him. He would take everything away from her, and she would be a slave in his house. The man was a dead man; there was no life in him; he could bring only death and he would bring it to Elisabeth, but before he did he would make her wish for death. When she wanted anything, he would block her way; when she sought help from her family, he would turn her family against her. Bit by bit she would find herself alone with no one to help her and no strength of her own to escape. She might beg her own slaves to help her, but they would not help her. No one could help her against the power of this man.

Mambo Pitou stopped speaking. She lowered her head so that she was looking up at Elisabeth from beneath her heavy brows. Then her eyes rolled up beneath their lids, exposing the whites, and Elisabeth made herself look away. She could see the people against the walls, quiet now, their attention fixed on Mambo Pitou, and she could hear the drum, louder, more intense. A few of the listeners found it irresistible and began to move their feet and shoulders to the beat. A coal exploded in the brazier, giving off a quick burst of red light and heat. Elisabeth looked again at Mambo Pitou. To her surprise she found the big woman had come back to herself completely. She was drinking from her gourd, her eyes on Elisabeth, but now her expression was calm, almost dreamy, and not unfriendly. What she had said, Elisabeth thought, was true. Hermann would be the death of her; he was a dead man. How could this woman who had never seen him know so much about him? While she listened to Mambo Pitou, Elisabeth had felt that Hermann was being conjured up before her eyes, that any moment he might appear, even now, even here. There must be some escape, surely. If Mambo Pitou knew all this, she must know how to put a stop to it. Elisabeth leaned forward, so intent on her desire to have an answer that she rested her hands on the slats of the wooden box. Mambo Pitou leaned forward too, as if to meet her, her eyes growing wide and luminous in the unsteady light of the candles. "Will you help me?" Elisabeth said softly. She raised her face to meet the dark lips that approached her face, that might, it seemed to her, change her life with a kiss.

But she received no kiss. Instead, to her shock, the lips that seemed pursed to kiss her sprayed her face with wine. Elisabeth fell back on her haunches, crying out, but no one, not even Lucinde, made a move to help her. She wiped her face and hair with her hand while the dreadful woman drank another gourd full of wine and sprayed it out of her mouth in every direction. She began muttering in her impenetrable language, though Elisabeth caught a word or two she understood to be curses. She rolled her eyes and waved her hands before her, as if pushing someone away. Elisabeth heard a man say, "The spirit comes to ride his horse now," and another voice, a woman's, said, "This white woman get what she want." She looked behind her and found Lucinde only a few steps away, her eyes intent on Elisabeth, as if she read her thoughts, knew she wanted to run as fast and as far from this room as she could. "Don't move," she said. "Stay where you are."

Mambo Pitou stopped her gyrations, called a young man to her side, and whispered into his ear. He watched Elisabeth closely as he listened; then he knelt near some of the candles and gathered up from their bases the hot black wax, which he formed into a ball and brought to Mambo Pitou. She took the ball and began pressing and shaping it, her big shoulders hunched over her work, as preoccupied as an artisan. When she was finished, she held it out to Elisabeth. It was a man, a crude figure, but it seemed to Elisabeth to bear a striking resemblance to Hermann. There was something in the posture, the straightness of the back and the angle of the head, so unexpected and amazing that she smiled. "Yes," she said, "that's Hermann." Mambo Pitou pressed the figure on Elisabeth, who took it, uncertain what to do. It was still warm but hard. She turned it over in her hands. Was this all she needed? Was she to take it away? From somewhere in her skirts Mambo Pitou drew out a small knife, which she held out to Elisabeth, insistently. She was speaking again; she seemed angry. The man who had gathered the wax drew closer. Lucinde came up from behind and leaned over Elisabeth. "Take the knife," she said. Elisabeth reached out, took the knife in her hand. The room had grown still. There was only the ceaseless drone of Mambo Pitou's unintelligible rant and the insistent, endless beating of the drum.

Elisabeth felt weak, exhausted. What did these people want from her? She sank back until she was leaning against Lucinde, who whispered to her, something, what was it, that she was to cut herself with the knife so that her blood could moisten the little figure. "I can't do it," Elisabeth replied. "I just can't do it." Now Lucinde was kneeling behind her and her arms came about Elisabeth's waist, drawing her down. She let her body fall until her head rested against her friend's breasts. She could hear Lucinde's soft voice, "It's all right, my child. Lucinde will do it for you. Just rest, just be still." As her body relaxed, her hands fell open in her skirts. The figure rolled to the floor; the knife lodged in her lap. The man bent over her, taking up the doll; then she felt his hand searching her skirt for the knife. Lucinde's hands held her wrists; her warm lips caressed her cheeks. She had been right to come here. This was the only way, and Lucinde would make it easy for her. Elisabeth was enveloped in a sensuous, perfumed darkness to which she willingly surrendered. There was the sharp stab of pain as the man passed the knife across her arm, but it was so quick, so neatly executed, the only emotion she felt was gratitude, for she could not have done it with such ease. She watched as he pressed the figure against the cut, turning it carefully so that it was thoroughly smeared with blood. Mambo Pitou had risen to her feet, and Elisabeth gazed up at her dreamily. Mambo Pitou looked enormous; the flowing red of her robe seemed to pour down toward Elisabeth like a river of blood. The man had given her the bloodied figure, which she held out to Elisabeth, scowling. "Get up," she said. "Come with me." Lucinde pushed her forward; the man helped her up by taking her hand. They were all being kind to her now, she thought. They knew she believed in this, whatever it was, and that she would see it through. Mambo Pitou led the way to the brazier, but she moved jerkily, as if her feet were too heavy and her upper body light. She stopped, turned halfway toward Elisabeth, held out the figure. Suddenly she seemed struck by powerful spasms that knit her stomach and snapped her head back, forward, then back again. Her eyes were wide, focused not on Elisabeth but on something

behind her, and her lips parted slightly in a smile of sensual pleasure. Elisabeth heard someone say, "Now the spirit is on her," and
she agreed, for it was as if Mambo Pitou had been transformed.
Lucinde put her arm about Elisabeth's waist and whispered,
"When she offers you her hand, take it, and hold on tight. The
spirit may come through her to you." Elisabeth was willing, more
than that. "Yes," she said, "I will."

Mambo Pitou faced the brazier. Her body continued to jerk
spasmodically and she had begun to hum in a high voice that
seemed too girlish for her large frame. She took up an earthen dish
from a pile of bowls and plates on the floor and, placing the wax
figure upon it, set it on the lid of the brazier. Elisabeth stood close
to her, though the heat was unbearable, like the breath of an infernal creature, a dragon or a devil. The crowd drew closer as well,
moving randomly yet in strange concert, driven by the pulsing
drum. Mambo Pitou held her arms out before her, moving her
hands in quick, sharp motions directed at the stove. She was singing a high-pitched, incantatory melody, the words of which were
familiar to her audience, for one by one their voices joined in. She
turned slowly in a circle, taking in the room with her motions;
then, when she faced the brazier again, she stopped. Her eyes were
wild, unfocused; again they rolled up, showing the whites. She
pointed at the dish Elisabeth knew she could not see and cried out,
her voice now harsh and deep. As her audience followed her in-
struction and gave their attention to the contents of the dish, there
were other cries. The singing faded away; only the drum continued. Elisabeth heard the word *petro* passed from one to the other
behind her. Lucinde, who still held her, whispered something she
could not understand, but this word, *petro,* was part of it. Elisabeth
studied the faces around her, afraid to see what they saw, what
evidently surprised, alarmed, yet gratified them, what they recognized and named. At last she followed their eyes to the wax figure
on the stove.

It had begun to melt, of course, but not into a formless pool.
Somehow the rough head and limbs of the figure had become

elongated. The back had sagged in, and, as Elisabeth watched, a thin stream of wax ran out, curving down over the back, then up toward the rim of the dish. Now the body was sleek, the head heavy; the limbs seemed powerful and sinewy. It was a black cat, his hind legs drawn in beneath his belly, his forelegs extended, head and tail lowered, ready to spring. For a moment the figure was as clear as if it had been carved; in the next, the lines began to blur, the hind legs and tail ran together, the body became flaccid, the head merged with the forelegs to form a shape like a flattened cone. But she had seen it; they had all seen it. Though no one spoke to her, Elisabeth understood from the charged atmosphere of the room that this momentary apparition meant her suit would be answered. She turned to Mambo Pitou, who was singing again, moving her shoulders and hips in a convulsive manner that seemed beyond her control. She was smiling, and her eyes were fixed on some phantom in the air before her, something so beautiful and powerful that she could not look away, and as she stood transfixed she held one hand out to Elisabeth. "Take her hand," Lucinde said, though it wasn't necessary, for Elisabeth had already reached out willingly, eagerly, as a drowning man reaches out, regardless of danger.

She could remember that moment clearly, and she could see her own hand, which, in the eerie light of the oppressive room, appeared opalescent, like carved marble. It disappeared into the grip of Mambo Pitou's dark hand and she was pulled forward to her knees, her arm nearly separated from its socket. After that her memory came up against a wall of black.

As she lay in her comfortable old bed, safe in her parents' home, the warm sunlight streaming through the pale lace curtains at the window, Elisabeth tried to persuade herself that the whole nightmarish scene had been just that, a nightmare. But her arms and neck ached, she felt as if she'd taken a beating, and there was the thin red line of the cut on her arm. Lucinde had brought her home; she had a dim memory of changing carriages in front of the Cathedral, of being supported, weeping and barely conscious, be-

tween Lucinde and her own coachman, across the rough cobble-
stones. Fortunately her parents had retired for the evening, and
only the houseboy, who opened the door and waited in the hall
while Lucinde helped her up the long staircase, had seen her. Of
course he knew where she had been, Elisabeth thought, and they
all knew by now, all the house servants. She had come home at
midnight, disheveled, bleeding, clinging to the arm of her hairdresser; that was all they needed to know to guess the rest.

As she sat up in her bed and poured a glass of water from the
carafe, she remembered something else, something Lucinde had
said in the carriage on the frantic, bumpy ride back to town. There
were good spirits and bad spirits, weak and strong. The one that
had come to Elisabeth was one of the cruelest and strongest. That
was why everyone had been surprised, and why it had gone
roughly on Elisabeth. He was a young spirit, a *petro* spirit; he had
come into existence in the new world. Before that time there had
been no need of him. Some said he was the spirit of rage against
imprisonment.

Elisabeth gulped down the water and poured another glass.
Her throat was parched, as if she had been screaming. She heard a
door open at the end of the hall, then rapid footsteps moving
toward her bedroom. What time was it? How late had she slept?
She could hear voices downstairs, moving toward the dining room,
raised, unfriendly. Something was wrong. She brought her legs
over the side of the bed and stood as the footsteps stopped before
her door. There was a knock, soft yet insistent. "Come in," Elisabeth said.

The door opened and her mother stepped in, closing it carefully behind her. Her face was filled with anxiety, alarm. She approached her daughter, speaking softly, as if she feared being overheard. "You must get dressed at once," she said. "Let me help you.
Your husband has come to take you home."

43

It did not take long before news of Bessie, Elisabeth's unfortunate young maid, reached the attentive ear of André Davillier. He took particular interest in her fate because she was born on his plantation, the daughter of his cook Rosalie. Bessie had lived at Rosedawn until she was ten, at which time she was sold to M. Boyer to be trained for his daughter's service. Though no one asked her opinion, Rosalie was not unhappy with this transaction, as it put her daughter in a good house in the town and meant there might be the occasional opportunity to see her when Elisabeth came to visit.

André Davillier took an enlightened view of the management of his slaves; on this subject he had even written a small treatise, privately published and circulated among his neighbors, in which he recommended that slaves be well cared for and comfortably lodged. Part of his recommendation was a step-by-step description of the proper treatment of yaws and scurvy, the two "mortal distempers that most frequently attacke the negroe." It irritated André that his pamphlet was more popular for the remedies than for the strength of its argument in favor of proper diet and ventilation, an argument he felt he had advanced irresistibly. "We see all those who understand the government of horses give an extraordinary attention to them," he maintained. "In the cold season they are well covered and kept in warm stables. In the summer they have a cloth thrown over them to keep them from dust, and at all times good litter to lie upon.

"If you ask these masters why they bestow so much pains upon beasts they will tell you that, to make a horse serviceable to you, you must take a good deal of care of him."

This analogy to the horse was the linchpin of André's argument. A rebellious horse might be brought into line with a combination of force and kindness; on this everyone agreed. How was a rebellious slave any different? "Punish them in proportion to the fault they have done," he recommended, "yet always with humanity. When a negroe comes from being whipped, cause the sore parts to be washed with vinegar mixed with salt. Jamaica pepper, which grows in the garden, and even a little gunpowder." The goal for the slaveholder and horse owner was, after all, the same: to produce a willing, reliable, healthy servant. What good was a slave who was ill nourished, broken of spirit, resentful, and likely to run away at the first opportunity?

Because he held these strong views, André was especially chagrined to learn that the redress of Bessie's crime was a punishment so callously administered it had left her unfit for service. Hermann had not, as he threatened, turned her over to the police. When he found his wife had run to her parents, he decided to settle the matter himself. He had Bessie whipped, then locked her in a small storage room that no one was allowed to enter until he returned from New Orleans with Elisabeth. By that time the girl was nearly starved and delirious with fever. The cuts from the beating, which had never been washed, were infected. On her return, Bessie's mistress tried to treat the girl herself, but to no avail; she grew worse every day until finally, despairing, Elisabeth sent for the doctor from Saint Francisville. It was from this doctor, Claude Lanier, an old school chum who came to Rosedawn to attend one of his daughter's indispositions, that André Davillier got the whole story. Dr. Lanier was well acquainted with his friend's ideas about slave management, as well as his habitual interest in the personal lives of those creatures, equine and human, who had been born at Rosedawn. Over an afterdinner brandy in Rosedawn's spacious dining room, he told André of his attendance at Montague. By his vigilance, Bessie had survived, but she was lame and her right arm was paralyzed, leaving her of no use to anyone.

"The man is mad," André grumbled. "What inexcusable waste."

"He wants to get rid of her now, of course," Dr. Lanier said. "But who would buy her?"

As they spoke André noticed that his butler, who was clearing away the dinner dishes, was listening to the conversation, for his hand paused over a butter dish, fluttered over to a fork, which he failed to pick up, then back to the dish. "Edward," André said testily, "what are you doing?"

Edward grabbed the dish and backed away from the table. "Sir" was all he could bring himself to reply.

"Oh, go on." André waved his hand, dismissing him. "Go and tell her the girl is still alive, anyway. And she has Dr. Lanier here to thank for it." Edward slipped out the door, his eyes down. "Surely there's something to be done with her," André said. "She's young. Could she still bear a child?"

"She could," Dr. Lanier assured him. "No reason that she couldn't."

André sipped his brandy thoughtfully. He had too many babies at Rosedawn, and not enough old folk to look after them. He did not allow the mothers to take their babes into the fields as some owners did, because, he maintained, the mothers were thereby distracted and didn't work well. He kept the babies at the cabins, supervised by the oldest slaves, who could no longer work much. The babies who were not weaned were attended by one or two wet nurses. He had a strong young woman, a good worker, as a wet nurse now. It was a waste of her strength, but what could he do? If he had another nurse, it occurred to him, he could free this excellent girl for field work.

"I could marry her off here," André suggested. "Then while she's pregnant she could supervise the children. I've got a mess of them this year, too young to sell yet. When her babe is born, she can stay on as a wet nurse."

Dr. Lanier nodded over his brandy. "She could certainly do that," he agreed. "There's nothing wrong with her, reproductively speaking." Then he laughed at his own remark.

"Schlaeger would sell her pretty cheaply, I dare say."

"As I said," Dr. Lanier agreed, "he wants to be rid of her. But she's not his to sell. She's Elisabeth's. That's what all this running home to Papa was about."

"And do you think Elisabeth would sell her to me?"

"I think so," Dr. Lanier said, rubbing his brow. "But I can't be sure. Elisabeth is not what she was."

"Is she ill?"

"Not ill," Dr. Lanier said, swallowing the last of his brandy. "But changed. Go and see for yourself. I would be interested to have your opinion of her condition."

So the next morning, André composed a brief note to Elisabeth, explaining that he needed a wet nurse and that he understood she might be willing to part with her maid Bessie, who would be suitable for such work. He made no mention of Bessie's condition nor of how he had come by the information that she might be for sale. Elisabeth replied in the next post. Bessie was indeed for sale. She had been ill, and the unfortunate result of her illness, a paralysis in the right arm, left her unfit to do any housework adequately. But she was otherwise fit and strong and would serve very well as a wet nurse. Elisabeth encouraged André to visit at his earliest convenience, judge the girl's condition for himself; if he was pleased, a price could be easily agreed upon. "I'd like a good home for Bessie," Elisabeth concluded, "and I know you will provide one for her. She's an honest girl, although a little inclined to nervousness."

André set out for Montague the following morning. It was a hot, sunny day, and his horse had begun to lather by the time he came to the end of his own property. He felt sleepy and contented; he spent a few moments mulling over the virtues of the new hat he was wearing, a better fit all around and not so heavy as his old one. He was at peace with himself, with his horse, his family, the busy, populous, prosperous world of his plantation, the easy pace of his days, the cultivated charm of his evenings. He considered his mission, which was a pleasing one.

After his dinner with Dr. Lanier, he had found Rosalie weeping in the kitchen. It was a strange sort of weeping, for she made no sound, only sat at the table with her hands in her lap while tears poured down her face like sweat. She knew all about her daughter's trouble at Montague and had known from the start. It was amazing how these people kept track of one another. She had carried on as usual, cooking the meals, planning her menus for the week ahead, while she knew her daughter was being beaten, locked up, starved. She had said nothing, had made no effort to save her, for indeed, André had to admit, there was nothing she could have done. When she saw André, who stood in the doorway feeling unaccountably nervous to find her in such a state, she took up a napkin and began dabbing at her eyes. Though it was his practice never to confide his plans to his slaves, even when these plans concerned their own circumstances, faced with the voiceless grief of this stoic woman, André found himself overcome with a need to reassure her. "I'll try to get her back, Rosalie," he said. She raised her wet eyes to his and gave him a look that was neither gratitude nor pleading, but something other, something that smote his conscience and made him turn away, feeling oddly sour. It was not until the next evening, when he sat down to a supper comprising dishes Rosalie knew to be his favorites, that he excised from his memory the look she had given him and replaced it with one he found more pleasing. He had been mistaken. It was not reproach he had seen in her eyes. Here, in the stuffed loin of pork, the thick gumbo, in this blancmange, was the proof of her sincere, her proper gratitude.

André arrived at Montague by noon. He had sent a boy the night before to announce his visit, and he fully expected to stay for the midday meal, which he looked forward to. The long ride had given him an appetite, and Hermann's cook was a good one. Elisabeth would certainly put herself out for his visit. As the house came into view at the end of the avenue of oaks, he roused himself from his reverie. It was a fine house, he couldn't deny that, but the millwork the builder had attached to every possibly surface made it look ludicrous, like an old woman in too much rouge and lace. As he approached, he saw a boy get up from the veranda and pound on the front door. A moment later the door opened and Charles came out. He sent the boy running for the stable man and came out to the steps to greet his master's neighbor. Charles, André reflected, had seen a lot. He'd practically run Montague when old deClerc went mad, and he'd found his master's body after the suicide. Presumably he'd been in the house throughout Bessie's incarceration and must have heard her suffering, for Dr. Lanier had told him the girl was raving when he got there, that he heard her screams from the front hall. Indeed, when André had tied up his horse and climbed the stairs, he observed that Charles had aged remarkably in the six months or so since he had last seen him. His hair was turning white, and his posture, which had always been erect, was sadly stooped, as if he had been carrying a heavy burden and only just set it down. As he ushered André to the door, Charles gave him a shy smile of greeting and expressed his hope that the ride had been uneventful. "Most agreeable," André assured him, "but a little hot. Please make sure my horse is cooled down properly, will you, Charles?" They entered the cool, dark hall; for a moment André paused, allowing his eyes to adjust to the pleasant change, for the light outside was brutal in comparison. Then he looked up the wide staircase and saw Elisabeth, who stood on the landing perfectly still, as if, he thought, she had been standing there for hours.

Elisabeth. But how changed.

She was thinner, paler, she looked tired, but these changes were the superficial evidence of a more serious, a profound alteration. Later, when he tried to describe his impression to Dr. Lanier, he said, "The light in her eyes has gone out," and his friend agreed, for they both remembered what Elisabeth had been, how stimulating the keen intelligence of her regard, so charged with irony and wit, so playful and engaging. As André stood before this new, this altered Elisabeth, he felt he was looking at a shell, like a burned-out house in which all that remained of once elegant furnishings were a few charred sticks, bits of broken glass, and ashes.

If Elisabeth noticed her old friend's dismay, she made no mention of it. She came down the stairs to him, her hand extended, an artificial smile and a few obligatory words of welcome on her lips. As André stepped forward to take her small cold hand in his they both heard heavy footsteps on the porch. Elisabeth's eyes met André's only for a moment, but it was long enough for him to see that her strange lifelessness was a cover for something akin to pure terror. In the next moment the door behind him flew open and Hermann Schlaeger burst in. André was not to meet Elisabeth's eyes again. He turned to Hermann, who greeted him with a show of enthusiasm André could neither entirely trust nor resist. He was such a big, crude fellow it was hard to credit him with the intelligence and cunning necessary to sham a feeling he did not have.

Charles opened the dining room doors noiselessly and stood aside as Hermann ushered his friend and his wife into the room. It had been redecorated since his last visit, to Elisabeth's fine taste, André observed. Everything was light and airy, the colors delicate, soft blues and grays. He would never have thought to put such patterns and shades together, yet the effect was one of remarkable naturalness. Elisabeth smiled her new vacant smile on receiving his compliments and looked about her at her own handiwork as if she were seeing it for the first time. Hermann accepted André's praise for her; André thought he seemed more pleased than she was. They took their seats at the long table—André across from Elisabeth, her husband next to her—and Charles filled the glasses with wine and water. Hermann raised the subject about which he had long wanted to ask André's opinion: the vicissitudes of the price of cotton. As the first course, a soup of mushrooms and shallots, was served, the two men fell into conversation, moving easily from one subject to another, for they had many interests in common. Elisabeth was silent, though she looked from one to the other as they spoke, and she did address a few words, leaning away from her husband, to Charles as he cleared away the courses. André sent an occasional furtive look in her direction, but he found her eyes always lowered demurely. The food, as he had expected, was excellent. He ate heartily, washing down everything with great gulps of wine. By the time coffee was served he was feeling so relaxed and amiable, he had nearly forgotten the reason for his visit.

But Hermann had not, and when at last he brought it up, his cordiality seemed to evaporate. "We must get this matter of Bessie settled," he said. "It is an unpleasant business." He scowled, taking in his neighbor and his wife, as if, André thought, he suspected them of being in league against him. Elisabeth kept her eyes on her coffee cup. When she lifted it to her lips, André noticed that her hand was trembling.

"Let's conclude it swiftly, then," André suggested. "I don't think we shall have much difficulty." Hermann agreed, rising from the table and sorting through the formidable collection of keys he wore on a ring beneath his coat. André and Elisabeth followed him across the hall to the drawing room doors, where he stopped and, to the astonishment of his guest, though not of his wife, opened the lock with one of the keys.

What sort of man kept his drawing room locked in the middle of the day, André wondered. Charles, who followed them into the room, set about opening the French doors onto the veranda. The room was warm, the air stale from being closed up, though the furniture gleamed and everything was in perfect order. It was like a show room, kept only for display. Hermann took a chair near one of the windows, and André followed his example. He watched Elisabeth closely. She stood in the doorway, apparently uncertain about her role in the forthcoming transaction. Hermann spoke to her curtly. "Sit down, please," he said. "Charles will bring her in." Then he extracted another key, this time from his coat pocket, which he handed to Charles, who stood stiffly behind his chair. "Go and get her," he said.

Charles disappeared down the hall, and the three sat for a moment in an oppressive silence. André expected Elisabeth to dispel the gloom with light banter, drawing her guest out by a subtle combination of interest and sympathy, but this new Elisabeth settled resolutely into the silence. She sat staring into the hallway, waiting for her slave to appear, and there was a stubbornness in her posture that suggested she was willing to let the silence swallow the room, the house, the world, rather than break it. André noted that Hermann had fixed his eyes intently on his wife's profile. He too showed no inclination to speak. This was the ordinary state of affairs between them, André thought.

They heard doors opening and closing in the back of the house, then footsteps moving toward them down the hall. Hermann gave up staring at Elisabeth and turned to André. "Bessie has been ill," he said. "I'm afraid she's not entirely recovered."

"Elisabeth wrote me to that effect," André replied. "I have a use for her."

"I know," Hermann interrupted. "I read your letter." And hers as well, André thought. Then he forgot his annoyance at the proprietary remark, for Charles appeared in the open doorway bringing with him cause for a more powerful emotion.

Bessie stood half in the room, her head lowered, her eyes on the floor. Her body was twisted at impossible angles, one hip several inches higher than the other, one hand hanging stiffly, palm out, the fingers drawn up in a permanent fist. Her shoulder was raised so high that her chin rested against her collarbone. She was gaunt; her skin seemed darker than André remembered; her face was drawn. There were circles, nearly black, beneath her eyes. Someone had cropped her hair very close, probably to avoid the bother of brushing it when she was too sick to care for herself, and it gave her a boyish look, though no one would ever mistake her for a young person again. She raised her sad eyes, but she kept her head jammed down against her shoulder—apparently she couldn't lift it—and cast a quick look at Elisabeth before returning her attention to the carpet.

André struggled against a torrent of outrage and anger. If a man had used a horse so ill as this, he thought, he would beat him. Only a few months ago this pathetic, wasted creature had been a healthy, lively young woman with a lifetime of good service in her; now she was worthless. He looked from Bessie to Charles, who stood beside her, his eyes focused on some spot in the air, to Elisabeth, who leaned forward in her chair, her face half hidden in her hand, to Hermann, who appeared relaxed, his head resting comfortably against the back of his chair, so that he looked down his nose at his guest, his expression cold, a steely insolence in his hard gray eyes. He's pleased with himself, André thought.

The silence in the room was stifling. André had to clear his throat to break through it. "She is marvelously changed," he said.

"I had my own physician in to attend to her," Hermann replied. "Doctor Claude Lanier. I believe he is a friend of yours."

André got to his feet wearily. This was a rotten business, and the sooner it was over, the better. He approached Bessie, who stood immobile, fixed in her unnatural posture. "I am Monsieur Davillier, Bessie," he said. "Do you remember me?"

"Yes, sir," she said at once.

He took her clenched hand in his own, finding it as cold and hard as iron. "Can you move your fingers at all?"

"No, sir," she said.

He touched her cheek, patting her softly, as if he were calming a nervous animal, then ran his thumb under her upper lip and bent down to look at her teeth. "You eat well enough now, I suppose?" he said.

She waited until he had moved his hand away from her mouth. "Yes, sir," she said. "I do."

He stepped back and stood looking her up and down. He could marry her off easily enough; he even had a fellow in mind, a house servant, as she had been. He would give her first son his freedom on his majority—that would make her a desirable match —and when the boy was out on his own, with any luck he would buy his old mother away and André would be relieved of the expense of her. "I'm going to take you back to Rosedawn, Bessie," he said.

She looked up at André, then cast a questioning glance behind him at Elisabeth, who said, "I think that will be for the best."

André addressed Elisabeth. "What do you want for her?"

Elisabeth named a low figure. Hermann stirred in his chair. It had dawned on him that his display of temper was going to cost money. "Surely she's worth more than that?" he said.

André stood rubbing his chin, as if he found the figure too high. "Not anymore," he said to Hermann. "Certainly not to me." To Elisabeth he said, "Although you are welcome to try for a better price."

Elisabeth shook her head gravely, while Hermann grumbled about the cost of sending a slave to auction.

"Then we are agreed?" Elisabeth said.

"I'll send a wagon for her in the morning," André replied.

Hermann got to his feet. He was clearly annoyed by André's subtle insistence on dealing only with Elisabeth. He waved the back of his hand at Charles impatiently. "Take her back to her room," he said. The two slaves disappeared down the hall; André could hear Charles's even step and Bessie's halting one as she dragged her twisted leg toward her last night in the hated room at Montague. Hermann moved behind Elisabeth's chair and rested his hand on her shoulder in the manner of an affectionate husband, but André observed the flinch of distaste that went through her, and he saw that the look her husband bent upon her was anything but warm. Dr. Lanier had told him Hermann had gotten the best of her family when he went to New Orleans to bring her back. He had suggested that Elisabeth was nervous, unstable—her running away without warning in the middle of the night was evidence—and that M. Boyer knew his daughter was not entirely sound when he'd tried to block the marriage by lowering her dowry. If Elisabeth hoped to retain her property, Hermann explained, she'd best understand that future rebellions would raise in her husband's mind serious doubts about her competence to administer her own affairs.

And that was all it took. The Boyers backed down. Elisabeth's father told her she would not be welcomed at home unless she came with her husband's permission.

André looked sadly at Elisabeth. She was eerily still, her back straight, her eyes fixed in that disturbing and empty way on the arm of her chair. Now Hermann attempted to cajole his neighbor into another coffee, or perhaps a brandy, but André demurred. He had business in Saint Francisville and would have to be off at once if he was to arrive before dark. As they walked out onto the veranda, Elisabeth and André discussed arrangements for the deed transfer. Hermann had sent for André's horse, but it was a few moments in arriving, and while they stood on the wide porch André noticed that Charles was closing the drawing room doors. Elisabeth seemed unaware of this, or else she ignored it, as she ignored so much, André imagined, because if she let herself notice, she really would go mad. And it struck him as cruelly ironic that she had contrived, in spite of her husband, to send poor Bessie home to her mother, a trick she had not had the power to arrange for herself. As his horse was brought around, he watched a flicker of interest, a trace of a smile pass across her features; she was a passionate horsewoman, he recalled, one of the best riders in the state. But she suppressed her interest at once, and the vacant stare returned. She held her hand out to André as he took his leave, but there was neither warmth nor pressure in it, and her goodbye was as soft and toneless as the fall of a leaf. He climbed onto his horse and turned his back on this unhappy place, this Montague, which did seem a cursed house where nothing could prosper. A pang of guilt smote him, for he had brought this miserable couple together. He looked back and saw them, standing side by side, waving dully, mechanically, like those doomed and dreadful puppets André had seen in the traveling shows, who so often represented a married couple, trapped on a claustrophobic stage, where they were condemned to battle each other pointlessly, forever, with no escape, no recourse, no rest, not even the hope of death.

44

Camille had already opened the exhibit gate when she realized something was wrong with Magda. The leopard was crouched at the back of her night cage, waiting, but as the gate rose before her she did not make her usual dash for freedom. She moved forward quickly, but hit the side wall with a low thud, fell back, then scrambled to her feet and lurched through the gateway. Camille noticed the uneaten meat stick in the corner of the cage. She let the other cats go out, one by one. All had eaten their dinners and left the night house in the usual way, anxious or furious by turns. She took the two-way radio from the hook next to the door and walked out past the yard, where an elephant stood absentmindedly beating hay against his knees, through the old arch that was one of the few surviving structures from the original zoo, then along the narrow, shady walk that separated the public from the secret world of those responsible for maintaining the illusion they paid to see. The public hadn't been let in yet, though there were probably a few already waiting at the gates. As she walked quickly along the path to the Asian exhibits, Camille breathed in the damp morning air and, in the midst of her misgivings about Magda, noted that the empty zoo was a touchingly beautiful place. She rehearsed a fantasy, that the world was only zoos, and that half the population spent its time visiting while the other half was employed in zoo maintenance. The problem was, of course, what did the visiting public do to earn enough money to support the zoos? She smiled at this, the single flaw in her grand scheme, as she arrived in front of Magda's exhibit.

At first she didn't see the leopard. Magda was in the back, behind a tree and an outcropping of fake rock, and she was not moving. Camille could make out only her flank and one forepaw. As she watched, the leopard appeared between the two obstructions and walked toward Camille. Again she misjudged the distance on her right side and collided with the rock. She sat down, confused by her error. As Camille raised the radio to punch in the hospital number, Magda watched her with what looked like interest. The muscle at the corner of her mouth twitched, revealing one formidable canine; it was clearly an involuntary motion. She yawned, opening her mouth so wide her eyes were forced closed and Camille could see down her red throat. When she closed her mouth, she left a bit of her tongue out, like a house cat.

There was a blare of static as Camille put the radio to her ear, then Ellen's voice, sounding tired, saying, "Hospital." It was early, Camille reflected. She felt shy. She had never spoken to Ellen without going through her supervisor. Magda sat watching her impassively. Her mouth twitched again.

"This is Camille," she said. "Something's wrong with Magda, the black leopard."

"What's going on?" Ellen said.

"She hardly ate last night. When she went out this morning,

she staggered against the wall, and she did it again in the exhibit. Her mouth is twitching. Otherwise she seems okay. Maybe dazed a little; she looks confused."

"I'm on my way," Ellen said.

Camille was gratified by the prompt seriousness with which Ellen responded to her call, but she felt guilty for having let Magda into the exhibit without noticing something was wrong. Getting her back into the night house would be impossible, and if Ellen chose to sedate her it would be equally impossible to get a dart in her; there were too many hiding places in the exhibit. Camille was anxious on two other counts: she had called the vet without notifying her supervisor, and, most seriously, she was sure something really was wrong with Magda. It was the last worry that she felt in the pit of her stomach, a gnawing, burning sensation that made her shift her weight from foot to foot, as if she could stamp it out. Magda began to pace in a disoriented fashion, flaring her nostrils and emitting odd, groaning sounds. Camille saw that her mouth was twitching regularly now. If only Ellen would come, she thought, looking toward the walk where she expected her to appear. To her relief, she saw three brown-uniformed figures, two women, Ellen and the technician Beth, and a man, her supervisor, walking briskly toward her. As they came up, Camille addressed her supervisor. "I'm sorry," she said, "I didn't notice anything until I'd already gotten her out. Then I was so worried I forgot to call you." It didn't matter, he assured her, and Ellen, who was watching Magda, consternation knitting her brow, said, "You did the right thing to call me."

"What's wrong with her?" Camille asked.

Ellen gave her a quick, speculative look. "That's what I hope to find out," she said.

Magda had stopped pacing and stood before the high ledge, her favorite sleeping spot, where she often spent an entire day, showing her curious visitors only her tail or, occasionally, a forepaw. Slowly she backed away from it and made a running start, the beginning of her spectacular midair turn-leap, but when the moment came for the concentrated and precise spring, her hind legs failed to deliver the required momentum. After rising only a few feet, she veered off and fell on her side, her legs sprawled out, and made a hollow thud and a low grunt as the air was forced from her lungs.

"Jesus," Camille said.

The four humans watched as the cat struggled to her feet. Saliva poured from her mouth in a thin stream, and her eyes were unfocused, though she looked warily at the ledge as if she suspected it of having moved.

"Did any of the other cats eat from the same feline tube last night?" Ellen asked Camille.

"Antonella and Paolo did."

Ellen spoke to Beth, though she kept her eyes on the leopard. "Call the hospital and get a stretcher over here. We're going to take her in."

"Do you want the gun?" Beth said, taking the radio Camille handed her.

"We may not need it," Ellen said. "She's starting to seizure."

And as they watched, the leopard appeared to be losing consciousness. She sat down clumsily; her head dropped down between her shoulders. Ellen started moving away, toward the night house, giving orders to Beth as she went. Camille followed along, feeling useless and terrified. She knew how quickly wild animals died when they became ill; their ability to mask symptoms was a survival mechanism. Once they were sick enough to show it, there was often little time left. As they passed through the arch, Ellen said to Camille, "Go have a look at Paolo and Antonella. Look for anything odd, any facial twitching, heavy salivation; see if they look dazed, you know, star gazing, anything like that. Watch them for a few minutes, then meet us back here. If we've gone already, come over to the hospital."

"Yes, ma'am," Camille said, turning back. Though she hated to leave Magda, it made her feel better to have something to do. As she walked back across the exhibit, Magda, still sitting in that exhausted, dazed position, head down, stared vacantly into space. Camille paused to look at her, but only for a moment; then she took off at a run for the lion exhibit.

Now a few visitors had begun to enter the zoo, and they looked curiously at the young woman in uniform who ran past them, her expression so intent and serious. She rushed past the sun bears and up the wide wooden ramp between the big cats and a smaller exhibit, more like a large fenced yard, where a few deer lifted their heads at the sound of her hurried footsteps and a heron stalked about idly, picking among the thin patches of grass. Sonya, the white tiger, only a few yards away, lounged on her fake rock, indifferent to her gathering audience. She treated them to a great yawn, which caused a murmur of admiration to go up. Camille slowed to a brisk walk, for the lion exhibit was next. As she came around the turn, she saw Paolo crouched at the edge of the moat, lapping water placidly like a great golden dog. Antonella stood a few feet behind him, gazing up at the ramp. Camille placed herself near her line of vision, but she couldn't tell whether the lioness was looking at her. If she was, she quickly lost interest. After a moment she turned her attention to her mate, who had finished his drink and was ambling toward her, his big head lowered as he pulled himself up the sloping path he'd worn in the carefully tended grass that ran to the water's edge. He climbed toward his mate, glanced briefly back at the ramp. Camille strained to see his face. He looked, she thought, as he always looked, old, weary, majestic. His mane was thin now, and he was inclined to put on weight, but Camille knew his teeth were still impressive. He never entered the night house without making a leaping and snarling mock attack at the window in the iron door; it was part of his routine. Camille remembered how, when she first started her job, this ritual of his had frightened her. Now she hardly noticed it. He turned away, bumping Antonella's shoulder with his head as he went by. She gave way at once and followed him to an outcropping of fake rock where a thin stream of water flowed continually into a buried pipe.

It was the coolest spot in the exhibit. Paolo stretched out near the water while Antonella amused herself by tearing at the big, weathered, much-chewed and clawed log anchored in concrete beneath the small Jerusalem thorn tree, which was wrapped in wire mesh to protect it from just such amusements. There was a clatter on the ramp; a little boy ran toward Camille, followed by his mother, who was slowly pushing a baby carriage. "Mom!" the boy shouted. "Look! Lions!" He stopped close to Camille, hanging over the rail. "Look!" he shouted. "He's playing with that log."

Camille frowned at the boy, who seemed indifferent to her. "That's a female," Camille said. "It's a she." The boy gave her a sidelong look full of suspicion, then called back to his mother. "Look, Mom, he's playing with that log." His mother drew up, smiling blandly. She looked exhausted, Camille thought. The boy's attention span was very short; he was already bored with the lions. His restless eyes raked over the exhibit; when he looked ahead, he saw the frieze of elephants that led to the next part of the Asian domain. "Elephants!" he cried out, and was gone. His mother, who had hardly noticed the lions, steered the carriage toward the ramp and followed him, calling weakly, hopelessly, "Peter, don't go so fast. Wait for me."

Camille watched the lions for another minute. Paolo was napping, and Antonella, bored by her log, took her turn at the water's edge. There was no facial twitching; her eyes were clear. When she raised her head from drinking, she looked right at her keeper, and Camille had the sense that she recognized her. The lioness watched her attentively. "Antonella," she said. "Hey, girl." She pushed off the rail and started back, walking quickly. "So it wasn't poison," Camille said.

She heard the hurried, synchronized beat of their footsteps before she saw them bearing Magda down the sidewalk toward the hospital. She ran to catch up and took a place at the back of the stretcher, gripping the pole, which her supervisor relinquished to her, and throwing her weight into it as they went up a low incline.

She noticed that Beth held in her free hand the catchpole, which was looped around Magda's neck. Ellen was carrying her black case. "How are the lions?" Ellen said over her shoulder.

"They look fine," Camille replied. "Paolo's sleeping, but he was awake when I got there and looked okay. Antonella was ripping at her log."

"We'll send a sample of the feline tube to the lab anyway," Ellen said. They rounded the last corner and rushed past the squawking hawks and owls, who rattled their jesses as they hopped from their perches to express their disapproval of this disturbance. Beth stepped ahead to hold the door open and assisted Ellen in bringing the stretcher through the doorway. Another technician, the young man Camille had seen before, stood holding back the heavy treatment-room door. They maneuvered the stretcher carefully inside and set it down on the steel operating table. Then, as they gathered around and began shifting the leopard from the stretcher, Camille got her first look at Magda's face.

She wasn't unconscious. Her jaws were slack; the flow of saliva had formed a pool beneath her head. It was obvious that she couldn't move, but her eyes were wide open and seemed, in a flat, distant way, to see. She was there and not there, neither dead nor in any ordinary sense of the word alive. She was trembling from head to foot, as if from a chill. When Camille slipped her hand under the animal's shoulder, she recoiled momentarily from the quavery feel of it, but she looked up to find Ellen's eyes on her and understood this was no time for squeamishness. Ellen began filling syringes from various bottles while Beth drew startling red blood from Magda's foreleg, one, two, three tubes, which she handed to the young man, who took them down the hall.

Camille and her supervisor stood watching as the two women seemed to swarm over the leopard. Ellen bent over her, listening through the stethoscope, examining Magda's mouth, while Beth injected two syringes into her shoulder. "Get a catheter in her," Ellen said. Beth drew up the IV stand and began fastening a plastic bag of clear liquid to a long, flexible tube. Ellen pulled up another machine, a black box full of dials and screens with wires sticking out.

"That's the EKG machine," Camille's supervisor said.

Camille looked at him, nodded, dry-mouthed. She felt a strong resistance to knowing anything about these machines, these needles and tubes being brought to bear on the mystery of Magda, who lay in a trance beyond the reach of their voices, in some dark, unpeopled world. Yet Camille felt complete confidence in the ability of this science to bring Magda back to ordinary life, which, she realized, she wanted more than anything. Since she called Ellen, everything had happened at a furious pace, leaving her standing uselessly on the sidelines, her fingers crossed and her heart in her throat, like a gambler who has put everything on a horse he knows nothing about; all she could do was stand back and watch the professionals. Her supervisor sensed her discomfort, for after a brief consultation with Ellen he told Camille she could leave. "I'll be over in a little while," he assured her.

She glanced quickly at Ellen, who was taping the wires from the black box to the leopard's side and chest. Her mouth was set in a resolute line. She was determined to bring Magda back.

Everyone in the room was aware of what would happen if the leopard suddenly regained consciousness. Beth stood by ready to apply the gas mask; Camille's supervisor held the catchpole. There was a sense in which the still, deathlike creature laid out so carelessly on the steel table was not Magda at all, yet she possessed the potential to be Magda. Camille imagined Magda springing to her feet, wires and needles flying in all directions, the humans fleeing for their lives. She looked up at the clock; then, overcome with embarrassment for Magda, she left. As she went out across the sidewalk, past the petulant hawks and owls, it occurred to her that Magda could never know what it was to be embarrassed.

45

Camille sat hunched forward on a chair, her face hidden in her hands. She'd gotten her wish; she was spending the night in the night house, but like the wishes granted by the malevolent gods of fairy tales and fables, this one had come with a devastating hitch. All around her the cats paced nervously, all but Magda, who lay still, as she had for many hours, on the concrete floor of her cage.

The light from the bare bulbs overhead was harsh, too bright, not the perfectly black night the cats were accustomed to, into which, presumably, they could see. The light made them nervous, irritable. Camille sat hour after hour, as they growled, paced, shit, slapped at one another, paced some more. Now and then she heard a low scratching sound; rats, she thought, carrying out their nightly raids on the feed room, heedless of the light, but she didn't want to look at them. Once she thought she heard the sharp snap of one of the traps.

She raised her head wearily to check the clock near her feet. It was almost two, the hour when her shift would end.

She had come on at ten, replacing her supervisor, who stayed a few minutes, talking to her softly, as if he didn't want to disturb the agitated animals. "Not much to do here," he said. "You should have brought a book."

Camille looked in at Magda's still form. She lay on her side, stiff, facing the front of the cage, but her eyes were open, and Camille could detect the slight rise and fall of breath in her chest. "How's she doing?" she asked.

"Nothing's changed," he said. "Ellen said she didn't expect anything, not until morning. But if you notice any change, even if she just starts blinking, call her at home."

"Does she know what's wrong with her yet?"

"No, I don't think so."

Camille swallowed uncomfortably. All morning she had struggled with a tightness in her throat. She unscrewed the cap on the water bottle she'd brought with her and offered it to her supervisor, who shook his head. "No, thanks," he said. She brought the bottle to her lips, drank a little, but it didn't seem to help. As soon as she swallowed, her throat felt dry again. "I'm so thirsty today," she said.

Her supervisor picked up a canvas bag he had left by his chair. "I'd better get home," he said. "Ellen will be here at two." Camille followed him to the door, as if, she thought, he were a guest in her house. Then she went back to the chair and took her seat. She was tired but not sleepy. She did not think she would have difficulty staying awake.

It had been a harrowing day. In the afternoon Magda was returned to the night house, where she regained consciousness briefly. First she staggered about, breathing heavily, the corner of her mouth twitching spasmodically, shaking her head and working her jaws, from which a steady stream of saliva poured over the floor. Camille called Ellen, hoping she would take Magda back to the hospital, but when she arrived, carrying the dart case and another smaller bag, she only stood before the cage, frowning. "Is she getting worse?" Camille asked.

She never got an answer, for the leopard suddenly charged the front of the cage, snarling, claws out, furious, though her eyes were unfocused and she did not appear to be attacking the two women who watched her. It was something else, something she alone could see. Her head hit the bars, throwing her back on her haunches. She gathered herself up and took off at a wild run, tearing around the cage, leaping in the air. When she got to the back wall she rose up against it, clawing the concrete as if she could pull it apart.

"I'm going to have to knock her down," Ellen said, more to herself than to Camille. She opened the case and began unpacking the dart gun.

Later, when Magda was unconscious and Beth arrived to assist in more tests, more medication, Camille overheard their brief exchanges. They seemed to be ruling out possibilities. It wasn't peritonitis, lead or arsenic poisoning. They didn't think it was toxoplasmosis, though the lab results weren't in yet. Camille's supervisor arrived and conferred with Ellen about the night watch. They decided it was best to leave Magda in the night house.

The day had dragged on. At five Camille brought in all the cats and fed them. The air was full of the smell of meat, the sounds of their powerful jaws, the muscles in their throats choking down their dinners as fast as possible. Camille stood in front of Magda's cage and watched her. How could she lie so motionless with all this energy around her? Surely the effects of the anesthesia had worn off by now. The leopard's unearthly stillness afflicted Camille; it was so unlike sleep. She rubbed her eyes with her fingertips and became aware of Sonya, sitting close by, rolling out growl after growl like a current of disapproval. Camille went back to the feed room, where she busied herself cleaning buckets and washing out the ice chest. Every few minutes she stopped her work and walked over to look at Magda. By six, when her supervisor arrived, she'd rearranged the feed room, a job she had wanted to finish for some time. But she felt no sense of accomplishment. They looked at

Magda together, and Camille told her supervisor what had happened during Ellen's visit. He'd seen something like this before, he said, manic behavior punctuated by seizures.

"Is she going to die?" Camille asked.

"I hope not," he said. "I surely hope not."

On the short bus ride to her mother's house, Camille seemed to be moving through a fog, not an unpleasant sensation, as it softened the world she ordinarily found harsh and unsympathetic. At home she swallowed an unappetizing meal, indifferent to the taste of it and to the torrent of abuse she provoked when she announced that she was going back to work. Her mother simply didn't believe it. This story of a sick leopard was a ruse. Who would trust her with such an important job, anyway? She was going out to meet some worthless friends, to disgrace herself and humiliate her mother, who failed to understand why she knew no one presentable enough to bring home. Camille smiled at this picture of herself, the center of a vivacious group of ne'er-do-wells. She rarely responded to her mother's accusations—it only made things worse—but this time she found she didn't care. "Do you seriously imagine that I have any friends?" she asked. She thought of Eddie, whom she had not seen in a month.

She was thinking of Eddie again as she glanced at the round wind-up clock near her feet, Eddie and his wife. Perhaps he'd only made up the wife to be rid of her. She stood; her back ached from sitting on the hard chair, and she stretched her arms, bending from side to side, her eyes on Magda. Then she dropped her arms and stepped closer to the bars of the cage. Magda hadn't moved, but something was different. Her body looked flat, as if it had sunk into the floor. Her mouth was open a little wider than before, and the red tongue and gums looked dry. Her yellow eyes were open, as they had been, but they were without luster; they looked darker, dull. Camille strained to see the slight rise and fall of breath in the leopard's side. She thought she saw it; then she wasn't sure. "Oh, Jesus," she said. She looked about her helplessly at the other cats, who continued their pacing. Antonella and Paolo were engaged in a game that involved pressing their heads together and growling. She started toward the feed room, where the phone was, but stopped halfway. There was no point in calling Ellen; she was surely on her way. She went back to Magda. Now the golden eyes appeared to be focused on her, or was she imagining it? "Magda," she said, but of course the leopard didn't respond. Perhaps she had only drifted into a deeper unconsciousness. Camille stood wringing her hands, her upper teeth pressed hard into her lower lip, her eyes narrowed. "Don't let her die," she said.

She picked up the clock. There was no mistake; it was two o'clock. She set it on the chair. Sonya, who was pacing the length of her cage, made an angry rush at the bars. She was so close, Camille could have touched her. "Shut up," she said. "Why don't you just relax for a change?" The tiger tilted her big head, fixing her keeper with icy blue eyes, behind which there was nothing but murder. Camille turned back to Magda, but she couldn't look at her. She noted only that the leopard had not moved.

There was a sudden loud rapping on the metal door, so startling that Camille felt the blood drain from her knees and her heart thud against her chest. It sent all the cats into a frenzy; even the placid Flo leaped to her feet and screamed with her neighbors. "Thank God," Camille said, rushing down the aisle. She leaned into the heavy door and pushed it open to reveal Ellen, standing in the square of light that poured out from the doorway.

"Thank God you're here," Camille said, breathlessly.

"Is something wrong?" Ellen asked, as she stepped inside and Camille let the door close behind them.

"I didn't call you because I knew you'd be on your way," Camille said, following Ellen along the aisle, past the sun bears, to Magda's cage. "It's only been a few minutes. I don't know what it is. She just looks different. She hasn't moved or even made a sound."

They came to a stop before the cage. Ellen looked at Magda quickly, then bent a mild, incredulous look on Camille. "She's dead," she said flatly.

Camille flinched and stepped back, as if to avoid a blow. She brought her hands to her eyes. Her throat was tight; she gasped for air. Ellen was occupied in pulling the latch at the front of the cage. As she opened the gate, the steel screeched in the track, a sound that set the cats off in a new frenzy of growling and pacing. Ellen climbed into the cage and knelt beside Magda.

Not Magda any longer, Camille thought, as she followed, but Magda's empty body. And where was the force that had been Magda? Somehow, while she was sitting in the chair, watching, it had slipped away. Camille stood behind Ellen, looking about the cage, at the concrete ledge where Magda had preferred to eat her meals, the half-full water dish at which she had crouched, lapping up water, her golden eyes moving from side to side as if she thought it might be dangerous to be so exposed. That was all there was, the bars, the metal water dish, and near the front of the cage a woman bent over the motionless body of a leopard. Ellen lifted a stiffening foreleg, pressed her ear against the animal's side. "You were right," Ellen said. "She hasn't been gone long. Just a few minutes, I'd guess."

Camille looked down at the leopard's frozen jaws, the flat, glassy eyes. "I'm sorry," she said.

Ellen stood up. "There's nothing to be sorry about. There's nothing you could have done."

"I didn't know," Camille said. What was it she didn't know? She knelt beside Magda and rested her hand on the leopard's shoulder. Then she did what she had never been able to do before; she stroked Magda's head, running her fingers behind her ears, across her brow, petting her as she might pet a house cat. It was another wish fulfilled in perverse circumstances. Tears ran silently down her cheeks into the open neck of her shirt. Ellen made no move to leave. She stood looking down at the brokenhearted girl, feeling a combination of sympathy and vexation, for she did not know what had killed this animal and she was determined to find out. It was a cruel irony that she had a better chance of finding out now that Magda was dead. She cast her thoughts over Magda's history, which she had studied closely, searching for a clue. "She was wild caught," she said.

Camille looked up, but Ellen didn't seem to be addressing her, so she made no reply.

"I didn't know that until today," Ellen went on. "It was completely illegal, of course, so it's hard to tell when it happened. She could have changed hands a few times before she turned up in Saint Louis. That's where her records start, at the zoo there."

Camille imagined Magda, terrified, thoroughly wild, locked up in a makeshift cage in the back of one truck after another, moving through the exotic back streets of African towns and cities, loaded into the roaring black hold of an airplane, sedated, no doubt, for she was a valuable animal and it was important to keep her alive. She touched one of Magda's canine teeth, found it as dry and hard as ivory. Just pressing lightly against its point made an indentation in her finger. It was designed, Camille thought, for one thing, sinking into flesh.

"Zoos don't like to buy wild-caught animals," Ellen continued, "but if they don't, there's no telling what will happen to them. Ethically it's a bind. The Saint Louis zoo was glad to get her. There's not a lot of genetic diversity in the captive leopard population, and they had two males. They thought she could be mated, but that didn't work out."

Camille continued to stroke Magda, listening gratefully to Ellen's narration of her history. There were old stories, she knew, of spirits who lingered among the living to hear talk of themselves. Camille didn't want Ellen to stop talking. She wanted Magda to hear. When Ellen fell silent, Camille searched for a question to make her go on. "Why wasn't she mated?" she asked, without lifting her eyes or her hands from Magda's body.

"Well, actually, she was, in a way. She wouldn't let either of the males near her. She tried to kill them. So she was kept apart. But she was artificially inseminated. She had one pregnancy, two cubs. One was born dead, the other died a week later. They tried a second time, but she miscarried early in the pregnancy. Then the Saint Louis people wanted to get rid of her. They didn't have an exhibit space for one cat. We had no leopards, so she was sent here. That was eight years ago. The exhibit really could serve for two cats, but she could never adjust to sharing it. Leopards aren't social in the wild. They're loners, not like lions. A few years ago we tried to house her with another female we had on loan, but it was just impossible. We wound up keeping Magda in the yard for six weeks." The yard was the enclosed area just outside. It was Camille's favorite place in the zoo. There was a big old cage there, so old the concrete floor was cracked and the grass came through in patches. It was set in the shade of two crape myrtle trees, where it was always cool, even on the hottest days. So Magda had spent six weeks there, away from the other cats, sleeping under the moon and the stars, probably the only nights she'd spent in the open air during her ten years of captivity.

Ellen had stopped speaking. Camille understood that the brief sketch of Magda's life, which had constituted a kind of eulogy, was over. The other cats had quieted down; the night house was unusually still. Camille stood up, rubbing her palms against her jeans. She wasn't sobbing, her breathing was regular, but her tears continued to fall. She tried to brush them away, to no avail. She might have been ashamed, but Ellen didn't appear concerned or surprised by her behavior. She followed Ellen, stepping down from the cage to the aisle. Without thinking, she began to pull the heavy gate closed behind her. Ellen touched her shoulder. "Leave it open," she said. "There's no reason to close it now."

Camille released the cold iron of the bars. It pleased her that the cage was to be left open.

"I'll do the necropsy in the morning," Ellen said. "But I'll have to get her in the cooler tonight. We'd better go get a stretcher."

"Sure," Camille said, walking with Ellen down the hall to the door. When they came out, it was raining, not hard, but steadily.

Ellen went out into the yard without a pause. Camille hesitated, then dashed out, easily catching up with Ellen. They walked side by side along the broken sidewalk and under the walkway.

It was dark, wet, and silent, and as Camille and Ellen made their way to the hospital, neither of them spoke. The lights were on, giving the white building the look of an outpost in a jungle. The women went inside, took up the stretcher from the surgery room, and went out into the rain again. They moved quickly, but by the time they got back to the night house, they were thoroughly soaked. The cats paced and growled, irritated by the continued intrusion into their night, unaware, Camille thought, that their diminishing numbers were down by one more. Magda's body seemed to have become more inert, heavy and stiff-looking. Now no one could mistake her rigidity for sleep. Ellen and Camille put down the stretcher and bent over her. As Camille ran her hand across the rough back and haunch, the unyielding, uncompromising hardness of death was communicated to her through her fingertips. This creature, who had been in life the definition of agility and litheness, was now as heavy and dull as stone. Ellen had her hands under the shoulders and head, waiting for Camille to get a grip on the hips. She passed one hand down over Magda's tail, holding the upper leg; then, sliding her other hand under the hip, nodded to Ellen that she was ready. They lifted the leopard easily, as if she were carved from a board, and laid her on the stretcher. Taking the poles of the stretcher between them, they stood up; Camille was surprised at how light it felt. They retraced their steps, down the hall, past the living, breathing, agitated cats, to the door, where Ellen pushed the light switch off with her elbow, then out into the dark, rainy night, back under the walkway to the small concrete building near the hospital, up to the door where a neat black plaque read NECROPSY ROOM. Ellen balanced one pole inside her elbow to get the door open, then directed Camille to lay the stretcher on the floor. She turned back to the door, found the light switch, and flicked it on.

It was an operating room, very like the one in the hospital, orderly, sterile, but different. There was no x-ray equipment, no setup for syringes, no oxygen tank. Instead, there were cutting tools of all sizes, knives and saws, and a wall of specimen jars. Ellen went to a long white case, like a freezer, opened the lid, then joined Camille, who stood blinking confusedly in the harsh light, which seemed to throw the grim purpose of the room into relief. Nothing was to be hidden here. As she helped Ellen lift Magda's body and carry it to the cooler, Camille fought down a rush of nausea. The image of Magda, so black against the gleaming, white interior of the cooler, seemed to burn into her eyeballs.

"I'll do it early tomorrow," Ellen said, closing the lid. "Before you get to work."

Camille only nodded, picturing the scene. Magda would be removed from the cooler and brought to the table to be cut open, taken apart, subjected to one final examination. The hacked-up remains would be shipped to Baton Rouge to be incinerated. Another indignity, Camille thought. Magda should be buried at midnight, by candlelight. For a moment she allowed herself a plan: she would come back after Ellen was gone and drag Magda out into the park for a proper burial. Save the flickering light of the candles, everything in this fantasy was black, black sky, black soil beneath the shovel, and Magda herself, black, being lowered into the black hole Camille would have dug for her.

But of course she couldn't do this. The park was patrolled by police, and Magda was too heavy for her to carry any distance. She stood idly, her hands dangling at her sides, her shoulders slumped forward, entertaining strange visions, unable to carry them out or give them up.

"Can I give you a ride home?" Ellen asked.

Camille came back to herself. Her first thought was that she did not want anyone to see the dreary house she shared with her mother. The second was that she didn't intend to go home. But she could think of no excuse, and Ellen was waiting. She stuttered out, "Yes, thanks."

As Camille and Ellen made their way to the hospital parking

lot neither of them spoke. They climbed into Ellen's car, an old rundown vehicle, not what Camille had imagined. Ellen threw her black bags in the back among a confusion of objects, some medical, some surprisingly domestic. Camille noticed a vacuum cleaner attachment and a pair of red sneakers.

"Which way?" Ellen asked as she started the engine.

"Down Magazine," Camille said. "It's not far. It's Lyons Street."

"I know where that is," Ellen said.

As they drove out into the empty, rainy streets, Camille tried to concentrate on the unusual sensation of riding in a car so late at night, but her thoughts veered resolutely back to Magda. She imagined the morning, only a few hours away, when she must go in to find the empty cage. She rubbed her eyes. She had stopped crying, she didn't know when, but her eyes burned and ached. They felt hot, and she knew they must be red and swollen. "I didn't think she would die," she said.

Ellen glanced at her, then looked back out at the street. The windshield wipers clicked repeatedly, an irritating mechanical punctuation in the soft, melodious patter of the rain. "It was fast," Ellen said. "I'm not sure what it was. I think it was viral. It could have been something she was carrying for years."

"From when she was in the wild?"

Ellen frowned. "That's a long time. It's unlikely, but it's possible."

"How many leopards are left?" Camille asked.

"In the wild?" Ellen replied. "It's hard to say. They're such solitary animals and they hunt at night, so it's hard to count them. Not many, though. Like all the big cats, they live mostly on reserves. Off the reserves they get killed because they run afoul of people, bother cattle, or get killed for their hides—that sort of thing."

Camille leaned her cheek against the cool car window. "Will they survive?" she asked.

"It's a gamble," Ellen replied. "I'd say not a good one. Theoretically, captive breeding programs could increase diversity, but, especially with the big cats, we're too successful. There's no place to put the surplus animals. Habitats are shrinking by the minute. We can't return them to the wild; there's just no place for them to go. That's why so many of our cats are on implants. If leopards are to survive, the world needs more leopards, but zoos don't. We won't have any trouble replacing Magda."

Camille listened to Ellen distantly, trying not to hear what she was saying; the sense of it penetrated her resistance. Wild animals, particularly the bigger ones, the dangerous ones, who took up space, were doomed. Zoos operated as arks, holding animals for the future, but it was a future that would never come. "Why is this happening?" Camille said.

"In a word?" Ellen said, a smile playing around her mouth. "Hamburger."

Outside the car the cluttered storefronts drifted by. They passed a bar Camille had been in once, and a small restaurant where the word *pizza* was spelled out in blue neon on a sign that gleamed coolly in the rain. Everyone who looks at it has to think the word *pizza,* Camille thought. She was annoyed at having been taken in by the sign. She looked at Ellen's profile in the dim light from the dashboard. She was sure of herself, Camille thought. Her husband had left her, Camille had heard one of her daughters had been arrested, but she didn't seem to miss a beat. The daughter had started appearing at the zoo in the afternoons, assisting Ellen, the rumors went. Camille had seen her once, walking alongside her mother, their heads inclined toward each other, talking amiably. The daughter said something Camille couldn't hear, but when she looked toward the path where Camille was pushing a wheelbarrow loaded with chicken wire, Camille saw that she was laughing. How strange that must be, Camille thought, to have a mother who makes you laugh.

"Don't you ever want to give up?" Camille said softly.

Ellen caught on Camille's averted face an expression of such intensity that she did not reply at once lest she give the wrong answer. Camille looked down at her hands, white and lifeless in the dark pool of her lap. Perhaps, she thought, Ellen had not heard her question.

The clicking windshield wipers began to squeak against the glass, a sound so irritating that Ellen slapped the handle to turn them off. "No," she said, "I don't want to give up. I don't like some of the compromises I have to make. But that's the deal."

They had come to the corner of Lyons Street. Ellen asked, "Right or left?"

"Right," Camille said. A panic seized her. She had to think of a way to escape. She could see her mother's house; the light was still on. She was awake, of course, waiting, growing angrier by the minute. Camille let the house go by. She fished a key out of her back pocket and gestured toward the houses on the next block. "It's on the left," she said. She chose a bigger double with a covered doorway off to the side, partly obscured by a bottle brush tree. "That one," she said. Ellen pulled the car up to the curb. "Come by the hospital tomorrow afternoon," she said. "I may have some answers for you."

"Sure," Camille said. "Thanks for the ride." She threw the car door open and slammed it behind her, darting through the rain to the porch. Ellen leaned across the seat to see that she got there. The tree obscured her view, but she saw Camille go up the steps. She couldn't see the door. She waited a moment; then she thought she saw a light go on in the house. Camille, she thought, was a little like Celia; she took things hard. She made a U-turn to get back to Magazine. The rain was letting up. By the time she got home it would probably be over.

46

Camille jumped off the porch steps and walked into the darkness at the back of the house. She stumbled over a hose coiled near a drainpipe, and fell to one knee in the wet grass. A light went on in the house. She stayed perfectly still, listening to the sound of water running through the pipes. The light went out, and she got to her feet. She went back to the sidewalk, pausing only to ascertain that Ellen was gone, and walked back toward Magazine, passing her mother's house on the far side of the street. The rain was letting up —it was only a drizzle—but she was wet and chilled. She saw the light shining in her mother's window, in what she called the den, a word that always struck Camille as appropriate, the place where she lay in wait, gazing vacantly at the flickering images on the television screen, pouring out another glass of gin, ready to spring. Camille was exhausted and heartbroken; she would have liked to lie down and rest, but the thought of the gauntlet she would have to run to get to her uncomfortable sofa bed was more than she could bear. She didn't know where she was going, only that she wasn't going home.

Magazine Street was well lit, wide, empty. She knew the buses ran only every hour. It was an impossibly long walk to Canal Street, but she preferred to keep moving. Her wet clothes clung to her, the light rain ran down her cheeks and dripped from the ends of her hair, but she was only dimly aware of it. She thought of Magda, of her cold, still body lying in the softly humming cooler, in the dark, empty room, no more than meat now, like the slices of cows and pigs in refrigerators all over town. Or like the rabbits Magda herself had once delighted in ripping apart, lying on her slab in the night house, her yellow eyes nearly closed with pleasure.

A car passed Camille, the tires hissing on the wet asphalt, then another. She looked back, but there was no bus in sight. She crossed Napoleon Avenue, after which the street quickly deteriorated. It grew darker, certainly more dangerous; the buildings were disreputable and dingy. But Camille felt impervious to danger. She passed two men coming out of a bar, arguing loudly. They didn't seem to notice her. Perhaps, she thought, her grief made her invisible. Over her shoulder this time, several blocks away, she could see the lights of the bus coming toward her. She had plenty of time to reach the next stop, where she stood patiently, clutching the change she dug out of her jeans pocket, until the bus pulled up and the doors snapped open before her. The driver, a black woman, scarcely looked at her as she dropped her coins into the machine. The bus was empty; the air was frigid from the air conditioning. Camille took a seat near the front, close to the aisle, as far from the vent as she could get.

It was a long ride to Canal Street, but it seemed to Camille to pass quickly. They stopped only twice, to pick up two women near Touro Hospital, then to discharge them near Thalia Street. By the time the bus reached Canal, the rain had stopped. Camille's clothes were still damp, and she was so cold her teeth chattered, yet her eyes and the inside of her mouth felt hot. As she stepped down to the pavement, the jolt that came up from her feet passed through her body like an electric shock. Her head snapped back and a puff of air burst from her throat. She looked around nervously, wondering if anyone had seen her, had noticed her discomposure, but save a young couple who leaned against a wall absorbed in each other, there was no one about. She crossed Canal Street hurriedly; it was too open, too exposed, and she wanted most of all to be unseen, to disappear. This would be possible once she got into the Quarter. Even if she began talking to herself, which she knew was a distinct possibility, no one would notice her there. Her head was filled with a rushing sound, like a strong wind, or water crashing relentlessly against a rocky, recalcitrant shore. She was both afraid and fearless. When she turned the corner onto Chartres she felt she was plunging into an abyss, yet she did not hesitate. She stopped at the first bar she came to, an ugly, dark room where a few men and one loud, worn-out woman were arguing heatedly about whether the woman had been within her rights to hit the man she lived with. As she took a stool at the bar, Camille underwent a cursory inspection from the bleary, violent eyes of this group. She noticed that the woman had a thin, dark brown scar, raised like a vein in a dry leaf, running from the inside corner of one eye across her cheek nearly to her ear. Camille looked away hastily at the bartender, a wizened, mean-looking man, who said suspiciously, "What do you want?"

She had two drinks, swallowing them down quickly, keeping her eyes on the smeared red plastic surface of the bar. By the time she finished the second, the noise in her head had smoothed out to a steady buzz. She paid the bill, slipped off the stool, and went back out into the street. The air was still damp, but the clouds had disappeared, leaving the black smooth dome of the sky glittering with stars, but Camille scarcely noticed it; indeed, she could hardly see it, for the street was well lit. None of the people who walked along the sidewalk, moving from bar to bar, thought of looking up; nor, if they were asked the next day what sort of night it had been, would they have been able to say. In the branches of the trees, which brooded together in small groups, on the old courthouse

lawn, in the occasional patio or playground, the birds were quiet;
the world had gone to sleep. Some creatures stirred; this was their
time, rats and waterbugs, roaches, a few cats not so domesticated
they had forgotten how to hunt, and the sleepless, restless humans
who like Camille dreaded the coming of daylight.

She walked to Toulouse Street and went into another bar, one
she had been in before, with Eddie. He had disappeared weeks ago,
nor had she really any wish to see him, but the place made her
remember the brief period of happiness she had enjoyed, when she
had felt herself desired and imagined that she was in love. Now she
saw what an illusion that had been, how absurd she must have
seemed, with her unsolicited appearances, her unwanted presents,
her yearning for domesticity and affection. Where had she gotten
the idea that the simple daily happiness she imagined was possible?
From television, she supposed, and advertisements. It was certainly
not from the observation of actual people, or from her slight acquaintance with literature, in which happiness was always as she
had found it to be, elusive, imaginary, a lie designed by some
malevolent force, God or possibly the author, to drive the characters to despair.

She found a place at the bar, which was not crowded, though
there were several people talking and laughing together at one end.
It was a less volatile place than the first bar, and she was less
noticeable. She ordered her drink and sat over it, drinking slowly
now, oblivious of her surroundings.

A man sitting at the far end of the bar got up and moved next
to her. She looked at him absently as he climbed onto the barstool;
he was middle-aged, balding, overweight, drunk, unattractive in
every way and serenely unaware of it. "Can I buy you a drink?" he
said.

"Sure," Camille said, assessing her half-empty glass. "But I
don't want to talk to you."

"Oh," he said, pretending dismay. "Why not?"

Camille leaned away from him, for he had stretched out his
hand to touch her. She kept her head lowered, but her eyes focused

coldly on his face, and she felt her upper lip lift at the corner, drawing in a warning hiss of air. This seemed momentarily to sober the man, who dropped his hand to the bar, saying, "Oh, hey. It's nothing to get upset about."

Camille slipped down from the barstool. "You can pay for that one," she said, indicating the glass on the bar. She went out into the street.

She walked back across Chartres Street to the bar she liked most, where the old waiter was always polite and she could take a small table on the street or in the patio. The drinks were more expensive, but she knew she would be allowed to sit in peace. There were a few people inside, a couple at a table and two men at the bar. Camille took the table beneath the painting of Judas's hands. As she waited for her drink she thought of the unpleasant man, of how he had been taken aback by her look, because, clearly, he knew there was something wrong with her, something off. He had thought her anger out of proportion to his provocation. Lucky for him, she thought, I don't carry a gun. And then she thought— and it seemed odd to have such a thought—that there were millions of people in the world who had actually killed another person.

She drank steadily, quietly, signaling now and then to the waiter for another, or watching the few patrons drift out. This bar, unlike so many, was not open all night. It closed for a few hours at four, which was rapidly approaching. At last the waiter brought her the check, setting it on the table without comment. Camille pulled several bills from her pocket and studied them carefully. She was running out of money; if she left only a small tip, she could have two, maybe three drinks somewhere else.

When she got to her feet she understood that she was drunk, but not so much that she couldn't find her way to the bathroom. After she had relieved her bladder, she sat for a few moments trying to read the graffiti on the walls. It was the usual confusion, declarations of love, mini-debates on the subject of lesbianism, an outrage to one woman, a religion to another. Some women had simply written their names and the date of their visits, adding compliments to the city: LOVE YA' NEW ORLEANS, or GREAT TOWN. Near the door handle someone had scrawled, in red ink, DYSLEXICS UNTIE. Camille read this a few times before she understood it. For the first time that day, she laughed. "That's pretty good," she said. Her voice sounded strange, distant. She stood up to arrange her clothes, and her stomach churned and lurched dangerously. At the sink she found her own reflection gazing back at her mournfully. Her hair was dry, but it hung limp and uneven around her pale, sad face. She combed it with her fingers, then bent down over the sink and splashed water over her cheeks and eyes. When she reached for a towel, she found the dispenser was empty. "Of course," she said, wiping her face against the sleeve of her blouse. She went out of the bathroom to find the dark, cool room empty, and as she passed the patio she could hear the light clinking of the glasses the old waiter was gathering up on a tray. It seemed quiet, serene, utterly safe, and for a moment she wanted to stay. Perhaps the waiter would sit with her and have one last drink; they would talk; he would take a liking to her; they would become friends. As she had this thought he appeared in the doorway, taking slow, careful steps, gripping the tray in both hands. He looked weary beyond speech and so absorbed in the task of getting the tray to the bar without dropping any of the glasses that he didn't even notice Camille, who crossed the room quickly and let herself out at the closed doors.

The street was empty as well, though it did not have the comfortable atmosphere of the old bar. It was cool, damp, and sinister. She walked along as briskly as she could toward the Cathedral, but the sidewalk was uneven and she stumbled, reaching out to steady herself against a lamppost, and again against the glass front of a shoe store. She found herself gazing confusedly at a colorful display of expensive shoes, arranged as if they had been kicked off by tired party-goers. A single gold high-heeled shoe stood upright on a raised display, like a black velvet throne, surrounded by a corona of fake jewels. Camille battled down a wave of nausea, and she felt a clammy, sickish relief as a line of perspiration broke over her forehead. It was important, she thought, to keep moving.

The street opened out gracefully at its juncture with Jackson Square, and the lights aimed at the façade of the Cathedral reflected on the strip of flagstone before it, so that the scene was as bright as day. Camille hurried across it, feeling she had stumbled onto a stage. She was eager to get into the wings before it was discovered that she did not know her lines. There was no one about, not even a policeman. Through the padlocked gates of the dark, tree-shrouded square, she could see the Café du Monde, lit up as always and far from empty. A clatter of cups and soft voices drifted out across the wide street. As Camille approached she saw a young woman in a floor-length dress of green satin, bare-shouldered and blond, lean over the shoulder of a handsome man in a tuxedo and playfully shake the powdered sugar from her beignet onto his perfectly pleated trousers. He struggled to his feet, laughing and complaining, twisting her arm until, with a shriek of mock pain, she agreed to give up the bit of fried bread.

Camille moved away from this spectacle toward the river. She climbed the broad steps to the platform, surprising a couple locked in an embrace on one of the benches. The woman, who Camille noted was neither young nor beautiful, gave her a quick, critical glance, then returned her attention to the man, whose hands were occupied in a frenzied and continual kneading of her large breasts. Camille ducked her head and walked to the railing, where she could look down over the slow, black, roiling expanse of the river.

Everything was too close together, she thought, beauty to ugliness, death to life. Or perhaps it was only that she was peculiarly placed to notice. The woman in the green dress, only steps away, would never be in a position to see this coarse public mating which Camille had blundered into and which continued now behind her. She could hear the couple struggling with their clothes, the man's guttural groaning. No one seemed to care what she saw or what she thought. She didn't want to turn back, for there was no way to leave without passing the couple, so she went down the steps to a wooden walkway, across the railroad tracks, to the rocks at the river's edge. Here it was dark and still; the bright world of the café seemed far away. As she looked down at the rocks, she could detect a sinuous motion; then, as her eyes adjusted to the darkness, she saw that there were rats moving about near the walkway. She counted four. They too were indifferent to her; they seemed urgent, darting from one hiding place to another, or engaged in burrowing in the oily black silt that glittered poisonously among the scattered rocks. The walkway ended here, perhaps twenty feet from the river. The water lapped and swirled up continuously over the rocks near her feet. The ugly rats moved darkly, busily. A line from a poem she had studied in school came to her: "And I the while, the sole unbusy thing." It was about a man, she recalled, the poet himself, watching birds, or perhaps it was bees. She thought of Magda. If Magda could stand on this spot, she would know exactly what to do. She'd have a rat for dinner and then a long cool drink from the river. Nothing here would appall her, and she would be able to see perfectly well in the dark.

Camille felt she was perched at the edge of the known world. Beyond this, everything was exploration. She stepped out onto the slippery rocks.

Immediately she fell forward, throwing out her hands to keep from pitching face down. One hand found grimy sand, and she supported herself on it, but the other slipped between two rocks and encountered something sharp. She winced as she felt the skin of her palm give. The cut was sudden, sharp, and deep. She fell back on her knees. The ooze gave way beneath her as her sneakers sank into the wet sand, and she clutched her injured hand to her chest. She could see the blood, which looked black, welling up quickly, and felt the pain behind it like a shout from the horrified nerve ends. She looked back toward the walkway, then out at the water. If she crawled a few feet she would reach a shallow grassy pool where she could bathe her hand. She knew the river was so polluted that it was a kind of antiwater, not useful for cleaning anything, but the pain drove her out to it. She plunged her injured hand into the cool water and held it there a moment while a soft breeze lifted her hair from her face. Her mouth and throat were so dry she could hardly swallow. She brought her hand up to look at it, and for a moment, before the blood started up again, she could see the cut. It was small, squarish, a puncture deep in the fleshy part of her palm. If only she had a handkerchief. A rush of nausea reminded her of how much she had drunk. She had only time to turn away from the pool before her stomach contracted violently and she vomited, leaning over a depression made by the contiguity of three rocks, like a bowl that opened into the river, a serendipitous arrangement for which she was pathetically grateful. Gradually she became clearheaded, but dislocated, for she was certainly in a world she hardly recognized. She turned back to the pool, crouching low over the water, leaning on her good hand, using her injured hand to push the water toward her mouth. At first she thought only to rinse her mouth, but the water was cool and did not taste as bad as she had expected, so she swallowed some of it. She heard the scratching of the rats nearby, though none came close to her, and the sudden cry of a bird flying low along the shore line. She raised her head, wary but unafraid. Across the river she could see the bright lights of the ferry just leaving the Algiers landing. It whirled out into the water, looking gay and light, but Camille knew the engines were noisy and powerful and battled the current all the way. If she waded out into the river, she would not go far before she would be swept off her feet, carried away, rolled down to the sandy bottom like a bit of scrap wood. She might not surface until she reached the Gulf of Mexico. The vision was both so horrifying and attractive that it brought her to her feet. She scrambled back over the rocks to the wooden walkway, holding her wounded hand closed and away from her side.

The platform marked a border between two worlds, and as Camille stood looking down at herself she saw that what was inevitable in one was unacceptable in the other. Her jeans and shoes were muddy and wet, her shirt was stained with blood. She made her way back to the stairs. Her hand throbbed, and the roaring in her head recommenced as she staggered up into the confusion of light and sound on the platform. The couple was gone. Camille sank down, breathless, on the bench they had vacated.

Once more she thought of Magda, and a memory came unbidden, a small incident that had happened only a few weeks before when she was passing her lunch hour, as she often did, standing in front of Magda's exhibit. The leopard was stretched out on her cliff, showing her small audience only the tip of her tail and one paw, when suddenly she leaped to the ground and began pacing back and forth across the front of the exhibit. She went to her fake stream, crouched and lapped at the water, then, seeming sleepy and indifferent, she sat down, facing the delighted onlookers. Murmurs of approval passed among them; this was something to see. As Camille stretched forward over the rail to get a better view, Magda's head came up abruptly; she saw and recognized her keeper. She stood, took a step forward, her yellow eyes fixed intently on Camille, her ears up and alert to catch the sound of her breath, her nostrils flared to take in her smell. A boy standing nearby turned to Camille. "He's watching you," he said.

Camille felt her cheeks warm and flushed with pleasure as she looked down at the boy's sweat-smudged face, into his curious and admiring eyes. "I'm her keeper," she said. "I take care of her. She knows me."

"I take care of her," Camille said, to no one now, to the dark night around her, and the words tasted bitter in her mouth. I'm so tired, she thought. She stretched out on her side, her legs curled up, her cheek resting on the raised part of the seat. The sound of voices from the café drifted past her, but she couldn't make out what they said. When she closed her eyes, she was immediately asleep.

"You can't sleep here," the man was saying. "Come on. You have to get up." He had his hand on her shoulder, shaking her, though not roughly. She sat up on the bench without protest. "I'm sorry," she said.

"What did you do?" he asked. "Take a swim in the river?"

Camille looked down at her muddy clothes, which were still wet. Her shoes were caked with mud. "I fell," she said.

"You'd better move on," he said. "Go on. Otherwise I'll have to take you in."

She got to her feet. The pain in her hand was sharp, but she kept it closed. She didn't want the policeman to see it. "I'm going," she said, moving toward the café. The taste in her mouth was so foul, she kept her face averted. The policeman didn't follow. He went down toward the river where she had been. Looking for a body, Camille thought.

There were a few people about on the sidewalk. She was careful not to look at them as she sidled past, keeping close to the buildings, her head down, her shoulders hunched forward as if she expected a beating. Soon it was not so brightly lit, though there was an opacity to the air that meant dawn was not far away. She knew a bar farther down on Decatur Street that never closed and was always dark. The clientele were the worst sort of people, dangerous and desperate. Most of them had good cause to avoid light. No one would notice her there, or if they did, they would take her for one of their own. A man would buy her a drink. This time she wouldn't refuse.

47

The painter, Jack, was heading back to his apartment after a late breakfast with a prospective buyer. He was in a foul humor, which was not unusual for him, but this time he had something to focus his energy on; the buyer had been, as he expected, rich, spoiled, and stupid. She reminded him of the women in his own family, all of whom he despised. Ordinarily he would have tried to make himself pleasant to her to facilitate the sale, but five minutes into the meeting he saw that this wasn't necessary. She was the kind who thrived on rudeness; she thought it proved he was a real artist. So in spite of his distaste for her he managed to enjoy himself, being spectacularly rude, working himself into a near frenzy of abuse for her milieu, for everything she represented, with her diamonds, her expensive clothes, and her impertinent characterization of herself as a patron of the arts. She would come to his studio, of course, and stand among the canvases making absurd remarks about his compositions or the dark brooding of his palette, and he would give her a little bourbon and then fuck her, which was, as they both knew, what she was actually paying for. He was muttering to himself, even flailing his arms to express his complete exasperation, as he rounded the corner of Barracks Street and stepped hard on Camille's left ankle.

For a moment he didn't know it was Camille. She was lying curled up like a sleeping child against a few low concrete steps that led to the door of the corner house. Her face was hidden in the crook of her arm. A street person, the painter thought. They should be hosed out of the Quarter with the rest of the trash. But as he was about to go on, she raised her arm and he recognized her.

"Good God," he said, "what are you doing here?" She rubbed her eyes with the back of one filthy hand, and he saw that she was rubbing away tears, for she left two streaks of moistened dirt across her cheeks. "And what are you crying about?" he added.

"You hurt my ankle," she said.

"Well, you shouldn't be lying on the sidewalk like that."

"And I hurt my hand," she added, opening her other palm carefully. The painter could see the black dried blood and, even through the dirt, the swollen red flesh around it. The cut was well on the way to infection. Camille tried to lift herself to one elbow but failed, falling back helplessly to the pavement with a whimper of pain. "I can't get up," she said.

"What happened to you?" the painter asked impatiently. The more he looked at her, the worse she seemed. Her clothes were bloody and filthy, her jeans were torn, her face looked bruised and bluish. Perhaps it was the contrast she presented to the well-heeled woman he had just left, or perhaps it was her resemblance to the tortured, muddy figures in his own paintings—he was never to know—but something about her touched his ordinarily unresponsive sensibilities. "This is pitiful," he said, bending over her. "You can't lie out on the street like this. The police will come and take you in."

"They don't want me," Camille murmured. Her eyes were closed; she seemed to be drifting away.

"I hate to touch you, you're such a mess," he said, but he did touch her. He pulled her shoulders up from the concrete and propped her against the wall. She opened her eyes briefly, with an expression so dazed and panicked she made him think of a trapped animal. "Do you know who I am?" he asked.

"I bit you," she said flatly.

"Yes, well, don't remind me of that. I'm going to try to get you to your feet, and if you bite me again I'll leave you to rot. You understand that much?"

"Yes," she said. She bent her knees and pushed herself up against the wall as he raised her by her armpits. She leaned against his side while he passed an arm reluctantly around her waist. A rank odor mixed of sweat, vomit, blood, and semen rose from her body and her clothes, offending his nostrils. "God, you stink," he said.

"That doesn't surprise me," she replied. Then she took a few steps, wincing at each one.

"Why can't you walk?" he asked, for she didn't seem to be favoring one foot over the other. She made no reply, and he saw that it was taking all her energy to make this slow progress. His apartment was three blocks away. At this rate, he thought, we'll never get there. And what was he going to do with her when he got there? Wash her; that much was certain. After that he would have to get rid of her.

Camille hobbled along at his side, sunk in confusion and fatigue. She tried to remember how she had arrived at the corner, but only lurid, disconnected flashes came to her. She remembered sitting at one bar, then another. A man had taken her into an alley and forced his penis into her mouth. There was another man there too, who held her hands. Though she had no money, she had never been without a drink. She hadn't eaten, and she had vomited until her stomach was empty; she remembered throwing up into a toilet somewhere. Part of her difficulty in walking was the pain in her stomach, which made it hard for her to straighten up. She thought it strange that she could remember clearly everything about the painter, but the recent events remained obscure. How long had she been lying on the sidewalk?

They arrived at the apartment. She leaned against the wall while the painter opened the gate. It was broad daylight; the sun was bright and hot in her face. By now, she thought, they knew she wasn't coming in. Her supervisor would have let the cats out and called in a volunteer to clean out the cages. Magda had already been cut up, put in a bag, and sent to the incinerator. "She is no more," Camille said.

The painter pulled her arm over his shoulder and helped her through the gate. "What are you talking about?" he said. He was having second thoughts about bringing her home, but he could think of nothing else to do with her. "I should have brought you to Shelbourne," he said. "You're his discovery, after all."

As they struggled to the staircase, the fountain in the patio bubbled joyfully, cooling the air, and the big plantain trees blocked the sun. Camille looked wearily back. "How beautiful it is here," she said.

The painter pulled her on. "I'd give you the tour," he said, "but I don't think you're up for it."

She laughed. "No," she said, "I guess I'm not." A stab of pain in her stomach twisted her smile into a grimace. "Oh, Jesus," she said, clutching the painter's shoulder.

"Did you get hit in the stomach?"

"No," she said. "I think I drank poison."

The pain diminished, and for a moment she could see clearly. When they got to the stairs, she was able to pull herself up by using the rail. The painter went ahead, unlocked and opened the door, and helped her up the last few steps.

"This is very nice of you," Camille said as she stepped into the cool, darkened foyer.

"I'll say," he agreed. "I must be out of my mind."

He closed the door and locked it. Camille heard the bolt shoot into the latch, a sound that had a pleasing quality of decision and finality to it. She looked around at the three graceful arches. Through the one in front of her she could see the gleaming fixtures of the kitchen sink. "Could I have a glass of water?" she said.

"You need more than a glass," the painter said. "You need a tubful." He went ahead of her into the kitchen. "Come this way," he said. "And take off those clothes."

Camille followed him. She was still unsteady on her feet, but she could lean on the wall as she went along, so she wasn't afraid of falling. Just off the kitchen was a small bathroom; she hadn't seen it before. The painter bent over the tub, turning the faucets and testing the water with his open palm. Camille went to the sink and filled the glass she found there, drank it quickly, then filled it again and drank half of that. She caught her reflection in the mirror over the sink; it startled her. Her skin was as white as milk; her eyes were sunken, dark, and lifeless. She looked down anxiously at her blood-and-dirt-encrusted hand.

"Do you want a shower or a bath?" the painter asked.

"I think I'd better start with a shower."

He stood up, pulling the shower curtain across the tub. Camille crouched down to untie her shoelaces while he stood watching. "Can you do it by yourself?" he asked.

"Yes. I think so. The water made me feel better."

"Leave this door open," he said, going out. "I don't trust you."

Camille undressed slowly, like an old person, she thought. She had to hold on to the sink with one hand and pull her jeans off with the other. She felt relieved to see her own body. Her clothes had protected it from dirt. It looked strong, young, inviolate. There was an ugly scrape on her knee such as children often have, but she was otherwise unmarked. She passed her hand over her breasts, down to her stomach, feeling mystified by her own vitality. How could she feel so wretched and still look so alive? She leaned into the tub, flipped the shower valve, and, holding on to a towel bar for support, climbed into the tub.

For a few moments she tried to ignore the confusion of her

thoughts, which surged in her head so densely as to seem almost tangible, and she felt she could detect their pressure behind her eyes and at her eardrums. She concentrated on the sensation of the warm water cascading over her head and shoulders and on the mundane business of washing her hair, which she accomplished with one hand, keeping her injured hand dry. When she had finished, she flicked the shower valve and closed the tub drain. She sat down carefully, easing herself into the steadily rising water, braced for the pain as she submerged her wounded hand, but it was not as bad as she feared. Sitting stiffly, she waited for the tub to fill, her legs stretched out before her, her shoulders hunched over, hopelessly sick, too weak even to lift the washcloth from the rack, too exhausted to cry. At length she turned off the water and leaned against the wall of the tub. She closed her eyes, but the lurching giddiness and the torrent of frightening images that accosted her in the darkness made her open them again at once. "Great," she said softly. "I can't close my eyes." The room was quiet. She could hear only the dripping of the tap and an occasional sound from the other room, the painter moving something. He was in his studio, she guessed.

She reached for the soap floating near her side. How odd that he used this old-fashioned soap, she thought, and odder still that it floated. What did they do to make it so light? She rubbed the bar back and forth over the hole in her hand until all the bits of dried blood and dirt dissolved and she could see the cut itself. It looked bad, but it would heal. She had always been healthy. She touched the cut, pressing the edge of it lightly.

She remembered falling on the rocks by the river, but why had she gone down there?

A condition of calm expectancy settled over her, easing the pressure of anxiety. A solution, she understood, was about to come to her. She took up the cloth and washed herself. The thing to do now was to finish this bath. Then, if she could sit alone for a few minutes, she would figure it all out.

When she stepped out of the tub, a wave of dizziness hit her, and she was forced to sit down on the closed toilet seat, her head over her knees. Still she kept her eyes open until she began to feel better. She reached up to pull a towel from the bar next to her and dropped it over her head and shoulders, too weak to bother arranging it. When she felt a shadow fall across the room, she looked up from under the towel to find the painter in the doorway, raising his cigarette to his impatient, cynical lips. "You're feeling better," he observed.

"I was dizzy," Camille replied. She eased the towel down under her arms and pulled it closed across her torso. "But I'm better now."

"What exactly happened to you?" he asked.

"I'm just trying to remember that."

He snorted. "You were drunk," he said.

Camille nodded agreeably. "That's true," she said, "but I'm trying to remember before that."

"You look like hell." He stepped into the narrow room, leaning across her to flick his cigarette ash into the sink. He had abandoned his role as her protector and resumed the one he clearly preferred, the put-upon, bored, but willing seducer and master sergeant. First he would insult her a little, then start giving orders. She remembered it perfectly. She leaned away from him, holding the towel to her breasts and casting a hopeless look past him toward the kitchen. If only he would offer her something to eat. She was weak from hunger, and she couldn't bear for him to approach her in this way just when she was on the brink of understanding what had brought her here, to this particular dead end. She had nothing, no money, no place to go, or no place she wanted to go. The painter stepped back, still watching her, formulating, she thought, a plan for her.

"Go and lie down on the bed," he said, turning away from her. "I'll check on you in a few minutes."

To her relief, he left. He went into his studio, and the sounds she had heard, of cans and jars being moved around, began again.

Perhaps she was wrong about him, she thought. She got up and walked wearily through the kitchen to his bedroom. He was right; she should lie down and get to the bottom of it all.

But the bottom, she knew, was always a little farther, a little deeper, than anticipated. So she had fallen in and through one illusion after another until she had come to this pleasant, quiet room, which was to be hers only for a few moments. She wished the painter would stay away, that she could sleep for a long, long time, undisturbed and unmolested. Perhaps when she woke up, she would find a way to untangle one thread from the vicious weave of her imagination and follow it to a conclusion. She perched on the edge of his bed, looking down at the night table. His cigarette pack and a plate of ashes cluttered the smooth dark surface of the wood.

She knew, of course—how could she have missed it—that there was something wrong with her, that she was inadequate and unlovable. This knowledge had stunted her, had crippled her, and though she had railed against it in her hopeless, incompetent way, like the explorer thrashing about in quicksand, her struggles had only made things worse. Now rage deserted her, and she was left with the dull conviction of her own worthlessness. She could hear the painter cracking ice into the kitchen sink. Before her, on the round table, there were a few carnations in a cut-glass vase. Once they had been beautiful, but they'd been left too long; the water was yellow, the petals faded, brown at the edges as if singed by a match, and they gave off an acrid odor of decay, which, combined with the smell of the ashes in the ashtray, was pervasive and sickening. A consummate weariness invaded her. She thought of Magda giving in to the anesthetic, lying on her stomach on the concrete floor, saliva pouring off her tongue, her front legs working helplessly, long after her back legs were useless to her, so that she dragged herself around in a circle, trying to escape the steady, relentless, all-conquering dark. Don't fight so hard, Camille had thought, watching her. Just give it up.

And she remembered Ellen's reply in the car—she seemed to

hear her cool, confident voice—"No, I don't want to give up." Then something else. Something about compromise. She didn't like it, but that was the deal.

Camille smiled at the recollection. It was true enough; that was the deal: nothing but compromise as far as she could see, stretching on forever, unlimited and illimitable compromise. Or so it must seem to someone like Ellen, who had, in fact, something, an ideal, a principle, some shred of dignity, that could be compromised. But Camille felt herself to be beyond that now. Perhaps this was a kind of liberty, she thought.

She could hear the painter, moving out of the kitchen, coming toward her. The ice tinkled gaily in the glass he was carrying. She didn't have much time. Quickly she reached out and opened the drawer of the night table, and there it was, just as she remembered. He would be surprised, probably wouldn't recall that he had let her see it. That was ironic. So much the worse for him, she thought.

When the painter arrived at the doorway, holding two drinks, his mouth dropped open so suddenly that his lighted cigarette fell onto the expensive carpet at his feet, but he didn't even look down to see it, couldn't drag his eyes away from Camille. She was naked —the towel had fallen away—and she sat awkwardly on the edge of the bed, holding his revolver across her lap. As he watched, she brought it up and laid the muzzle gently against her temple. Then she moved it slightly, settling it into the curve of bone beneath the skin. "Camille," he said. It was all he had time to say, but she didn't hear him, wasn't looking at him, and it was already too late. She had successfully concentrated all the remaining energy in her body into the simple and final task of squeezing the trigger.

After Elisabeth returned to Montague with her husband, her life became entirely a prison. In her brief absence Hermann had called in a locksmith, who had equipped her bedroom door with a lock that could be opened only from the outside. Every night and during the day, while Hermann was inspecting his fields, Elisabeth was closed up in this room. When Hermann was in the house she was required to be in his sight at all times. She still managed the housekeeping, supervised the servants, the purchasing, the menus. Occasionally she was allowed to play the piano after dinner. She carried on her regular correspondence, though every letter she sent or received was scrutinized by her husband.

She was given her liberty only once, on the day that André Davillier came to buy her servant Bessie. She hoped that this visit might signal a change, that her punishment might come to an end, but no sooner was André out of sight at the end of the long drive to

Montague than Hermann led her silently back up the stairs and locked her away again.

So she waited, alone in her room, day after day, with no one to talk to and no one she could trust. She slept little, read a great deal. Time passed very slowly.

She tried various strategies to disarm Hermann, to make him relent: reason, pleading, promises, anger, indifference. Nothing worked, yet every day she woke up feeling hopeful. She did not neglect her appearance, though she could no longer take any pleasure in it. Her beauty, she reflected, had brought her to this pass.

Hermann remained a mystery to her, as obdurate and implacable as stone. He saw to her comfort and was elaborately polite to her before the servants, but when they were alone he was silent and brutal. Sometimes at night, after he left her, she leaned on the window, looking down into the quiet moonlit yard and stroking her cheek, as her mother had done when she was a child, remembering the gentle, sweet, pleasure-laden life she had once enjoyed, detail by detail: the scent of the orange trees in her mother's garden, the sound of laughing voices pouring up the stairs while she dressed for a dinner party, the giddy rush of sensual confidence as she took the arm of a gentleman and turned out toward the other couples chatting gaily on the freshly polished floor while the violins raced up and down a scale or two and the dancing began. Bitter tears rose to her eyes, and she rubbed them away impatiently. It was useless to long for the past, but she was too wretched to rest in the present. Gradually her thoughts and energies coalesced on the only real hope she had: the promise Mambo Pitou had given her in that hot, frightening, feverish room on the last night of her freedom. The spirit that had come to her that night, leaving her unconscious in Lucinde's arms, would come again. She turned from the window and threw herself down on the carved prie-dieu before the two statues of the Virgin and Saint Michael that had belonged to her grandmother and prayed fervently, to these and to all the saints, that the spirit might come to rescue her soon.

But only her husband came to her. Night after night he sat across the dining table watching her. He seemed fascinated by the change captivity had wrought upon her. She gave up all artifice, all pretense of pleasure in his company. Later, when he came to her room, she would turn her back on hearing his key in the lock. When he spoke to her, she answered coldly or not at all. When he embraced her, she did not struggle, nor did she give in. She turned to ice in his arms. This did not displease him; in fact, her indifference seemed to increase his passion. He sweated and moaned over her, called her name as if she were dear to him. Then, when he was spent, he got up silently and left her, carefully locking the door behind him.

It was after just such a visit, on a humid, hot night in July, that Elisabeth's prayers were answered.

Hermann had come to her, forced himself upon her, and left without speaking. She got up from her bed, sick with hatred, and went to her basin to wash herself. She took down her dressing gown and pulled her hair up off her neck, fastening it loosely with a comb. After she had washed carefully between her legs, she sponged her neck and shoulders, letting the lukewarm water run down over her breasts and her back. Hermann had nailed the windows in her room so that they could be opened only a foot or so. The heat was stifling; it combined with her anger to take her breath away. Still wet from her bath, she went to the window and looked out hopelessly at the flat black sky, the milky, luminous moon. She covered her eyes with her fingertips, for her head was throbbing, and she stood very still, listening to her own thoughts. Then she heard something beyond this litany of rage, something outside her head, a rustling in the hot, still air, leaves and grass moving gently but unmistakably. She dropped her hands and looked down into the garden. Something moved at the edge of the trees; but then, as she watched, her mouth open with astonishment, her eyes wide in disbelief, the animal stalked onto the open lawn.

It was a great black cat, moving toward the house. As she

watched, it stopped, looked off to the trees, turned back, lifted its head, and fixed its strange bright eyes suddenly on her face.

She wanted to speak, to welcome her deliverer, but when she opened her mouth no words came to her. She breathed slowly, trying to control her fear. As she watched, the motionless body of the leopard seemed to fade into the darkness around it until only the eyes, which never flickered, remained, glowing eerily in the night. A combination of terror and elation drained her limbs, and she slid down against the sill to her knees. Her throat tightened; she coughed. The leopard's mouth opened slightly, and she saw the gleam of its canine teeth, heard the rasp of air deep in its throat, but still it did not move. The golden eyes, like twin shafts of light, penetrated with uncanny accuracy the darkest corners of her pounding, incredulous heart. She closed her eyes. Her head was filled with unruly images, violent and cruel. She opened her eyes at once. Nothing had changed. The leopard was still there, and she was kneeling on the carpet, mesmerized by the animal's unblinking, determined regard. One of us has to move, she thought, and she tried to move, to lift her hand, but she couldn't do it. Then come to me, she thought, giving up all resistance, for I can't come to you.

She closed her eyes again, but this time there was only darkness and the sound of her own breathing, even and deep. She was weary, her head ached, and she realized dimly that she was hungry. When was the last time she had eaten? She opened her eyes again. She was outside on the lawn, looking up at the figure of a woman she did not recognize, looking away at the world around her through the leopard's golden eyes.

And the world was entirely different. The night was as bright as day; she could hear everything, even the smallest movement of a leaf, the flickering of a mouse's whisker in the thicket nearby. She could smell something strong, something dead. The smell assailed her and tempted her; she was ravenously hungry. She followed it along the narrow path near the garden wall, around the side of the house to the front porch. She was cautious, alert. She did not ordinarily go anywhere near human habitations. She had done that once and awakened in a cage. But the smell was so enticing, she couldn't resist. She crept carefully up the walkway, up onto the steps of the porch.

The door was open; all was darkness within. As she crouched low, she saw framed by the doorway, like an offering, the bloody carcass of a rabbit on the porch floor. Heedlessly, she rushed up the stairs and fell upon the dead animal. She gripped the head between her strong forepaws and tore into the hip; she could feel the satisfying snap as the bone separated from the socket. A sensation of well-being flooded through her. Hunger had driven her, would drive her again, but now she experienced only the deep, sensual pleasure of eating.

There was a movement inside the house at the top of the stairs. She raised her head, the bloody haunch dangling from her jaws, and looked up into the darkness. A man appeared, carrying a lamp. He did not see her—she was as black as the shadows that shrouded her—but he seemed agitated nonetheless. He called out a name, took a few steps down, stopped on the landing, called again, gruffly, imperiously.

She dropped the rabbit. The man heard the soft thud as it hit the floor and turned toward her. She knew him; he was the man who took everything away. He would try to take her rabbit. A hard, smoldering coal of rage flamed up in her head. She crouched again, low, her stomach nearly touching the floor, and crept forward soundlessly, steadily, first one step, then two more. The man held the lamp out before him, but he couldn't see past the foot of the stairs. He was sweating from heat and fear; she could smell it. Another step, another. She was inside the doorway. She could hear the shift in his breathing from deep to shallow as his heart rate increased. His mouth opened slightly; she heard his tongue touch the back of his teeth. She stretched her forelegs, shifting her weight onto her powerful hind legs. Every muscle, every fiber of her body was intention; her concentration was complete. There was nothing but the man and her perfect apprehension of the man. He could feel it now himself, though he didn't know it. He lowered the lamp and, stretching out one hand to touch the stair rail, leaned forward. She felt the slight motion of his shoulders, the delicate imbalance in his legs. It was her signal to move. Still in her crouched position, she ran swiftly, silently, across the remaining space to the foot of the stairs. Adrenaline flushed into her veins like an intoxicating liquor, and the air parted around her, creating a pathway she poured herself into, up the stairs, her big paws scarcely touching the carpet, and up into the air at the man's confused, gesticulating body. In a delirium of purpose, her claws, her teeth found their marks, and she held on to him as he let out one startled cry and fell sideways onto the landing. He fought her, kicked her, his fists pounded her head, but she hung on, her eyes closed, steadily tightening her jaws while the blood filled her mouth and poured down her throat. The beating of her own heart filled her ears, growing stronger, louder, faster, even as the man's heart flagged beneath her paws. His struggles diminished, became only the unfocused twitches and reflexes of defeat. Gradually she loosened her grip on him, opened her jaws, lifted her head, and peered into the dark, still air of the house.

She listened. Nothing stirred. The only sound was her own labored breathing. The man's corpse lay staring up at her, his face contorted in a grimace of terror, his throat a gaping, bleeding hole. She looked down at her hands, which were spread wide over his chest, covered in blood, and, with a sinking sensation of nausea and disgust, she realized her mouth was full of blood. She gagged, lowered her head, and spat. Dropping back on her knees, she wiped her mouth on her sleeve. Calmly, she got to her feet and adjusted the open bodice of her dressing gown. She was tired and thirsty, but she felt lightheaded, giddy, as if she had drunk too much wine. Hermann's keys lay next to her bare feet on the carpet; she pushed at them with her toes, then stooped down to pick them up, turning away from her husband for good, she thought, forever.

She would have a glass of sherry, then some music. Her spirits soared. She could already hear the triumphant, joyous strain of the music she would play, abandoning herself to it, as she had not done for so long, with the pure concentration of a mind and soul at peace, entirely and perfectly free.

49

Paul stopped the microfiche and backed it up to the small headline that had caught his attention: ANIMALS MISSING FROM TRAVELING EXHIBITION. He brought his face close to the screen, squinting at the smaller print beneath it. "Mr. James Renault," he read, "who has for so many years provided our population with fascinating spectacles in the line of fireworks and fighting animal exhibitions, regrets to inform the public that three animals escaped from his menagerie on Wednesday, April 2, at his temporary quarters near Port Hudson. The missing animals were, to wit: one strong Attakapas bull, one black Asian leopard, and one Canadian bear. These animals are extremely dangerous and valuable, and Mr. Renault would appreciate any information leading to their recovery."

Paul sat back in his chair. "I'll be damned," he said.

He knew all about this Renault fellow. His handbills were not difficult to come by. There had once been a big rotunda out near the river where he staged his shows, which were popular with everyone, even children, who were admitted at half price. Paul had seen one of the bills at the archives downtown not long ago, advertising what was described as "an interesting exhibition." He remembered the sequence: "first, a bull against six dogs; second, six bull dogs against a Canadian bear; third, a beautiful tiger against a black bear." He had been struck by that description, "a beautiful tiger." If the tiger survived, he was pitted against a bull, and if the bull was unfortunate enough to survive that match, Renault announced his intention to attach fireworks to his back, which would produce, he promised, "a most entertaining amusement."

There were certainly some things about history that were worth forgetting, Paul thought. He rarely mentioned events of this kind in his romantic evocations of the past. His readers had a vested interest, as he did himself, in the notion that the past had something to offer the present, that it was not merely the record of how vicious the human animal has always been. Paul spared his readers this conclusion, but lately he had begun to wonder if he wasn't being unfair to them by doing so. He had never allowed himself to dwell on the dark side of his historical discoveries—to do so would be another kind of lie—rather, he hinted at it, allowed it to be glimpsed in the distance, through a lace curtain or grillwork, or at the end of a long alley of trees.

He copied out the brief notice and checked the date and the name of the newspaper. Tomorrow he'd scour the issues that covered the two months prior to and after this article. It was a lucky break, a lucky day. He had been looking in the Port Hudson paper for some record of the arrest of a slave who had run away from André Davillier's plantation and instead he had found this surprising notice, which, he knew at once, was the key to the mystery of Hermann Schlaeger's violent death.

But was it possible? Port Hudson wasn't more than twenty miles from Saint Francisville. The date of the article was four months before Hermann's death. That would mean the leopard had not gone far but had somehow managed to elude all efforts, and these may have been considerable, toward its recapture. It must also have left little or no evidence of its continued existence, for Paul felt sure this was the only reference to its being at large in the area. How could that have happened? The leopard might have been recaptured and kept captive by someone who had a use for it. It might have been stolen to begin with. Or it might have laid low, living on what it could kill, and there would have been plenty of game in the dense wilderness between the two towns.

Tomorrow, Paul decided, he would check on those possibilities. For tonight he only wanted to speculate. He switched off the machine and carried the plastic sheet to the desk. Mrs. Wharton smiled at him, as she did every day. She had read all his books and was herself an amateur historian of the local area. He nodded to her, dropping the sheet into the box on the counter. Perhaps she wouldn't like his next book, he thought, but it might be good for her.

He walked out into the parking lot and spent a few aggravating minutes trying to remember where he had put his car. Then he spotted it, only two rows from where he thought it must be. The air around him was cool, dry, breezy, coming in from the north, over the lake, and right down his shirt collar. He ducked into the car, slammed his door against the wind, turned on both the engine and his tape player. Instantly the closed space was flooded with sound. It was Mahler, revving up to a fever pitch of longing. Paul switched on the headlights and eased the car out of the space, comfortably enclosed in his own perfectly controlled, intensely interesting, mobile little world.

As he drove away from the university, he decided to take the longer route across town, along Bayou Saint John and past the park, which was scenic, and all the way up Carrollton Avenue, which was always slow. On the way he would try to fit this remarkable, unexpected piece of the puzzle of Hermann Schlaeger's murder into its proper place.

For it was murder; he was convinced of that, though Elisabeth was not, as she believed to the end, the murderer. A dozen scenarios presented themselves. As was his habit, Paul tried to elaborate the most practical, the least fantastic.

The few reports on Elisabeth's conduct after her arrest stressed two points: her insistence on her own guilt, and her calm, proud demeanor. Though her statements were the wildest mumbo-jumbo, Paul knew enough about the superstitious inclinations of the population to suspect that any attempts to discredit her story of transformation were largely for show. Somehow she had caused the death of her husband; on this everyone was agreed. What struck Paul most about her brief statement was that she'd gotten it wrong. At the ceremony she had attended with Lucinde, she had been visited by a spirit, and she claimed it was this spirit which had come again the night of her husband's murder. But anyone who had made, as Paul had, even a cursory study of voodoo knew that, while animal spirits might occasionally visit humans, "riding" them like horses into all sorts of mischief, human spirits did not ever enter animals.

But if, as Paul now believed, Hermann was actually killed by the leopard that escaped from Mr. Renault's collection, it was not surprising that Elisabeth, who had been promised deliverance by a supernatural force, should, when she saw the leopard, conclude she was responsible for its appearance. How bizarre, Paul thought, smiling to himself. What an incredible coincidence.

There remained a few questions. The most obvious were: Why had the leopard approached the house? Who had opened the front door? And how had Elisabeth escaped from her bedroom?

Paul came to Claiborne Avenue, where he no longer turned left to go home. He had made the turn unconsciously, so regularly, and for so long that he sometimes found himself changing lanes to be ready for it. It made him think of Ellen every time. Today those thoughts were bitter, for he had spoken to her that morning on the subject of Celia's court case, which had been resolved unexpectedly and favorably, without a trial. The lawyer had found a technicality, something having to do with the arrest itself, and the judge had dismissed the charge. "Saving the taxpayers' money," Paul had joked, but Ellen responded testily, "That depends on which taxpayers you mean. I got the lawyer's bill this morning." Between the divorce lawyer and Celia's lawyer, the added expense of his new apartment, and the steady rise in the girls' school tuition, money was a problem for both of them now, and Ellen did not try to hide her resentment. Paul changed the subject whenever possible. He asked about Celia. Her grades were up; the last time she had lunch with him she was nearly cheerful. She liked working at the zoo with her mother, had made a friend of Beth, the technician, who took her horseback riding on weekends. Surely this was something to be pleased about, something for which Ellen could take some credit. He tried to compliment her on the success of her strategy for bringing Celia through a difficult time, but Ellen only responded testily, "She's not out of the woods yet."

What woods? Paul thought impatiently as he accelerated past the corner. His daughters had everything they could possibly want. They were young, good-looking; soon they would be off on their own; but Ellen spoke of them as if they were recovering from a fatal illness.

Every time he talked to her he wound up irritated. She never called him, never sounded pleased to hear from him. Yet several times a day he thought of things he wanted to tell her. He resolved to call her less often, to make a list of matters that concerned them both and bring them up all at once. He wondered how long she would wait if he didn't make the effort to call. He asked her questions about her work, her problems with the house, the girls, the pets; she never asked him anything about his life. She seemed to think he didn't have one anymore, or that Donna was his life. And of course he was never supposed to mention Donna's name. If he did, he could feel the temperature drop through the phone.

In this agitated state he arrived at his new home. Donna's car was in the driveway. She left work at five and usually had dinner ready by seven, unless he called to say he would be late. When he opened the front door the aroma of something cooking—something delicious, he knew, for she was an excellent cook—drifted down the steep uncarpeted stairwell and enticed him up the stairs. She would be glad to see him; she always was, as if, he sometimes thought, she was surprised that he came back. Now and then he caught a glimpse of himself through her eyes, a highly flattering perspective in which he was a romantic figure, mature, confident, an intellectual, a good catch. Perhaps the routine into which they had so immediately fallen was disconcerting. She had rearranged the furniture, painted and even papered the walls of the apartment herself, hung complicated heavy draperies that matched the bedspread. The apartment had a decorator look to it now. She consulted on these matters with the landlady, who had taken a liking to her at once, but she never asked Paul's opinion. She seemed blithely confident of her own taste, of her ability to turn a room, the apartment, the world, into a place where Paul would be comfortable.

He shrugged as he entered the kitchen, shrugging off a small, foolish misgiving. And there she was, standing at the stove, her long hair pulled back in a ponytail for ease while cooking. She turned, spoon in hand, her pretty face flushed from the heat, and smiled at him. "They had beautiful okra at the market," she said. "I'm making seafood gumbo."

At dinner he told her of his discovery: there actually was a real leopard loose in the area at the time of Hermann Schlaeger's death. She expressed surprise, enthusiasm, but when it came to speculating on the possibilities introduced by this new information, she seemed timid, even a little bored. Paul gave in. Really, he thought, it was not surprising that she was tired of the story of Hermann and Elisabeth. She wanted to show him some travel books she'd taken from the library, all about Egypt, with fascinating pictures. She was planning their trip as she had planned their bedroom, down to the thread count.

Later, after a delicious dinner, discussion of travel plans, some dalliance on the couch while listening to Brahms and Fauré, Donna yawned, stretched, kissed him affectionately, and went off to bed.

Paul sat for a while, drinking the wine left over from dinner, his mind wandering, his mood expansive and relaxed. He thought about Elisabeth Boyer, the beautiful, lively young woman whom Hermann had met at the Davilliers' dinner party, and Elisabeth Schlaeger, the grim, silent madwoman who stood impassively on the scaffold that rainy morning in Saint Francisville. Two different women, yet the second had been created from the first, like rock, under pressure. She made only one statement after the arrest, left an ordinary will, returning her estate and Hermann's as well, for she had inherited it, to her family.

Paul got up, went to his desk, turned on the lamp, and took a sheaf of pages from the side drawer: his notes, which had accumulated at an astounding rate. Donna had tried to persuade him to use a computer or to let her put them on a computer for him, but he refused. "My method resists mechanization," he explained. "And I like it that way."

He turned to André Davillier's description of what he had found in the house that morning. There was no mention of the heavy ring of keys that Hermann always had about him. The police inquest didn't mention the keys either. The investigator had been more concerned with documenting the quantity and location of every drop of Hermann's blood. What puzzled him was a smear of blood on the porch floor, in front of the open door. Presumably it had dripped from Elisabeth's hands, perhaps been smeared by the Davillier clan as they came to investigate. But why would Elisabeth have gone out to the porch after Hermann was dead?

Paul closed his eyes, leaning over the confusion of his notes, his head resting between his hands. Who else could have known about the leopard? Who was in the house that night? His head buzzed with details. He had seen the house; he knew exactly where the body lay, where the bedrooms were, Elisabeth's on one side of the landing, Hermann's on the other. He had seen how the front door opened into the entranceway, giving a view of the graceful curving staircase as well as the long hall that led back past the dining room to the kitchen, the larder, and the three small rooms where the house servants were lodged.

Paul sat back in his chair, his eyes opened wide. "It was Charles," he said.

Of course. It was Charles. He was in the house that night, though, like all the other servants, he had been found hiding in his room. He had everything he needed, including a motive, for Hermann had forced him to be an accomplice in the miserable business of Bessie and even of keeping Elisabeth locked up. He had many reasons, besides the ordinary ones any slave might have, to wish his master dead.

Paul began to work out the most likely explanation. The night was hot, airless. Charles, having retired to his room, stood at the window, like Elisabeth, longing for a breath of air. He saw the movement in the trees, then the leopard moving cautiously near the garden. He had a few keys, one to the larder and one to the front door. His own room was never locked; indeed, there was no lock in the door. At once a simple plan came to him. He left his room, crossed to the larder, and took out a piece of meat, perhaps part of a freshly butchered pig or a dressed rabbit. A rabbit, Paul decided; that would be the obvious choice, something wild for something wild. Charles carried the limp, furry carcass carefully, silently, down the long hall to the front door, which he opened wide. He was taking a risk and he knew it. But one thing was certain: the only person in the house who would come down the stairs to see what was happening was Hermann. Elisabeth couldn't; the cook, a heavy sleeper, wouldn't; and he intended to stay in his room no matter what happened until it was over. He dropped the meat onto the porch, backed down the hall, closed the door of his room, sat on his narrow cot, and waited.

The leopard was cautious, but the smell of blood was irresistible. It crossed the garden, slunk along the wall of the house, around the hedge to the front steps. There was the meat, the open door, the silent, sleeping house. Nervously the cat crossed the little distance and fell upon the rabbit. Ordinarily it would have taken this dinner away, to be devoured in secret, but hunger overrode natural caution. The leopard sunk its teeth into the rabbit's side and began to devour it.

Something woke Hermann up. Perhaps it was the noise the leopard made; perhaps he was just restless, as power-mad men often are. He got out of his bed, lit a candle, and went out onto the landing. When he looked down, he couldn't see the leopard—the candlelight was too dim, the animal too black—but he could see that the door was open, and he could hear the sound of something moving, something, could it be, eating. It was a frightening, bestial sound; it was loud in the still heat of the house. Hermann took a few steps down, holding his candle out before him. "Charles," he called, softly at first, then, growing annoyed at his situation and particularly at the impudence of the butler's opening the front door in the middle of the night, with more determination, "Charles."

The leopard stepped into the doorway, a bloody haunch dangling from its mouth. Hermann heard the thud as the strong jaws opened and the meat dropped to the porch floor. Before he could even turn back, a pure force like black light swarmed up the stairs and knocked him over. He clung to the rail, cried out for help, but the humans who heard his brief struggle made no effort to help him. Elisabeth lay in a swoon on the floor of her bedroom, the cook incorporated his cries into a dream, and Charles, who knew what was going on, sat on the edge of his bed, his arms clasped around his torso, his eyes closed, rocking back and forth like a child who has been sent to his room, waiting for his punishment to end.

When the house was still again, Charles got up and went to his window. After what seemed like a long time, he saw the sinuous movement of the leopard, like a sudden ribbon of black darting rapidly away from the house. Quietly, carefully, he opened his door and crept out into the hall. At the stairs he stood still and listened. Hermann's candle had fallen and guttered; he could see it white against the dark carpet on the first step. Hermann's body lay sprawled above him, dark, bulky, bleeding, a horrible sight, but Charles was entirely unmoved. He climbed the stairs and looked down at the wide, staring eyes, the contorted mouth, the bloody remains of a throat, and felt only relief. This master would not be calling his name again. At the end of one outstretched arm, as if Hermann had been reaching for it even at the moment of his death, was the heavy ring of keys. Charles eased around the body, pressing close against the rail so as not to touch it, reached down, and took the keys.

Paul leaned back in his chair and yawned. While working this out, he had finished his glass of wine. He got up and went to the kitchen to refill it, examining the explanation he had fabricated and elevating it from fantasy to theory. It was a good theory too, he decided. It made sense of all the details. As he filled his glass, he tied in the last two. Charles had unlocked Elisabeth's door after Hermann was dead, but he did not open it. He passed the corpse a second time and returned to his room to wait. Elisabeth, waking from a state that must have been a kind of ecstasy, wandered out onto the landing and found her enemy as she had been told she would, vanquished forever. She bent over him in the dark, touched the bloody shirt, brought her face close to the wound at his throat, touched her lips to it. Paul did not like to think that even in this moment of her triumph she would have gone so far as to drink her husband's blood. He smiled as he poured out the last drops of wine. No, he wouldn't say it, but his readers would draw their own conclusions. He went back to his desk and began sorting through the pages, stopping to read over the description of the Davilliers' arrival at Montague that morning. The front door was closed, he noted. So either Charles or Elisabeth had closed it.

Probably Charles, he thought. Elisabeth wouldn't have been in a state to notice such things. He gathered up the papers and stuffed them into the drawer, worrying an old question like a bone, the one he always dragged out to gnaw over in his historical adventures: What about the mosquitoes? There was rarely any mention of them in the letters and diaries he read, yet, particularly in the undrained swamp that was the city, they must have been a constant plague. And indeed they brought plague. Only a few days after Elisabeth's arrest, there was an outbreak of yellow fever that carried away the citizens of New Orleans at the rate of five hundred a day.

Enough for tonight, Paul thought, as he closed the drawer on the Schlaeger murder. This afternoon he had purchased a new recording of two Beethoven quartets. He had looked forward to the agreeable sense of possession he would experience as he opened the plastic wrapping and examined the liner notes. He knew the recording would be a good one—it was the Tokyo Quartet—and he had waited until now to listen to it because he wanted to give it his full attention. As he unwrapped the slender package and fitted the disc into the niche of the CD player, he confessed to himself another reason for wanting to be alone while listening to these quartets. They were Ellen's favorites. Her interest in music was sketchy, at best, though she certainly had no aversion to it; she had not, as he had, made a study of it. But these two quartets, he knew, she had loved.

Still loved, he thought, as the first tremulous notes rose into the air. It annoyed him when he found himself thinking of her in the past tense. Almost unconsciously, as he minded the music, he had drifted close to his bookshelves. He looked about him—at the empty room, the open doorways at either end, one of which led to the stairs to the bedroom—as if he thought someone might be watching him, but of course no one was. Donna was fast asleep. Stealthily he reached behind the books on the shelf at eye level and drew out a small cardboard box, an old stationery box, in which he kept a few photographs of Ellen. He brought the box to his desk, sat down, and opened it.

There weren't many. She never liked to be photographed, only rarely looked into a camera. He thumbed through the few on top, Ellen with Celia or Lillian, to one he particularly liked. She was sitting on the sidewalk in front of the zoo hospital, her legs crossed, leaning on one arm, her face turned away, toward a hawk, who sat on his perch gazing back at her intently. Their expressions, bird and woman, were eerily similar. "Two hawks," he called this picture.

Now as he looked at this photograph, his head filled with the somber yet triumphant music she loved so well, he gave himself over to missing his wife, missing her so viscerally that tears rose to his eyes. He looked away from the picture; it was painful to see her, so serious, so confident. Instead, he looked inward and asked himself seriously and openly how he had come to this inexplicable pass.

He had wanted, he admitted, to be torn. And why had he wanted it? Why not be satisfied with the charms and rewards of domestic felicity? Certainly he had enjoyed these. He could recall long stretches when he had required nothing more. But time passed, a kind of stagnation set in with the calm, and he panicked, like a man who, drifting at sea in a tiny vessel, succumbs to drinking sea water, though he knows it will be the death of him.

So he went out, now and then, and risked his happiness, because the sensation of being torn was sweet to him, and it became finally a part of the way he loved Ellen. He understood that he had been driven by his vanity, by his fear of boredom, of being ordinary, like Joe DeMott, a type, the domesticated academic who performed meaningless tricks for the benefit of his family and his students, whose reward was the occasional dinner party or published monograph or petty promotion. He had required a secret life, in which he was different, at liberty, his ordinary existence at risk. He had once told Joe he could not live without a secret life, but added that there was nothing to fear because the important thing was that it remain a secret. He was careful, discreet. Ellen didn't know. Sometimes it was difficult; he would find himself attached to another woman, and then he did suffer. But it made him love Ellen more, and he felt no guilt, for he made the sacrifice at her feet; it was for her that he brought the affair to an end.

It was true, he saw this now, that as he got older he became incautious, overeager; he had wanted to fall in love, just once more, with the impetuosity of youth, that heady, reckless abandon and desire, and he had done it. He was on the other side of it, having risked everything. Nor did he regret it. He loved Donna, the way she looked, the way she moved, her soft voice and open, cheerful manner, her energy, her youth. At times he felt he wanted to devour her, to suck her life into his own. But in loving her he was aware of a futility, a desperation he knew was neither youthful nor attractive.

The first movement had ended. There was a moment of silence; then the languorous, sad, mysterious adagio began. Paul sat at his desk wistfully holding the photograph of the woman he had loved for twenty years. He wanted to speak to her now, to tell her how much he missed her, how empty his world was without her, but he knew he couldn't pick up the phone and dial her number. She didn't want to hear from him, certainly not at this time of night and not in this condition. He touched the photograph lightly with his thumb, touching her face, which was so small it disappeared, and then the tiny gray area that was her torso.

His heart ached. He had wanted to be torn; it seemed harmless enough. But here was the result: he was sick with longing. He had torn his life in half.

50

In the dream Ellen was digging. She was standing knee-deep in a hole, making rapid progress, for she had a good shovel and the dirt was soft. It was dark; there were trees all around. She wasn't sure where she was, but she thought it must be in the zoo, the back part, near the river, where the public was not allowed. Gradually the work became more difficult. The ground was harder; she was getting out the dirt in small quantities. She was anxious, frightened. She must dig quickly; otherwise she would be too late. The shovel only scratched off the surface of the earth, which seemed to be wet, thickening, setting, like concrete. In frustration she threw the shovel out of the hole and fell on her hands and knees, clawing at the hardening ground with her fingers. To her surprise the dirt began to give. Soon she was scooping it out in handfuls. Then she could feel something just beneath the surface. She scratched around it frantically; this was what she was looking for. It was cold, hard, the top divided in branches like a root. She couldn't make it out in the dark, but she was clearing away the dirt easily now. The back part of it was cylindrical, and it seemed to go down and down. The moon came out from behind a cloud, pouring a pearly light on the scene, and Ellen fell back on her heels. She could see what it was sticking up out of the rough soil, as pale and bloodless as marble, but it wasn't marble.

It was a human hand.

She woke with a little shout that she heard as she broke through the smooth surface of consciousness, a squeak like a frightened rodent. It took a moment to recover. Her eyes searched the darkness behind her eyelids, and the world turned to veins. In terror, she opened her eyes, and the room was there, shadowy and familiar, bathed in a rosy light. It was just after dawn.

She breathed a long sigh of relief. She could still see the lifeless hand jutting up through the soil, the fingers splayed wide apart, as eloquent of horror as a scream. "Jesus," she said, turning over on her side. She pulled the other pillow close to her stomach and wrapped herself around it. "That was a bad one," she said.

Waking up was more and more like an escape from hell. She lay motionless while her body, drained by fear, recovered. If Paul had been there, if she could have reached out to find his warm shoulder, then the fear set loose by the dream would have evaporated like mist. But he wasn't there, and in his absence the fear bit into her like a gnawing animal. Had she locked the garage door? What was that creaking sound in the attic? Were the girls both safe in their beds? She searched her memory; yes, they were both home. Lillian had come in late, at midnight, but she was fine. While she lay trying to remember things, she had the misfortune of turning up why Paul wasn't there, and, then, where he was.

She had not been invited to the apartment, of course, but one night, after a few drinks with Beth and Gina, she had driven by alone. It was the second floor of the house, Lillian had told her, a big old house with a wide, tree-shaded screened porch across the front. The entrance was on the side. She parked across the street, turned off the car lights, and looked up at the windows. There were two lights on in the back, two cars in the driveway. Everyone thinks I'm so strong, she thought. But here I sit. She tried to imagine what was going on in the apartment; then, discovering how good she was at this exercise, she tried to stop. At last she started the engine and drove away, feeling she had come to a new, a secret, low.

She pushed the pillows away resolutely and reached for the clock. It was four A.M., too early to get up. She had two more hours if she wanted them. But who wanted to stay in bed with such entertainments as the buried hand on the other side of sleep? It was Camille, she thought. I was trying to get her back. As she swung her legs over the side of the bed, she had another thought. It was me, buried alive.

She sat there going over the dream. It did have to do with Camille; she felt certain of that, because there was so much dirt in the dream and what had struck her as ironic about Camille's funeral was that there was so little dirt involved. The priest had a handful in his pocket, in a plastic sandwich bag, which he withdrew at the proper moment, scattering it over the coffin lid. The compressed pellets rattled like cascading marbles on the mausoleum floor. Ellen glanced up at Camille's mother, aghast that she should be exposed to such a mockery of burial, but this sad, broken-down woman didn't seem to notice. Ellen had gone up to her before the ceremony to introduce herself and to offer her condolences. Camille's mother extended her hand automatically, but she didn't look at Ellen, and when the obligatory handshake was over she turned away, confused, as if she expected there to be someone behind Ellen, someone in a line.

There was no one. Only Ellen and Camille's mother and the priest. The mausoleum sent out some hired pallbearers, who wheeled an accordion platform into place and transferred the cheap, shiny gray coffin onto it. The priest said a short service and added a few words, very few, Ellen thought, on the subject of God's intentions in taking away one so young. Then he emptied his bag of garden dirt over the coffin. The attendants began to crank up the lift, for Camille's slot, narrow and gaping like an open post office box, was on the second level. As the lift raised the coffin on one end so that it would slide into the marble opening, Camille's body could be heard to shift inside, a sound so unexpected and dismal that even the pallbearers flinched.

It was obscene, Ellen thought. Couldn't they find a better way to do it? It occurred to her that it might be a good idea to order seat belts as part of one's funerary equipment, and she had to stifle a smile. To sober herself she glanced again at Camille's mother, who stood staring blankly at the wall of marble.

She was a small woman, of a compact build, as Camille had been, dressed entirely in black and wearing a black hat with an old-fashioned half veil that jutted out over her forehead like a cloud. Her face was pale, puffy; her dark eyes were rimmed in red. She looked as though she had been weeping for days, and she was weeping now, though she made no sound. As Ellen watched, she approached the wall, put her hand out to touch the marble, leaned against it, her head down, while a long shudder passed through her and she covered her face with her other hand. This was as close as she could ever get to her daughter now. The pallbearers, lowering their automatic lift, kept their eyes on their work; the priest, behind them, waited patiently to lead the stricken woman away. He was used to this, Ellen thought, but even he seemed touched by the quiet spectacle of the mother's grief. She stood motionless until at last the priest went to her and touched her arm. As she moved away from the wall, her gaze fell on Ellen, but without recognition or interest. Ellen met her eyes and saw there a desolation so profound it sought no comforting. Without a word to the priest, who stood ready to offer her the solace of religion, she walked away, out across the marble floor to the concrete steps. Ellen looked after her, then back at the priest. He raised his eyebrows, indicating his willingness to exchange a few remarks, but Ellen felt too low to take him up on it. She wanted to get home, to see her own daughters, to reassure herself that she might not ever share this woman's unbearable fate. She nodded, acknowledging his unspoken pleasantry, but said nothing. Then she followed Camille's mother, who was walking aimlessly, though in the general direction of the parking lot, across the wide, sun-drenched drive.

Ellen reached for her robe. She didn't like to remember this lonely figure, or the miserable funeral, one of the saddest and certainly the shortest she had ever attended. The dream had faded, but it left her feeling weak, dull, full of aches. She went into the bathroom and stood in a daze before the mirror, pushing her hair back from her face. She looked like a fright, she thought. A fright who had seen a fright. She gave her attention to the task of getting the toothpaste onto the toothbrush. As usual, one of the girls had squeezed all of the paste out of the top of the tube, and she had to work it up from the bottom.

By the time she was dressed the sun was up, but there was a haze over the sky and the air was cool. She went down to the kitchen and opened the refrigerator, closed it, went to the counter, and plugged in the electric kettle. It was Saturday. Normally she would not have to go in to work, but she was keeping a twenty-four-hour watch on the new jaguar, Minx, who had not been in quarantine three full days before he began to exhibit the same facial twitching that had characterized Magda's fatal illness. The lab reports on Magda had never been conclusive. All attempts at virus isolation had failed, but Ellen felt pretty sure it was viral encephalitis. When she noticed Minx's mouth twitching and the way he sat staring at the top of his enclosure, Ellen was so frustrated, she cursed. Beth, who was with her, looked at her with amused surprise. "I'm sorry," Ellen said. "I just don't want to go through this again."

Ellen opened the raisin bread package and dropped a slice into the toaster. Maybe, she thought, she had gotten to Minx sooner than she'd gotten to Magda, or maybe since he was younger he would be able to throw it off. She'd sedated Minx at once, done a complete workup on him, and started him on Sulkamyin and Daraprim, because she couldn't rule out toxoplasmosis. All his blood work and serum chemistry values came back normal. She returned him to the quarantine enclosure and had somebody watch him for the rest of the day. In the afternoon, Lenny, the new keeper in the Asian domain, came running into the hospital. "Something's wrong with him," he said. "He's going round in circles."

By the time Ellen got there, Minx had seizured. She started him on Valium, which was effective. Fifteen minutes later he was trying to get up. He was groggy, confused. The facial twitching continued, but he managed to sit up, and he tried to groom himself, always, Ellen told Lenny, who was interested in everything about the cats, a good sign.

After they had agreed on the shifts and the procedure should anything change, Ellen left the zoo. If she heard nothing, she would return at eight A.M. There was no way to call in; the quarantine area was a long walk from the hospital, and she had no reason to call, yet she felt anxious and distrustful. She remembered the night she had come in to find Camille pacing as nervously as all the cats, apparently unaware that the animal she was watching was already dead.

The toast popped up. Ellen pulled it out absentmindedly and took down a cup from the cabinet, for the kettle had started whistling. As she poured the water into the cup, she heard sounds from upstairs, the bathroom door opening, water running. One of the girls was up, but, she felt sure, not for long. Sleeping in on Saturdays was a privilege they both guarded with a nearly religious fervor.

But to her surprise she heard the pad of bare feet on the staircase and turned to find Celia leaning sleepily in the doorway.

"Did I wake you up?" Ellen asked.

"No. I couldn't sleep. I've been awake for hours. When I heard you I decided to get up."

"Do you want some hot milk?"

"No," Celia said, crossing to the stove. "I want some coffee."

"Honey," Ellen protested, "don't drink coffee at four-thirty in the morning on an empty stomach. You'll make yourself sick."

"My stomach is made of iron," Celia said. "Do I ever get stomachaches? No. I get headaches."

"Well, it will give you a headache too, and you'll never get back to sleep."

"So I'll stay up," Celia replied. "What are you going to do?"

Ellen stirred milk into her tea and poured a little into a cup to heat for Celia's coffee. "I was thinking of going in early."

"You're worried about that jaguar."

"I am," Ellen admitted. "I want to have a look at him. I could relieve Beth, give her a chance to get some sleep if we have to keep up the watch."

"I'll go with you," Celia said.

"You might get stuck there for hours." Ellen said this as an argument against going, but Celia seemed to have worked out the possibilities.

"If I get dressed now," she said, "and we go, we won't get there until five-thirty. If nothing's going on, Beth and I can go get some breakfast, and we could bring you something. Then she can drop me off here. It's on her way home."

"That's true," Ellen agreed.

"And if something is happening and you need x-rays or something, I can help."

Ellen smiled. There was not much likelihood that x-rays would be required, but Celia was always eager to take them. It was something of a joke in the hospital. Beth had taught her how to assist in placing the animal, how to fill out the labels, how to set the plates in the development tanks. Whenever an animal came in, even if the problem was a flesh wound or a skin irritation, if Celia was on hand she would say, "Looks like x-ray material to me," or, "You'll want some pictures of that, right?" As she stood at the counter fussing over her coffeepot, Ellen looked at her daughter hopefully, curiously. "What is it about x-rays that you like so much?" she said.

Celia considered the question. "I like seeing what can't ordinarily be seen," she said. "And I like getting a good, clear picture."

She was good at it too, Ellen thought. Sometimes she could tell which plates Celia had assisted in, they were so carefully done. She seemed to know intuitively how to get the animal flat enough so that everything showed up. The microwave bell went off. Ellen opened it, took out the milk, and handed it to Celia, who grasped the hot cup gingerly. "All right," Ellen said. "You drink up your cup of acid, then get dressed, and we'll go."

As she was closing her case, Ellen saw the book she had been reading before she went to sleep, a collection of essays about zoos, about their function as arks, trying to carry endangered species over the flood to a time when it would be safe to return them to the world. A hopeless mission. The author made this clear in the opening paragraphs, quoting the grim statistics. Ellen was familiar with this information, the worst of bad news, but perhaps reading it once again just before sleep had not been a good idea. She remembered her dream in which the earth was turning into concrete, not such an imaginative flight, given the import of her bedtime reading. She picked up the book and looked at the cover painting, an update on the Peaceable Kingdom, only more animals, more people, all shoved together in a narrow space. In the front a whale was rising out of a blue pool, as if eager to get into the picture. The animals all looked harmless and happy. A bluebird perched on a woman's hand; a snake was coiled on a camel's hump. It was a joke, she thought. The only thing realistic about it was how crowded the animals and the people were. They couldn't all fit in the picture.

She heard Celia leave the bathroom and go down the stairs. Because she was more cheerful these days and doing well in school, Paul thought everything was fine, problem solved, close the book.

But she hardly slept at all, ate poorly and irregularly, and suffered from headaches so severe that she occasionally came home from school and spent the afternoon lying in a darkened room with a cool cloth over her eyes. She had a routine for it: a bowl of ice water, the cloth she preferred, the pillows arranged in a certain way. Since her father was no longer available to do it, Celia was learning to take over the hard job of comforting Celia. She hadn't forgiven him, still referred to him as "the creep" or "the juvenile delinquent," but she was learning to do without him.

And so are we all, Ellen thought as she followed her daughter down the stairs. Whether we like it or not.

Celia left a note for Lillian, and they got into the car and drove out into the early morning air. The city was marvelously quiet; there was still a fog over the monuments in the graveyard, so the angels and animals seemed to be materializing from the mist. Celia busied herself sorting through Ellen's tapes, looking for something she could listen to. "You're worse than Dad," she said. "Nothing but Beethoven and Brahms."

"That's not true," Ellen defended herself. "I have two Doctor Johns and a Neville Brothers."

Celia nodded; she'd found one. "This is good," she said, pushing a tape into the deck. There were a few electronic beeps; then Dr. John's version of a voodoo chant came gushing out. It was good, Ellen agreed. Just the thing for five A.M. As they drove beneath the big oaks that lined the park, the music made the spooky world seem spookier. Religion always rendered nature both more and less threatening, Ellen thought. It purported to explain our tie to the earth, but more often than not its effect was to cut those ties. People who believed they could summon the spirits of animals to set them free had already accepted that they were, in an important way—something having to do with volition—not animals. The word was out. The animals certainly knew it, even if the people did not. The separation papers had already been filed; the great divorce was under way.

Celia was tapping one hand against the other in time to the music. "Do you think there's still voodoo in New Orleans?" she asked.

Ellen smiled. "Oh, yes," she said. "No doubt about it."

They arrived at the gates of the zoo. Ellen parked the car near the hospital, next to Beth's battered old truck. They got out and walked along the sidewalk until it ran out, then followed a dirt path past a series of chain-link enclosures hidden among the low trees, the scruffy bushes, and the tall bamboo. The fog was thick, they were close to the river, and it would be a while before the sun burned it off. As they passed a crosspath they could hear a heavy swishing sound, as well as the quick light step of human feet, but it was too foggy to see. Ellen recognized the sound and knew what was coming, but Celia did not. She peered through the fog and let out a soft *wow* as the mist parted and she saw the great gray head, the huge legs like moving columns, the sensitive flexible trunk sweeping along the ground. It was Tula, the elephant, going out for his morning constitutional. His trainer walked hurriedly at his side; this was exercise for man and beast. When he saw the two women, he waved his stick. "Good morning," he called. "You're up early."

Ellen only smiled, but Celia said, "Good morning." The trainer quickened his step, tapping Tula's foreleg to remind him of the turn. As the elephant came whirling past them, the ground shook. He was so close they could have touched him, so intent on his walk he seemed not to notice them, though his trunk lifted from the dirt, waving amiably as he went by.

Ellen moved on, and Celia, falling into step beside her, said, "That was something."

Ellen opened her hands before her, indicating the park. "It's a jungle out here," she said. Celia looked back over her shoulder to see Tula disappearing into the fog, as if he were made from it. Then she turned ahead to where the path widened into a patch of low wild grasses. They could see the row of quarantine cages off to one side and the dirt walkway in front of them. Celia stepped out ahead. She had spotted Beth sitting on a folding chair, and she hurried to her across the narrowing space. Ellen watched her daughter's back, picking up the pace as always, and she saw Beth smile and wave, an expression of calm good will on her features, which, Ellen thought, Celia needed and had come to rely on, the sincere welcome of the admired, older friend.

"You're early," Beth said as Ellen came into earshot.

"We couldn't sleep," Celia answered for her mother, and Ellen added, "So I thought if I couldn't maybe you should."

"Well," Beth said, looking gay, almost mischievous, "we may all get some rest if my guess is right."

"How is he?" Ellen said.

Beth pointed toward the cage; it was only a few steps away. "See for yourself," she said.

And there was Minx, the young jaguar, sitting calmly in a grassy patch of the enclosure, studying, without nervousness or aggression, the three women who gathered in front of the wire. "How long has he been like this?" Ellen asked.

"Almost three hours," Beth said. "He slept for a long time. When he woke, he seemed dizzy, but he was determined to get up. He walked a few steps; then I think he figured it was best to sit down."

"Any twitching?"

"None. I've been watching his face a lot. It hasn't happened once since he woke up. He hasn't been staring into space, either. He's been keeping his eye on me, mostly, and anything else that moves."

"That's good," Ellen said.

As they watched, the jaguar got to his feet, took a step, another, slowly, as if testing his balance. He stood still, then turned his attention from the women to the full bucket of water that stood about ten feet away in the shade of a crape myrtle tree.

Ellen watched him closely. His eyes were clear, focused, and after a few shaky steps his stride seemed to level out. He went to the bucket, lowered his face to the water, and began lapping it up, urgently at first, then, when his thirst was assuaged, with intense concentration, as if it were now his obligation to drink the entire bucket.

Ellen and Beth exchanged speculative looks. "So what do you think, Mom?" Celia said. "Is he going to be all right?"

Ellen knew that a relapse was possible; it was certainly too soon to say. But the improvement was marked; the animal was young, appeared to possess a calm temperament, and looked strong. Ellen felt a surge of emotion as she watched him quietly drinking from his water bucket in the soft, early morning light. The only sound was his tongue working against the water and the occasional twitter of birds in the trees nearby. She leaned closer in to see the jaguar's face, and as she did he stopped drinking. He lifted his head, the water pouring in two thin streams from his slightly open jaws. He gave her a long, steady look, his yellow eyes betraying nothing of his sentiments, if he could be said to have any. In fact, Ellen thought, his look was the opposite of sentiment. This was the look that sees no moment beyond the present, that contemplates the world in an eternal *now,* the natural, healthy, straightforward, and increasingly rare regard of the wild and predatory cat.

Hers was a small, a pitiful triumph, Ellen thought. Of course she knew that. In the face of what was coming it was laughable, a joke, like struggling to scoop out a thimbleful of water from a sinking ship, from the *Titanic,* just before the great stern slipped beneath the icy black water and the prow began to rise in the frigid air; that was how sure she was this ship would sink. So why did this little victory feel so satisfying, so important? Ellen put her arm around her daughter, who, adding to the overwhelming and sudden fund of her happiness, did not pull away. She leaned into her mother, her eyes still on the cat, impatient for the answer to her question. "Well," she asked, "what do you think?"

It wasn't much, Ellen thought. Why did she feel such joy, such unexpected and overpowering joy? Her heart seemed to swell with it, and her throat was tight. "I think," she said, but her voice broke. She cleared her throat and tried again. "I think," she said firmly, "this time, we win."